WITH A FOREWORD BY EUDORA WELTY

PENGUIN BOOKS

Penguin Books Ltd., Harmondsworth, Middlesex, England
Penguin Books, 625 Madison Avenue, New York, New York 10022, U.S.A.
Penguin Books Australia Ltd, Ringwood, Victoria, Australia
Penguin Books Canada Ltd, 2801 John Street, Markham, Ontario, Canada
L3R 1B4
Penguin Books (N.Z.) Ltd, 182-190 Wairau Road, Auckland 10, New Zealand

First published in the United States of America and Canada by
Doubleday & Company, Inc., 1981
First published in Great Britain by Penguin Books Ltd 1983
Published in Penguin Books by arrangement with
Doubleday & Company, Inc.
Published in Penguin Books 1983

Printed in Canada by Webcom Limited

To Robert Phillips
Encourager and Friend

Acknowledgment is made to the editors of *The New Yorker* for the following stories, which first appeared in their pages: "The Little Brown Girl," "The Eclipse," "First Dark," "A Southern Landscape," "Ship Island," "The Fishing Lake," "The Adult Holiday," "The Pincian Gate," "The Absence," "A Bad Cold," "Sharon," "The Finder"; *McCall's* for "Moon Rocket" and "The Bufords"; *Texas Quarterly* for "The White Azalea"; *Prairie Schooner* for "The Visit"; *Shenandoah* for "Presents"; *Delta Review* for "On the Gulf"; *Mississippi Review* for "Instrument of Destruction"; *Journal of Canadian Fiction* for "Go South in the Winter"; *Southern Review* for "A Kiss at the Door," "Mr. McMillan," "Prelude to a Parking Lot," "Indian Summer"; *1976: New Canadian Stories* for "I, Maureen"; *Atlantic* for "A Christian Education" and "Port of Embarkation"; *Chatelaine* for "The Search"; *Ontario Review* for "The Girl Who Loved Horses." A shortened version of "Knights & Dragons" first appeared in *Redbook*. "The Day Before," "Judith Kane," and "Wisteria" first appeared in *Ship Island and Other Stories* (McGraw-Hill, 1968).

CONTENTS

PART III 1965–1971

PART IV 1972–1977

PREFACE

Looking back on the times of writing these stories means looking back on the novels that were being written also, either in my head or actually, means looking back, too, on the events and feelings of all those years. Back then it was all a certain way, but later on something changed all that, and so on until . . . Until what? "You certainly can't know where you are till you know where you were." So Marilee Summerall, who crops up here and there in these pages, might observe.

Where *I* was, obvious after two lines of the first story, was Mississippi; in many ways, I'm there still. The pasture the child of the first story looks across to find her playmate in the yellow dress is the same as the one where the girl races her calico pony in the last story. There are images—especially, it seems, to Southerners—that never go away; they do not even fade.

Some writers invent their new terrains; I preferred to go and look for mine. First and last, for me it was Italy. One after another, scenes I remember from that abundant Mediterranean world have wound up in my work, a sojourner's baggage getting itself unpacked and shared. There's a second country for everybody, one way or another.

What I'm talking about now is how you take up residence in the world. It comes to that, I think, for all of us, whether we stay put or not; though "the South," our much perused literary land, is still there, findable, and enduring, apparently, even if gnawed at by prosperity and change.

I had tried to get my Southern experience down with youthful urgency back in the years that ended in 1956 when *The Voice at the Back Door* was published. This was the last of three Mississippi novels, the others being *Fire in the Morning* and *This Crooked Way*. The "Southern Renaissance" was in full tide back then and lent its radiance to any serious work undertaken there; it made the South itself seem enough and more as subject to explore, as object of some ultimate vision.

But by 1956 I had wound up in Italy where a Guggenheim Fellowship had landed me and marriage to an Englishman who worked there had indefinitely detained me. Without meaning to I had got unstuck. Had I also, by accident, become that fashionable person, an Exile? No, it was absence; that was all. So what on earth did it mean, Marilee, except that I wasn't down home any more to visit relatives and talk about the cotton crop? For me it meant the breaking up of those long tides of existence in one locale that have yielded up countless novels, out of which the novel seems to unfurl so naturally, so rhythmically, so right. My experience was now broken into pieces, no less valid, perhaps no less interesting—perhaps even more relevant, I was tempted to speculate, to the restless life of the world? Short stories seemed a better way to get at this sort of thing than novels, at least a better way to start. When "The Little Brown Girl," first rejected by *The New Yorker* in 1944, was taken by that magazine in 1957, I felt the stir of new possibilities for work, and other stories followed. Like "First Dark" and "A Southern Landscape," *The Light in the Piazza* was meant to be a short story—it became, under its own momentum, a long story which *The New Yorker* published, then, separately, with some expansion, a novel. After "The White Azalea," another Italian piece, I stopped to look around and found we'd moved to Montreal.

"Ship Island" marked a return to a South which was not the one I left; some alchemy, for better or worse, had set in. I could now, though, move at will from the old home-scapes of the Gulf Coast islands or the fishing lakes of north Mississippi, to the Italy of "The Visit," "The Pincian Gate," and "Knights & Dragons." This last too started as a story and wound up a novel. Time out again. A new start.

From 1965 to 1972 I was involved with two novels many scenes of which were written for each before I finished either. *No Place for an Angel* wings back and forth with its restless cast of friends who come together and part, may turn up in New York or Rome or Texas or

Washington or Miami. *The Snare,* published in 1972, is fixed in the thick atmosphere of New Orleans, and never, I think, loses its hold on that place, which is its measure. But stories, too, kept coming along, all around and between the novels. The clear light of "The Absence" followed the grim spell of "Knights & Dragons"; nostalgia for the world of Marilee may have prompted "The Day Before," "The Bufords," "Presents," and "On the Gulf," though there are darker currents running in stories like "Judith Kane," "The Finder," and "Instrument of Destruction," relating these to *The Snare* and to a late story like "I, Maureen."

After *The Snare* the first story I wrote was "A Christian Education," based on a childhood memory, and from there on, through the "imagined" stories which follow, I feel a oneness, though what its nature is escapes saying, unless it is something like acceptance, the affirming of what is not an especially perfect world for these seeking girls and women, but at least is possible, livable, living.

To place this many stories in the order in which they were written (not necessarily the order of publication) may suggest that the writer thinks she has started out low and lowly but mounted high. It isn't meant that way. I think rather of walking down a certain path, a personal road. Any art, however quietly practiced, is a progress in one sense, but the best parts come when and where they may be found, like encounters. The road itself is always moving on.

ELIZABETH SPENCER
Montreal, 1979

FOREWORD

Elizabeth Spencer is from North Mississippi and I am from Central Mississippi, so there needed to be a modest coincidence to bring us together. This occurred. Elizabeth came as a student to Belhaven College in Jackson and was unerringly made president of the Belhaven Literary Society; it was the year I published my first book, and I lived right across the street facing the College. Elizabeth made a telephone call to ask if I'd please step over to a session of the Literary Society so they could meet a real writer and seek my advice. It would have been unneighborly to stay home.

I met then a graceful young woman with a slender, vivid face, delicate and clearly defined features, dark blue eyes in which, then as now, you could read that Elizabeth Spencer was a jump ahead of you in what you were about to say. She did as nice Southern girls, literary or unliterary, were supposed to do in the Forties—looked pretty, had good manners (like mine, in coming when invited), and inevitably giggled (when in doubt, giggle). But the main thing about her was blazingly clear—this girl was serious. She was indeed already a writer.

As a matter of fact, she was all but the first writer *I'd* ever met, and the first who was younger than I was. (The other was Katherine Anne Porter.) Elizabeth offered me my first chance to give literary advice. But my instinct protected us both. This free spirit, anybody could tell, would do what she intended to do about writing. What else, and what better, could a writer know of another writer? It was all I was sure of about myself. I imagine she was glad not to get advice.

Instead of advising each other, we became friends. To leap over something like a decade's difference in age proved no more trouble to either than crossing Pinehurst Street. It wasn't long before Elizabeth herself, with degrees from Belhaven and Vanderbilt, published her own first book, the novel *Fire in the Morning:* she'd gone right on her way as she'd known she would, and as she always has.

In the Southern branching-out way, we met each other's families; in particular, Elizabeth and I appreciated each other's mothers. In Jackson in my family home, in Carrollton in her family home, and, over the years, on the Mississippi Gulf Coast, in New York, in Florence, in London, in Montreal where she lives now, sometimes by trustworthy coincidence and sometimes by lucky planning, we'd meet, and though we might not have written each other a line, we knew right where to take up the conversation. It was as refreshing as a picnic—indeed it often *was* a picnic, and we talked over lunch on the banks of the Pearl.

Even though Elizabeth dedicated her book of stories *Ship Island* to me, I see no reason why my pride in this honor should prevent me from giving expression to my joy in the timely appearance of this full collection. It is as her fellow writer that I see so well what is *unerring* about her writing. The good South, bestowing blessings at the cradle of storytellers, touched her most tenderly with the sense of place. Elizabeth evokes place and evokes it acutely in that place's own choice terms—take, for example, her story title "First Dark." She can faultlessly set the social scene; she takes delight in making her characters reveal themselves through the most precise and telling particulars. I think she would agree that Southern writers really don't have much excuse for writing vaguely or unobservantly or without enlightenment about human relationships, when they thrive in the thick of family life. They comprehend "identity" because it's unavoidable. One reason why Elizabeth has never hesitated in her writing is that she began by knowing who she is. In her scrutiny of recalcitrant human nature there's an element of participating joy in that nature's very stubbornness, or in the way it yields every time to the same old tunes. She cannot go wrong about the absurd. All these are Southern blessings—perhaps. But equally valuable to this writer is a gift *not* characteristic of the Southerner: this is her capacity for cool detachment.

It was never surprising that she has felt well able, early on, to strike out from her Mississippi base, to find herself new territories: her fiction has consistently reached toward its own range, found its own scope, its own depth. What she'll do next, after the broad variety of her accomplishments, is still unpredictable.

It would have been as reckless to predict for Elizabeth as it would have been to offer her advice, and for the same good reason. Indeed, how *could* I have guessed, for one thing, that a schoolgirl so fragile-looking (though she went with a determined walk that made her hair bounce) could have had so much *power* to pour into her stories? Without any sacrifice of the sensitivity and the finely shaded perceptions we expect of her, her cool deliberateness to pull no punches will time after time take the reader by surprise. Katherine Mansfield stunned readers by a like combination of means; and I should say Elizabeth Spencer has earned with these stories a place in her rare company.

EUDORA WELTY
April, 1980

PART I

1944–1960

THE LITTLE BROWN GIRL

Maybeth's father had a business in the town, which was about a mile from where they lived, but he had about forty acres of land below the house that he planted in cotton and corn. The land was down the hill from the house and it was on two levels of ground: twenty acres, then a bluff covered with oak sprouts and vines, then a lower level, which stretched to the property line at the small creek. You could see it all from the house—the two fields and the creek, and other fields beyond the creek—but from the upper field you could just see as far as the willows along the creek bank.

For nine months of the year, Maybeth's father hired a Negro named Jim Williams to make the crop. Jim would work uptown in the mornings and come in the afternoons around two o'clock—a black, strapping Negro in blue overalls, stepping light and free and powerful on the road from town. He would go around the house to the back to hitch up the black mule in spring, or file on the hoe blade in summer, or drag a great dirty-white cotton sack to the field in the fall. Spring, summer, and fall they saw him come, until he became as much a part of the household as Maybeth or Brother or Lester Junior or Snookums, the cook; then, after the last pound of cotton was weighed in the cold fall twilight, the Jim they knew would vanish. In winter, they sometimes spoke to a town Negro as Jim, and he would answer back, pleasant as you please, but it was no use pretending he was the same. The cotton stalks stood black and sodden in the field, and the cornstalks broke from the top, and there was nothing for a little girl to do in the afternoons but grow all hot and stuffy by the fire or pester Mother for things to eat or study schoolbooks sometimes. There wasn't anybody much to play with out where they lived.

At last, the spring day would come when Maybeth could leap away from the school bus and the ugly children in the bus, and run up the drive to the house, then down the hill, under the maple trees, to the field. Jim would be in the field, plowing with the middlebuster, and she would get to follow behind him for the first time in the year. Jim did a lot of funny things out there in the field. Up ahead, where the rows ended at the top of the bluff, Jim sometimes stopped when he had pulled the plow out of the ground, and while the black mule circled in the trace chains he would fling up his head and sing out, rich and full, as loud as he could sing, "Ama-a-zi-in' grace–" The air would quiver for the next line to come, but Jim would be well into the field by then, driving the plow down the furrow with a long, swinging stride.

Once, Maybeth tried to tell him the next line. "It goes 'How sweet the sound,' Jim," she said, trying to put her little shoes in Jim's broad tracks.

But all Jim Williams said was, "Git up, Jimson Weed!" Other times, he called the mule Daisy Bell, and that was funny, too, because the mule's name was Dick, and Dick was a man mule, Maybeth was sure. But when she told Jim that, he only said, "Lawd, Lawd," as though she had told him something he had never heard before, or something he had only half heard when she said it. You couldn't tell which.

But most of the time Maybeth was asking Jim questions. When she got like that with Mother, Mother would finally say, "Now, what on earth made you think of that?" Daddy would laugh at her questions and say, "I don't know, honey." But Jim knew the answer to everything. He knew why the jaybird bounced on the air when he flew and why the mule swept his nose along the ground when he turned and why the steel plow slid out of the earth as clean as when it entered. Sometimes Maybeth knew that Jim was making up, but most of the time she believed him word for word, like the catechism in Sunday School.

One spring afternoon, a few days before Maybeth's seventh birthday, Jim was sporting a new red bandanna in the back pocket of his overalls. Even before Maybeth reached him, she spotted it, and she asked about it first thing.

"My little girl give me that," he said. He spoke in his making-up voice, but he looked perfectly straight-faced.

Maybeth hurried very fast behind him. "Aw, Jim, you ain't got a little girl, have you? How old is she?"

"She be eight nex' fall," he said, very businesslike. "Gee, mule."

"How big is she?"

"She jes' 'bout your size, honey."

A little brown girl in a starched blue-and-white checked dress stepped smiling before Maybeth's eyes. From then on, Maybeth's questions all went in one direction, and if Jim had any peace, it was only because he was Jim.

"When will I get to see her, Jim? When will she come and play with me?"

"Some day nex' week, I reckon."

"What day next week?"

"Long 'bout the middle part of the week, I spec'."

"Aw, you're just foolin', Jim. Aren't you just foolin'?"

"Ama-a-zi-in' grace –" sang Jim Williams as the black mule turned in the trace chains against a low and burning cloud. And that night, when Jim had eaten his supper in the kitchen and gone, the little brown girl in the blue-and-white checked dress stayed on.

"Mother, guess what Jim told me today," said Maybeth, opening her arithmetic book before the fire. "He said he had a little girl. She's coming and play with me."

"Oh, honey, Jim's just fooling you. Jim hasn't got any children, has he, Lester?"

"Not that I ever heard of," said Daddy. "It's a good thing, too–the way he drinks and carries on every Saturday night."

"He's fooling you," said Mother.

Maybeth bent quickly to her sums. "I know it," she said.

And in a way she had known it all along. But in another way she hadn't known it, and the not knowing still remained along with the knowing, and she never thought it out any further. Nothing was changed, and she and the little brown girl played together before she went to sleep at night, in dull moments at school, and when she was being quiet on the bus, riding home with the noisy children. The little girl was the first thing to ask questions about when she ran to the field after school, the warm sun on her yellow hair, and her feet already uncomfortable to be out of their shoes.

The first thing, that is, until the Friday came when Maybeth was seven. It was a perfect birthday. Under her plate at breakfast that morning she found two broad silver dollars. The class sang "Happy Birthday" to her in school, and that night Snookums, the cook, who usually finished work in the afternoon, returned from her house to cook supper, and they all had fried chicken and rice and gravy and a coconut birthday cake.

Maybeth ran into the kitchen to show her silver dollars to Snookums and Jim. "Look, Snookums! Look, Jim!" she said.

"Lawd-ee!" said Snookums. She was a young, bright Negro with a slim waist and straight black hair.

"My, *my!*" said Jim. "That's ringin' money, ain't it, Snookums?"

"Lawd-ee!" said Snookums.

"Which you druther have, Snookums," said Jim, "ringin' money or foldin' money?"

The door was open to the dining room, and Maybeth heard her big brother laugh and holler back, "Either one'll do to buy Saturday-night liquor, won't it?"

Jim and Snookums just fell out laughing, and Maybeth somehow felt ashamed.

After supper, she put the two silver dollars in a little box inside a bigger box and put them in the very back right-hand corner of her drawer in the bureau.

The next day was Saturday, and it rained, so Jim stayed in the barn and shelled corn for the chickens, and Maybeth watched.

"I *wuz* gwine bring my little girl to play with you nex' week," said Jim.

Maybeth was stricken. "How come you can't, Jim? Oh, how come you can't?"

"She ain't got no fine dress like you is. She ain't got nothin' 'cept one ole brown dress. She say she shame to come."

Maybeth broke the stubborn grains of corn from a cob one at a time, and her heart beat very fast. "Have you sure 'nough got a little girl, Jim?"

Jim did not answer. "There's dresses at the Jew store," he went on mournfully. "But they's nigh onto two dollars. Take the nigger long time to make up that money."

A few minutes later, Maybeth was hurrying back to the house in the rain.

She took the two silver dollars out of the little box within the larger box, and ran back to the barn.

"What you fixin' to do?" Jim Williams asked, holding the two coins in his open palm and cutting his eyes toward her.

"For the dress," Maybeth said. "You know. For your little girl's dress, Jim."

"Your daddy ain't gwine like you playin' around with this money," he said.

"He ain't going to know," said Maybeth.

"You *sure?*" he asked, snapping shut the three clasps on his little leather purse.

"I'm not going to tell him," said Maybeth.

"Gwine git her a yalla dre-ess," sang Jim softly, and the corn poured out of his fingers in rich handfuls and rattled against the side of the scuttle as fast as the rain on the tin roof.

Maybeth did not know why she had given Jim the money. It was like when you are playing mud pies by yourself and you get real salt and pepper for the pies, or when you are dressing up to play lady and you make a mess of all the closets and cedar chests trying to get something real and exactly right—the high-heeled button shoes or the hat with the plume. She and Jim were playing that Jim had a little girl. But when the playing was over, Jim did not give the money back, and, of course, she did not really know that she had expected him to, so she never asked. And because she wasn't exactly sure what money meant, her sorrow centered on the two little empty boxes in the corner of the dresser drawer.

She thought of them with an empty feeling when she rode to school on Monday morning in the pickup with Daddy and saw a yellow dress in the Jew-store window. When she rode back from school on the bus, she looked again, and something went queer inside her, because the yellow dress was gone.

Maybeth ran so hard down the hill to the field that afternoon that the pound of her feet shook her all over and she could hardly stop running at the fence. All the way home in the bus, all the way through the yard and down the hill, she could picture Jim plowing with the little girl in the yellow dress behind him in the furrow, and they would look up when Maybeth came. From the fence, she could see that Jim was plowing down at the far corner, where the land was lowest; he was almost through busting the upper field. She could just see the top of his head following Dick's flapping ears up the slope. Maybeth crawled through the barbed wire and caught a snag in her dress. When she had pulled it free, and looked up, Jim was in full view on the higher ground, and he was alone.

Maybeth came slowly out of the maple shade into the hot sun. As she crossed the rows, the clods made her stumble once or twice. She fell in behind him at last.

"I tore my dress. See?" she said, holding up the snagged hem.

He glanced back, the sweat big on his temples and catching the sun on his cheek. "Sho' did," he said. "You shorely did."

They were back beside the bluff before she asked, "How come your little girl didn't come today, Jim?"

He had stopped, with the plow in the new furrow, to cut himself a plug of tobacco. He jerked his kinky head toward the creek. "She down there," he said.

"Down there?"

"She shame to come till you come. She say she gwine set in the bushes and watch for you. She be comin' on in a minute now."

Maybeth ran to the edge of the bluff, among the honeysuckle vines, and stared and stared down toward the low willows along the creek bank, until their sharp spring green blurred in her eyes.

"Where, Jim, where?"

Jim hooked the lines over the plow handle. "Whoa, mule," he said. He walked away from her along the edge of the bluff and stood on the highest point, bigger than anything from sky to sky. He pointed.

"See," he said, and his tone was infinite. "Look yonder. She setting on the groun'. See. She done crossed her legs."

"Has she got on a–a yellow dress?"

"Yes'm! Yes'm! You sees her! You sees her sho'!"

"Is she sitting under that bigges' clump of willow, right over yonder? Sitting cross-legged?"

"Yes'm! That's right! By that bigges' clump."

"Sort of with one hand on the ground?"

"Yes, ma'am! You sees her sho'!"

Then, in two strides, he was back at the plow. "She'll come. My little girl'll come. Gee, mule. She knows we done seen her, and she'll come. Gee up, sir!"

The plow ran into the earth, and Maybeth, still standing on the bluff, could hear from somewhere the creak of the harness, and the tearing of little roots as the soft ground was severed. She stood staring, and the green blur beyond the lower field fanned out and then closed together around the shape of something—was it something?—like a still image under the willow trees. Humming to himself, Jim Williams passed farther down the slope, but Maybeth stayed on the bluff, as motionless as the fluted honeysuckle bloom beside her hand and the willows across the lower field standing up in the windless air.

She saw something move under the willows.

Maybeth began to walk, and then she began to run, faster and faster. The rows, with their heavy chunks of clodded earth, flew beneath her, trying to trip her, to keep her from the hill and the white house on the hill and Mother.

She caught her breath a little in the yard, and then she went in and found Mother in the kitchen, drinking some water.

"Why, precious, why are you so hot?" Mother said. "Why did you come back from the field?"

How could you tell about the yellow dress and something coming alive beneath the willows? "I—I got hungry," said Maybeth.

Mother gave her a piece of cold corn bread and sent her out on the back steps. There was a sound around the corner of the house. A Bantam rooster stepped toward her on the flagstone walk. Maybeth jumped up, trembling, and flung the muffin to him and ran into the house, through one room and another.

"Mother!" she called. "Mother!"

"In here, honey."

When she came into the room, her mother looked up at her. Then she laid aside her darning basket and took Maybeth into her arms and rocked her in the rocking chair.

THE ECLIPSE

Anybody would have noticed them, they were both so pretty. The young lady was immaculate and fresh, out of choice, or perhaps you could say out of disdain for people who weren't; gloves snow white and stocking seams straight—she would stay just so all summer. The boy with her might or might not. He was small but growing, possibly about twelve years old, and could reach a new phase any minute. He was by nature blond and bright as a daisy, and soap and water had been recently at work, for the tuft of hair at his crown was springing erect again, strand by strand. What had made him content to scrub so well? She, obviously, was the answer.

She rode backward for the time being (later they would swap), reading a slick-paged magazine, and he looked out the window, but remarks occurred to them; they exchanged glances as though by signal. His feet were reassuring: honest, puppylike, clumsy. One thought pleasantly of them bare below rolled blue jeans, splotched with dust and watermelon juice. From behind the magazine page she drank in the soft-cut lines of his profile. Her eyes fell away the instant before he caught her staring. Somebody could come very near to them without their noticing. Somebody did. "Dorothy Eavers! Don't you remember *me?*"

The train passed through a landscape that looked empty, partly because they were moving so fast; it gave them only a slight rocking motion as a sign of its power. Since the interior of the sealed air-conditioned coach was not cluttered by the sound of rails, there was no need for the woman to shout, much less get up and cross the aisle. But she had done both. Never mind; the two traveling companions recovered almost at once. She was not a threat. By some feat, the immaculate girl was even able to recall her name.

"Ina Pearl! I didn't see you."

"Well, I saw *you*. The reason it took me so long, I couldn't believe my eyes. Not that you've changed a bit, now that I see you up close. I just didn't know you lived down here any more. I didn't know you had a little boy, either. I declare! He's almost as tall as you."

"But he's not mine! This is my student, my pupil."

"Music!" said Ina Pearl. "It always just thrilled me to death to hear you play. But weren't you going to New York and go on the stage?"

Dorothy Eavers winced. This came of college-girl exchanges, confidences given that would be quoted with no regard for accuracy.

"I never thought of the stage," she said. "I had hoped to do concert work, but I couldn't make a go of it. I took a job teaching public school music in Stilton. Quite a change! I give some private lessons, too—to Weston, for instance." She touched his hair. "I wasn't good enough for New York, I guess."

"Oh, now, I bet you were, too!" cried Ina Pearl.

"The funny thing is I give more concerts now than I ever did," said Dorothy Eavers. "Weston, here"—her smile at the boy, meeting his eyes, was like a wink of agreement on Ina Pearl—"Weston has put me in my place. I'm his accompanist. No one can get enough of hearing him sing. We're going to New Orleans now to audition for this famous boys' choir—oh, I'm sure you've heard of them. They—"

"Do you know," Ina Pearl inquired of her, comfortably regarding Weston, "since I saw you last, I've had two? They're just about his size. One might be a little bit bigger and the other a little bit littler. Sing! You couldn't make them stop yelling long enough to *sing* anything."

Having thus established her children as indubitably superior to boys who did stop yelling and sing, she went on to tell everything else about them. Weston knew himself out of it now. He turned his attention from the fleet landscape and examined her, this talkative intruder. She was nothing like Miss Eavers. He went through an appalling catalogue of her faults, arriving at the conclusion that she wasn't in the least attractive. When she opened her purse and took out her compact, powder sprinkled into an unwholesome tangle of junk. Her fingernails were painted bright, and three of them were chipped. He could think of other, even worse things that probably were wrong with her, too—he had got quite a supply from watching his mother—and from every single one of them Miss Eavers was absolutely free, which was why everybody back in town said she was "stuck-up."

Oh, he had heard them talking. From the upstairs window after supper, sitting where they said he oughtn't to, because the screen might not be strong enough, he had heard them.

"Stuck-up thing!" (Mother.)

"Got mighty pretty ankles, Miss Mamie." (Mr. Harry Buford, from across the street.)

"Bob Nabors begged her for a date, like several others when she first came, but Bob especially. . . . Just crazy about her. Why would it hurt to give him a date? She thinks because she's lived in New York and knows about music." (Mother.)

Cigar glow down in the dark. (Mr. Harry, thinking about her.) "Maybe she likes 'em older, more mature."

"I got nothing against her. I just wish Weston wasn't quite so enthusiastic. He ought not to put all of his time on music." (Daddy.)

"She's stuck-up, if you ask me. Just plain stuck-up." (Mother.)

From the window in the dark, Weston could look up into the clean, brilliant September sky. He knew better than anybody. Miss Eavers was no more stuck-up than a star.

When the woman called Ina Pearl got off at the next station stop, they did not converse about her.

"Where's this?" asked Weston, leaning out.

"Picayune, I think," said Miss Eavers.

"I wouldn't like to live here, either," said Weston.

"What do you mean, 'either'?"

"Either here or Stilton." He did not choose to watch the exit of Ina Pearl from his life—how she was greeted by two little boys with suckers in their jaws, how she scrambled into a car beside a man in shirt sleeves. Weston looked ahead of him. His mouth was softly closed; his lashes were thick as June grass; his summer freckles lingered just below the skin, like a thin wash of gold. He waited to move on again. "Or any place else in Mississippi," he murmured.

Miss Eavers glanced up in something like alarm from the enameled page of the latest musical arts magazine. She occasionally felt twinges of her responsibility for him, but their relationship had galloped from the first, and except to instruct him in range, scales, breathing, voice projection, and allied matters, she had never exerted her natural authority.

"But you've never been out of it!" she exclaimed.

He did not accept the reproof, if that was what it was. He had got his idea from her, after all, if never in so many words.

"I'm going out now," he said superbly.

He was obviously headed for a lot of trouble.

The first he knew of it, the trouble had already happened. It was at the audition—for that hour they had talked about for so long did finally, actually, roll around. Weston's fine concluding high note had been sent aloft to fade, he had heard his little discreet applause from the handful of listeners who sat in the auditorium with their notebooks out, and he had made his little bow. He and Miss Eavers were leaving the stage of the auditorium when she and her music books brushed past him into the wings. A man was coming into the wings from another direction, stooping to enter a small door that opened into the backstage area from the auditorium itself. A short flight of steps brought him quickly level with them.

"Dorothy Eavers!" he said. "I couldn't believe it."

"Sh-h-h!" said Miss Eavers, a bit teacherish. "You'll have to whisper."

"When I came through the door and saw you up there on the stage, I said, 'I'm right back in college and late for convocation.' You always played the Alma Mater."

"I saw you when you came in. From the corner of my eye. Can you imagine! I recognized you right away."

Weston was hurt. That she could have been free to notice anybody while he was singing, even out of the corner of her eye! And where had she been looking all the other times she accompanied him? Oh, he was very hurt.

Some quality in the season, in the spring air that was so much heavier this far south than what they had left in Stilton, liberated him. He felt he was dreaming, so he did not try to be polite. He certainly did not want to go along while Miss Eavers had lunch with this newspaperman she used to go to college with. He said he would go back to the hotel; he took advantage of an artist's right to weariness. He would go by himself, too. He had got around Jackson, after all, more than once; he knew that cities, like mechanical toys, never gave you any problem you couldn't figure out. He did not wave good-by when he parted from them on St. Charles Avenue, though he felt sure that she had turned and was looking back anxiously, had turned and turned again, until the man's big hand pressed her back below the shoulder blades and she moved on. "If anything should happen to him . . ." He did not hear her say it, but if she was saying anything, that was it—not "But I want to be with Weston." Just let a man who wasn't from Stilton come along and she became exactly like all the others *in* Stilton. Maybe she was stuck-up after all. He was tremendously successful in reaching the hotel.

The only thing he was not successful in doing was staying alone in his room. He had absolutely nothing to say to himself. If he didn't mind being alone at home, in Stilton, it was only because somebody was always wondering about him. He went down into the lobby and wandered about among the palms. He bought some chewing gum, some Life Savers, and a pack of cigarettes, just to see how it felt. He sat down at a desk in the writing room and wrote, on a picture postcard of the hotel, "I have slipped away from Miss Eavers and tonight I am going to some HOT SPOT. Oh, boy!"

Then he could not think of anybody to address it to. A year ago, there would have been three or four. But now they all knew the truth: He Sang. It was her fault that he couldn't make the card sound right. Oh, hadn't she been awful? She had cut him off from everybody except herself; then she had gone off and left him. He tore the card in two and went to buy a newspaper. He sat on the edge of a sofa, sinking down between the armrest and the big leather cushion. The paper was all about a world as troubled as his own, though much less concentrated.

"See anything good, sonny?"

There was a man sitting at the far end of the sofa from him. He spoke with a Northern accent and he was whacking away on a stick of gum.

"Want to read it?" Weston asked.

"No, thanks. Already seen it. Just making conversation. Killing time. You meeting someone?"

"I was meeting my teacher. But she won't come now."

"I thought boys always wanted to get away from their teachers. Maybe you're teacher's pet. Or maybe your teacher's a pet. Ha-ha!"

Weston had never actually heard anybody say "Ha-ha!" before. He had read it lots of times, mainly in the funny paper. This gave him confidence. "I'm just crazy about Miss Eavers," he confided mournfully. "Only she's so much older than I am that naturally we can't get married. She likes me a lot, though. She won't give anybody in town a date, but when I come to take a lesson, that makes her happy. I know it does. She says so. I can sing real well, see? Miss Eavers says if I'm not a genius, I'm the closest thing to it she's ever heard sing. We came down to New Orleans to audition me for this real famous boys' choir. Everybody at home just knows I'll get in. I can make people cry. Then, this morning, right while I was singing, this man her own age came in. She'd already met him a long time ago, and–" He found the next too grisly to relate.

"Now she's gone off with him," said the man, as easy as that. "So you didn't get the prize?"

"The what?"

"Did you win the money? Did they take you on? You know what I mean."

"Oh, the choir director. I don't know. He said for us all to come back this afternoon and they would tell us which ones. But I don't care about it. It was all on account of her I was doing so well."

"Look, now, kid, you can't look at it that way. You gotta get in there and win, see? By golly, maybe you *are* a genius. All you gotta do is get in there and show 'em."

"It would make her feel a lot worse if I didn't," said Weston, though it had never seriously entered his head that they wouldn't take him. Too many people had told him how good he was, some even from Out of the State. He was greatly in demand for civic clubs and had given a concert in Jackson. "However, I will," he added.

"That's the spirit."

The Northern man, who was waiting for space on an airplane to Denver, Colorado, took him to the hotel drugstore and bought him a sandwich and an ice-cream soda. Then he seemed to forget that Weston was there at all. Perhaps longer conversations than the one they had exchanged were unknown to him. He hauled himself back to attention by means of a tremendous yawn. "I think you're really stuck on this schoolteacher, kid."

Weston did not answer.

"Yes, sir, got a real old-timey crush. But she's perfectly right, you know–going off with that fellow her own age. Look at it from her standpoint. Anyway, you got to learn to be realistic. Y'know, if I've got a motto, that's it. *Be Real-isstic!"* The man leaned close to pronounce this thoroughly, and revealed very bad breath and tartar more than halfway down each tooth.

"Thank you for the chicken salad sandwich and chocolate ice-cream soda," said Weston. "I better hurry on back now. I hope you have a nice trip and all. Good-by."

He walked hastily out of the drugstore, bumping into stools. He wished he had not told the Yankee man anything. He had turned out to be just as bad as Mother and Daddy. Never mind. Weston *did* sing better than anybody else, and he had only to go to the auditorium and hear them say so.

When he rejoined Miss Eavers outside the auditorium that afternoon, she was alone. She looked as cool as ever, in her spring silk dress that had something like water lilies printed on it, and her new little curly straw hat. She had bought all this for their trip, just as he had not worn until now his blue-and-beige checked flannel coat and gabardine trousers. His underwear was new, too, if anybody wanted to know. Miss Eavers held her long spring wrap over her arm, but otherwise she looked just the same as when she walked away with the man she used to know in college. Maybe her forehead was a little rosy and her hair shaken a bit forward, as though by a breeze or agitation, but this might have resulted naturally from having said to the man, "I have to hurry on back now," and leaving him with a disappointed feeling, just as Weston had left the Yankee in the drugstore. At any rate, neither of them told each other about it.

"Hello, Miss Eavers."

"Weston." She touched his lapel, which he knew to be perfectly straight. "They say we can go in and have a seat. In a few minutes they'll tell us who has been chosen."

He held the door for her.

Going back, they had the lounge car to themselves most of the time. It got dark along about Picayune, and Weston tried to think of some way to make Miss Eavers not notice when they got to Stilton, so that they could go on to Chicago together in the coach with the soft gray rugs and the green easy chairs and the lamplight, and maybe never come home at all. She could change her printed silk dresses for black satin.

It would be as simple as that. Better and better night clubs would pay them more and more. They would show the world.

The fact was that the director of the boys' choir had not chosen Weston after the audition; worse still, he had not mentioned him at all. But now that Weston and Miss Eavers had been through every detail of the audition four times and had decided that the director, if not actually crazy, knew nothing about his job, he began to feel drowsy and comforted, just as he felt after any other kind of misfortune—a bump on the head, for instance. In Chicago, they all came around to his dressing room to shake hands.

Presently, in the swaying twilight where they so comfortably were, he became aware that Miss Eavers was talking. He even knew that she had begun to speak after a sigh. "I had such a good time today. It was a wonderful surprise to see Frank. I hadn't seen him in years. He took me to such a nice place to eat. We had good food. Later, we rode out along the lake in his car. We had a lot to talk about. I want to live like that. I want somebody nice, who knows where to go and what to order, to ask me out every now and then. I miss that kind of thing in Stilton." She sighed again, and the two sighs formed the proper setting around her words.

He leaned toward her. She must be told right away about Chicago. He finished splendidly, drawing out his wallet. "You didn't know, but Daddy gave me fifty dollars extra, to have in reserve in case we needed it. So we've got a start, see?"

"Weston." Her face had the expression he could always bring to ladies' faces in every audience by singing one of the old ones, like "Old Black Joe" or, more successful yet, "Danny Boy." He had even made her cry. She reached across and caught his hand. "Weston." She said it again.

He looked down at her hand on his; it might as well have been the chilly white touch of an aunt. She even patted. He knew then they would not be going to Chicago, let alone trying to sing in night clubs. They would get off when the train stopped at Stilton.

"We planned this trip for two months," he said, "and you went off with the first man that came along."

"Oh, Weston, do try to look at it from my standpoint."

"All this time you made me think I could sing better than anybody else in the world."

"I thought you could. You can! I still think you can!"

She was going to have answers to everything, and he would have to believe them. All that, too, came of her being older.

He left Miss Eavers and began to wander as freely as a chimpanzee on the loose through the dark, night-traveling train. When they reached the outskirts of Stilton, just at the point where he knew that the train broke over the rise and all the watchers at the station could see, he had found the right way to release the emergency brakes. Having previously read, on a printed card beside the handle, all the penalties that pertained to this action, along with the directions on how to perform it, he was not surprised at the wrath of the conductor, or at how more and more officials kept appearing from various distances along the train. When at last they pulled into the Stilton station, even the engineer came down from the engine to join the others, all on account of Weston. He could tell the engineer by the great big cuffs on his gloves.

The conductor hauled Weston down the steps by one arm. Not until then did Miss Eavers appear. "Where's yer husband, lady? Is his daddy here?" they all asked her, but she only shook her head in a dazed way, as though there had really been a wreck. She never did tell them that she wasn't anything but his music teacher.

Then everybody left off speaking to her, because Weston's father was there, saying, "I'm his daddy. You don't mean *he* did it? You don't say! You *don't* say!" He could not have been happier if he were making eggnog on Christmas morning. He lighted a cigar and offered others to the conductor and the engineer and the stationmaster, and cheerfully signed all the papers about how he would have to pay the twenty-five-dollar fine. After the train left, all the men who had come down to meet it hung around the station for a long time, talking. They all could tell about similar things they had done, and all of them said that when they were boys they had wanted to stop a train some way or other but never had. Mr. Robert Littleton had tried to flag one once, but it hadn't paid any attention. Finally, Daddy and Weston went home together.

"How did you stop her, son?" Daddy asked on the way home. "How did you reach the handle?"

"I stood on a suitcase in the car platform," Weston said.

It was quite some time before anybody thought to ask him how he had done in the music contest.

The next afternoon, Miss Eavers called to say that he had not come to his music lesson and that she thought he might be sick, but his mother said no, he wasn't sick, but he wasn't in the house right then and he would call her later. Weston was there, however. He was lying flat on his stomach on the glider on the side porch, listening to every word, but he was incapable, through something that seemed a good deal like laziness, of opening his mouth to say so.

In the following days, he rallied. He sang for the Kiwanis Club at Scott's Hotel on Friday, as scheduled, and, the next week, went with Miss Eavers to Clinton, Mississippi, to give a program for the Junior Chamber of Commerce. But the weather kept getting hotter. School sped inexorably toward June. What had it all meant? Nothing could completely focus his attention. He took to playing the radio, listening to any old thing.

During May, some newspaperman came up all the way from New Orleans twice to see Miss Eavers; the postmistress said that letters were being exchanged. Nobody was surprised when she resigned from the school in June. The only question was how Weston would "take it"; to everybody's relief, Weston did not seem overly concerned. As a matter of fact, he believed himself to be secretly glad of it, though only in a minor way, like finishing typhoid shots. Whenever he had wanted to do something, it seemed he always had a lesson or a program. Naturally, he couldn't put *all* of his time on music.

So neither anybody nor anything warned him about the anguish that struck him like chills and fever one hot summer night when he awoke wondering, *How did she get home?*

Nobody had seen her leave the station that night they got back. (What would she have to say to men who swapped stories while they waited around to meet the train, or to railroad conductors, or to the engineer in his big dirty gloves?) She had simply withdrawn. He saw her now, carrying the suitcase through all the poor parts of Stilton, at last turning into the pretty street where she lived. Now she passed alone under the trees, sweet as an arrow, and started up the walk to her rooming house. The yard around her rested fragrant and damp with spring; the bridal wreath hung whiter than moonlight. The porch was wooden and hollow, but she did not make much noise crossing it, and in a bit of moonlight she saw where to fit her key. She turned sideways to get the suitcase through. Then she closed the door behind her. The house was big and dark and quiet; lots of people lived there, but he knew where her room was–right above the front porch. The street said nothing, all its length. In the yard, the flowers did not stir. No light came on.

From the town he watched–from just what point he did not know, but he knew he watched–and no light ever came on. She might as well have walked through the false front of a house and fallen a mile, the way they did in movie cartoons. She might as well have died on the stair.

Miss Eavers! Miss Eavers! Oh, wait, wait, wait, wait, wait!

On the hot, coverless July bed Weston lay, and a tongue of lightning flickered in the far sky.

FIRST DARK

When Tom Beavers started coming back to Richton, Mississippi, on weekends, after the war was over, everybody in town was surprised and pleased. They had never noticed him much before he paid them this compliment; now they could not say enough nice things. There was not much left in Richton for him to call family—just his aunt who had raised him, Miss Rita Beavers, old as God, ugly as sin, deaf as a post. So he must be fond of the town, they reasoned; certainly it was a pretty old place. Far too many young men had left it and never come back at all.

He would drive in every Friday night from Jackson, where he worked. All weekend, his Ford, dusty of flank, like a hard-ridden horse, would sit parked down the hill near Miss Rita's old wire front gate, which sagged from the top hinge and had worn a span in the ground. On Saturday morning, he would head for the drugstore, then the post office; then he would be observed walking here and there around the streets under the shade trees. It was as though he were looking for something.

He wore steel taps on his heels, and in the still the click of them on the sidewalks would sound across the big front lawns and all the way up to the porches of the houses, where two ladies might be sitting behind a row of ferns. They would identify him to one another, murmuring in their fine little voices, and say it was just too bad there was nothing here for young people. It was just a shame they didn't have one or two more old houses, here, for a Pilgrimage—look how Natchez had waked up.

One Saturday morning in early October, Tom Beavers sat at the counter in the drugstore and reminded Totsie Poteet, the drugstore clerk, of a ghost story. Did he remember the strange old man who used to appear to people who were coming into Richton along the Jackson road at twilight—what they called "first dark"?

"Sure I remember," said Totsie. "Old Cud'n Jimmy Wiltshire used to tell us about him every time we went 'possum hunting. I could see him plain as I can see you, the way he used to tell it. Tall, with a top hat on, yeah, and waiting in the weeds alongside the road ditch, so'n you couldn't tell if he wasn't taller than any mortal man could be, because you couldn't tell if he was standing down in the ditch or not. It would look like he just grew up out of the weeds. Then he'd signal to you."

"Them that stopped never saw anybody," said Tom Beavers, stirring his coffee. "There were lots of folks besides Mr. Jimmy that saw him."

"There was, let me see . . ." Totsie enumerated others—some men, some women, some known to drink, others who never touched a drop. There was no way to explain it. "There was that story the road gang told. Do you remember, or were you off at school? It was while they were straightening the road out to the highway—taking the curves out and building a new bridge. Anyway, they said that one night at quitting time, along in the winter and just about dark, this old guy signaled to some of 'em. They said they went over and he asked them to move a bulldozer they had left across the road, because he had a wagon back behind on a little dirt road, with a sick nigger girl in it. Had to get to the doctor and this was the only way. They claimed they knew didn't nobody live back there on that little old road, but niggers can come from anywhere. So they moved the bulldozer and cleared back a whole lot of other stuff, and waited and waited. Not only didn't no wagon ever come, but the man that had stopped them, he was gone, too. They was right shook up over it. You never heard that one?"

"No, I never did." Tom Beavers said this with his eyes looking up over his coffee cup, as though he sat behind a hand of cards. His lashes and brows were heavier than was ordinary, and worked as a veil might, to keep you away from knowing exactly what he was thinking.

"They said he was tall and had a hat on." The screen door flapped to announce a customer, but Totsie kept on talking. "But whether he was a white man or a real light-colored nigger they couldn't say. Some said one and some said another. I figured they'd been pulling on the jug a little earlier than usual. You know why? I never heard of *our* ghost *saying* nothing. Did you, Tom?"

He moved away on the last words, the way a clerk will, talking back over his shoulder and ahead of him to his new customer at the same time, as though he had two voices and two heads. "And what'll it be today, Miss Frances?"

The young woman standing at the counter had a prescription already out of her bag. She stood with it poised between her fingers, but her attention was drawn toward Tom Beavers, his coffee cup, and the conversation she had interrupted. She was a girl whom no ordinary description would fit. One would have to know first of all who she was: Frances Harvey. After that, it was all right for her to be a little odd-looking, with her reddish hair that curled back from her brow, her light eyes, and her high, pale temples. This is not the material for being pretty, but in Frances Harvey it was what could sometimes be beauty. Her family home was laden with history that nobody but the Harveys could remember. It would have been on a Pilgrimage if Richton had had one. Frances still lived in it, looking after an invalid mother.

"What were you-all talking about?" she wanted to know.

"About that ghost they used to tell about," said Totsie, holding out his hand for the prescription. "The one people used to see just outside of town, on the Jackson road."

"But why?" she demanded. "Why were you talking about him?"

"Tom, here—" the clerk began, but Tom Beavers interrupted him.

"I was asking because I was curious," he said. He had been studying her from the corner of his eye. Her face was beginning to show the wear of her mother's long illness, but that couldn't be called change. Changing was something she didn't seem to have done, her own style being the only one natural to her.

"I was asking," he went on, "because I saw him." He turned away from her somewhat too direct gaze and said to Totsie Poteet, whose mouth had fallen open, "It was where the new road runs close to the old road, and as far as I could tell he was right on the part of the old road where people always used to see him."

"But when?" Frances Harvey demanded.

"Last night," he told her. "Just around first dark. Driving home."

A wealth of quick feeling came up in her face. "So did I! Driving home from Jackson! I saw him, too!"

For some people, a liking for the same phonograph record or for Mayan archaeology is enough of an excuse to get together. Possibly, seeing the same ghost was no more than that. Anyway, a week later, on Saturday at first dark, Frances Harvey and Tom Beavers were sitting together in a car parked just off the highway, near the spot where they agreed the ghost had appeared. The season was that long, peculiar one between summer and fall, and there were so many crickets and tree frogs going full tilt in their periphery that their voices could hardly be distinguished from the background noises, though they both would have heard a single footfall in the grass. An edge of autumn was in the air at night, and Frances had put on a tweed jacket at the last minute, so the smell of moth balls was in the car, brisk and most unghostlike.

But Tom Beavers was not going to forget the value of the ghost, whether it put in an appearance or not. His questions led Frances into reminiscence.

"No, I never saw him before the other night," she admitted. "The Negroes used to talk in the kitchen, and Regina and I—you know my sister Regina—would sit there listening, scared to go and scared to stay. Then finally going to bed upstairs was no relief, either, because sometimes Aunt Henrietta was visiting us, and *she'd* seen it. Or if she wasn't visiting us, the front room next to us, where she stayed, would be empty, which was worse. There was no way to lock ourselves in, and besides, what was there to lock out? We'd lie all night like two sticks in bed, and shiver. Papa finally had to take a hand. He called us in and sat us down and said that the whole thing was easy to explain—it was all automobiles. What their headlights did with the dust and shadows out on the Jackson road. 'Oh, but Sammie and Jerry!' we said, with great big eyes, sitting side by side on the sofa, with our tennis shoes flat on the floor."

"Who were Sammie and Jerry?" asked Tom Beavers.

"Sammie was our cook. Jerry was her son, or husband, or something. Anyway, they certainly didn't have cars. Papa called them in. They were standing side by side by the bookcase, and Regina and I were on the sofa—four pairs of big eyes, and Papa pointing his finger.

Papa said, 'Now, you made up these stories about ghosts, didn't you?' 'Yes, sir,' said Sammie. 'We made them up.' 'Yes, sir,' said Jerry. 'We sho did.' 'Well, then, you can just stop it,' Papa said. 'See how peaked these children look?' Sammie and Jerry were terribly polite to us for a week, and we got in the car and rode up and down the Jackson road at first dark to see if the headlights really did it. But we never saw anything. We didn't tell Papa, but headlights had nothing whatever to do with it."

"You had your own *car* then?" He couldn't believe it.

"Oh no!" She was emphatic. "We were too young for that. Too young to drive, really, but we did anyway."

She leaned over to let him give her cigarette a light, and saw his hand tremble. Was he afraid of the ghost or of her? She would have to stay away from talking family.

Frances remembered Tommy Beavers from her childhood—a small boy going home from school down a muddy side road alone, walking right down the middle of the road. His old aunt's house was at the bottom of a hill. It was damp there, and the yard was always muddy, with big fat chicken tracks all over it, like Egyptian writing. How did Frances know? She could not remember going there, ever. Miss Rita Beavers was said to order cold ham, mustard, bread, and condensed milk from the grocery store. "I doubt if that child ever has anything hot," Frances's mother had said once. He was always neatly dressed in the same knee pants, high socks, and checked shirt, and sat several rows ahead of Frances in study hall, right in the middle of his seat. He was three grades behind her; in those days, that much younger seemed very young indeed. What had happened to his parents? There was some story, but it was not terribly interesting, and, his people being of no importance, she had forgotten.

"I think it's past time for our ghost," she said. "He's never out so late at night."

"He gets hungry, like me," said Tom Beavers. "Are you hungry, Frances?"

They agreed on a highway restaurant where an orchestra played on weekends. Everyone went there now.

From the moment they drew up on the graveled entrance, cheerful lights and a blare of music chased the spooks from their heads. Tom Beavers ordered well and danced well, as it turned out. Wasn't there something she had heard about his being "smart"? By "smart," Southerners mean intellectual, and they say it in an almost condescending way, smart being what you are when you can't be anything else, but it is better, at least, than being nothing. Frances Harvey had been away enough not to look at things from a completely Southern point of view, and she was encouraged to discover that she and Tom had other things in common besides a ghost, though all stemming, perhaps, from the imagination it took to see one.

They agreed about books and favorite movies and longing to see more plays. She sighed that life in Richton was so confining, but he assured her that Jackson could be just as bad; *it* was getting to be like any Middle Western city, he said, while Richton at least had a sense of the past. This was the main reason, he went on, gaining confidence in the jumble of commonplace noises–dishes, music, and a couple of drinkers chattering behind them–that he had started coming back to Richton so often. He wanted to keep a connection with the past. He lived in a modern apartment, worked in a soundproof office–he could be in any city. But Richton was where he had been born and raised, and nothing could be more old-fashioned. Too many people seemed to have their lives cut in two. He was earnest in desiring that this should not happen to him.

"You'd better be careful," Frances said lightly. Her mood did not incline her to profound conversation. "There's more than one ghost in Richton. You may turn into one yourself, like the rest of us."

"It's the last thing I'd think of you," he was quick to assure her.

Had Tommy Beavers really said such a thing, in such a natural, charming way? Was Frances Harvey really so pleased? Not only was she pleased but, feeling warmly alive amid the music and small lights, she agreed with him. She could not have agreed with him more.

"I hear that Thomas Beavers has gotten to be a very attractive man," Frances Harvey's mother said unexpectedly one afternoon.

Frances had been reading aloud–Jane Austen this time. Theirs was one house where the leather-bound sets were actually read. In Jane Austen, men and women seesawed back and forth for two or three hundred pages until they struck a point of balance; then they got married. She had just put aside the book, at the end of a chapter, and risen to lower the shade against the slant of afternoon sun. "Or so Cud'n Jennie and Mrs. Giles Antley and Miss Fannie Stapleton have been coming and telling you," she said.

"People talk, of course, but the consensus is favorable," Mrs. Harvey said. "Wonders never cease; his mother ran away with a brush salesman. But nobody can make out what he's up to, coming back to Richton."

"Does he have to be 'up to' anything?" Frances asked.

"Men are always up to something," said the old lady at once. She added, more slowly, "In Thomas's case, maybe it isn't anything it oughtn't to be. They say he reads a lot. He may just have taken up with some sort of idea."

Frances stole a long glance at her mother's face on the pillow. Age and illness had reduced the image of Mrs. Harvey to a kind of caricature, centered on a mouth that Frances could not help comparing to that of a fish. There was a tension around its rim, as though it were outlined in bone, and the underlip even stuck out a little. The mouth ate, it took medicine, it asked for things, it gasped when breath was short, it commented. But when it commented, it ceased to be just a mouth and became part of Mrs. Harvey, that witty tyrant with the infallible memory for the right detail, who was at her terrible best about men.

"And what could he be thinking of?" she was wont to inquire when some man had acted foolishly. No one could ever defend accurately the man in question, and the only conclusion was Mrs. Harvey's; namely, that he wasn't thinking, if, indeed, he could. Although she had never been a belle, never a flirt, her popularity with men was always formidable. She would be observed talking marathons with one in a corner, and could you ever be sure, when they both burst into laughter, that they had not just exchanged the most shocking stories? "Of course, *he*—" she would begin later, back with the family, and the masculinity that had just been encouraged to strut and preen a little was quickly shown up as idiotic. Perhaps Mrs. Harvey hoped by this method to train her daughters away from a lot of sentimental nonsense that was their birthright as pretty Southern girls in a house with a lawn that moonlight fell on and that was often lit also by Japanese lanterns hung for parties. "Oh, he's not like that, Mama!" the little girls would cry. They were already alert for heroes who would ride up and cart them off. "Well, then, you watch," she would say. Sure enough, if you watched, she would be right.

Mrs. Harvey's younger daughter, Regina, was a credit to her mother's long campaign; she married well. The old lady, however, never tired of pointing out behind her son-in-law's back that his fondness for money was ill-concealed, that he had the longest feet she'd ever seen, and that he sometimes made grammatical errors.

Her elder daughter, Frances, on a trip to Europe, fell in love, alas! The gentleman was of French extraction but Swiss citizenship, and Frances did not marry him, because he was already married—that much filtered back to Richton. In response to a cable, she had returned home one hot July in time to witness her father's wasted face and last weeks of life. That same September, the war began. When peace came, Richton wanted to know if Frances Harvey would go back to Europe. Certain subtly complicated European matters, little understood in Richton, seemed to be obstructing Romance; one of them was probably named Money. Meanwhile, Frances's mother took to bed, in what was generally known to be her last illness.

So no one crossed the ocean, but eventually Tom Beavers came up to Mrs. Harvey's room one afternoon, to tea.

Though almost all her other faculties were seriously impaired, in ear and tongue Mrs. Harvey was as sound as a young beagle, and she could still weave a more interesting conversation than most people who go about every day and look at the world. She was of the old school of Southern lady talkers; she vexed you with no ideas, she tried to protect you from even a moment of silence. In the old days, when a bright company filled the downstairs rooms, she could keep the ball rolling amongst a crowd. Everyone—all the men especially—got their word in, but the flow of things came back to her. If one of those twenty-minutes-to-or-after silences fell—and even with her they did occur—people would turn and look at her daughter Frances. "And what do you think?" some kind-eyed gentleman would ask. Frances did not credit that she had the sort of face people would turn to, and so did not know how to take advantage of it. What did she think? Well, to answer that honestly took a moment of reflection—a fatal moment, it always turned out. Her mother would be up instructing the maid, offering someone an ashtray or another goody, or remarking outright, "Frances is so timid. She never says a word."

Tom Beavers stayed not only past teatime that day but for a drink as well. Mrs. Harvey was induced to take a glass of sherry, and now her bed became her enormous throne. Her keenest suffering as an invalid was occasioned by the absence of men. "What is a house without a man in it?" she would often cry. From her eagerness to be charming to Frances's guest that afternoon, it seemed that she would have married Tom Beavers herself if he had asked her. The amber liquid set in her small four-sided glass glowed like a jewel, and her diamond flashed; she had put on her best ring for the company. What a pity no longer to show her ankle, that delicious bone, so remarkably slender for so ample a frame.

Since the time had flown so, they all agreed enthusiastically that Tom should wait downstairs while Frances got ready to go out to dinner with him. He was hardly past the stair landing before the old lady was seized by such a fit of coughing that she could hardly speak. "It's been—it's been too much—too *much* for me!" she gasped out.

But after Frances had found the proper sedative for her, she was calmed, and insisted on having her say.

"Thomas Beavers has a good job with an insurance company in Jackson," she informed her daughter, as though Frances were incapable of finding out anything for herself. "He makes a good appearance. He is the kind of man"—she paused—"who would value a wife of good family." She stopped, panting for breath. It was this complimenting a man behind his back that was too much for her—as much out of character, and hence as much of a strain, as if she had got out of bed and tried to tap-dance.

"Heavens, Mama," Frances said, and almost giggled.

At this, the old lady, thinking the girl had made light of her suitor, half screamed at her, "Don't be so critical, Frances! You can't be so critical of men!" and fell into an even more terrible spasm of coughing. Frances had to lift her from the pillow and hold her straight until the fit passed and her breath returned. Then Mrs. Harvey's old, dry, crooked, ineradicably feminine hand was laid on her daughter's arm, and when she spoke again she shook the arm to emphasize her words.

"When your father knew he didn't have long to live," she whispered, "we discussed whether to send for you or not. You know you were his favorite, Frances. 'Suppose our girl is happy over there,' he said. 'I wouldn't want to bring her back on my account.' I said you had to have the right to choose whether to come back or not. You'd never forgive us, I said, if you didn't have the right to choose."

Frances could visualize this very conversation taking place between her parents; she could see them, decorous and serious, talking over the fact of his approaching death as though it were a piece of property for agreeable disposition in the family. She could never remember him without thinking, with a smile, how he used to come home on Sunday from church (he being the only one of them who went) and how, immediately after hanging his hat and cane in the hall, he would say, "Let all things proceed in orderly progression to their final confusion. How long before dinner?" No, she had had to come home. Some humor had always existed between them—her father and her—and humor, of all things, cannot be betrayed.

"I meant to go back," said Frances now. "But there was the war. At first I kept waiting for it to be over. I still wake up at night sometimes thinking, I wonder how much longer before the war will be over. And then—" She stopped short. For the fact was that her lover had been married to somebody else, and her mother was the very person capable of pointing that out to her. Even in the old lady's present silence she heard the unspoken thought, and got up nervously from the bed, loosing herself from the hand on her arm, smoothing her reddish hair where it was inclined to straggle. "And then he wrote me that he had gone back to his wife. Her family and his had always been close, and the war brought them back together. This was in Switzerland—naturally, he couldn't stay on in Paris during the war. There were the children, too—all of them were Catholic. Oh, I do understand how it happened."

Mrs. Harvey turned her head impatiently on the pillow. She dabbed at her moist upper lip with a crumpled linen handkerchief; her diamond flashed once in motion. "War, religion, wife, children—yes. But men do what they want to."

Could anyone make Frances as angry as her mother could? "Believe what you like then! You always know so much better than I do. *You* would have managed things somehow. Oh, you would have had your way!"

"Frances," said Mrs. Harvey, "I'm an old woman." The hand holding the handkerchief fell wearily, and her eyelids dropped shut. "If you should want to marry Thomas Beavers and bring him here, I will accept it. There will be no distinctions. Next, I suppose, we will be having his old deaf aunt for tea. I hope she has a hearing aid. I haven't got the strength to holler at her."

"I don't think any of these plans are necessary, Mama."

The eyelids slowly lifted. "None?"

"None."

Mrs. Harvey's breathing was as audible as a voice. She spoke, at last, without scorn, honestly. "I cannot bear the thought of leaving you alone. You, nor the house, nor your place in it—alone. I foresaw Tom Beavers here! What has he got that's better than you and this place? I knew he would come!"

Terrible as her mother's meanness was, it was not half so terrible as her love. Answering nothing, explaining nothing, Frances stood without giving in. She trembled, and tears ran down her cheeks. The two women looked at each other helplessly across the darkening room.

In the car, later that night, Tom Beavers asked, "Is your mother trying to get rid of me?" They had passed an unsatisfactory evening, and he was not going away without knowing why.

"No, it's just the other way around," said Frances, in her candid way. "She wants you so much she'd like to eat you up. She wants you in the house. Couldn't you tell?"

"She once chased me out of the yard," he recalled.

"Not really!"

They turned into Harvey Street (that was actually the name of it), and when he had drawn the car up before the dark front steps, he related the incident. He told her that Mrs. Harvey had been standing just there in the yard, talking to some visitor who was leaving by inches, the way ladies used to—ten minutes' more talk for every forward step. He, a boy not more than nine, had been crossing a corner of the lawn where a faint path had already been worn; he had had nothing to do with wearing the path and had taken it quite innocently and openly. "You, boy!" Mrs. Harvey's fan was an enormous painted thing. She had furled it with a clack so loud he could still hear it. "You don't cut through my yard again! Now, you stop where you are and you go all the way back around by the walk, and don't you ever do that again." He went back and all the way around. She was fanning comfortably as he passed. "Old Miss Rita Beavers' nephew," he heard her say, and though he did not speak of it now to Frances, Mrs. Harvey's rich tone had been as stuffed with wickedness as a fruitcake with goodies. In it you could have found so many things: that, of course, he didn't know any better, that he was poor, that she knew his first name but would not deign to mention it, that she meant him to understand all this and more. Her fan was probably still somewhere in the house, he reflected. If he ever opened the wrong door, it might fall from above and brain him. It seemed impossible that nowadays he could even have the chance to open the wrong door in the Harvey house. With its graceful rooms and big lawn, its camellias and magnolia trees, the house had been one of the enchanted castles of his childhood, and Frances and Regina Harvey had been two princesses running about the lawn one Saturday morning drying their hair with big white towels and not noticing when he passed.

There was a strong wind that evening. On the way home, Frances and Tom had noticed how the night was streaming, but whether with mist or dust or the smoke from some far-off fire in the dry winter woods they could not tell. As they stood on the sidewalk, the clouds raced over them, and moonlight now and again came through. A limb rubbed against a high cornice. Inside the screened area of the porch, the swing jangled in its iron chains. Frances's coat blew about her, and her hair blew. She felt herself to be no different from anything there that the wind was blowing on, her happiness of no relevance in the dark torrent of nature.

"I can't leave her, Tom. But I can't ask you to live with her, either. Of all the horrible ideas! She'd make demands, take all my time, laugh at you behind your back–she has to run everything. You'd hate me in a week."

He did not try to pretty up the picture, because he had a feeling that it was all too accurate. Now, obviously, was the time she should go on to say there was no good his waiting around through the years for her. But hearts are not noted for practicality, and Frances stood with her hair blowing, her hands stuck in her coat pockets, and did not go on to say anything. Tom pulled her close to him–in, as it were, out of the wind.

"I'll be coming by next weekend, just like I've been doing. And the next one, too," he said. "We'll just leave it that way, if it's O.K. with you."

"Oh yes, it is, Tom!" Never so satisfied to be weak, she kissed him and ran inside.

He stood watching on the walk until her light flashed on. Well, he had got what he was looking for; a connection with the past, he had said. It was right upstairs, a splendid old mass of dictatorial female flesh, thinking about him. Well, they could go on, he and Frances, sitting on either side of a sickbed, drinking tea and sipping sherry with streaks of gray broadening on their brows, while the familiar seasons came and went. So he thought. Like Frances, he believed that the old lady had a stranglehold on life.

Suddenly, in March, Mrs. Harvey died.

A heavy spring funeral, with lots of roses and other scented flowers in the house, is the worst kind of all. There is something so recklessly fecund about a south Mississippi spring that death becomes just another word in the dictionary, along with swarms of others, and even so pure and white a thing as a gardenia has too heavy a scent and may suggest decay. Mrs. Harvey, amid such odors, sank to rest with a determined pomp, surrounded by admiring eyes.

While Tom Beavers did not "sit with the family" at this time, he was often observed with the Harveys, and there was whispered speculation among those who were at the church and the cemetery that the Harvey house might soon come into new hands, "after a decent interval." No one would undertake to judge for a Harvey how long an interval was decent.

Frances suffered from insomnia in the weeks that followed, and at night she wandered about the spring-swollen air of the old house, smelling now spring and now death. "Let all things proceed in orderly progression to their final confusion." She had always thought that the final confusion referred to death, but now she began to think that it could happen any time; that final confusion, having found the door ajar, could come into a house and show no inclination to leave. The worrisome thing, the thing it all came back to, was her mother's clothes. They were numerous, expensive, and famous, and Mrs. Harvey had never discarded any of them. If you opened a closet door, hatboxes as big as crates towered above your head. The shiny black trim of a great shawl stuck out of a wardrobe door just below the lock. Beneath the lid of a cedar chest, the bright eyes of a tippet were ready to twinkle at you. And the jewels! Frances's sister had restrained her from burying them all on their mother, and had even gone off with a wad of them tangled up like fishing tackle in an envelope, on the ground of promises made now and again in the course of the years.

("Regina," said Frances, "what else were you two talking about besides jewelry?" "I don't remember," said Regina, getting mad.

"Frances makes me so mad," said Regina to her husband as they were driving home. "I guess I can love Mama and jewelry, too. Mama certainly loved *us* and jewelry, too.")

One afternoon, Frances went out to the cemetery to take two wreaths sent by somebody who had "just heard." She drove out along the winding cemetery road, stopping the car a good distance before she reached the gate, in order to walk through the woods. The dogwood was beautiful that year. She saw a field where a house used to stand but had burned down; its cedar trees remained, and two bushes of bridal wreath marked where the front gate had swung. She stopped to admire the clusters of white bloom massing up through the young, feathery leaf and stronger now than the leaf itself. In the woods, the redbud was a smoke along shadowy ridges, and the dogwood drifted in layers, like snow suspended to give you all the time you needed to wonder at it. But why, she wondered, do they call it bridal *wreath?* It's not a wreath but a little bouquet. Wreaths are for funerals, anyway. As if to prove it, she looked down at the two she held, one in each hand. She walked on, and such complete desolation came over her that it was more of a wonder than anything in the woods—more, even, than death.

As she returned to the car from the two parallel graves, she met a thin, elderly, very light-skinned Negro man in the road. He inquired if she would mind moving her car so that he could pass. He said that there was a sick colored girl in his wagon, whom he was driving in to the doctor. He pointed out politely that she had left her car right in the middle of the road. "Oh, I'm terribly sorry," said Frances, and hurried off toward the car.

That night, reading late in bed, she thought, I could have given her a ride into town. No wonder they talk about us up North. A mile into town in a wagon! She might have been having a baby. She became conscience-stricken about it—foolishly so, she realized, but if you start worrying about something in a house like the one Frances Harvey lived in, in the dead of night, alone, you will go on worrying about it until dawn. She was out of sleeping pills.

She remembered having bought a fresh box of sedatives for her mother the day before she died. She got up and went into her mother's closed room, where the bed had been dismantled for airing, its wooden parts propped along the walls. On the closet shelf she found the shoe box into which she had packed away the familiar articles of the bedside table. Inside she found the small enameled-cardboard box, with the date and prescription inked on the cover in Totsie Poteet's somewhat prissy handwriting, but the box was empty. She was surprised, for she realized that her mother could have used only one or two of the pills. Frances was so determined to get some sleep that she searched the entire little store of things in the shoe box quite heartlessly, but there were no pills. She returned to her room and tried to read, but could not, and so smoked instead and stared out at the dawn-blackening sky. The house sighed. She could not take her mind off the Negro girl. If she died . . . When it was light, she dressed and got into the car.

In town, the postman was unlocking the post office to sort the early mail. "I declare," he said to the rural mail carrier who arrived a few minutes later, "Miss Frances Harvey is driving herself crazy. Going back out yonder to the cemetery, and it not seven o'clock in the morning."

"Aw," said the rural deliveryman skeptically, looking at the empty road.

"That's right. I was here and seen her. You wait there, you'll see her come back. She'll drive herself nuts. Them old maids like that, left in them old houses—crazy and sweet, or crazy and mean, or just plain crazy. They just ain't locked up like them that's down in the asylum. That's the only difference."

"Miss Frances Harvey ain't no more than thirty-two, -three years old."

"Then she's just got more time to get crazier in. You'll see."

That day was Friday, and Tom Beavers, back from Jackson, came up Frances Harvey's sidewalk, as usual, at exactly a quarter past seven in the evening. Frances was not "going out" yet, and Regina had telephoned her long distance to say that "in all probability" she should not be receiving gentlemen "in." "What would Mama say?" Regina asked. Frances said she didn't know, which was not true, and went right on cooking dinners for Tom every weekend.

In the dining room that night, she sat across one corner of the long table from Tom. The useless length of polished cherry stretched away from them into the shadows as sadly as a road. Her plate pushed back, her chin resting on one palm, Frances stirred her coffee and said, "I don't know what on earth to do with all of Mama's clothes. I can't give them away, I can't sell them, I can't burn them, and the attic is full already. What can I do?"

"You look better tonight," said Tom.

"I slept," said Frances. "I slept and slept. From early this morning until just 'while ago. I never slept so well."

Then she told him about the Negro near the cemetery the previous afternoon, and how she had driven back out there as soon as dawn came, and found him again. He had been walking across the open field near the remains of the house that had burned down. There was no path to him from her, and she had hurried across ground uneven from old plowing and covered with the kind of small, tender grass it takes a very skillful mule to crop. "Wait!" she had cried. "Please wait!" The Negro had stopped and waited for her to reach him. "Your daughter?" she asked, out of breath.

"Daughter?" he repeated.

"The colored girl that was in the wagon yesterday. She was sick, you said, so I wondered. I could have taken her to town in the car, but I just didn't think. I wanted to know, how is she? Is she very sick?"

He had removed his old felt nigger hat as she approached him. "She a whole lot better, Miss Frances. She going to be all right now." Then he smiled at her. He did not say thank you, or anything more. Frances turned and walked back to the road and the car. And exactly as though the recovery of the Negro girl in the wagon had been her own recovery, she felt the return of a quiet breath and a steady pulse, and sensed the blessed stirring of a morning breeze. Up in her room, she had barely time to draw an old quilt over her before she fell asleep.

"When I woke, I knew about Mama," she said now to Tom. By the deepened intensity of her voice and eyes, it was plain that this was the important part. "It isn't right to say I *knew,*" she went on, "because I had known all the time—ever since last night. I just realized it, that's all. I realized she had killed herself. It had to be that."

He listened soberly through the story about the box of sedatives. "But why?" he asked her. "It maybe looks that way, but what would be her reason for doing it?"

"Well, you see—" Frances said, and stopped.

Tom Beavers talked quietly on. "She didn't suffer. With what she had, she could have lived five, ten, who knows how many years. She was well cared for. Not hard up, I wouldn't say. Why?"

The pressure of his questioning could be insistent, and her trust in him, even if he was nobody but old Miss Rita Beavers' nephew, was well-nigh complete. "Because of you and me," she said, finally. "I'm certain of it, Tom. She didn't want to stand in our way. She never knew how to express love, you see." Frances controlled herself with an effort.

He did not reply, but sat industriously balancing a match folder on the tines of an unused serving fork. Anyone who has passed a lonely childhood in the company of an old deaf aunt is not inclined to doubt things hastily, and Tom Beavers would not have said he disbelieved anything Frances had told him. In fact, it seemed only too real to him. Almost before his eyes, that imperial, practical old hand went fumbling for the pills in the dark. But there had been much more to it than just love, he reflected. Bitterness, too, and pride, and control. And humor, perhaps, and the memory of a frightened little boy chased out of the yard by a twitch of her fan. Being invited to tea was one thing; suicide was quite another. Times had certainly changed, he thought.

But, of course, he could not say that he believed it, either. There was only Frances to go by. The match folder came to balance and rested on the tines. He glanced up at her, and a chill walked up his spine, for she was too serene. Cheek on palm, a lock of reddish hair fallen forward, she was staring at nothing with the absorbed silence of a child, or of a sweet, silver-haired old lady engaged in memory. Soon he might find that more and more of her was vanishing beneath this placid surface.

He himself did not know what he had seen that Friday evening so many months ago—what the figure had been that stood forward from the roadside at the tilt of the curve and urgently waved an arm to him. By the time he had braked and backed, the man had disappeared. Maybe it had been somebody drunk (for Richton had plenty of those to offer), walking it off in the cool of the woods at first dark. No such doubts had occurred to Frances. And what if he told her now the story Totsie had related of the road gang and the sick Negro girl in the wagon? Another labyrinth would open before her; she would never get out.

In Richton, the door to the past was always wide open, and what came in through it and went out of it had made people "different." But it scarcely ever happens, even in Richton, that one is able to see the precise moment when fact becomes faith, when life turns into legend, and people start to bend their finest loyalties to make themselves bemused custodians of the grave. Tom Beavers saw that moment now, in the profile of this dreaming girl, and he knew there was no time to lose.

He dropped the match folder into his coat pocket. "I think we should be leaving, Frances."

"Oh well, I don't know about going out yet," she said. "People criticize you so. Regina even had the nerve to telephone. Word had got all the way to her that you came here to have supper with me and we were alone in the house. When I tell the maid I want biscuits made up for two people, she looks like 'What would yo' mama say?' "

"I mean," he said, "I think it's time we left for good."

"And never came back?" It was exactly like Frances to balk at going to a movie but seriously consider an elopement.

"Well, never is a long time. I like to see about Aunt Rita every once in a great while. She can't remember from one time to the next whether it's two days or two years since I last came."

She glanced about the walls and at the furniture, the pictures, and the silver. "But I thought you would want to live here, Tom. It never occurred to me. I know it never occurred to Mama . . . This house . . . It can't be just left."

"It's a fine old house," he agreed. "But what would you do with all your mother's clothes?"

Her freckled hand remained beside the porcelain cup for what seemed a long time. He waited and made no move toward her; he felt her uncertainty keenly, but he believed that some people should not be startled out of a spell.

"It's just as you said," he went on, finally. "You can't give them away, you can't sell them, you can't burn them, and you can't put them in the attic, because the attic is full already. So what are you going to do?"

Between them, the single candle flame achieved a silent altitude. Then, politely, as on any other night, though shaking back her hair in a decided way, she said, "Just let me get my coat, Tom."

She locked the door when they left, and put the key under the mat—a last obsequy to the house. Their hearts were bounding ahead faster than they could walk down the sidewalk or drive off in the car, and, mindful, perhaps, of what happened to people who did, they did not look back.

Had they done so, they would have seen that the Harvey house was more beautiful than ever. All unconscious of its rejection by so mere a person as Tom Beavers, it seemed, instead, to have got rid of what did not suit it, to be free, at last, to enter with abandon the land of mourning and shadows and memory.

A SOUTHERN LANDSCAPE

If you're like me and sometimes turn through the paper reading anything and everything because you're too lazy to get up and do what you ought to be doing, then you already know about my home town. There's a church there that has a gilded hand on the steeple, with the finger pointing to Heaven. The hand looks normal size, but it's really as big as a Ford car. At least, that's what they used to say in those little cartoon squares in the newspaper, full of sketches and exclamation points—"Strange As It Seems," "This Curious World," or Ripley's "Believe It or Not." Along with carnivorous tropical flowers, the Rosetta stone, and the cheerful information that the entire human race could be packed into a box a mile square and dumped into Grand Canyon, there it would be every so often, that old Presbyterian hand the size of a Ford car. It made me feel right in touch with the universe to see it in the paper—something it never did accomplish all by itself. I haven't seen anything about it recently, but then, Ford cars have got bigger, and, come to think of it, maybe they don't even print those cartoons any more. The name of the town, in case you're trying your best to remember and can't, is Port Claiborne, Mississippi. Not that I'm *from* there; I'm from *near* there.

Coming down the highway from Vicksburg, you come to Port Claiborne, and then to get to our house you turn off to the right on State Highway No. 202 and follow along the prettiest road. It's just about the way it always was—worn deep down like a tunnel and thick with shade in summer. In spring, it's so full of sweet heavy odors, they make you drunk, you can't think of anything—you feel you will faint or go right out of yourself. In fall, there is the rustle of leaves under your tires and the smell of them, all sad and Indian-like. Then in the winter, there are only dust and bare limbs, and mud when it rains, and everything is like an old dirt-dauber's nest up in the corner. Well, any season, you go twisting along this tunnel for a mile or so, then the road breaks down into a flat open run toward a wooden bridge that spans a swampy creek bottom. Tall trees grow up out of the bottom—willow and cypress, gum and sycamore—and there is a jungle of brush and vines—kudzu, Jackson vine, Spanish moss, grapevine, Virginia creeper, and honeysuckle—looping, climbing, and festooning the trees, and harboring every sort of snake and varmint underneath. The wooden bridge clatters when you cross, and down far below you can see water, lying still, not a good step wide. One bank is grassy and the other is a slant of ribbed white sand.

Then you're going to have to stop and ask somebody. Just say, "Can you tell me where to turn to get to the Summerall place?" Everybody knows us. Not that we *are* anybody—I don't mean that. It's just that we've been there forever. When you find the right road, you go right on up through a little wood of oaks, then across a field, across a cattle gap, and you're there. The house is nothing special, just a one-gable affair with a bay window and a front porch—the kind they built back around fifty or sixty years ago. The shrubs around the porch and the privet hedge around the bay window were all grown up too high the last time I was there. They ought to be kept trimmed down. The yard is a nice flat one, not much for growing grass but wonderful for shooting marbles. There were always two or three marble holes out near the pecan trees where I used to play with the colored children.

Benjy Hamilton swore he twisted his ankle in one of those same marble holes once when he came to pick me up for something my senior year in high school. For all I know, they're still there, but Benjy was more than likely drunk and so would hardly have needed a marble hole for an excuse to fall down. Once, before we got the cattle gap, he couldn't open the gate, and fell on the barbed wire trying to cross the fence. I had to pick him out, thread at a time, he was so tangled up. Mama said, "What were you two doing out at the gate so long last night?" "Oh, nothing, just talking," I said. She thought for the longest time that Benjy Hamilton was the nicest boy that ever walked the earth. No matter how drunk he was, the presence of an innocent lady like Mama, who said *"Drinking?"* in the same tone of voice she would have said *"Murder?"* would bring him around faster than any number of needle showers, massages, ice packs, prairie oysters, or quick dips in December off the northern bank of Lake Ontario. He would straighten up and smile and say, "You made any more peach pickle lately, Miss Sadie?" (He could even say "peach pickle.") And she'd say no, but that there was always some of the old for him whenever he wanted any. And he'd say that was just the sweetest thing he'd ever heard of, but she didn't know what she was promising—anything as good as her peach pickle ought to be guarded like gold. And she'd say, well, for most anybody else she'd think twice before she offered any. And he'd say, if only everybody was as sweet to him as she was. . . . And they'd go on together like that till you'd think that all creation had ground and wound itself down through the vistas of eternity to bring the two of them face to face for exchanging compliments over peach pickle. Then I would put my arm in his so it would look like he was helping me down the porch steps out of the reflexes of his gentlemanly upbringing, and off we'd go.

It didn't happen all the time, like I've made it sound. In fact, it was only a few times when I was in school that I went anywhere with Benjy Hamilton. Benjy isn't his name, either; it's Foster. I sometimes call him "Benjy" to myself, after a big overgrown thirty-three-year-old idiot in *The Sound and the Fury*, by William Faulkner. Not that Foster was so big or overgrown, or even thirty-three years old, back then; but he certainly did behave like an idiot.

I won this prize, see, for writing a paper on the siege of Vicksburg. It was for the United Daughters of the Confederacy's annual contest, and mine was judged the best in the state. So Foster Hamilton came all the way over to the schoolhouse and got me out of class—I felt terribly important—just to "interview" me. He had just graduated from the university and had a job on the paper in Port Claiborne—that was before he started work for the *Times-Picayune* in New Orleans. We went into an empty classroom and sat down.

He leaned over some blank sheets of coarse-grained paper and scribbled things down with a thick-leaded pencil. I was sitting in the next seat; it was a long bench divided by a number of writing arms, which was why they said that cheating was so prevalent in our school—you could just cheat without meaning to. They kept trying to raise the money for regular desks in every classroom, so as to improve morals. Anyway, I couldn't help seeing what he was writing down, so I said, " 'Marilee' is all one word, and with an 'i,' not a 'y.' 'Summerall' is spelled just like it sounds." "Are you a senior?" he asked. "Just a junior," I said. He wore horn-rimmed glasses; that was back before everybody wore them. I thought they looked unusual and very distinguished. Also, I had noticed his shoulders when he went over to let the window down. I thought they were distinguished, too, if a little bit bony. "What is your ambition?" he asked me. "I hope to go to college year after next," I said. "I intend to wait until my junior year in college to choose a career."

He kept looking down at his paper while he wrote, and when he finally looked up at me I was disappointed to see why he hadn't done it before. The reason was, he couldn't keep a straight face. It had happened before that people broke out laughing just when I was being my most earnest and sincere. It must have been what I said, because I don't think I *look* funny. I guess I don't look like much of any one thing. When I see myself in the mirror, no adjective springs right to mind, unless it's "average." I am medium height, I am average weight, I buy "natural"-colored face powder and "medium"-colored lipstick. But I must say for myself, before this goes too far, that every once in a great while I look Just Right. I've never found the combination for making this happen, and no amount of reading the make-up articles in the magazines they have at the beauty parlor will do any good. But sometimes it happens anyway, with no more than soap and water, powder, lipstick, and a damp hairbrush.

My interview took place in the spring, when we were practicing for the senior play every night. Though a junior, I was in it because they always got me, after the eighth grade, to take parts in things. Those of us that lived out in the country Mrs. Arrington would take back home in her car after rehearsal. One night, we went over from the school to get a Coca-Cola before the drugstore closed, and there was Foster Hamilton. He had done a real nice article—what Mama called a "write-up." It was when he was about to walk out that he noticed me and said, "Hey." I said "Hey" back, and since he just stood there, I said, "Thank you for the write-up in the paper."

"Oh, that's all right," he said, not really listening. He wasn't laughing this time. "Are you going home?" he said.

"We are after 'while," I said. "Mrs. Arrington takes us home in her car."

"Why don't you let me take you home?" he said. "It might–it might save Mrs. Arrington an extra trip."

"Well," I said, "I guess I could ask her."

So I went to Mrs. Arrington and said, "Mrs. Arrington, Foster Hamilton said he would be glad to drive me home." She hesitated so long that I put in, "He says it might save you an extra trip." So finally she said, "Well, all right, Marilee." She told Foster to drive carefully. I could tell she was uneasy, but then, my family were known as real good people, very strict, and of course she didn't want them to feel she hadn't done the right thing.

That was the most wonderful night. I'll never forget it. It was full of spring, all restlessness and sweet smells. It was radiant, it was warm, it was serene. It was all the things you want to call it, but no word would ever be the right one, nor any ten words, either. When we got close to our turnoff, after the bridge, I said, "The next road is ours," but Foster drove right on past. I knew where he was going. He was going to Windsor.

Windsor is this big colonial mansion built back before the Civil War. It burned down during the 1890s sometime, but there were still twenty-five or more Corinthian columns, standing on a big open space of ground that is a pasture now, with cows and mules and calves grazing in it. The columns are enormously high and you can see some of the iron grillwork railing for the second-story gallery clinging halfway up. Vines cling to the fluted white plaster surfaces, and in some places the plaster has crumbled away, showing the brick underneath. Little trees grow up out of the tops of columns, and chickens have their dust holes among the rubble. Just down the fall of the ground beyond the ruin, there are some Negro houses. A path goes down to them.

It is this ignorant way that the hand of Nature creeps back over Windsor that makes me afraid. I'd rather there'd be ghosts there, but there aren't. Just some old story about lost jewelry that every once in a while sends somebody poking around in all the trash. Still it is magnificent, and people have compared it to the Parthenon and so on and so on, and even if it makes me feel this undertone of horror, I'm always ready to go and look at it again. When all of it was standing, back in the old days, it was higher even than the columns, and had a cupola, too. You could see the cupola from the river, they say, and the story went that Mark Twain used it to steer by. I've read that book since, *Life on the Mississippi,* and it seems he used everything else to steer by, too—crawfish mounds, old rowboats stuck in the mud, the tassels on somebody's corn patch, and every stump and stob from New Orleans to Cairo, Illinois. But it does kind of connect you up with something to know that Windsor was there, too, like seeing the Presbyterian hand in the newspaper. Some people would say at this point, "Small world," but it isn't a small world. It's an enormous world, bigger than you can imagine, but it's all connected up. What Nature does to Windsor it does to everything, including you and me—there's the horror.

But that night with Foster Hamilton, I wasn't thinking any such doleful thoughts, and though Windsor can be a pretty scary-looking sight by moonlight, it didn't scare me then. I could have got right out of the car, alone, and walked all around among the columns, and whatever I heard walking away through the weeds would not have scared me, either. We sat there, Foster and I, and never said a word. Then, after some time, he turned the car around and took the road back. Before we got to my house, though, he stopped the car by the roadside and kissed me. He held my face up to his, but outside that he didn't touch me. I had never been kissed in any deliberate and accomplished way before, and driving out to Windsor in that accidental way, the whole sweetness of the spring night, the innocence and mystery of the two of us, made me think how simple life was and how easy it was to step into happiness, like walking into your own rightful house.

This frame of mind persisted for two whole days—enough to make a nuisance of itself. I kept thinking that Foster Hamilton would come sooner or later and tell me that he loved me, and I couldn't sleep for thinking about him in various ways, and I had no appetite, and nobody could get me to answer them. I half expected him at play practice or to come to the schoolhouse, and I began to wish he would hurry up and get it over with, when, after play practice on the second night, I saw him uptown, on the corner, with this blonde.

Mrs. Arrington was driving us home, and he and the blonde were standing on the street corner, just about to get in his car. I never saw that blonde before or since, but she is printed eternally on my mind, and to this good day if I'd run into her across the counter from me in the ten-cent store, whichever one of us is selling lipstick to the other one, I'd know her for sure because I saw her for one half of a second in the street light in Port Claiborne with Foster Hamilton. She wasn't any ordinary blonde, either–dyed hair was in it. I didn't know the term "feather-bed blond" in those days, or I guess I would have thought it. As it was, I didn't really think anything, or say anything, either, but whatever had been galloping along inside me for two solid days and nights came to a screeching halt. Somebody in the car said, being real funny, "Foster Hamilton's got him another girl friend." I just laughed. "Sure has," I said. "Oh, Mari-leee!" they all said, teasing me. I laughed and laughed.

I asked Foster once, a long time later, "Why didn't you come back after that night you drove me out to Windsor?"

He shook his head. "We'd have been married in two weeks," he said. "It scared me half to death."

"Then it's a mercy you didn't," I said. "It scares *me* half to death right now."

Things had changed between us, you realize, between that kiss and that conversation. What happened was at least, the main thing that happened was–Foster asked me the next year to go to the high school senior dance with him, so I said all right.

I knew about Foster by then, and that his reputation was not of the best–that it was, in fact, about the worst our county had to offer. I knew he had an uncommon thirst and that on weekends he went helling about the countryside with a fellow that owned the local picture show and worked at a garage in the daytime. His name was A. P. Fortenberry, and he owned a new convertible in a sickening shade of bright maroon. The convertible was always dusty–though you could see A.P. in the garage every afternoon, during the slack hour, hosing it down on the wash rack–because he and Foster were out in it almost every night, harassing the countryside. They knew every bootlegger in a radius of forty miles. They knew girls that lived on the outskirts of towns and girls that didn't. I guess "uninhibited" was the word for A. P. Fortenberry, but whatever it was, I couldn't stand him. He called me into the garage one day–to have a word with me about Foster, he said–but when I got inside he backed me into the corner and started trying it on. "Funny little old girl," he kept saying. He rattled his words out real fast. "Funny little old girl." I slapped him as hard as I could, which was pretty hard, but that only seemed to stimulate him. I thought I'd never get away from him—I can't smell the inside of a garage to this good day without thinking about A. P. Fortenberry.

When Foster drove all the way out to see me one day soon after that—we didn't have a telephone in those days—I thought he'd come to apologize for A.P., and I'm not sure yet he didn't intend for me to understand that without saying anything about it. He certainly put himself out. He sat down and swapped a lot of Port Claiborne talk with Mama—just pleased her to death—and then he went out back with Daddy and looked at the chickens and the peach trees. He even had an opinion on growing peaches, though I reckon he'd given more thought to peach brandy than he'd ever given to orchards. He said when we were walking out to his car that he'd like to take me to the senior dance, so I said O.K. I was pleased; I had to admit it.

Even knowing everything I knew by then (I didn't tell Mama and Daddy), there was something kind of glamorous about Foster Hamilton. He came of a real good family, known for being aristocratic and smart; he had uncles who were college professors and big lawyers and doctors and things. His father had died when he was a babe in arms (tragedy), and he had perfect manners. He had perfect manners, that is, when he was sober, and it was not that he departed from them in any intentional way when he was drunk. Still, you couldn't exactly blame me for being disgusted when, after ten minutes of the dance, I discovered that his face was slightly green around the temples and that whereas he could dance fairly well, he could not stand up by himself at all. He teetered like a baby that has caught on to what walking is, and knows that now is the time to do it, but hasn't had quite enough practice.

"Foster," I whispered, "have you been drinking?"

"Been *drinking?*" he repeated. He looked at me with a sort of wonder, like the national president of the W.C.T.U. might if asked the same question. "It's so close in here," he complained.

It really wasn't that close yet, but it was going to be. The gym doors were open, so that people could walk outside in the night air whenever they wanted to. "Let's go outside," I said. Well, in my many anticipations I had foreseen Foster and me strolling about on the walks outside, me in my glimmering white sheer dress with the blue underskirt (Mama and I had worked for two weeks on that dress), and Foster with his nice broad aristocratic shoulders. Then, lo and behold, he had worn a white dinner jacket! There was never anybody in creation as proud as I was when I first walked into the senior dance that night with Foster Hamilton.

Pride goeth before a fall. The fall must be the one Foster took down the gully back of the boys' privy at the schoolhouse. I still don't know quite how he did it. When we went outside, he put me carefully in his car, helped to tuck in my skirts, and closed the door in the most polite way, and then I saw him heading toward the privy in his white jacket that was swaying like a lantern through the dark, and then he just wasn't there any more. After a while, I got worried that somebody would come out, like us, for air, so I got out and went to the outside wall of the privy and said, "Foster, are you all right?" I didn't get any answer, so I knocked politely on the wall and said, "Foster?" Then I looked around behind and all around, for I was standing very close to the edge of the gully that had eroded right up to the borders of the campus (somebody was always threatening that the whole schoolhouse was going to cave off into it before another school year went by), and there at the bottom of the gully Foster Hamilton was lying face down, like the slain in battle.

What I should have done, I should have walked right off and left him there till doomsday, or till somebody came along who would use him for a model in a statue to our glorious dead in the defense of Port Claiborne against Gen. Ulysses S. Grant in 1863. That battle was over in about ten minutes, too. But I had to consider how things would look—I had my pride, after all. So I took a look around, hiked up my skirts, and went down into the gully. When I shook Foster, he grunted and rolled over, but I couldn't get him up. I wasn't strong enough. Finally, I said, "Foster, Mama's here!" and he soared up like a Roman candle. I never saw anything like it. He walked straight up the side of the gully and gave me a hand up, too. Then I guided him over toward the car and he sat in the door and lighted a cigarette.

"Where is she?" he said.

"Who?" I said.

"Your mother," he said.

"Oh, I just said that, Foster. I had to get you up someway."

At that, his shoulders slumped down and he looked terribly depressed. "I didn't mean to do this, Marilee," he said. "I didn't have any idea it would hit me this way. I'm sure I'll be all right in a minute."

I don't think he ever did fully realize that he had fallen in the gully.

"Get inside," I said, and shoved him over. There were one or two couples beginning to come outside and walk around. I squeezed in beside Foster and closed the door. Inside the gym, where the hot lights were, the music was blaring and beating away. We had got a real orchestra specially for that evening, all the way down from Vicksburg, and a brass-voiced girl was singing a 1930s' song. I would have given anything to be in there with it rather than out in the dark with Foster Hamilton.

I got quite a frisky reputation out of that evening. Disappearing after ten minutes of the dance, seen snuggling out in the car, and gone completely by intermission. I drove us away. Foster wouldn't be convinced that anybody would think it at all peculiar if he reappeared inside the gym with red mud smeared all over his dinner jacket. I didn't know how to drive, but I did anyway. I'm convinced you can do anything when you have to—speak French, do a double back flip off a low diving board, play Rachmaninoff on the piano, or fly an airplane. Well, maybe not fly an airplane; it's too technical. Anyway, that's how I learned to drive a car, riding up and down the highway, holding off Foster with my elbow, marking time till midnight came and I could go home without anybody thinking anything out of the ordinary had happened.

When I got out of the car, I said, "Foster Hamilton, I never want to see you again as long as I live. And I hope you have a wreck on the way home."

Mama was awake, of course. She called out in the dark, "Did you have a good time, Marilee?"

"Oh yes, ma'am," I said.

Then I went back to my shed-ceilinged room in the back wing, and cried and cried. And cried.

There was a good bit of traffic coming and going out to our house after that. A. P. Fortenberry came, all pallid and sober, with a tie on and a straw hat in his hand. Then A.P. and Foster came together. Then Foster came by himself.

The story went that Foster had stopped in the garage with A.P. for a drink before the dance, and instead of water in the drink, A.P. had filled it up with grain alcohol. I was asked to believe that he did this because, seeing Foster all dressed up, he got the idea that Foster was going to some family do, and he couldn't stand Foster's family, they were all so stuck-up. While Foster was draining the first glass, A.P. had got called out front to put some gas in a car, and while he was gone Foster took just a little tap more whiskey with another glassful of grain alcohol. A.P. wanted me to understand that Foster's condition that night had been all his fault, that instead of three or four ounces of whiskey, Foster had innocently put down eighteen ounces of sheer dynamite, and it was a miracle only to be surpassed by the resurrection of Jesus Christ that he had managed to drive out and get me, converse with Mama about peach pickle, and dance those famous ten minutes at all.

Well, I said I didn't know. I thought to myself I never heard of Foster Hamilton touching anything he even mistook for water.

All these conferences took place at the front gate. "I never saw a girl like you," Mama said. "Why don't you invite the boys to sit on the porch?"

"I'm not too crazy about A. P. Fortenberry," I said. "I don't think he's a very nice boy."

"Uh-*huh*," Mama said, and couldn't imagine what Foster Hamilton was doing running around with him, if he wasn't a nice boy. Mama, to this day, will not hear a word against Foster Hamilton.

I was still giving some thought to the whole matter that summer, sitting now on the front steps, now on the back steps, and now on the side steps, whichever was most in the shade, chewing on pieces of grass and thinking, when one day the mailman stopped in for a glass of Mama's cold buttermilk (it's famous) and told me that Foster and A.P. had had the most awful wreck. They had been up to Vicksburg, and coming home had collided with a whole carload of Negroes. The carnage was awful—so much blood on everybody you couldn't tell black from white. They were both going to live, though. Being so drunk, which in a way had caused the wreck, had also kept them relaxed enough to come out of it alive. I warned the mailman to leave out the drinking part when he told Mama, she thought Foster was such a nice boy.

The next time I saw Foster, he was out of the hospital and had a deep scar on his cheekbone like a sunken star. He looked handsomer and more distinguished than ever. I had gotten a scholarship to Millsaps College in Jackson, and was just about to leave. We had a couple of dates before I left, but things were not the same. We would go to the picture show and ride around afterward, having a conversation that went something like this:

"Marilee, why are you such a nice girl? You're about the only nice girl I know."

"I guess I never learned any different, so I can't help it. Will you teach me how to stop being a nice girl?"

"I certainly will not!" He looked to see how I meant it, and for a minute I thought the world was going to turn over, but it didn't.

"Why won't you, Foster?"

"You're too young. And your mama's a real sweet lady. And your daddy's too good a shot."

"Foster, why do you drink so much?"

"Marilee, I'm going to tell you the honest truth. I drink because I like to drink." He spoke with real conviction.

So I went on up to college in Jackson, where I went in for serious studies and made very good grades. Foster, in time, got a job on the paper in New Orleans, where, during off hours, or so I understood, he continued his investigation of the lower things in life and of the effects of alcohol upon the human system.

It is twenty years later now, and Foster Hamilton is down there yet.

Millions of things have happened; the war has come and gone. I live far away, and everything changes, almost every day. You can't even be sure the moon and stars are going to be the same the day after tomorrow night. So it has become more and more important to me to know that Windsor is still right where it always was, standing pure in its decay, and that the gilded hand on the Presbyterian church in Port Claiborne is still pointing to Heaven and not to Outer Space; and I earnestly feel, too, that Foster Hamilton should go right on drinking. There have got to be some things you can count on, would be an ordinary way to put it. I'd rather say that I feel the need of a land, of a sure terrain, of a sort of permanent landscape of the heart.

MOON ROCKET

A cone of light fell on the open tablet, its page blank except for the formula $x=\frac{\pi}{r^2}$ printed across the top line. Bill looked up from his desk at the white wall before him. An equation, short and simple as this one, had divided the atom. It lifted huge rockets from their launching pads, roaring flame, their noses true upon the zenith, with the great oiled cylinder below, turning, turning, turning, silent in the tremendous certainty of power.

And with him inside!

Just back of the nickel and sapphire plated nose, in a room rife with instruments and gauges, in a chair no larger than this one . . . He trembled, right down through his shoe soles, and had turned back to his equation, when a knock sounded at his door.

Everybody had to knock. If they didn't, he would turn into Dongoo, the flying saucer pilot, and speak nothing but Orion. "That's because you wouldn't knock," he would explain. "It wasn't *me,* Bill," his sister would argue. "It was Mother that didn't knock." "I don't care!" he would say, sometimes in English, sometimes in Orion. Once he had gone everywhere on all fours speaking Orion and, from time to time, barking. He at last explained, getting up after he had driven a splinter into his knee, that he was Zoa, faithful dog of Dongoo, the flying saucer pilot. His father, who had an aunt by marriage named Zoa, said that it was a girl's name and wouldn't do. "Let's not make it any *more* complicated," his mother advised. "Anyway, dogs can't talk," his sister said. She thought she had him there: she was very dumb. "They can on Orion," he hardly took the trouble to reply.

So now they knocked.

"Come in!" he remembered to say.

The door cracked softly open. It was his mother. "Did you forget about Trick or Treat?" she asked.

"Oh!" He turned around in his chair like a busy executive and rapidly stroked his palm across that part of his head where a forelock would have grown if he had not had a crew cut. It was a sign he was worried.

"They called you twice," she told him. "They waited a long long time."

He remembered now, back through the ages, the centuries, the great wash and wallow of clouds swirling, streaming, foaming, forming–breaking now like the wash of the ocean against rocks, now blown aside to expose the deep naked sky itself, shot into the immense reaches with worlds that turned to lights in green in red in blue in crystal white, as far as thought could reach to them, where meteors like Cadillacs scorched by, and white gleaming stuff fell into his face like snow, and anybody could see the answer to No. 9, though No. 10 looked hard enough to keep him for a while . . . he remembered back to ten minutes or twenty or no time at all ago when the children all came into the living room, as they had promised, to get his sister and him. The breath of cheerful cold in the house had come back all the way to where he was. He was happy they had come. He heard the murmur of their voices answering things his mother and father asked them, and now he would go out and see all the costumes, the masks, and smell up close the chilly excitement.

All the candy!

He jumped up and snatched from the bed where it was laid out for him, his red cloak with the black band at the top that buttoned closely at the throat, like Mandrake the Magician's cape, in the funny books, only not nearly so long. He put on his horrible mask, tying a careful knot to shorten the rubber band. The band prickled as it rolled on his crew cut down the slope of his head at the back. The coarse stiffened paper of the mask cut into the bridge of his nose. But in the mirror, didn't he look awful? He tried to make things worse, sticking out his tongue, making his ears waggle or his hair bristle straight up. He tossed on his black cowboy hat and drew the string up tight under his chin, bringing the brim down so no skin showed between the top of the mask and the hat. The results satisfied him perfectly. He stopped making faces, and thought that now, now was the moment to dash out among them, spin through and around them, admire them and be admired. He loved them. It would help his love along not even to know them in their masks and puffy long sleeves, or witches' skirts, and white ghost draperies. Should he wear his cowboy boots and maybe even take his gun? He didn't know. He took off the cape and laid it carefully on the bed, took off his hat and mask, and went to get the cowboy boots out of his closet. Then he sat down at the desk again and began to finish No. 10, the one he hadn't quite seen the answer to, though it would only take a minute. It had been sometime during this minute that his sister and his mother and his sister again had come and knocked and called and knocked again. "Just a minute," he had said. Hadn't he already foreseen everything that would happen, known already all the admiring and the love? It wasn't time yet to think beyond that.

Now it was too late. They were gone. He was filled with regret, though the solution to the problem stood beautifully, unassailably true on the top line of the new sheet. He sat stroking his hair.

His mother, who had prepared herself for this very thing, told him that all the others would be at Dicky Martin's house right now, for Dicky's mother had asked them to come there first and have some hot chocolate with gingerbread men–goblins and witches and ghosts, all the different shapes–she had heard about it on the telephone. That would make everything all right, wouldn't it? "Yes," he agreed, after considering it. "I believe it would."

When he went out the door, he tried to plant one of his great big smacks on his mother's cheek, but the horrible mask got in the way.

"Is he all squared away?" his father asked, as she came back into the living room.

"I think I broke through the sound barrier," she said. "He'll be O.K. now."

"Do you think he gets any *worse?*" he asked.

"He's just the same as he always was," she said. She kept up an amused tone–perhaps a good thing.

Bill had not gone far toward Dicky Martin's house when he ran into Janey. Janey was a Korean war orphan who had been adopted by some people who didn't have any little girl or little boy either. She had a face like the moon, broad with craters here and there on it: he thought this especially after he had seen the pictures of the far side of the moon, for her hair came down, making a fringe of shadows, and the front side of the moon had a man's face, broad and jolly, if petrified.

"Hey, Janey," he said, "what are you?"

"I'm a goblin," she said. She had a squeaky voice. It turned out that Janey was late because her mother hadn't finished her costume when the others came by. Bill's mother said that Janey was more American than her mother, whose name was plain Mrs. Brown, and who was never on time with a single thing.

"What's your name in Korean, Janey?" he asked her. He had asked her this a lot of times, for he liked to hear her reply, something that sounded like a little mouse telling you *its* name.

"You forgot your Trick or Treat basket," he said. "Everybody has to have one, to put all the candy in. You had one last year, remember?"

"Mother forgot," said Janey. She stopped short. "I'll go back."

"No, you can have mine," he said. "I'll carry it and you tell everybody it's yours."

"Then where are you going to put your candy?" she wondered in falsetto.

"In with yours. We'll divide later."

"O.K."

Walking together, step in step, with long matched strides, they ascended the rising street, but when they reached the corner to turn down to Dicky Martin's house, Bill kept right on going. The Martins' lights were near, just a few houses below, and you could hear giggles and shrieks of laughter. Janey had stopped. Bill turned back to her. "This way," she said, pointing.

"O.K.," he said, "in a minute. I want to go up here just a little way first. Come on. Janey, come on with me."

She hesitated a long time, but in the end she came, without asking any questions either. They had been friends all along, ever since he had brought her home with him from school without asking anybody, and his mother had been in bed sick and had sent Janey home because she couldn't stand noise in the house, any noise at all. Later, his mother had worried for fear Janey would think she had been discriminated against and sent away for being a Korean, so she acted especially nice to Janey after that and had a long talk with Bill to get him to be especially nice to Janey too. He did not pay any attention because none of this had anything to do with him and Janey.

He took Janey with him to the very top of the hill where the street ended. Here there was a barricade of crossed lumber, carelessly knocked together, and flares burned in low black pots, ugly as mines. They made a ghostly light leaping up against the sky now and again, turning the night black, even making the neatly drawn finish of the suburban street look ragged, unprecise, and open to flickering marvels. The children observed this without fear. They had always lived in a suburb, no house of which was more than ten years old: they could remember when the very trees were no taller than they themselves were now. If they had seen a real ghost, they would have thought only that it was one of their friends, dressed up, desiring candy.

Though the barrier and the flares seemed to mark the end of the hill, for the light rendered everything beyond itself a blank, Bill knew that the hill continued, and it became a new sort of terrain, strangely satisfying. He approached the lowest point of the barrier and stepped across. "Come on," he looked back to say.

"I can't," Janey squeaked. "It says Do Not Trespass."

He walked back and took her hand. Like her face, her hand was broad, and warmer than was usual for hands, as though her Oriental skin had a temperature all its own. She came forward slowly, like a blind person might, not mistrusting him, but simply hesitant in herself, though when he stepped over the barrier she came right over too. They stood together past the light and black-smelling smoke of the flares, hand in hand, in their strange garb, facing outward. Soon they could see the night for the first time, a large sky with strong, rapid masses of cloud, and a good many stars. Now, too, the land they stood on opened before them, and presently they could see it all.

It was a bare, dry land, with no trees, nothing growing on it. To the right, sinking down the fall of the hill, stood a row of small square houses, all dark. Some had timbers stacked near them, and large crate-like boxes for mixing cement. Pipes came down the raw sides of one or two, but were not joined to anything. Plank sidewalks had been laid for the workmen who came in the daytime to roll their wheelbarrows along from house to house. All the doors were empty and all the windows were black.

To the left the land was bare even of houses. It fell away more sharply, but large mounds of fresh earth marked it, like dunes, and long fissures scarred it, cracks such as an earthquake might make. Straight ahead of them was a little square house sitting on two large rollers, and towering behind it, a bulldozer and a machine with a long neck for biting the earth up and dumping it elsewhere. Bill knew the names of all the things here and he also knew exactly what was being done here: what they called a new subdivision. In the afternoons when he walked home from school the warm fall sun would be full of the sound of long buzzes and pauses that the machines made. He sometimes climbed up to the barrier and watched their ponderous maneuvers.

Yet now as he took a fresh grip on Janey's hand and drew her forward, he said: "You know where we are? This is the moon!"

"Really?" Janey said.

"Look up there," he said, pointing to the sky. "You don't see any moon up there, do you?"

She examined the sky while the clouds pushed silently on, and agreed.

"That's because we're *on it!*" He was terribly excited. He almost shouted.

He wanted to run forward with Janey in the marvelous floating giant steps of everybody's dreams. Perhaps, from that moment on, he might actually have made this his normal method of motion, to the astonishment of everybody in the whole world; for strange things are happening every day.

But Bill had taken only one or two such steps when he noticed something new at a little distance before them: a wheelbarrow maybe, sitting just back of one of the dunes. Then he saw when it moved, straightening up, that it wasn't a wheelbarrow at all, but somebody, grown up but not a man like their daddies, short but not a child like themselves, and though wearing tight black pants and a sweater of exaggerated weight and size, not to be thought of as in a costume, even on Halloween. Bill had seen boys like him by daylight. They were in the upper grades of schools he was still too young to attend. They grouped talking in front of little hole-in-the-wall cafés in an older part of town where the movie houses were, down below the new shopping center. He was not surprised to find one on the moon.

The boy backed off a step or two, bending almost double at the waist, seeking shadow. "Get away!" he whispered to them and made a shooing motion with his hands. "Get on away from here!"

"Who are you?" Bill asked, right out loud, but the boy continued to whisper, "I'm the night watchman. You little devils are not supposed to be here. Get out!"

"If you're the night watchman," Bill asked, "where is your flashlight?"

At that the boy decided to run at them in earnest. Bill knew now what to do; for all of us when we get to the moon will know exactly how to act. Out there on the distant fields of the heavens, chivalry still lives. Innocent maidens tremble in their little space suits at the approach of the wicked, and it is up to a stalwart rocket man to stand his ground. "Get behind me, Janey," he said, and pulled her back of him until they were standing like two slices of bread in a sandwich. Though he called her Janey, he had already decided that she was Thera the Moon Maiden.

He called out to the boy: "We're just children in Halloween suits, and we don't want to hurt anything."

On the low horizon far beyond the hill, the lights of a city were flashing up upon the clouds. This would be one of the great moon cities, lighted with sun borrowed from the other hemisphere, and surrounded by such high walls that from the earth they looked like barren craters. The boy would be one of those people who had killed somebody or robbed a bank or something in the city and had been condemned to walk out of it. He had been sent out alone while the policemen watched him. He had walked up a ramp to the towering plate glass gates, at a certain point breaking the electric current, so that the gates slid up automatically, and then he took one last bitter look back at the green city full of gardens and swimming pools with water sprays on everybody's lawn, with rainbows in ten colors playing in them, and then he walked out and the gates sank down again. So now he was out here in the dry chilly dark, trying to scare Dongoo and his friend Thera, who only wanted to reach the city.

Since the boy would not listen to the truth, but kept coming on at them, Bill leaned down and picked up a good-sized chunk of moon-hardened earth and threw it at him, to stop him. When the earth struck him, the boy leaned down in turn, saying something ugly, and caught up what looked like a club. He was coming on faster now, and when Dongoo charged at him to catch his arm he hurled the club at them.

The weapon missed Dongoo, but Thera the Moon Maiden gave a

little cry and fell down. The next instant, Dongoo had plunged with flailing arms into the criminal from the moon city, who though at first in retreat, taken by surprise, rallied and struck Dongoo such a whack on the side of his head that he went off spinning and turning crazily, and fell down with his head reeling. When he could look up, he had begun to cry without deciding to, because the blow had been ugly and it had hurt. The quality that was so ugly had been the relentlessness—no instant of softening consideration that here was only a little boy in a Halloween suit. Was it only the dizziness or were there really not one bad boy, but lots of them, who had been thronging the shadows just out of sight, and now were running away? He didn't know. "Mean, mean, mean!" he tried to cry out, after them all, and running a few steps now this way, now that, he looked for wherever they might have gone to, and wished for his daddy and Janey's daddy to come and do all the things to them that he was too little to do himself. His mask was knocked to one side, his brave cape was in a sorry tangle about his arm. His broad black hat had fallen in the dust and been stepped on. He picked it up with a sob.

Then he heard a whimpering sound behind him and looked back.

Thera the Moon Maiden was sitting up, right where she had fallen. With her head in her hands, she was making the little sound, over and over. It was the exact sound, though she did not remember it, that she had been making in the debris of a burning Korean village, when a voice had said, "Well, whadayaknow!" and a pair of hands had reached down to her, and lifted her whole and safe without a scratch on her anywhere, out of a building where no two splinters were left together and every stone was blasted as fine as face powder. This sound, it seemed, always had the most marvelous results. When he heard it, Dongoo knew exactly what to do again.

He went to her and helped her up, dusting all the dirt off her space suit and out of her hair and off her cheek. Then he picked up the club the mean boy had thrown (it was an old corn stalk, with roots like bird claws clutching a heavy portion of dried earth). He put it in his Trick or Treat basket, in case he needed it, for defense. Then, once more, they set out together.

When they got to Dicky Martin's house, everybody was gone. Dicky Martin's mother came out on the front steps and admired their costumes. She offered to make them some more hot chocolate, but said that all the gingerbread men were eaten up. "No, thank you," Bill said. She made them promise to go straight home and not to look for the others, because it was Saturday night, after all, and there had been some bad neighborhood gangs of boys wandering around even in this district and she didn't know what the country was coming to.

Down the Martins' sidewalk and later on the street itself, Bill kept walking ahead of Janey with long steps, now circling back and around her, while she moved chunkily along in her orange goblin suit, and once when he circled her he heard her say, in her little voice:

"The night watchman threw a rock at us, but you chased him away."

He did not try to correct her, though he knew that none of it was true, even to the rock. It was what *was* true that kept worrying him, that he was trying to cast off by taking longer and longer steps, furling his cape in the night air, but still he could not feel any better. Back of all his painful new knowledge stood two ideas: one was that children in Halloween suits ought not to be thrown at and knocked down; the other was that Dongoo, the Rocket Man, ought to Win.

When they got to Janey's house, "This is where I live," she said and stopped, but he felt for the first time he could remember that it was necessary to be with somebody rather than to be alone. So he asked Janey to go to the drugstore and get something to eat, a chocolate milk shake maybe. And he continued to worry, all the while, and not to say anything.

Janey wanted a strawberry ice cream soda instead of a milk shake and he ordered one scoop of ice cream in a dish for himself, as he had known all along he would have to, because he just had a quarter. While they were waiting, Janey began telling him a long story about how her daddy caught a cold sitting up without any socks on to watch the late movie. When the soda came, she had to stand up on her knees on the seat to reach the straw.

Watching her, little by little, Bill began to feel O.K. again. He took off his horrible mask to eat the ice cream. At last he said, his eyes narrowing humorously, though he was tinged through with that knowledge which is always a lot like sadness: "You're from the moon."

"I'm not either," she said. "I'm from Green Avenue, just the same as you are."

"Your name is Thera," he pursued.

"It's not either," she said, and finished her ice cream soda with a snort of the straw. "My name is Janey Brown."

Taking up the long spoon, she began to eat the ice cream remaining in the tall glass, bending forward until her broad face hung almost directly over the mouth of the glass, the spoon moving into her mouth with the mysterious quickness of thinking about it. Only the slight motion of her jaw betrayed what pleasure she took in the flavored mixture, juicy with strawberry, tingling with carbonated foam.

THE WHITE AZALEA

Two letters had arrived for Miss Theresa Stubblefield: she put them in her bag. She would not stop to read them in American Express, as many were doing, sitting on benches or leaning against the walls, but pushed her way out into the street. This was her first day in Rome and it was June.

An enormous sky of the most delicate blue arched overhead. In her mind's eye—her imagination responding fully, almost exhaustingly, to these shores' peculiar powers of stimulation—she saw the city as from above, telescoped on its great bare plains that the ruins marked, aqueducts and tombs, here a cypress, there a pine, and all round the low blue hills. Pictures in old Latin books returned to her: the Appian Way Today, the Colosseum, the Arch of Constantine. She would see them, looking just as they had in the books, and this would make up a part of her delight. Moreover, nursing various Stubblefields—her aunt, then her mother, then her father—through their lengthy illnesses (everybody could tell you the Stubblefields were always sick), Theresa had had a chance to read quite a lot. England, France, Germany, Switzerland, and Italy had all been rendered for her time and again, and between the prescribed hours of pills and tonics, she had conceived a dreamy passion by lamplight, to see all these places with her own eyes. The very night after her father's funeral she had thought, though never admitted to a soul: *Now I can go. There's nothing to stop me now.* So here it was, here was Italy, anyway, and terribly noisy.

In the street the traffic was really frightening. Cars, taxis, buses, and motor scooters all went plunging at once down the narrow length of it or swerving perilously around a fountain. Shoals of tourists went by her in national groups–English schoolgirls in blue uniforms, German boys with cameras attached, smartly dressed Americans looking in shop windows. Glad to be alone, Theresa climbed the splendid outdoor staircase that opened to her left. The Spanish Steps.

Something special was going on here just now–the annual display of azalea plants. She had heard about it the night before at her hotel. It was not yet complete: workmen were unloading the potted plants from a truck and placing them in banked rows on the steps above. The azaleas were as large as shrubs, and their myriad blooms, many still tight in the bud, ranged in color from purple through fuchsia and rose to the palest pink, along with many white ones too. Marvellous, thought Theresa, climbing in her portly, well-bred way, for she was someone who had learned that if you only move slowly enough you have time to notice everything. In Rome, all over Europe, she intended to move very slowly indeed.

Halfway up the staircase she stopped and sat down. Other people were doing it, too, sitting all along the wide banisters and leaning over the parapets above, watching the azaleas mass, or just enjoying the sun. Theresa sat with her letters in her lap, breathing Mediterranean air. The sun warmed her, as it seemed to be warming everything, perhaps even the underside of stones or the chill insides of churches. She loosened her tweed jacket and smoked a cigarette. Content . . . excited; how could you be both at once? Strange, but she was. Presently, she picked up the first of the letters.

A few moments later her hands were trembling and her brow had contracted with anxiety and dismay. *Of course, one of them would have to go and do this! Poor Cousin Elec,* she thought, tears rising to sting in the sun, *but why couldn't he have arranged to live through the summer? And how on earth did I ever get this letter anyway?*

She had reason indeed to wonder how the letter had managed to find her. Her Cousin Emma Carraway had written it, in her loose high old lady's script–*t*'s carefully crossed, but *l*'s inclined to wobble like an old car on the downward slope. Cousin Emma had simply put Miss Theresa Stubblefield, Rome, Italy, on the envelope, had walked up to the post office in Tuxapoka, Alabama, and mailed it with as much confidence as if it had been a birthday card to her next-door neighbor. No return address whatsoever. Somebody had scrawled American Express, Piazza di Spagna? across the envelope, and now Theresa had it, all as easily as if she had been the President of the Republic or the Pope. Inside were all the things they thought she ought to know concerning the last illness, death, and burial of Cousin Alexander Carraway.

Cousin Emma and Cousin Elec, brother and sister—unmarried, devoted, aging—had lived next door to the Stubblefields in Tuxapoka from time immemorial until the Stubblefields had moved to Montgomery fifteen years ago. Two days before he was taken sick, Cousin Elec was out worrying about what too much rain might do to his sweetpeas, and Cousin Elec had always preserved in the top drawer of his secretary a mother-of-pearl paper knife which Theresa had coveted as a child and which he had promised she could have when he died. *I'm supposed to care as much now as then, as much here as there,* she realized, with a sigh. *This letter would have got to me if she hadn't even put Rome, Italy, on it.*

She refolded the letter, replaced it in its envelope, and turned with relief to one from her brother George.

But alack, George, when *he* had written, had only just returned from going to Tuxapoka to Cousin Elec's funeral. He was full of heavy family reminiscence. All the fine old stock was dying out, look at the world today. His own children had suffered from the weakening of those values which he and Theresa had always taken for granted, and as for his grandchildren (he had one so far, still in diapers), he shuddered to think that the true meaning of character might never dawn on them at all. A life of gentility and principle such as Cousin Elec had lived had to be known at first hand. . . .

Poor George! The only boy, the family darling. Together with her mother, both of them tense with worry lest things should somehow go wrong, Theresa had seen him through the right college, into the right fraternity, and though pursued by various girls and various mamas of girls, safely married to the right sort, however much in the early years of that match his wife, Anne, had not seemed to understand poor George. Could it just be, Theresa wondered, that Anne had understood only too well, and that George all along was extraordinary only in the degree to which he was dull?

As for Cousin Alexander Carraway, the only thing Theresa could remember at the moment about him (except his paper knife) was that he had had exceptionally long hands and feet and one night about one o'clock in the morning the whole Stubblefield family had been aroused to go next door at Cousin Emma's call—first Papa, then Mother, then Theresa and George. There they all did their uttermost to help Cousin Elec get a cramp out of his foot. He had hobbled downstairs into the parlor, in his agony, and was sitting, wrapped in his bathrobe, on a footstool. He held his long clenched foot in both hands, and this and his contorted face—he was trying heroically not to cry out—made him look like a large skinny old monkey. They all surrounded him, the family circle, Theresa and George as solemn as if they were watching the cat have kittens, and Cousin Emma running back and forth with a kettle of hot water which she poured steaming into a white enameled pan. "Can you think of anything to do?" she kept repeating. "I hate to call the doctor but if this keeps up I'll just have to! Can you think of anything to do?" "You might treat it like hiccups," said Papa. "Drop a cold key down his back." "I just hope this happens to you someday," said Cousin Elec, who was not at his best. "Poor Cousin Elec," George said. He was younger than Theresa: she remembered looking down and seeing his great round eyes, while at the same time she was dimly aware that her mother and father were not unamused. "Poor Cousin Elec."

Now, here they both were, still the same, George full of round-eyed woe, and Cousin Emma in despair. Theresa shifted to a new page.

"Of course [George's letter continued], there are practical problems to be considered. Cousin Emma is alone in that big old house and won't hear to parting from it. Robbie and Beryl tried their best to persuade her to come and stay with them, and Anne and I have told her she's more than welcome here, but I think she feels that she might be an imposition, especially as long as our Rosie is still in high school. The other possibility is to make arrangements for her to let out one or two of the rooms to some teacher of good family or one of those solitary old ladies that Tuxapoka is populated with—Miss Edna Whittaker, for example. But there is more in this than meets the eye. A new bathroom would certainly have to be put in. The wallpaper in the back bedroom is literally crumbling off. . . ." (Theresa skipped a page of details about the house.) "I hope if you have any ideas along these lines you will write me about them. I may settle on some makeshift arrangements for the summer and wait until you return in the fall so we can work out together the best . . ."

I really shouldn't have smoked a cigarette so early in the day, thought Theresa, it always makes me sick. I'll start sneezing in a minute, sitting on these cold steps. She got up, standing uncertainly for a moment, then moving aside to let go past her, talking, a group of young men. They wore shoes with pointed toes, odd to American eyes, and narrow trousers, and their hair looked unnaturally black and slick. Yet here they were obviously thought to be handsome, and felt themselves to be so. Just then a man approached her with a tray of cheap cameos, Parker fountain pens, rosaries, papal portraits. "No," said Theresa. "No, no!" she said. The man did not wish to leave. He knew how to spread himself against the borders of the space that had to separate them. Carrozza rides in the park, the Colosseum by moonlight, he specialized . . . Theresa turned away to escape, and climbed to a higher landing where the steps divided in two. There she walked to the far left and leaned on a vacant section of banister, while the vendor picked himself another well-dressed American lady, carrying a camera and a handsome alligator bag, ascending the steps alone. Was he ever successful, Theresa wondered. The lady with the alligator bag registered interest, doubt, then indignation; at last, alarm. She cast about as though looking for a policeman: this really shouldn't be allowed! Finally, she scurried away up the steps.

Theresa Stubblefield, still holding the family letters in one hand, realized that her whole trip to Europe was viewed in family circles as an interlude between Cousin Elec's death and "doing something" about Cousin Emma. They were even, Anne and George, probably thinking themselves very considerate in not hinting that she really should cut out "one or two countries" and come home in August to get Cousin Emma's house ready before the teachers came to Tuxapoka in September. Of course, it wasn't Anne and George's fault that one family crisis seemed to follow another, and weren't they always emphasizing that they really didn't know what they would do without Theresa? *The trouble is,* Theresa thought, *that while everything that happens there is supposed to matter supremely, nothing here is supposed even to exist. They would not care if all of Europe were to sink into the ocean tomorrow. It never registered with them that I had time to read all of Balzac, Dickens, and Stendhal while Papa was dying, not to mention everything in the city library after Mother's operation. It would have been exactly the same to them if I had read through all twenty-six volumes of Elsie Dinsmore.*

She arranged the letters carefully, one on top of the other. Then, with a motion so suddenly violent that she amazed herself, she tore them in two.

"Signora?"

She became aware that two Italian workmen, carrying a large azalea pot, were standing before her and wanted her to move so that they could begin arranging a new row of the display.

"Mi dispiace, signora, ma . . . insomma. . . ."

"Oh . . . put it there!" She indicated a spot a little distance away. They did not understand. *"Ponere . . . la."* A little Latin, a little French. How one got along! The workmen exchanged a glance, a shrug. Then they obeyed her. *"Va bene, signora."* They laughed as they returned down the steps in the sun.

Theresa was still holding the torn letters, half in either hand, and the flush was fading slowly from her brow. What a strong feeling had shaken her! She observed the irregular edges of paper, so crudely wrenched apart, and began to feel guilty. The Stubblefields, it was true, were proud and prominent, but how thin, how vulnerable was that pride it was so easy to prove, and how local was that prominence there was really no need to tell even them. But none could ever deny that the Stubblefields meant well; no one had ever challenged that the Stubblefields were good. Now out of their very letters, their sorrowful eyes, full of gentility and principle, appeared to be regarding Theresa, one of their own who had turned against them, and soft voices, so ready to forgive all, seemed to be saying, "Oh, Theresa, how *could* you?"

Wasn't that exactly what they had said when, as a girl, she had fallen in love with Charlie Wharton, whose father had unfortunately been in the pen? Ever so softly, ever so distressed: "Oh, Theresa, how *could* you?" Never mind. That was long ago, over and done with, and right now something clearly had to be done about these letters.

Theresa moved forward, and leaning down she dropped the torn sheets into the azalea pot which the workmen had just left. But the matter was not so easily settled. What if the letters should blow away? One could not bear the thought of that which was personal to the Stubblefields chancing out on the steps where everyone passed, or maybe even into the piazza below to be run over by a motor scooter, walked over by the common herd, spit upon, picked up and read, or—worst of all—returned to American Express by some conscientious tourist, where tomorrow, filthy, crumpled, bedraggled, but still legibly, faithfully relating Cousin Elec's death and Cousin Emma's grief, they might be produced to confront her.

Theresa moved a little closer to the azalea pot and sat down beside it. She covered the letters deftly, smoothing the earth above them and making sure that no trace of paper showed above the ground. The corner of Cousin Emma's envelope caught on a root and had to be shoved under, a painful moment, as if a letter could feel anything—how absurd! Then Theresa realized, straightening up and rubbing dirt off her hand with a piece of Kleenex from her bag, that it was not the letters but the Stubblefields that she had torn apart and consigned to the earth. This was certainly the only explanation of why the whole curious sequence, now that it was complete, had made her feel so marvelously much better.

Well, I declare! Theresa thought, astonished at herself, and in that moment it was as though she stood before the statue of some heroic classical woman whose dagger dripped with stony blood. *My goodness!* she thought, drowning in those blank exalted eyeballs: *Me!*

So thrilled she could not, for a time, move on, she stood noting that this particular azalea was one of exceptional beauty. It was white, in outline as symmetrically developed as an oak tree, and blooming in every part with a ruffled, lacy purity. The azalea was, moreover, Theresa recalled, a Southern flower, one especially cultivated in Alabama. Why, the finest in the world were said to grow in Bellingrath Gardens near Mobile, though probably they had not heard about that in Rome.

Now Miss Theresa Stubblefield descended quickly, down, down, toward the swarming square, down toward the fountain and all the racket, into the Roman crowd. There she was lost at once in the swirl, nameless, anonymous, one more nice rich American tourist lady.

But she cast one last glance back to where the white azalea stood, blooming among all the others. By now the stone of the great staircase was all but covered over. A group of young priests in scarlet cassocks went past, mounting with rapid, forward energy, weaving their way vividly aloft among the massed flowers. At the top of the steps the twin towers of a church rose, standing clearly outlined on the blue air. Some large white clouds, charged with pearly light, were passing overhead at a slow imperial pace.

Well, it certainly is beyond a doubt the most beautiful family funeral of them all! thought Theresa. *And if they should ever object to what I did to them,* she thought, recalling the stone giantess with her dagger and the gouts of blood hanging thick and gravid upon it, *they've only to read a little and learn that there have been those in my position who haven't acted in half so considerate a way.*

PART II

1961–1964

THE VISIT

The children were playing through the long empty rooms of the villa, shuttered now against the sunlight during the hottest hour of the day. The great man had gone to take a nap.

Before she had come to Italy, Judy thought that siesta was the word all Latins used for a rest after lunch, but she had learned that you said this only in Spain. In Italy you went to *riposarsi,* and this was exactly what the great man had done.

It was unfortunate because Bill had built up so to this visit. To be invited to see Thompson was, for almost anyone in the academic world, the token of something superior; but in Bill's particular field, it was the treasure, the X mark on the ancient map.

Judy often thought that Bill had an "and-then" sort of career. Graduate courses, a master's degree. A dissertation, a doctorate. A teaching appointment, scholarly articles. And then, and then. Promotion, the dissertation published, and clearly ahead on the upward road they could discern the next goal: a second, solidly important, possibly even definitive book. A grant from the Foundation was a natural forward step, and Bill then got to take his wife to Italy for a year. In Italy, as all knew, was Thompson.

Bill and Judy Owens had arrived in October; now it was June. All year Bill had worked on his book, the ambitious one, all about ancient Roman portraiture; Judy had typed for him, and manuscript had piled up thickly. They went about looking at museums, at ancient ruins and new excavations. They met other attractive young American couples who were abroad on fellowships and scholarships, studied Italian, attended lectures, and frequently complained about not getting to know more of the natives.

But all the time Bill and Judy did not mistake what the real thread was, nor which and-then they were working on now. The book would get written somehow; but what prestige it would gain for Bill if only he had the right to make a personal reference to Thompson even once —and more than once would be overdoing it. Should it go in the introduction, or the preface, or the acknowledgments, or the text itself? This would depend on the nature of what Thompson, at last, yielded; and did it matter so much where the single drop of essence landed, when it would go to work for one anywhere, regardless?

Bill was always thorough—he was anything but aimless, but in this matter he became something he had never been before: he grew crafty as hell. He plotted the right people to write and the best month for them to receive a letter. He considered the number of paragraphs which should go by before Thompson was even mentioned. In some cases Thompson's name was not even allowed to appear; yet his presence (such was Bill's skill) would breathe from every word. Pressure could be brought to bear in some cases: Bill had not been in the academic world fifteen years for nothing; and everything in American life is, in the long run, as we all know, competitive. He poked fun at his scheming mind—yet the goal was important to him, and he pressed forward in an innocent, bloodthirsty way, as if it were a game he had to win.

At last, in May, just when it seemed that nothing would happen, a letter arrived from a Professor Eakins, Bill's mentor in graduate school. "By the way," Eakins wrote (after a certain number of paragraphs had gone by), "I had a letter from Thompson recently saying that if any one of my students would be in the neighborhood of Genoa during June, he would be most welcome at the villa. I could think of no one I would rather have call on him than you, Bill. Of course, if you are planning to be in Sicily at that time, you'll let me know, so that—"

But Bill was not planning to be anywhere near Sicily in June.

From Genoa, in June, Bill and Judy had gone straight to the village in the mountains nearest to Thompson's villa. This village was the usual take-off point for people who went to see Thompson. Judy had pointed out that another village nearby had, according to the guidebook, a more interesting church, with a cosmatesque cloister and a work in the baptistry attributed by some to Donatello (Judy loved Donatello), but Bill decided that this was no time for anything unorthodox. So they went to the usual village.

All kind of legends were attached to the place. Some people had waited there for a week or more in the only halfway decent *pensione*, had dispatched all the proper credentials to the villa, but had never received any word at all. They had finally had to leave, looking out of the rear window of the taxi all the way to the station, until the mountain shut out the village forever. But no one could ever be personally encountered to whom anything of the sort had happened, and Bill had decided that it was only a Kafka-like nightmare which had accrued of itself to the Thompson image—he put it out of his mind by force.

He refused to recall it, even after he and Judy had sat waiting in the village for two days. He read the books he had brought to read, and Judy typed the chapter she had brought to type; then they proofread it together. They went out in the evenings and ate outdoors before a little restaurant under a string of colored lights. Here Judy, who got on rather well in Italian, answered all the waiter's questions about their son Henry, who had nine years and was now in care of his aunt in the *Stati Uniti*. The waiter said that she was much too young to have a nine-year-old son, and that her husband was a great scholar—one could see it *subito*. Judy enjoyed herself and drank up most of the wine. Light lingered in the mountains. They walked around and looked down at the view, an aspect of a splendid, darkening valley.

Bill threw himself down on a bench. Perhaps, he reflected aloud, Eakins was the wrong one to recommend him to Thompson. Who, after all, valued Eakins' work as highly as Eakins did? Eakins' large, fleshy, cultivated face all but materialized, with the thin, iron-gray hair and the thin waxed mustaches. It could be that Thompson thought so little of Eakins that any letter from or about Eakins could easily be tossed aside.

As he sat torturing himself this way, Judy leaned her elbows on the rough wall, looking far down at some twinkling lights. She said that if only they were religious instead of scholastic they would have come off better, since anyone at all could get an audience with the Pope. In fact, the problem seemed to be how to get out of one. In Rome, you might just pull a thread by accident and wind up buying a black veil and checking to see if you had the right gloves and shoes.

Bill said that scholastic was not the right word; it particularly connoted the Middle Ages. As Judy had finished only two years of college, Bill often had to put her right about things.

On their return to the *pensione,* the maid ran out and handed them a letter. *"È arrivata,"* she said. It was somewhat embarrassing to be clearly seen through. Nonetheless, Bill's hour had struck. He and Judy were invited to lunch with Thompson on the following day.

Instead of driving their own car up to the villa, they took a taxi, as the proprietor of the *pensione* advised. He said that the way was extremely steep and dangerous. There were falling rocks, sharp curves, few markers. Their tires might be cut to pieces on the stones. Their water might boil away out of the radiator. They might lose the way entirely.

"How symbolic can you get?" Bill remarked. "Besides, his brother probably owns the taxi."

But all the proprietor said proved to be literally true. Bill and Judy were flung against each other several times on the curves. As the road threaded higher and higher, they dared not look out of the windows.

"I have to keep reminding myself," said Bill, shuddering away from a frightful declivity, "that this road may be leading me to the Thrace mosaics."

Judy knew about those mosaics, all from having typed so many letters. She knew as much as anybody. How they had been whatever the polite word was for smuggled out of the Middle East; how large the sums were that had gone for them, some over tables and some under; how museums and authorities of every nation could agree on no one but Thompson to receive them. Now they were at the villa. Some visitors had been allowed to peep at them, some even to have a brief try, as with a jigsaw puzzle, at matching this to that—a foot here, an arm there, and what prestige when the thing was talked about afterward!

"If only you could see them," Judy said.

"I can't think of any reason why I shouldn't," Bill said. The road had stabilized somewhat and he spoke with greater confidence, leaning back and crossing his legs. Judy smoothed her hair and agreed with him, then they were there.

The road flattened; a green plateau appeared before them, and set in it, at a fair distance, the villa. It looked like a photograph of itself. The tawny, bare façade was facing directly toward them. A colonnade ran out toward the left like a strong arm; it broke and softened the long savage drop of the mountain behind and framed in a half-embrace the grassy courtyard. There in the background, a hundred yards or so behind the villa, hung the ruin, the old castle. Rough and craggy, it was unused except artistically, as a backdrop, or to show people through (some visitors had reported being shown through), or perhaps for children to play in. Thompson's daughter, whose husband, the Prince of Gaeta, owned the villa, was said to have two children, and as if to prove that this was so, they at once appeared, a boy and girl, dressed in identical loose gray pinafores and long black stockings. They came out from among the shadows of the colonnade.

The radiator cap on the taxi had been removed for the journey, and Bill and Judy now chugged at a decorous pace into the courtyard, trailing a long plume of smoke. A dark man wearing English flannels came out of the villa and hastened to the colonnade, taking from behind a pillar a large green watering can. He poured water into the radiator of the taxi, then the cab driver handed him the radiator cap through the window, and he screwed it in place. *"È il principe,"* said the driver, over his shoulder. The prince himself!

"Buon giorno," said the prince to the driver, sticking his head through the window.

"Buon giorno, signor principe," returned the driver.

"Notizie?"

Judy knew enough to follow that the prince was asking what was new and the driver was saying that nothing much was going on. Then the driver gave the prince a package of letters tied with a string.

The prince greeted his guests in English, opening the car door for them. The children had joined him and were standing nearby, side by side, looking at the newcomers, with dark eyes, brilliant in their pale, inquisitive faces.

"Perhaps," said the prince, "you'd like to see our position before going inside?" He led the way across the courtyard to the right, where they saw the land drop completely away. Portions of a road, perhaps their own, could be seen arranged in broken bits along the sheer slopes, and far below, between boulders, they saw the silent blue and white curling of the sea.

They were received in a small sitting room furnished with much-satin overstuffed furniture and opening out on a large terrace. The prince had them sit down and the two children, having been already formally presented in the courtyard, tucked themselves away on stools. Though they did not stare, they certainly watched: two more, they were clearly saying to themselves, had arrived.

Flashing dark, affable smiles, the prince said that he sometimes rode back down to the village with the taxi driver but that it must be hot below. Judy and Bill agreed: the nights were cool but at midday especially it was indeed hot below. Presently Madame Thompson came in—one said "Madame" instead of "Mrs." or "Signora" possibly to give her the Continental flavor she deserved, though she was not French but German, and Thompson was American. Her long straight gray hair was screwed into a loose knot at the back. She was wrapped in a coarse white shawl. They should all move out to the terrace, she suggested, because the view was "vunderful." They moved out to the terrace and soon two young women came in. The one with the tray of aperitifs was a servant; the other, the one wearing bracelets and smoking a cigarette, was Thompson's daughter, the princess.

From the opposite end of the terrace, making all turn, Thompson himself strode in.

He was grizzly and vigorous, with heavy brown hands. He wore a cardigan, crumpled trousers that looked about to fall down, and carpet slippers. He advanced to the center of the group and halted, squinting in the strong sun.

Judy dared not look at Bill. She had seen him at many other rungs of the ladder, looking both fearful and hopeful, both nervous and brave, in desperate proportions only Bill could concoct, and her heart had gone out to him. But now, as he confronted the Great Man at last, she looked elsewhere. She knew that he was transferring his glass to his left hand; she knew that his grasp would be damp, shaky, and cold.

Almost as much as for Bill, however, Judy was anxious for herself. Why, she now wondered, had she thought it necessary to look so well? Bill, in carefully pressed flannels, with crisp graying hair and heavy glasses, looked as American as naturally as a Chinaman looked Chinese, but with her the thing had taken some doing, and, inspired by the idea of helping him, she had worked at it hard. Brushes and bottles and God knows what had got into it and what with her best costume, a cream-colored linen sheath with loose matching jacket, a strand of pearls, gold earrings, and shimmering brown hair, she looked ready to be mounted in an enlargement on a handsome page; but what had that to do with scholarship? The princess and her mother, Judy felt certain, did not own one lipstick between them. They dressed like peasants, forgetting the whole thing.

It's only that I know how little I know to talk about, Judy thought. That's why I was so careful. What if they found out about all those books I haven't read? She shook hands with Thompson, but didn't say anything: she only smiled.

Bill, who used to be good at tennis–he and Judy had met one summer on a tennis court–found a means of cutting off the small talk with an opening question like a serve, something about a recent comparison of Byzantine and Roman portraiture. A moment later he was trotting off at Thompson's side, off toward the library, while words like monograph and research grant, Harvard and Cambridge, frothed about in their wake.

Judy was left alone with the family.

She asked them about their daily routine. The princess said she went down each afternoon to bathe in the sea. "But how do you get down?" Judy wanted to know. "Oh, by a stairway in back of the castle. It's quite a walk, but good for my figure." "Then do you walk back up?" "Oh no. There's a ski lift a half-mile from the beach. It lands me on a plateau, a sort of meadow. Beautiful. You've no idea. In the spring it is covered with flowers. I love it. Then I walk back through the castle and home."

"So there's skiing here, too?" she asked the prince.

"Oh no!" said the prince.

"He brought an old ski lift home from the Dolomites," the princess explained. "Just so I could ride up from the beach."

"Do you have a farm here?" Judy asked.

"Oh no!" said the prince.

"He did at one time," said the princess.

"At one time, I did, yes. Then I spent some years in England. In England they are all so kind to the animals. Oh, very kind. When I came back for the first time I saw how cruel our peasants were. Not that they meant to be cruel. Yet they were–they were cruel! I tried to change them. But they would not change. So at last I sold the animals and sent away all the peasants."

"That's one solution," Judy agreed.

"He vill never eat the meat," said Madame Thompson. She smiled, deeply, like the Mona Lisa. "Never!"

"Oh yes, the impression was a strong one. Also I am interested in Moral Rearmament. In England now there are so many thinking in this way. Now I oppose war and I will never eat meat again. *Carne? Mai!*"

It was not surprising, then, that they had pasta for lunch, followed by an omelet. Thompson sat at the head of the table.

"You should go to Greece," Thompson said to Bill. "Don't you plan to?"

"Greece isn't my field," Bill explained. "And of course my fellowship–"

"Fields and fellowships," said Thompson and gulped down some wine. "Fellowships and fields."

Bill remarked with a wry smile that Thompson himself had had one or two grants. "Oh, live on 'em!" Thompson cried. "Absolutely live on 'em. You people keep coming up the mountain–coming up the mountain. We must make it all work. How else?" His eye roved savagely around until it lighted on Judy: she felt as if her clothes were cracking suddenly away at the seams. Still observing her, Thompson said to Bill, "I'll tell you a subject that ten years ago I wouldn't have given a second thought to–at your age I would have derided it. The relation of art to economics."

"Oh, Lord, no," said Bill at once. "Not after 'The Byzantine Aesthetic.' "

"Very odd," said Thompson; "I feel exactly the same about one subject as the other." He sighed. "Well, don't tell Eakins on me, will you?"

"He'd think I was joking," Bill said.

"That summer in Paris," Thompson said, "when we met Eakins. When was that?" He addressed his wife. Madame Thompson had said nothing, it seemed to Judy, since her remark about the meat the prince would not eat; but now she began with patient, devoted, humorless accuracy to trace out what was wanted. Her voice rolled out in heavily muffled phrases, like something amplified through clouds.

"It vas in 1927, the summer Eugene, your secretary for ten years, had died at Cologne of pneumonia on the last day of February. You decided to bring three articles later called 'Some Aspects of the Renaissance'–"

"God!" Bill breathed, showing that he recognized the title.

"–to rewrite in Paris. After Eugene's death you thought alvays of the sculptures in the Louvre."

Memory rushed into Thompson, a back-lashing wave. The wine of that long ago summer seemed to be crisping his tongue. "Oh yes, and there was Eakins wanting all the same books as I in the Bibliothèque Nationale. He carried a sandwich in his briefcase. Very poor. One meal a day. Some *poule* or other was giving him that. No fellowships then. Nothing but fields. Some very green." He gave a short laugh. "I don't say he *read* the books, of course. That might be asking too much of Eakins."

The maid was putting the dessert around, a *crème caramel.* Thompson said he never ate dessert and went shuffling out in his carpet slippers. They all sat eating in silence. The princess said she would soon be going down for a swim if the Owens would care to join her. "I know I shouldn't so soon after eating, but the walk is good for me." She drew herself in smartly. Bill's refusal included the hint that he intended to have more of a talk with Thompson before the visit was over. "Oh, but he has gone to rest," they all said. "He must have his rest."

Bill looked concerned, and the prince promised to take him into the library, where Thompson would certainly come the moment he got up. Then the prince took Judy out to see his roses. The garden was in back of the castle ruins, in a sheltered area between the mountain and the ruined wall, opening out toward the south. The prince had gone to a great deal of trouble. Roses were especially hard to cultivate in Italy. But he had admired them so in England. His were ravishing–broad blooms of pink, white, red, and yellow. Here they could distinctly hear the sea.

In the pauses between his bits of information the prince looked inquiringly at Judy as if he was wondering if there was something else he could do for himself. His life so far would have been like the sweep of a windshield wiper. Of course, he was a prince; of course, he had a villa and a castle, with the daughter of a famous man for his wife and roses and two beautiful children, and Moral Rearmament and English flannels, and if the peasants did not understand, he sent them away. If that was not enough, he did not eat the meat. Was there something else?

Judy noticed this, but felt the lack of anything to suggest to him. She stood wondering whether, since the peasants and the animals were gone, the roses too were financed by the foundations, but she decided this line of thought was ungracious.

The children appeared from nowhere. "Now they will take you round the castle, if you like," the prince kindly said. "It is mainly in shadow, so you won't grow tired. But mind you don't let them tempt you to climb. They love it, but they are like cats. Say, 'No, no, come down!' "

He turned away, toward nothing.

Clambering around the castle, Judy came on a sort of enclosure, sunlit and quiet. She could smell warm earth beneath the grass. The air was sweet and soft, what Italians called *dolce*. There were some beautiful old broken chunks of ruin lying scattered about. Judy sat down on some ruined steps and rested her chin in her palm. The children called to her out of a tower but she said, "No, no, come down," so they did. The sky was radiant and gentle. She could glimpse the children at intervals, running past empty window gaps, until at last they leaped down on the grass before her.

Suddenly from behind the children, at a notch in the wall, the princess rose up. She was climbing; though as they could not see her feet, she seemed to be rising like a planet. She was rubbing her wet hair with a towel, and the sense and movement of the sea were about her.

Stopping still, she addressed a volley of Italian to the children. It would have been hard to convince anyone that her father was from Minnesota. Judy made out *"Che hai?" "Cattivo, tu!"* and *"Dammelo!"* which meant, she reasoned, that the children had something they shouldn't have which now was to be given to their mother. Then, as they at first hung back with their fists stuffed in the pockets of their pinafores, but finally obeyed, going forward and reaching out toward the princess, Judy glimpsed handful after handful of flashing blue stones, the purest, most vibrant blue she had ever seen. The color seemed to prank about the air for a moment with the freakish skip of lightning.

"Was the ski lift working?" a voice cried. Thompson himself was striding out to find them among the ruins. The princess came down from the wall and sat down quickly on a large fallen cornice. She had taken the stones, like eggs, in her towel, and now she quickly concealed them in it as well.

"It was working but not very well. It goes very *piano*. It also runs at an *angolo*."

"We must send Giuseppe down to look at the motor," Thompson said. "How was the sea?"

"Strong, but right," said the princess.

Judy saw from her watch that it was nearly three. Bill must be going nuts in the library, she knew; and here was Thompson grasping her arm and hustling her along a narrow path. They entered the villa by a side door and were at once standing facing one another in a narrow room with the remains of old frescoes peeling from the walls, a Renaissance chest in the corner, and a cold swept fireplace.

Thompson placed a hand like a bear's paw beneath her chin; his coarse thumb, raking down her cheek from temple to chin, all but left, she felt, a long scar. "Beauty," he remarked. His hand fell away and whatever she was expecting next did not occur.

"My husband," said Judy, "is waiting to see you. You know, don't you, that he is a terribly important scholar?"

"So Eakins said . . . but then I've never especially liked Eakins, do you? He says these things for some purpose. It is rather like playing cards. Perhaps it's all true. How am I to know? I was never a scholar." He confided this last somewhat eagerly, as though it had been the reason for finding her, and having her believe it mattered to him, Judy could not think why. He leaned back against the chest and folded his long arms. "You think I have to go and talk to him?" he debated with her. "You think that is the important thing?"

"I don't know. Oh, I really don't know!" She burst out with this–undoubtedly, the wrong thing–quite unexpectedly, surprising herself.

"Ummm," said Thompson, thinking it over. His eyes–large, pale, old, and, she supposed, ugly–searched hers. Unreasonable pain filled her for a moment: she longed to comfort him, but before she could think of how to, he tilted her head to an angle that pleased him, kissed her brow, and shambled off, though in truth he seemed to trail a length of broken chain.

She was left to lose her way alone.

Corridors, wrongly chosen, led her to a room, a door, a small courtyard, a stretch of gravel, a dry fountain. She walked halfway to the fountain and turned to look back at the façade, which like the other was sunburned and bare. It was surmounted by a noble crest, slightly askew–the prince's doubtless. I should have told Thompson, she thought, that the children had got into the mosaics, but suppose it wasn't true? How could you say such a thing and not make an idiot of yourself if you were wrong?

As she stood, her shadow lying faithfully beside her in the uncompromising sun, a door in the wing to her left swung open and two Hindus, splendidly dressed, the man in a tailored dark suit wearing a scarlet turban, the woman in a delicate spangled sari that prickled over the gravel, walked past the fountain, past Judy, and disappeared through a door in the façade. She had raised her hand to them, she had called, but they had not looked up.

Bill was disappointed to the point of despair by his visit, which had yielded him only a scant half-hour with Thompson and a dusty monograph, published in 1928. Even the subject matter–Greek vase painting–was not in Bill's field. Thompson had told him seriously that for a man of his age, he had a wonderful liver. If Eakins had lived in Europe as long as he (Thompson) had, his (Eakins') liver would look like a bloody sponge.

"He's an organized disappointment," Bill complained, "and not very well organized at that. He didn't want to talk to me because he can't compete any more. He's completely out of the swim."

"I liked him," said Judy. "I just loved him, in fact."

"Doubtless. He has a taste for pretty girls. You overdid it, dressing so well. Did he chase you through the upstairs ballroom? That's what it's used for nowadays."

The taxi having reappeared for them promptly at four, they were now speeding down the mountain at a suicidal clip; they clung to straps beside the windows, where many a scholarly pair had clung before. Leaping rocks and whipping around curves, the cab clanged like a factory.

"The children had got into the mosaics," Judy shouted.

"What?" Bill yelled. And when she repeated it, "That can't be true," he answered.

"Did you see the Hindu couple?" she asked, as they sped through a silent green valley.

"No," said Bill. "And please don't describe them." He said that he had a headache and was getting sick. He wondered if they would return alive.

From the corner of her eye, Judy saw a huge boulder, dislodged by their wheels, float out into a white gorge with the leisure of a dream.

SHIP ISLAND

The Story of a Mermaid

The French book was lying open on a corner of the dining room table, between the floor lamp and the window. The floor lamp, which had come with the house, had a cover made of green glass, with a fringe. The French book must have lain just that way for two months. Nancy, coming in from the beach, tried not to look at it. It reminded her of how much she had meant to accomplish during the summer, of the strong sense of intent, something like refinement, with which she had chosen just that spot for studying. It was out of hearing of the conversations with the neighbors that went on every evening out on the side porch, it had window light in the daytime and lamplight at night, it had a small, slanting view of the beach, and it drew a breeze. The pencils were still there, still sharp, and the exercise, broken off. She sometimes stopped to read it over. "The soldiers of the emperor were crossing the bridge: *Les soldats de l'empereur traversaient le pont.* The officer has already knocked at the gate: *L'officier a déjà frappé–*" She could not have finished that sentence now if she had sat right down and tried.

Nancy could no longer find herself in relation to the girl who had sought out such a good place to study, had sharpened the pencils and opened the book and sat down to bend over it. What she did know was how–just now, when she had been down at the beach, across the boulevard–the sand scuffed beneath her step and shells lay strewn about, chipped and disorderly, near the water's edge. Some shells were empty; some, with damp drying down their backs, went for short walks. Far out, a long white shelf of cloud indicated a distance no gull could dream of gaining, though the gulls spun tirelessly up, dazzling in the white light that comes just as morning vanishes. A troop of pelicans sat like curiously carved knobs on the tops of a long series of wooden piles, which were spaced out at intervals in the water. The piles were what was left of a private pier blown away by a hurricane some years ago.

Nancy had been alone on the beach. Behind her, the boulevard glittered in the morning sun and the season's traffic rocked by the long curve of the shore in clumps that seemed to burst, then speed on. She stood looking outward at the high straight distant shelf of cloud. The islands were out there, plainly visible. The walls of the old Civil War fort on the nearest one of them, the one with the lighthouse–Ship Island–were plain today as well. She had been out there once this summer with Rob Acklen, out there on the island, where the reeds grew in the wild white sand, and the water teemed so thick with seaweed that only crazy people would have tried to swim in it. The gulf had rushed white and strong through all the seaweed, frothing up the beach. On the beach, the froth turned brown, the color of softly moving crawfish claws. In the boat coming home through the sunset that day, a boy standing up in the pilothouse played "Over the Waves" on his harmonica. Rob Acklen had put his jacket around Nancy's shoulders–she had never thought to bring a sweater. The jacket swallowed her; it smelled more like Rob than he did. The boat moved, the breeze blew, the sea swelled, all to the lilt of the music. The twenty-five members of the Laurel, Mississippi, First Baptist Church Adult Bible Class, who had come out with them on the excursion boat, and to whom Rob and Nancy had yet to introduce themselves, had stopped giggling and making their silly jokes. They were tired, and stood in a huddle like sheep; they were shaped like sheep as well, with little shoulders and wide bottoms–it was somehow sad. Nancy and Rob, young and trim, stood side by side near the bow, like figureheads of the boat, hearing the music and watching the thick prow butt the swell, which the sunset had stained a deep red. Nancy felt for certain that this was the happiest she had ever been.

Alone on the sand this morning, she had spread out her beach towel and stood for a moment looking up the beach, way up, past a grove of live oaks to where Rob Acklen's house was visible. He would be standing in the kitchen, in loafers and a dirty white shirt and an old pair of shorts, drinking cold beer from the refrigerator right out of the can. He would eat lunch with his mother and sister, read the paper and write a letter, then dress and drive into town to help his father in the office, going right past Nancy's house along the boulevard. Around three, he would call her up. He did this every day. His name was Fitzrobert Conroy Acklen–one of those full-blown Confederate names. Everybody liked him, and more than a few–a general mixture of every color, size, age, sex, and religion–would say when he passed by, "I declare, I just love that boy." So he was bound to have a lot of nicknames: "Fitz" or "Bobbie" or "Cousin" or "Son"–he answered to almost anything. He was the kind of boy people have high, undefined hopes for. He had first seen Nancy Lewis one morning when he came by her house to make an insurance call for his father.

Breaking off her French–could it have been the sentence about *"l'officier"?*–she had gone out to see who it was. She was expecting Mrs. Nattier, their neighbor, who had skinny white freckled legs she never shaved and whose husband, "off" somewhere, was thought not to be doing well; or Mrs. Nattier's little boy Bernard, who thought it was fun to hide around corners after dark and jump out saying nothing more original than "Boo!" (once, he had screamed "Raw head and bloody bones!" but Nancy was sure somebody had told him to); or one of the neighbor ladies in the back–old Mrs. Poultney, whom they rented from and who walked with a cane, or Miss Henriette Dupré, who was so devout she didn't even have to go to confession before weekday Communion and whose hands, always tucked up in the sleeves of her sack, were as cold as church candles, and to think of them touching you was like rabbits skipping over your grave on dark rainy nights in winter up in the lonely wet-leaf-covered hills. Or else it was somebody wanting to be paid something. Nancy had opened the door and looked up, and there, instead of a dozen other people, was Rob Acklen.

Not that she knew his name. She had seen boys like him down on the coast, ever since her family had moved there from Little Rock back in the spring. She had seen them playing tennis on the courts back of the hotel, where she sometimes went to jump on the trampoline. She believed that the hotel people thought she was on the staff in some sort of way, as she was about the right age for that–just a year or so beyond high school but hardly old enough to work in town. The weather was already getting hot, and the season was falling off. When she passed the courts, going and coming, she saw the boys out of the corner of her eye. Were they really so much taller than the boys up where they had moved from, up in Arkansas? They were lankier and a lot more casual. They were more assured. To Nancy, whose family was in debt and whose father, in one job after another, was always doing something wrong, the boys playing tennis had that wonderful remoteness of creatures to be admired on the screen, or those seen in whiskey ads, standing near the bar of a country club and sleekly talking about things she could not begin to imagine. But now here was one, in a heavy tan cotton suit and a light blue shirt with a buttoned-down collar and dark tie, standing on her own front porch and smiling at her.

Yet when Rob called Nancy for a date, a day or two later, she didn't have to be told that he did it partly because he liked to do nice things for people. He obviously liked to be considerate and kind, because the first time he saw her he said, "I guess you don't know many people yet?"

"No, because Daddy just got transferred," she said–"transferred" being her mother's word for it; fired was what it was. She gave him a Coke and talked to him awhile, standing around in the house, which unaccountably continued to be empty. She said she didn't know a thing about insurance.

Now, still on the beach, Nancy Lewis sat down in the middle of her beach towel and began to rub suntan lotion on her neck and shoulders. Looking down the other way, away from Rob's house and toward the yacht club, she saw a man standing alone on the sand. She had not noticed him before. He was facing out toward the gulf and staring fixedly at the horizon. He was wearing shorts and a shirt made out of red bandanna, with the tail out–a stout young man with black hair.

Just then, without warning, it began to rain. There were no clouds one could see in the overhead dazzle, but it rained anyway; the drops fell in huge discs, marking the sand, and splashing on Nancy's skin. Each drop seemed enough to fill a Dixie cup. At first, Nancy did not know what the stinging sensation was; then she knew the rain was burning her. It was scalding hot! Strange, outlandish, but also painful, was how she found it. She jumped up and began to flinch and twist away, trying to escape, and a moment later she had snatched up her beach towel and flung it around her shoulders. But the large hot drops kept falling, and there was no escape from them. She started rubbing her cheek and forehead and felt that she might blister all over; then, since it kept on and on and was all so inexplicable, she grabbed her lotion and ran up the beach and out of the sand and back across the boulevard. Once in her own front yard, under the scraggy trees, she felt the rain no longer, and looked back curiously into the dazzle beyond the boulevard.

"I thought you meant to stay for a while," her mother said. "Was it too hot? Anybody would be crazy to go out there now. There's never anybody out there at this time of day."

"It was all right," said Nancy, "but it started raining. I never felt anything like it. The rain was so hot it burned me. Look. My face–" She ran to look in the mirror. Sure enough, her face and shoulders looked splotched. It might blister. I might be scarred for life, she thought–one of those dramatic phrases left over from high school.

Nancy's mother, Mrs. Lewis, was a discouraged lady whose silky, blondish-gray hair was always slipping loose and tagging out around her face. She would not try to improve herself and talked a lot in company about her family; two of her uncles had been professors simultaneously at the University of North Carolina. One of them had written a book on phonetics. Mrs. Lewis seldom found anyone who had heard of them, or of the book, either. Some people asked what phonetics were, and others did not ask anything at all.

Mrs. Lewis now said to her daughter, "You just got too much sun."

"No, it was the rain. It was really scalding hot."

"I never heard of such a thing," her mother said. "Out of a clear sky."

"I can't help that," Nancy said. "I guess I ought to know."

Mrs. Lewis took on the kind of look she had when she would open the handkerchief drawer of a dresser and see two used, slightly bent carpet nails, some Scotch Tape melted together, an old receipt, an unanswered letter announcing a cousin's wedding, some scratched negatives saved for someone but never developed, some dusty foreign coins, a bank deposit book from a town they lived in during the summer before Nancy was born, and an old telegram whose contents, forgotten, no one would dare now to explore, for it would say something awful but absolutely true.

"I wish you wouldn't speak to me like that," Mrs. Lewis said. "All I know is, it certainly didn't rain here."

Nancy wandered away, into the dining room. She felt bad about everything—about quarreling with her mother, about not getting a suntan, about wasting her time all summer with Rob Acklen and not learning any French. She went and took a long cool bath in the big old bathroom, where the bathtub had ball-and-claw feet painted mustard yellow and the single light bulb on the long cord dropped down one mile from the stratosphere.

What the Lewises found in a rented house was always outclassed by what they brought into it. Nancy's father, for instance, had a china donkey that bared its teeth in a great big grin. Written on one side was "If you really want to look like me" and on the other "Just keep right on talking." Her father loved the donkey and its message, and always put it on the living room table of whatever house they were in. When he got a drink before dinner each evening he would wander back with glass in hand and look the donkey over. "That's pretty good," he would say just before he took the first swallow. Nancy had often longed to break the donkey, by accident—that's what she would say, that it had all been an accident—but she couldn't get over the feeling that if she did, worse things than the Lewises had ever imagined would happen to them. That donkey would let in a flood of trouble, that she knew.

After Nancy got out of the tub and dried, she rubbed Jergens Lotion on all the splotches the rain had made. Then she ate a peanut-butter sandwich and more shrimp salad left over from supper the night before, and drank a cold Coke. Now and then, eating, she would go look in the mirror. By the time Rob Acklen called up, the red marks had all but disappeared.

That night, riding down to Biloxi with Rob, Nancy confided that the catalogue of people she disliked, headed by Bernard Nattier, included every single person—Miss Henriette Dupré, Mrs. Poultney, and Mrs. Nattier, and Mr. Nattier, too, when he was at home—that she had to be with these days. It even included, she was sad to say, her mother and father. If Bernard Nattier had to be mean—and it was clear he did have to—why did he have to be so corny? He put wads of wet, chewed bubble gum in her purses—that was the most original thing he ever did. Otherwise, it was just live crawfish in her bed or crabs in her shoes; anybody could think of that. And when he stole, he took things *she* wanted, nothing simple, like money–she could have forgiven him for that–but cigarettes, lipstick, and ashtrays she had stolen herself here and there. If she locked her door, he got in through the window; if she locked the window, she suffocated. Not only that, but he would crawl out from under the bed. His eyes were slightly crossed and he knew how to turn the lids back on themselves so that it looked like blood, and then he would chase her. He was browned to the color of dirt all over and he smelled like salt mud the sun had dried. He wore black tennis shoes laced too tight at the ankles and from sunup till way past dark he never thought of anything but what to do to Nancy, and she would have liked to kill him.

She made Rob Acklen laugh. She amused him. He didn't take anything Nancy Lewis could say at all to heart, but, as if she was something he had found on the beach and was teaching to talk, he, with his Phi Beta Kappa key and his good level head and his wonderful prospects, found everything she told about herself cute, funny, absurd. He did remark that he had such feelings himself from time to time–that he would occasionally get crazy mad at one of his parents or the other, and that he once planned his sister's murder down to the last razor slash. But he laughed again, and his chewing gum popped amiably in his jaws. When she told him about the hot rain, he said he didn't believe it. He said, "Aw," which was what a boy like Rob Acklen said when he didn't believe something. The top of his old white Mercury convertible was down and the wind rushed past like an endless bolt of raw silk being drawn against Nancy's cheek.

In the ladies' room mirror at the Beach View, where they stopped to eat, she saw the bright quality of her eyes, as though she had been drinking. Her skirts rustled in the narrow room; a porous white disc of deodorant hung on a hook, fuming the air. Her eyes, though blue, looked startlingly dark in her pale skin, for though she tried hard all the time, she never seemed to tan. All the sun did, as her mother was always pointing out, was bleach her hair three shades lighter; a little more and it would be almost white. Out on the island that day, out on Ship Island, she had drifted in the water like seaweed, with the tide combing her limbs and hair, tugging her through lengths of fuzzy water growth. She had lain flat on her face with her arms stretched before her, experiencing the curious lift the water's motion gave to the tentacles of weed, wondering whether she liked it or not. Did something alive clamber the small of her back? Did something wishful grope the spiral of her ear? Rob had caught her wrist hard and waked her—waked was what he did, though to sleep in the water is not possible. He said he thought she had been there too long. "Nobody can keep their face in the water that long," was what he said.

"I did," said Nancy.

Rob's brow had been blistered a little, she recalled, for that had been back early in the summer, soon after they had met—but the changes the sun made on him went without particular attention. The seasons here were old ground to him. He said that the island was new, however—or at least forgotten. He said he had never been there but once, and that many years ago, on a Boy Scout picnic. Soon they were exploring the fort, reading the dates off the metal signs whose letters glowed so smoothly in the sun, and the brief summaries of what those little boys, little military-academy boys turned into soldiers, had endured. Not old enough to fill up the name of soldier, or of prisoner, either, which is what they were—not old enough to shave, Nancy bet—still, they had died there, miserably far from home, and had been buried in the sand. There was a lot more. Rob would have been glad to read all about it, but she wasn't interested. What they knew already was plenty, just about those boys. A bright, worried lizard ran out of a hot rubble of brick. They came out of the fort and walked alone together eastward toward the dunes, now skirting near the shore that faced the sound and now wandering south, where they could hear or sometimes glimpse the gulf. They were overlooked all the way by an old white lighthouse. From far away behind, the twenty-five members of the adult Bible class could be overheard playing a silly, shrill Sunday-school game. It came across the ruins of the fort and the sad story of the dead soldiers like something that had happened long ago that you could not quite remember having joined in. On the beach to their right, toward the gulf, a flock of sandpipers with blinding-white breasts stepped pecking along the water's edge, and on the inner beach, toward the sound, a wrecked sailboat with a broken mast lay half buried in the sand.

Rob kept teasing her along, pulling at the soft wool strings of her bathing suit, which knotted at the nape and again under her shoulder blades, worrying loose the damp hair that she had carefully slicked back and pinned. "There isn't anybody in that house," he assured her, some minutes later, having explored most of that part of the island

and almost as much of Nancy as well, having almost, but not quite—his arms around her—coaxed and caressed her down to ground level in a clump of reeds. "There hasn't been in years and years," he said, encouraging her.

"It's only those picnic people," she said, holding off, for the reeds would not have concealed a medium-sized mouse. They had been to look at the sailboat and thought about climbing inside (kissing closely, they had almost fallen right over into it), but it did have a rotten tin can in the bottom and smelled, so here they were back out in the dunes.

"They've got to drink all those Coca-Colas," Rob said, "and give out all those prizes, and anyway—"

She never learned anyway what, but it didn't matter. Maybe she began to make up for all that the poor little soldiers had missed out on, in the way of making love. The island's very spine, a warm reach of thin ground, came smoothly up into the arch of her back; and it was at least halfway the day itself, with its fair, wide-open eyes, that she went over to. She felt somewhat historical afterward, as though they had themselves added one more mark to all those that place remembered.

Having played all the games and given out the prizes, having eaten all the homemade cookies and drunk the case of soft drinks just getting warm, and gone sight-seeing through the fort, the Bible class was now coming, too, crying "Yoohoo!" to explore the island. They discovered Rob hurling shells and bits of rock into the surf, while Nancy, scavenging a little distance away, tugged up out of the sand a shell so extraordinary it was worth showing around. It was purple, pink, and violet inside—a palace of colors; the king of the oysters had no doubt lived there. When she held it shyly out to them, they cried "Look!" and "Ooo!" so there was no need for talking to them much at all, and in the meantime the evening softened, the water glowed, the glare dissolved. Far out, there were other islands one could see now, and beyond those must be many more. They had been there all along.

Going home, Nancy gave the wonderful shell to the boy who stood in the pilothouse playing "Over the Waves." She glanced back as they walked off up the pier and saw him look at the shell, try it for weight, and then throw it in the water, leaning far back on his arm and putting a good spin on the throw, the way boys like to do—the way Rob Acklen himself had been doing, too, just that afternoon.

"Why did you do that?" Rob had demanded. He was frowning; he looked angry. He had thought they should keep the shell—to remember, she supposed.

"For the music," she explained.

"But it was ours," he said. When she didn't answer, he said again, "Why did you, Nancy?"

But still she didn't answer.

When Nancy returned to their table at the Beach View, having put her lipstick back straight after eating fish, Rob was paying the check. "Why not believe me?" she asked him. "It was true. The rain was hot as fire. I thought I would be scarred for life."

It was still broad daylight, not even twilight. In the bright, air-conditioned restaurant, the light from the water glazed flatly against the broad picture windows, the chandeliers, and the glasses. It was the hour when mirrors reflect nothing and bars look tired. The restaurant was a boozy, cheap sort of place with a black-lined gambling hall in the back, but everyone went there because the food was good.

"You're just like Mama," she said. "You think I made it up."

Rob said, teasing, "I didn't say that. I just said I didn't believe it." He loved getting her caught in some sort of logic she couldn't get out of. When he opened the door for her, she got a good sidelong view of his longish, firm face and saw the way his somewhat fine brows arched up with one or two bright reddish hairs in among the dark ones; his hair was that way, too, when the sun hit it. Maybe, if nobody had told him, he wouldn't have known it; he seemed not to notice so very much about himself. Having the confidence of people who don't worry much, his grin could snare her instantly—a glance alone could make her feel how lucky she was he'd ever noticed her. But it didn't do at all to think about him now. It would be ages before they made it through the evening and back, retracing the way and then turning off to the bayou, and even then, there would be those mosquitoes.

Bayou love-making suited Rob just fine; he was one of those people mosquitoes didn't bite. They certainly bit Nancy. They were huge and silent, and the minute the car stopped they would even come and sit upon her eyelids, if she closed her eyes, a dozen to each tender arc of flesh. They would gather on her face, around her nose and mouth. Clothlike, like rags and tatters, like large dry ashes of burnt cloth, they came in lazy droves, in fleets, sailing on the air. They were never in any hurry, being everywhere at once and always ready to bite. Nancy had been known to jump all the way out of the car and go stamping across the grass like a calf. She grew sulky and despairing and stood on one leg at a time in the moonlight, slapping at her ankles, while Rob leaned his chin on the doorframe and watched her with his affectionate, total interest.

Nancy, riddled and stinging with beads of actual blood briar-pointed here and there upon her, longed to be almost anywhere else—she especially longed for New Orleans. She always talked about it, although, never having been there, she had to say the things that other people said—food and jazz in the French Quarter, beer and crabs out on Lake Pontchartrain. Rob said vaguely they would go sometime. But she could tell that things were wrong for him at this point. "The food's just as good around here," he said.

"Oh, Rob!" She knew it wasn't so. She could feel that city, hanging just over the horizon from them scarcely fifty miles away, like some swollen bronze moon, at once brilliant and shadowy and drenched in every sort of amplified smell. Rob was stroking her hair, and in time his repeated, gentle touch gained her attention. It seemed to tell what he liked—girls all spanking clean, with scrubbed fingernails, wearing shoes still damp with white shoe polish. Even a fresh gardenia stuck in their hair wouldn't be too much for him. There would be all sorts of differences, to him, between Ship Island and the French Quarter, but she did not have much idea just what they were. Nancy took all this in, out of his hand on her head. She decided she had better not talk any more about New Orleans. She wriggled around, looking out over his shoulder, through the moonlight, toward where the pitch-black surface of the bayou water showed in patches through the trees. The trees were awful, hung with great spooky gray tatters of Spanish moss. Nancy was reminded of the house she and her family were living in; it had recently occurred to her that the peculiar smell it had must come from some Spanish moss that had got sealed in behind the paneling, between the walls. The moss was alive in there and growing, and that was where she was going to seal Bernard Nattier up someday, for him to see how it felt. She had tried to kill him once, by filling her purse with rocks and oyster shells—the roughest she could find. She had read somewhere that this weapon was effective for ladies in case of attack. But he had ducked when she swung the purse at him, and she had only gone spinning round and round, falling at last into a camellia tree, which had scratched her. . . .

"The Skeltons said for us to stop by there for a drink," Rob told her. They were driving again, and the car was back on the boulevard, in the still surprising daylight. "What did you say?" he asked her.

"Nothing."

"You just don't want to go?"

"No, I don't much want to go."

"Well, then, we won't stay long."

The Skelton house was right on the water, with a second-story, glassed-in, air-conditioned living room looking out over the sound. The sofas and chairs were covered with gold-and-white striped satin, and the room was full of Rob's friends. Lorna Skelton, who had been Rob's girl the summer before and who dressed so beautifully, was handing drinks round and saying, "So which is your favorite bayou, Rob?" She had a sort of fake "good sport" tone of voice and wanted to appear ready for anything. (Being so determined to be nice around Nancy, she was going to fall right over backward one day.)

"Do I have to have a favorite?" Rob asked. "They all look good to me. Full of slime and alligators."

"I should have asked Nancy."

"They're all full of mosquitoes," said Nancy, hoping that was O.K. for an answer. She thought that virgins were awful people.

"Trapped, boy!" Turner Carmichael said to Rob, and banged him on the shoulder. Turner wanted to be a writer, so he thought it was all right to tell people about themselves. "Women will be your downfall, Acklen. Nancy, honey, you haven't spoken to the general."

Old General Skelton, Lorna's grandfather, sat in the corner of the living room near the mantel, drinking a scotch highball. You had to shout at him.

"How's the election going, General?" Turner asked.

"Election? Election? What election? Oh, the election! Well–" He lowered his voice, confidentially. As with most deaf people, his tone went to extremes. "There's no question of it. The one we want is the one we know. Know Houghman's father. Knew his grandfather. His stand is the same, identical one that we are all accustomed to. On every subject–this race thing especially. Very dangerous now. Extremely touchy. But Houghman–absolute! Never experiment, never question, never turn back. These are perilous times."

"Yes, sir," said Turner, nodding in an earnestly false way, which was better than the earnestly impressed way a younger boy at the general's elbow shouted, "General Skelton, that's just what my daddy says!"

"Oh yes," said the old man, sipping scotch. "Oh yes, it's true. And you, missy?" he thundered suddenly at Nancy, making her jump. "Are you just visiting here?"

"Why, Granddaddy," Lorna explained, joining them, "Nancy lives here now. You know Nancy."

"Then why isn't she tan?" the old man continued. "Why so pale and wan, fair nymph?"

"Were you a nymph?" Turner asked. "All this time?"

"For me I'm dark," Nancy explained. But this awkward way of putting it proved more than General Skelton could hear, even after three shoutings.

Turner Carmichael said, "We used to have this crazy colored girl who went around saying, 'I'se really white, 'cause all my chillun is,'" and of course *that* was what General Skelton picked to hear. "Party's getting rough," he complained.

"Granddaddy," Lorna cried, giggling, "you don't understand!"

"Don't I?" said the old gentleman. "Well, maybe I don't."

"Here, Nancy, come help me," said Lorna, leading her guest toward the kitchen.

On the way, Nancy heard Rob ask Turner, "Just where did you have this colored girl, did you say?"

"Don't be a dope. I said she worked for us."

"Aren't they a scream?" Lorna said, dragging a quart bottle of soda out of the refrigerator. "I thank God every night Granddaddy's deaf. You know, he was in the First World War and killed I don't know how many Germans, and he still can't stand to hear what he calls loose talk before a lady."

"I thought he was in the Civil War," said Nancy, and then of course she knew that that was the wrong thing and that Lorna, who just for an instant gave her a glance less than polite, was not going to forget it. The fact was, Nancy had never thought till that minute which war General Skelton had been in. She hadn't thought because she didn't care.

It had grown dark by now, and through the kitchen windows Nancy could see that the moon had risen—a moon in the clumsy stage, swelling between three-quarters and full, yet pouring out light on the water.

Its rays were bursting against the long breakwater of concrete slabs, the remains of what the hurricane had shattered.

After saying such a fool thing, Nancy felt she could not stay in that kitchen another minute with Lorna, so she asked where she could go comb her hair. Lorna showed her down a hallway, kindly switching the lights on.

The Skeltons' bathroom was all pale blue and white, with handsome jars of rose bath salts and big fat scented bars of rosy soap. The lights came on impressively and the fixtures were heavy, yet somehow it all looked dead. It came to Nancy that she had really been wondering about just what would be in this sort of bathroom ever since she had seen those boys, with maybe Rob among them, playing tennis while she jumped on the trampoline. Surely the place had the air of an inner shrine, but what was there to see? The tops of all the bottles fitted firmly tight, and the soap in the tub was dry. Somebody had picked it all out—that was the point—judging soap and bath salts just the way they judged outsiders, business, real estate, politics. Nancy's father made judgments, too. Once, he argued all evening that Hitler was a well-meaning man; another time, he said the world was ready for communism. You could tell he was judging wrong, because he didn't have a bathroom like this one. Nancy's face in the mirror resembled a flower in a room that was too warm.

When she went out again, they had started dancing a little—a sort of friendly shifting around before the big glass windows overlooking the sound. General Skelton's chair was empty; he was gone. Down below, Lorna's parents could be heard coming in; her mother called upstairs. Her father appeared and shook hands all around. Mrs. Skelton soon followed him. He was wearing a white jacket, and she had on a silver cocktail dress with silver shoes. They looked like people in magazines. Mrs. Skelton held a crystal platter of things to eat in one hand, with a lace handkerchief pressed between the flesh and the glass in an inevitable sort of way.

In a moment, when the faces, talking and eating, the music, the talk, and the dancing swam to a still point before Nancy's eyes, she said, "You must all come to my house next week. We'll have a party."

A silence fell. Everyone knew where Nancy lived, in that cluster of old run-down houses the boulevard swept by. They knew that her house, especially, needed paint outside and furniture inside. Her daddy drank too much, and through her dress they could perhaps clearly discern the pin that held her slip together. Maybe, since they knew everything, they could look right through the walls of the house and see her daddy's donkey.

"Sure we will," said Rob Acklen at once. "I think that would be grand."

"Sure we will, Nancy," said Lorna Skelton, who was such a good sport and who was not seeing Rob this summer.

"A party?" said Turner Carmichael, and swallowed a whole anchovy. "Can I come, too?"

Oh, dear Lord, Nancy was wondering, what made me say it? Then she was on the stairs with her knees shaking, leaving the party, leaving with Rob to go down to Biloxi, where the two of them always went, and hearing the right things said to her and Rob, and smiling back at the right things but longing to jump off into the dark as if it were water. The dark, with the moon mixed in with it, seemed to her like good deep water to go off in.

She might have known that in the Marine Room of the Buena Vista down in Biloxi, they would run into more friends of Rob's. They always ran into somebody, and she might have known. These particular ones had already arrived and were even waiting for Rob, being somewhat bored in the process. It wasn't that Rob was so bright and witty, but he listened and liked everybody; he saw them the way they liked to be seen. So then they would go on to new heights, outdoing themselves, coming to believe how marvelous they really were. Two fraternity brothers of his were there tonight. They were sitting at a table with their dates—two tiny girls with tiny voices, like mosquitoes. They at once asked Nancy where she went to college, but before she could reply and give it away that her school so far had been only a cow college up in Arkansas and that she had gone there because her daddy couldn't afford anywhere else, Rob broke in and answered for her. "She's been in a finishing school in Little Rock," he said, "but I'm trying to talk her into going to the university."

Then the girls and their dates all four spoke together. They said, "Great!"

"Now watch," said one of the little girls, whose name was Teenie. "Cootie's getting out that little ole rush book."

Sure enough, the tiniest little notebook came out of the little cream silk bag of the other girl, who was called Cootie, and in it Nancy's name and address were written down with a sliver of a gold pencil. The whole routine was a fake, but a kind fake, as long as Rob was there. The minute those two got her into the ladies' room it would turn into another thing altogether; that she knew. Nancy knew all about mosquitoes. They'll sting me till I crumple up and die, she thought, and what will they ever care? So, when the three of them did leave the table, she stopped to straighten the strap of her shoe at the door to the ladies' room and let them go on through, talking on and on to one another about Rush Week. Then she went down a corridor and around a corner and down a short flight of steps. She ran down a long basement hallway where the service quarters were, past linen closets and cases of soft drinks, and, turning another corner and trying a door above a stairway, she came out, as she thought she would, in a night-club place called the Fishnet, far away in the wing. It was a good place to hide; she and Rob had been there often. I can make up some sort of story later, she thought, and crept up on the last bar stool. Up above the bar, New Orleans-style (or so they said), a man was pumping tunes out of an electric organ. He wore rings on his chubby fingers and kept a handkerchief near him to mop his brow and to swab his triple chins with between songs. He waved his hand at Nancy. "Where's Rob, honey?" he asked.

She smiled but didn't answer. She kept her head back in the shadows. She wished only to be like another glass in the sparkling row of glasses lined up before the big gleam of mirrors and under the play of lights. What made me say that about a party? she kept wondering. To some people it would be nothing, nothing. But not to her. She fumbled in her bag for a cigarette. Inadvertently, she drank from a glass near her hand. The man sitting next to her smiled at her. "I didn't want it anyway," he said.

"Oh, I didn't mean—" she began. "I'll order one." Did you pay now? She rummaged in her bag.

But the man said, "What'll it be?" and ordered for her. "Come on now, take it easy," he said. "What's your name?"

"Nothing," she said, by accident.

She had meant to say Nancy, but the man seemed to think it was funny. "Nothing what?" he asked. "Or is it by any chance Miss Nothing? I used to know a large family of Nothings, over in Mobile."

"Oh, I meant to say Nancy."

"Nancy Nothing. Is that it?"

Another teaser, she thought. She looked away from his eyes, which glittered like metal, and what she saw across the room made her uncertainties vanish. She felt her whole self settle and calm itself. The man she had seen that morning on the beach wearing a red bandanna shirt and shorts was standing near the back of the Fishnet, looking on. Now he was wearing a white dinner jacket and a black tie, with a red cummerbund over his large stomach, but he was unmistakably the same man. At that moment, he positively seemed to Nancy to be her own identity. She jumped up and left the teasing man at the bar and crossed the room.

"Remember me?" she said. "I saw you on the beach this morning."

"Sure I do. You ran off when it started to rain. I had to run, too."

"Why did you?" Nancy asked, growing happier every minute.

"Because the rain was so hot it burnt me. If I could roll up my sleeve, I'd show you the blisters on my arm."

"I believe you. I had some, too, but they went away." She smiled, and the man smiled back. The feeling was that they would be friends forever.

"Listen," the man said after a while. "There's a fellow here you've got to meet now. He's out on the veranda, because it's too hot in here. Anyway, he gets tired just with me. Now you come on."

Nancy Lewis was always conscious of what she had left behind her. She knew that right now her parents and old Mrs. Poultney, with her rent collector's jaw, and Miss Henriette Dupré, with her religious calf eyes, and the Nattiers, mother and son, were all sitting on the back porch in the half-light, passing the bottle of 6-12 around, and probably right now discussing the fact that Nancy was out with Rob again. She knew that when her mother thought of Rob her heart turned beautiful and radiant as a sea shell on a spring night. Her father, both at home and at his office, took his daughter's going out with Rob as excuse for saying something disagreeable about Rob's father, who was a big insurance man. There was always some talk about how Mr. Acklen had trickily got out of the bulk of his hurricane-damage payments, the same as all the other insurance men had done. Nancy's mother was probably responding to such a charge at this moment. "Now, you don't know that's true," she would say. But old Mrs. Poultney would say she knew it was true with *her* insurance company (implying that she knew but wouldn't say about the Acklen Company, too). Half the house she was renting to the Lewises had blown right off it—all one wing—and the upstairs bathroom was ripped in two, and you could see the wallpapered walls of all the rooms, and the bathtub, with its pipes still attached, had got blown into the telephone wires. If Mrs. Poultney had got what insurance money had been coming to her, she would have torn down this house and built a new one. And Mrs. Nattier would say that there was something terrible to her about seeing wallpapered rooms exposed that way. And Miss Henriette Dupré would say that the Dupré house had come through it all ab-so-lootly intact, meaning that the Duprés had been foresighted enough to get some sort of special heavenly insurance, and she would be just longing to embark on explaining how they came by it, and she would, too, given a tenth of a chance. And all the time this went on, Nancy could see into the Acklens' house just as clearly—see the Acklens sitting inside their sheltered game room after dinner, bathed in those soft bug-repellent lights. And what were the Acklens saying (along with their kind of talk about their kind of money) but that they certainly hoped Rob wasn't serious about that girl? Nothing had to matter if he wasn't serious. . . . Nancy could circle around all of them in her mind. She could peer into windows, overhearing; it was the only way she could look at people. No human in the whole human world seemed to her exactly made for her to stand in front of and look squarely in the eye, the way she could look Bernard Nattier in the eye (he not being human either) before taking careful aim to be sure not to miss him with a purseful of rocks and oyster shells, or the way she could look this big man in the red cummerbund in the eye, being convinced already that he was what her daddy called a "natural." Her daddy liked to come across people he could call that, because it made him feel superior.

As the big man steered her through the crowded room, threading among the tables, going out toward the veranda, he was telling her his life story all along the way. It seemed that his father was a terribly rich Yankee who paid him not to stay at home. He had been in love with a policeman's daughter from Pittsburgh, but his father broke it up. He was still in love with her and always would be. It was the way he was; he couldn't help being faithful, could he? His name was Alfred, but everybody called him Bub. The fellow his father paid to drive him around was right down there, he said, as they stepped through the door and out on the veranda.

Nancy looked down the length of the veranda, which ran along the side of the hotel, and there was a man sitting on a bench. He had on a white jacket and was staring straight ahead, smoking. The highway curled around the hotel grounds, following the curve of the shore, and the cars came glimmering past, one by one, sometimes with lights on inside, sometimes spilling radio music that trailed up in long waves and met the electric-organ music coming out of the bar. Nancy and Bub walked toward the man. Bub counseled her gently, "His name is Dennis." Some people in full evening dress were coming up the divided walk before the hotel, past the canna lilies blooming deeply red under the high, powerful lights, where the bugs coned in long footless whirlpools. The people were drunk and laughing.

"Hi, Dennis," Bub said. The way he said it, trying to sound confident, told her that he was scared of Dennis.

Dennis's head snapped up and around. He was an erect, strong, square-cut man, not very tall. He had put water on his light brown hair when he combed it, so that it streaked light and dark and light again and looked like wood. He had cold eyes, which did not express anything—just the opposite of Rob Acklen's.

"What you got there?" he asked Bub.

"I met her this morning on the beach," Bub said.

"Been holding out on me?"

"Nothing like that," said Bub. "I just now saw her again."

The man called Dennis got up and thumbed his cigarette into the shrubbery. Then he carefully set his heels together and bowed. It was all a sort of joke on how he thought people here behaved. "Would you care to dance?" he inquired.

Dancing there on the veranda, Nancy noticed at once that he had a tense, strong wrist that bent back and forth like something manufactured out of steel. She also noticed that he was making her do whatever it was he called dancing; he was good at that. The music coming out of the Fishnet poured through the windows and around them. Dennis was possibly even thirty years old. He kept talking the whole time. "I guess he's told you everything, even about the policeman's daughter. He tells everybody everything, right in the first two minutes. I don't know if it's true, but how can you tell? If it wasn't true when it happened, it is now." He spun her fast as a top, then slung her out about ten feet—she thought she would certainly sail right on out over the railing and maybe never stop till she landed in the gulf, or perhaps go splat on the highway—but he got her back on the beat and finished up the thought, saying, "Know what I mean?"

"I guess so," Nancy said, and the music stopped.

The three of them sat down together on the bench.

"What do we do now?" Dennis asked.

"Let's ask her," said Bub. He was more and more delighted with Nancy. He had been tremendously encouraged when Dennis took to her.

"You ask her," Dennis said.

"Listen, Nancy," Bub said. "Now, listen. Let me just tell you. There's so much money—that's the first thing to know. You've got no idea how much money there is. Really crazy. It's something, actually, that nobody knows—"

"If anybody knew," said Dennis, "they might have to tell the government."

"Anyway, my stepmother on this yacht in Florida, her own telephone—by radio, you know—she'd be crazy to meet you. My dad is likely off somewhere, but maybe not. And there's this plane down at Palm Beach, pilot and all, with nothing to do but go to the beach every day, just to pass away the time, and if he's not there for any reason, me and Dennis can fly just as good as we can drive. There's Alaska, Beirut—would you like to go to Beirut? I've always wanted to. There's anything you say."

"See that Cad out there?" said Dennis. "The yellow one with the black leather upholstery? That's his. I drive."

"So all you got to do," Bub told her, "is wish. Now, wait—now, think. It's important!" He all but held his hand over her mouth, as if playing a child's game, until finally he said, "Now! What would you like to do most in the world?"

"Go to New Orleans," said Nancy at once, "and eat some wonderful food."

"It's a good idea," said Dennis. "This dump is getting on my nerves. I get bored most of the time anyway, but today I'm bored silly."

"So wait here!" Nancy said. "So wait right here!"

She ran off to get Rob. She had all sorts of plans in her head.

But Rob was all taken up. There were now more of his friends. The Marine Room was full of people just like him, lounging around two big tables shoved together, with about a million 7-Up bottles and soda bottles and glasses before them, and girls spangled among them, all silver, gold, and white. It was as if while Nancy was gone they had moved into mirrors to multiply themselves. They were talking to themselves about things she couldn't join in, any more than you can dance without feet. Somebody was going into politics, somebody was getting married to a girl who trained horses, somebody was just back from Europe. The two little mosquito girls weren't saying anything much any more; they had their little chins glued to their little palms. When anybody mentioned the university, it sounded like a small country the people right there were running *in absentia* to suit themselves. Last year's Maid of Cotton was there, and so, it turned out, was the girl horse trainer—tall, with a sheaf of upswept brown hair fastened with a glittering pin; she sat like the mast of a ship, smiling and talking about horses. Did she know personally every horse in the Southern states?

Rob scarcely looked up when he pulled Nancy in. "Where you been? What you want to drink?" He was having another good evening. He seemed to be sitting up above the rest, as though presiding, but this was not actually so; only his fondness for every face he saw before him made him appear to be raised a little, as if on a special chair.

And, later on, it seemed to Nancy that she herself had been, among them, like a person who wasn't a person—another order of creature passing among or even through them. Was it just that nothing, nobody, could really distract them when they got wrapped up in themselves?

"I met some people who want to meet you," she whispered to Rob. "Come on out with me."

"O.K.," he said. "In a minute. Are they from around here?"

"Come on, come on," she urged. "Come on out."

"In a minute," he said. "I will in a minute," he promised.

Then someone noticed her pulling at his sleeve, and she thought she heard Lorna Skelton laugh.

She went racing back to Bub and Dennis, who were waiting for her so docilely they seemed to be the soul of goodness, and she said, "I'll just ride around for a while, because I've never been in a Cadillac before." So they rode around and came back and sat for a while under the huge brilliant overhead lights before the hotel, where the bugs spiraled down. They did everything she said. She could make them do anything. They went to three different places, for instance, to find her some Dentyne, and when they found it they bought her a whole carton of it.

The bugs did a jagged frantic dance, trying to climb high enough to kill themselves, and occasionally a big one crashed with a harsh dry sound against the pavement. Nancy remembered dancing in the open air, and the rough salt feel of the air whipping against her skin as she spun fast against the air's drift. From behind she heard the resonant, constant whisper of the gulf. She looked toward the hotel doors and thought that if Rob came through she would hop out of the car right away, but he didn't come. A man she knew passed by, and she just all of a sudden said, "Tell Rob I'll be back in a minute," and he, without even looking up said, "O.K., Nancy," just like it really was O.K., so she said what the motor was saying, quiet but right there, and definitely running just under the splendid skin of the car, "Let's go on for a little while."

"Nancy, I think you're the sweetest girl I ever saw," said Bub, and they drove off.

She rode between them, on the front seat of the Cadillac. The top was down and the moon spilled over them as they rode, skimming gently but powerfully along the shore and the sound, like a strong rapid cloud traveling west. Nancy watched the point where the moon actually met the water. It was moving and still at once. She thought that it was glorious, in a messy sort of way. She would have liked to poke her head up out of the water right there. She could feel the water pouring back through her white-blond hair, her face slathering over with moonlight.

"If it hadn't been for that crazy rain," Bub kept saying, "I wouldn't have met her."

"Oh, shut up about that goofy rain," said Dennis.

"It was like being spit on from above," said Nancy.

The needle crept up to eighty or more, and when they had left the sound and were driving through the swamp, Nancy shivered. They wrapped her in a lap robe from the back seat and turned the radio up loud.

It was since she got back, since she got back home from New Orleans, that her mother did not put on the thin voile afternoon dress any more and serve iced tea to the neighbors on the back porch. Just yesterday, having nothing to do in the hot silence but hear the traffic stream by on the boulevard, and not wanting a suntan, and being certain the telephone would not ring, Nancy had taken some lemonade over to

Bernard Nattier, who was sick in bed with the mumps. He and his mother had one room between them over at Mrs. Poultney's house, and they had stacks of magazines—the *Ladies' Home Journal, McCall's, Life,* and *Time*—piled along the walls. Bernard lay on a bunk bed pushed up under the window, in all the close heat, with no breeze able to come in at all. His face was puffed out and his eyes feverish. "I brought you some lemonade," said Nancy, but he said he couldn't drink it because it hurt his gums. Then he smiled at her, or tried to—it must have hurt even to do that, and it certainly made him look silly, like a cartoon of himself, but it was sweet.

"I love you, Nancy," he said, most irresponsibly.

She thought she would cry. She had honestly tried to kill him with those rocks and oyster shells. He knew that very well, and he, from the moment he had seen her, had set out to make her life one long torment, so where could it come from, a smile like that, and what he said? She didn't know. From the fever, maybe. She said she loved him, too.

Then, it was last night, just the night before, that her father had got drunk and made speeches beginning, "To think that a daughter of mine . . ." Nancy had sat through it all crouched in the shadows on the stair landing, in the very spot where the moss or old seaweed back of the paneling smelled the strongest and dankest, and thought of her mother upstairs, lying, clothed, straight out on the bed in the dark, with a headache and no cover on and maybe the roof above her melted away. Nancy looked down to where her father was marching up to the donkey that said, "If you really want to look like me—Just keep right on talking," and was picking it up and throwing it down, right on the floor. She cried out, before she knew it—"Oh!"—seeing him do the very thing she had so often meant to do herself. Why had he? Why? Because the whiskey had run out on him? Or because he had got too much of it again? Or from trying to get in one good lick at everything there was? Or because the advice he loved so much seemed now being offered to him?

But the donkey did not break. It lay there, far down in the tricky shadows; Nancy could see it lying there, looking back over its shoulder with its big red grinning mouth, and teeth like piano keys, still saying the same thing, naturally. Her father was tilting uncertainly down toward it, unable, without falling flat on his face, to reach it. This made a problem for him, and he stood thinking it all over, taking every aspect of it well into account, even though the donkey gave the impression that not even with a sledgehammer would it be broken, and lay as if on some deep distant sea floor, toward which all the sediment of life was drifting, drifting, forever slowly down. . . .

Beirut! It was the first time she had remembered it. They had said they would take her there, Dennis and Bub, and then she had forgotten to ask, so why think of it right now, on the street uptown, just when she saw Rob Acklen coming along? She would have to see him sometime, she guessed, but what did Beirut have to do with it?

"Nancy Lewis," he said pleasantly, "you ran out on me. Why did you act like that? I was always nice to you."

"I told them to tell you," she said. "I just went to ride around for a while."

"Oh, I got the word, all right. About fifty different people saw you drive off in that Cadillac. Now about a hundred claim to have. Seems like everybody saw those two characters but me. What did you do it for?"

"I didn't like those Skeltons, all those people you know. I didn't like those sorority girls, that Teenie and Cootie. You knew I didn't, but you always took me where they were just the same."

"But the point is," said Rob Acklen, "I thought you liked me."

"Well, I did," said Nancy Lewis, as though it all had happened a hundred years ago. "Well, I did like you just fine."

They were still talking on the street. There had been the tail of a storm that morning, and the palms were blowing. There was a sense of them streaming like green flags above the low town.

Rob took Nancy to the drugstore and sat at a booth with her. He ordered her a fountain Coke and himself a cup of coffee. "What's happened to you?" he asked her.

She realized then, from what he was looking at, that something she had only half noticed was certainly there to be seen—her skin, all around the edges of her white blouse, was badly bruised and marked, and there was the purplish mark on her cheekbone she had more or less powdered over, along with the angry streak on her neck.

"You look like you fell through a cotton gin," Rob Acklen continued, in his friendly way. "You're not going to say the rain over in New Orleans is just scalding hot, are you?"

"I didn't say anything," she returned.

"Maybe the mosquitoes come pretty big over there," he suggested. "They wear boxing gloves, for one thing, and, for another—"

"Oh, stop it, Rob," she said, and wished she was anywhere else.

It had all stemmed from the moment down in the French Quarter, over late drinks somewhere, when Dennis had got nasty enough with Bub to get rid of him, so that all of Dennis's attention from that point onward had gone exclusively to Nancy. This particular attention was relentless and direct, for Dennis was about as removed from any sort of affection and kindness as a human could be. Maybe it had all got boiled out of him; maybe he had never had much to get rid of. What he had to say to her was nothing she hadn't heard before, nothing she hadn't already been given more or less to understand from mosquitoes, people, life-in-general, and the rain out of the sky. It was just that he said it in a final sort of way–that was all.

"I was in a wreck," said Nancy.

"Nobody killed, I hope," said Rob.

She looked vaguely across at Rob Acklen with pretty, dark blue eyes that seemed to be squinting to see through shifting lights down in the deep sea; for in looking at him, in spite of all he could do, she caught a glimmering impression of herself, of what he thought of her, of how soft her voice always was, her face like a warm flower.

"I was doing my best to be nice to you. Why wasn't that enough?"

"I don't know," she said.

"None of those people you didn't like were out to get you. They were all my friends."

When he spoke in this handsome, sincere, and democratic way, she had to agree; she had to say she guessed that was right.

Then he said, "I was having such a good summer. I imagined you were, too," and she thought, He's coming down deeper and deeper, but one thing is certain–if he gets down as far as I am, he'll drown.

"You better go," she told him, because he had said he was on his way up to Shreveport on business for his father. And because Bub and Dennis were back; she'd seen them drift by in the car twice, once on the boulevard and once in town, silenter than cloud, Bub in the back, with his knees propped up, reading a magazine.

"I'll be going in a minute," he said.

"You just didn't realize I'd ever go running off like that," Nancy said, winding a damp Coca-Cola straw around her finger.

"Was it the party, the one you said you wanted to give? You didn't have to feel–"

"I don't remember any party," she said quickly.

Her mother lay with the roof gone, hands folded. Nancy felt that people's mothers, like wallpapered walls after a hurricane, should not be exposed. Her father at last successfully reached the donkey, but he fell in the middle of the rug, while Nancy, on the stair landing, smelling seaweed, asked herself how a murderous child with swollen jaws happened to mention love, if love is not a fever, and the storm-driven sea struck the open reef and went roaring skyward, splashing a tattered gull that clutched at the blast—but if we will all go there immediately it is safe in the Dupré house, because they have this holy candle. There are hidden bone-cold lairs no one knows of, in rock beneath the sea. She shook her bone-white hair.

Rob's whole sensitive face tightened harshly for saying what had to come next, and she thought for a while he wasn't going to make it, but he did. "To hell with it. To absolute hell with it then." He looked stricken, as though he had managed nothing but damaging himself.

"I guess it's just the way I am," Nancy murmured. "I just run off sometimes."

Her voice faded in a deepening glimmer where the human breath is snatched clean away and there are only bubbles, iridescent and pure. When she dove again, they rose in a curving track behind her.

THE FISHING LAKE

She was crossing the edge of the field, along the ridge, walking with a longer, more assured step now; she knew just about where he was. She knew because she had seen the jeep parked just off the road, where it got too soggy to risk and too narrow to go through without a limb batting you between the eyes, and she stopped the car about a stone's throw back from there. Something told her all along he would be at the lake. She cleared the ridge, and there he was just below her, down at the pier, tying up the boat. He didn't look up. She eased herself sidewise down the wet, loamy bank that released the heavy smell of spring with every step, and she was within a few feet of him before he said, still not looking up, "There ought to be a better boat down here. I spent half the time bailing. There used to be another boat."

"I think that's the same one," she said. "It's just that things get run down so in a little while. I bet the Negroes come and use it; there's no way to keep them from it."

"It's got a lock on it."

"Well, you know, they may just sit in it to fish. Either that or let the children play in it."

He had found the mooring chain now; it grated through the metal hook in the prow, and he snapped the lock shut and stepped out on the pier.

"Did you catch anything?"

He leaned down and pulled up a meager string–two catfish, a perch, one tiny goggle-eye. "The lake needs draining and clearing the worst kind. All around the bend there's the worst kind of silt and slime. The stink is going to get worse." He paused. "Or maybe you'd say that I'm the stinker."

"I didn't say that. I didn't say anything about it."

He stood with his back to her, hands hooked on his thighs, like somebody in the backfield waiting for the kickoff, and his hair, still streaked with color–sunburned, yellow and light brown–made him seem a much younger man than he would look whenever he decided to turn around. "I would tell you that I'm going to quit it," he said, "but you know and I know that that just ain't true. I ain't ever going to quit it."

"It wasn't so much getting drunk. . . . I just thought that coming home to visit Mama this way you might have put the brakes on a little bit."

"I intended to. I honestly did."

"And then, if you had to pick somebody out, why on earth did you pick out Eunice Lisles?"

"Who would you have approved of?" he asked. He looked off toward the sunset; it was delicate and pale above the tender, homemade line of her late uncle's fishing lake, which needed draining, had a leaking boat and a rickety pier.

"Well, nobody," she said. "What a damn-fool question. I meant, by the cool, sober light of day, surely you can see that Eunice Lisles–"

"I didn't exactly pick her out," he said. "For all I know, she picked me out." He lit a cigarette, striking the kitchen match on the seat of his trousers. He began to transfer the tackle box, the roach box, the worm can, and the minnow bucket from the boat to the pier. He next took the pole out of the boat and began to wind off the tackle. "Where we made our big mistake is ever saying we'd go out. We came to Mississippi to see your mother, we should have stayed with your mother."

"Well, I mean if it gets to where we can't accept an invitation–"

"It hasn't got to where anything," he said irritably. "I'm exactly the same today as I was yesterday, or a year ago. I'm a day or a year older. I've got a hangover worse than usual. And I would appreciate never having to hear anything more about Eunice Lisles."

Her uncle had made a bench near the pier–a little added thought, so very like him. It was for the older ladies to sit on when they brought their grandchildren or nieces and nephews down to swim, and he had had a shelter built over it as well, to shade their heads from the sun, but that had been torn down, probably by Negroes using it for firewood. She remembered playing endlessly around the pier when one of her aunts or her grandfather or Uncle Albert himself brought her down there, and at twilight like this in the summer seeing the men with their Negro rowers come back, solemn and fast, almost processional, heading home from around both bends in the lake, shouting from boat to boat, "Whadyacatch? Hold up yo' string! Lemme *see* 'em, man!" The men would have been secret and quiet all afternoon, hidden in the rich, hot thicket quiet of the brush and stumps, the Negroes paddling softly, holding and backing and easing closer, with hardly a ripple of the dark water. Then, at supper up at Uncle Albert's, there would be the fish dipped in corn meal, spitting and frying in the iron skillets and spewing out the rich-smelling smoke, and platter after platter of them brought in to the table. You ate till you passed out in those days, and there wasn't any drinking to amount to anything–maybe somebody sneaking a swallow or two off out in the yard. Her husband always told her she was wrong about this, that she had been too young to know, but she was there and he wasn't, she said, and ought at least to know better than he did. What she really meant was that her family and their friends and relatives had been the finest people thereabouts, and were noted for their generosity and fair, open dealings, and would never dream of getting drunk all the time, in front of people. He might at least have remembered that this was her home town.

She sat down carefully now on what was left of the bench her uncle had made. She opened her bag. "I brought you something." It was a slug of her sister-in-law's Bourbon she had poured out into a medicine bottle, sneaking as though it were a major theft, and adding a bit of water to the whiskey bottle to bring the level up again, nearly to where it was. She knew that all the family had their opinions. In the house she had kept as quiet as death all day, and so had they. The feeling was that gossip was flying around everywhere, just past the front gate and the back gate, looping and swirling around them.

"That was nice of you. By God, it was." He began to move methodically, slowly, holding back, but his sense of relief gave him a surer touch, so the top of the tackle box came clanging down in a short time, and he came up beside her, taking the small bottle and unscrewing the top. "Ladies first." He offered it to her. She laughed; he could always make her laugh, even if she didn't want to. She shook her head, and the contents of the bottle simply evaporated down his throat. "That's better." He sat companionably beside her; they had to sit close together to get themselves both on the bench.

"I reckon you feel like you get to the end of your rope sometimes," he sympathized. "I think maybe you might."

She had too much of a hangover herself to want even to begin to go into detail about what she felt.

"I don't feel any different toward you," he went on. "In fact, every time you do something like today–go right through your family without batting an eye, steal their whiskey for me out from under their noses, and come down here to get your fussing done in private–I love you that much more. I downright admire you."

She said, after a time, "You know, I just remembered, coming down here up past the sandpit that Uncle dug out to sand the lake with so we could swim without stepping ankle-deep in mud, there was this thing that happened. . . . I did it; I was responsible for it. I used to go there in the afternoons to get a suntan when we used to come and stay with Uncle Albert. And back then they had this wild dog–they thought for a long time it was a cooter, or some even said a bear–but it turned out to be a wild dog, who used to kill calves. So one day I was lying there sun-bathing and I looked up and there was the dog–that close to the house! It scared me half to death. I just froze. I went tight all over and would have screamed, but I couldn't. I remembered what they said about not getting nervous around animals because it only frightens them, so I didn't say anything and didn't move, I just watched. And after a while, just at the top of the hill where the earth had been busted open to get at the sand, the dog lay down and put its head on its paws–it must have been part bulldog–and watched me. I felt this peaceful feeling–extremely peaceful. It stayed there about an hour and then it went away and I went away. So I didn't mention it. I began to doubt if it had really seen me, because I heard somewhere that dogs' vision is not like humans', but I guessed it knew in its way that I was there. And the next time I went, it came again. I think this went on for about a week, and once I thought I would go close enough to pat its head. I had got so it was the last thing I'd ever be scared of, but when it had watched me climb to within just about from here to the end of the pier away from it, it drew back and got up and backed off. I kept on toward it, and it kept on drawing back and it looked at me–well, in a personal sort of way. It was a sort of dirty white, because of a thin white coat with blue markings underneath. It was the ugliest thing I ever saw.

"Then it killed some more calves, and they had got people out to find it, and more showed up when the word got round, bringing their guns and all, and there was almost a dance on account of it, just because so many people were around. A dollar-pitching, a watermelon-cutting–I don't know what all. I was only about fifteen, and I told on it."

"*Told* on it?"

"Yes, I said that if they would go down to the sandpit at a certain time they would see it come out of the woods to the top of the hill on the side away from the house. And they went out and killed it."

"That's all?"

"That's all."

"And that's the worst thing you ever did?"

"I didn't say that. I mean, I felt the worst about it afterwards."

"You might have thought how those poor calves felt."

"I thought of that. It's not the same thing The link was me. I betrayed him."

"You worry about this all the time?" He was teasing, somewhat.

"I hadn't thought of it in ten or maybe even fifteen years, until today, coming along the ridge just now. You can still see the sandpit."

At that moment, the bench Uncle Albert had built to make those long-dead ladies comfortable collapsed. They had been too heavy to sit on it, certainly, and shouldn't have tried. As though somebody had reached out of nowhere and jerked a chair from under them, just for a joke, it spilled them both apart, out on the pier.

They began to laugh. "Come out here next year," he said, in his flat-talking Georgia way, "there ain't going to be one splinter hanging on to one nail. Even the bailing can's got a hole rusted in it."

She kept on laughing, for it was funny and awful and absolutely true, and there was nothing to do about it.

THE ADULT HOLIDAY

That day there was a holiday for the college where he taught, but none for the schools, she was alone all day with her husband and he was angry with her. She had really never seen him so angry. A flush of rage had come over him soon after breakfast, and going into his office, just off the kitchen, she ran straight into it at the door, like a fiery wall, though his back was turned, his long hand sorting through some letters. "Oh," she thought, and "Oh," and "Oh," and "Oh . . ." even her thought fading, dissolving out to nothing, and then he turned and let her have it—a white lash of words during which she could only stand, try to catch her breath, try not to turn away, try to last it out, try in the end simply to survive.

Then it was over. It was the kind of thing she had never before experienced, something there was no apologizing for. If she had gone straight upstairs and packed a suitcase to go and get a job someplace, or to go back to her family and call a lawyer for a divorce, there was nothing he could have said to stop her, except possibly "I must be insane, and will go to a psychiatrist immediately." And he was not going to do that at all.

She clung about the house in corners all morning long, and finally fell to dusting the pictures. It had rained in the night, and the big maple on the back lawn stood pale green, enlarging itself in the new season. What did I do to start it, she wondered, as though by thinking of it in a small way, as just like any other quarrel, she might reduce it to being small. Had it been something about his mother? She knew that men were supposed to have deeply hidden sensibilities about their mothers. But all she said at breakfast was something mild about that lady's handwriting's getting worse—a fact they had often remarked upon before. Besides, he had always seemed more deeply aware of things about his father. Had she so much as alluded to his father? She did not think so. Had some chance association brought his father up? Had that arrogant face, ten years gone, intruded above her shoulder at breakfast to let her husband's vision cut through for once upon her, come straight into clear focus on the terrible creature that, for all she knew, she might really be? And had he not been able to bear that?

She didn't know . . . she didn't know. She turned herself all the way into a maid, and got out the silver to polish it. She did not wear her gloves and thought that now her hands would be splotched, which he didn't like but as he had let no stone of herself remain upon another in the general destruction, she felt that lamenting her hands would be like mourning the death of a kitten after the funeral of a child. She turned out a closet and straightened it, taking care to make no noise at all. She could not compose a grocery list, though she tried, and once she peeked down through a crack in the floor abovestairs and saw him eating lunch—he managed well enough alone. She fell to admiring how calmly he could assemble and digest everything. He had not forgotten the butter, nor the two kinds of bread—one for the salad, one for the meat and cheese—nor his favorite pepper mill. She lay hugged to the floor, thinking she would never eat again, but nonetheless admiring him, as a girl in the scullery might admire the lord of the castle. If she stayed on here, she would eventually have to speak to him; a word would have to crack through the voluminous stillness he had created in both their lives. She wondered what it would be. Eeny, meeny, miney, mo: "Did you mail the check for the gas?" "Let's go to the movies tonight." "My dearest wish was only that . . ."

But still she did not cross his path; she did not even cry until their little girl (the youngest, hence the earliest) came home from school and showed her the cutouts. Then her tears rolled down like rain.

"Why are you crying, Mother?"

"Well, I used to make cutouts at school, too," she said, sobbing.

The cutouts—witches, gingerbread men, clowns, and princesses—got smeared and wet in this torrent, which the child did not like, but grew cautious about. She went in to her father, having gathered up the stack of them. "Mother's crying," she said. "Do you know why?"

"She feels sad because it's my forty-fifth birthday," he said.

"But your birthday is not till tomorrow," said the child.

"I know that," he said, "but she was thinking of it."

There was a long silence. Soon she would have to come alive, to walk on her two numb legs back into his presence and thus concede that the thing had happened indeed and that she could and would go on living there, that dinner would somehow appear for them as usual. She heard the child and her husband building a fire.

"Listen, Daddy," said the child, "how do you feel about getting so old?"

"I don't like it," he said. "I thought that's why they were giving us the holiday, but of course it wasn't."

"The holiday is for Founder's Day."

"That's right, but I didn't go to the ceremony."

"Why didn't you?"

"Because I don't like being forty-five."

The child was silent, thinking all this over. He had a nice way with children—just whimsical enough without exactly trying to fool them; he let them know they were being made to think instead of being made fun of. He was also good at making a child aware of the joins and turns of an adult conversation.

"Does Mother really care *that* much if you're forty-five?" asked the child, and, listening, the mother could all but see just how the child looked when she said that—the downward look of thinking, the crinkle of the brow when she turned up her face. Those sobs had been incongruous with both the reasons given for them; the child would have felt that clearly all along.

He had not answered, but she knew by the crackling sound and the smell of woodsmoke that he had lighted the fire. "Anyway," said the child, to whom the problem still was a dense one, "she's just about thirty-seven herself."

"She should have gone away soon after I met her," he said, in his light, persistent way. "Then I wouldn't be here now."

"But where would you be?"

"Somewhere. Not here."

"Where would it be?" cried the child, gathering a sort of anxious interest, as if he had drawn her into a game.

"Wherever it is, it's not where you are the day before your forty-fifth birthday," he said. "It never is."

"Then where is it, Daddy?"

"If I knew, I'd go there."

"Would you take me?"

"Why would I take you? Of course not." He paused. "To be there I would have had to start going there the day your mother should have gone away."

Caught in a tangle of syntax almost like an enchantment, the child laughed uneasily, and tried to repeat: "To be there you . . . What now?"

"Try it," he said.

In the silence of the study, not called for by either of them, she remembered the very day he meant, a quite different spring from this one. He had come down to the office where she worked and waited in the gritty hallway outside for her to finish, had followed her all the way home, talking eagerly about his work, and she knew that he was in love with her, this studious, brilliant, earnest young man who (they said) had the world before him. All the things other people said faded, not mattering, and the two of them, walking together, passed every which way through a world of streams, muddy paths, and flowers, through short cuts that lengthened the way endlessly before them.

It was the deliberate association of that day with this that crushed in upon her, listening, and so all but made up, she felt, the final sum of her life. She put aside the sewing basket–she must have done a month's mending, very skillfully and accurately, in spite of the fact that her glasses were smeared with drying tears and she couldn't see anything. The child was attempting, as with a riddle, to get the syntax right, repeating, "For you to be there now you would have had . . . Wait. For you to be there now you would have had to start going there the day . . . Let me start over. For you to be there now . . ."

In another minute, she thought, the child would not only get it right but understand it, and then they all could vanish. She replaced her cleaned glasses and came to the living room door–a journey into the void. "I didn't leave that day because I didn't want to leave."

He at once said, trembling, "Darling, you didn't leave because I didn't want you to."

The child, greedy for happiness, looked up and smiled at them. Strung between them on a mended web of what they said, she abandoned the puzzle of her father's words forever.

THE PINCIAN GATE

It seemed to her impossible that you could, here in mid-twentieth century, enter a medieval wall through a tiny gate, having pulled an iron chain to jangle a bell high above you, be shouted at hoarsely to "*Vieni, vieni!*" and, having climbed a twisting narrow flight that smelled of Roman masonry—chilly the year round, exactly as it must have been in Byron's day—confront across the threshold the face of a boy you went to school with back in Arkansas. Only it was a little more complex than that. Sara thought that it was useless coincidence to have remembered Gowan Palmer from school; to all present purposes, he was just a nice man she and her husband had met a year ago at a party here in Rome. As for those bygone days, he seemed to like Sara and Paul in spite of having known them forever, and none of them had the bad taste of people who reminisce. She learned by way of somebody else that he had been married to a New York girl she would probably never see, just as she discovered that it was no romantic notion that had lured him to take a damp three rooms in the Roman wall near the Pincio, but a leftover lease from a fellow-artist, now in Greece, who wanted the place occupied even at a loss.

As for the problems he was now drifting into—financial, emotional, artistic, and otherwise—she would bet she was far more aware of them than he. She was always hearing things against him now, and this, in view of her and Paul's conviction that his work was about to break over into the big-name cluster, seemed particularly a shame. He had had for some months the air and countenance of an artist considered the best by the best. Sara had got the impression that people-who-knew, the experts, had so far spoken of his work only among themselves but would let the outside world in on it whenever they happened to think of it. As this, so far as she could see, was the only way in which a lay person could know about excellence in modern art, she had no complaints about it and rejoiced in Gowan's right to it.

In his studio now, out of the sun, she shivered and put on her jacket, while Gowan shook iron filings off a cushion and offered to heat up the espresso. He had been on a sculpture kick, as he called it, during the winter months, and she found herself angling to talk to him through a forest of elongated shapes in heavily beaten iron.

"Let's go up in the sun," she urged. "Don't you know it's warm? You just sit in here and work so much I bet you don't even know it's spring!"

"Not true. Somebody told me yesterday that it was spring. I'm not so helpless as you think."

"I always think you're going to get pneumonia in this place. I see myself carrying hot minestrone up through the wall in February."

"Oh, it can get warm enough. It's just that the traffic is so bad. That's the real reason I never entertain. At first, I felt I was on an island, with everything in Rome streaming past all day, and that at night I went under with it. The streetcars poured across my face, all iron wheels and clanging. Lambrettas snorted into my dreams. Now I sleep and work mainly on the park side, where there's less noise, but anyway I hardly hear it any more. Some part of your brain blocks out, I think. Here." He poured out coffee in tiny cups. "Let's go upstairs."

Above, they sat between the blunt teeth of masonry on a pair of rickety chairs and warmed their faces in the sun, sipping coffee.

"Who told you yesterday that it was spring?" She smiled, gently inquisitive.

"Francesca, of course. She drove by in the afternoon."

"Oh dear, maybe she's coming up today, too."

"Today she's in Viterbo, guiding an art photographer around."

"Our Italian career girl."

"She's doing well. Of course, she doesn't have to, with three villas and a palazzo."

It sounds like the perfect setup for you, Sara restrained herself from saying. For once started—a drink or two would have done the trick—she might have continued, It would be a world better for your money—or should we just say your backing?—to come from a source like

Francesca's family, who will never talk about it, than for you to go on borrowing from any number of people. You realize that this reputation you have gotten for living so lamely is setting people against you. In addition, Francesca's uncle is after all Mario Negalesco, who has certainly written enough art criticism to write something about you. He might just give you the one boost you need. Your whole life, as we see it, your career and all, is hanging on the brink of being what it ought to be, just what you've deserved all along. Can't you see it? And of course everyone, including Francesca, thinks you've every reason to make a serious relationship with her. There's even love to be thrown in, along with all the rest—even love!

"She laughs at all that *prepotente* stuff," he said. "One of the villas has cows in it, and all the furniture in the place is tied together with string. *La splendida famiglia, la principessa Negalesco.*"

But Sara noted that he broke into a smile he couldn't help—a good sign. "Have you met her uncle?" she asked.

"The critic? Oh, he's been by a couple of times. We got on O.K. He's a bit too Milanese for me."

There was a snarl of traffic below, intensifying to a wrangle of indecipherable noise from which, it seemed, no vehicle, however two-wheeled and tiny, could escape. They looked over the wall. He laughed out loud at the jam, which seemed to have gathered around two children who had wandered unescorted into the middle of the street, where they were both still standing, unhurt, one wailing, the other bewildered and pale. Now they were being liberated, handed out over the heads of Vespa riders, swung high by smiling strangers. An elderly Mercedes backed, having caught its bumper in the fender of a shiny new Fiat, which, in the silence that had inexplicably fallen, tore slowly open like a tin can. About fifty people had gathered on the sidewalk, forming a willing audience, from which there now ascended a chorus of groans. The driver came boiling up out of the Fiat, signaling the start of Act II.

"I often sit here and watch the show," said Gowan, leaning near her in the sun. He was wearing a blue blazer, his shirt open at the neck. She thought he must have grown his beard just for warmth; it was short and flat, like the pelt of a neat animal. He was the one bearded artist she could abide.

"The trouble is we can't talk here," he remarked.

They presently went for a walk in the park and, gravitating always downward, came to the jumping ring where horses could be seen daily, exercising. They were good horses, privately owned, and stabled in another part of the park. Today a groom was jumping a lively young chestnut gelding, richly maned and needing a workout. He flung his head repeatedly against the bit. A scarlet ribbon had been plaited into his forelock. The spring warmth came up out of the ground at them, and it was quiet here; they could hear the soft thudding of the hoofs on the ground, the cry of the rider ("Hup!") when the horse took the jumps, the occasional whack and ring of wood as a rail came down. Almost beyond the range of their hearing the city rumbled and echoed.

"Magnificent horse," said Gowan. *"Un cavallo magnifico."*

Indeed, the horse–his nervousness, his beauty, the swing of his neck, the red ribbon between his narrow, sensitive ears, the glint and powerful setting of his brightly shod hoofs–had almost succeeded in mesmerizing them both.

"You came down here because you wanted to talk," she reminded him. "Why don't we walk over that way?"

"Oh, I didn't want to talk *about* anything. Do you?"

"Well," she said, hesitating with a little laugh. "Why not?"

"Look here, Sara," he said, picking up a stone and hurling it out across the road, just the way he might have done, she suddenly thought, when he was a boy back at that school. "Look, Sara. Something's on your mind."

"Yes, you're right. It's just that Paul and I–well, we've been a little worried about you."

"Worried about me?" He came to a full stop.

"Well, we think–I don't know how to put it–that maybe you don't see yourself quite in perspective here in Rome, that maybe you don't see–many people don't; I know from time to time *I* don't–quite what's going on with you, the way friends at a little distance may be able to."

"You mean I don't hear the gossip," he said, short-circuiting her. "What a good thing I've got in Francesca, if only I knew how to take advantage of it."

She felt the rug pulled out from under her. "Something like that–only I wouldn't put it that way. It just seemed to us that maybe you were at more of a crossroads than you realized. I know that this has happened to Paul, in industry, and people speaking up, saying a word, has meant all the difference to him."

"And of course *he* never owed anybody any money," said Gowan.

She felt herself getting angry. "We've always, always, told you, let you know–"

"I know, I know. O.K., someday I'll fool you, close in on your kindness. . . ." He came to a halt, occasioned by a drop in the road and a line of shadow from a rise of hill, which they would in another moment have entered. "For God's sake, let's stay in the sun." He turned her around and walked them back to the horse ring. As they reached the rail, the horse swiftly cleared a low jump, front hoofs matched and proud, and, galloping straight at them, swerved off when almost dangerously near, flinging dirt (hard as a bullet, she thought, startled) against her cheek.

"God, I could stand here all day," said Gowan, glancing at his watch. "Lunch appointment; too bad. I'll tell you who it's with," he said, teasing her, making up, or trying to, for their near quarrel. "It's with a man who wants to arrange for me to take some of his English students during the summer. He has quite a list of them and is going back to London for a couple of months."

"Oh." Again she broke off saying what she wanted to. Obviously, if he started doing things like this, he was now destined to drift down into that indeterminate sediment of people who simply hung on in Rome, trying any and everything, living barely, living some way, year in and year out, until not even they could remember quite why they had come here in the first place. But it's none of my business, she said to herself. And she must have walked like that and held her head like that and kept silent like that, for he said with an amused air, "It's really none of your business, is it?"

She would have left him right then, except they had almost regained the wall and she remembered that she had left her gloves and scarf in his studio above. She was angry enough to wonder if she would ever really want to see him again at all, she and Paul having been, all this time, friends, true friends, forbearing friends, to Gowan Palmer.

"Oh, I'll get them for you," he offered when she mentioned going up, and ran up the stairs, leaving her on the narrow flight in the very middle of the wall–like something in a Poe story, she thought, sealed up in the masonry. He soon returned, laid the scarf and gloves in her hand, and in the close quarters of the stair turned her face abruptly up to his and gave her a long, staggering kiss, which was so unexpected and worked so well she even got swept into wondering for a moment if their shadow had not stamped itself against the wall.

Then he let her go. Her hands for a moment lay trembling against his blazer, and, turning upward, she got an uncertain final glimpse of his face and heard his voice ascending: ". . . not quite deteriorated, you must admit."

The door above her closed, and she went out into the street.

KNIGHTS & DRAGONS

PART ONE

1

Martha Ingram had come to Rome to escape something: George Hartwell had been certain of it from the first. He was not at all surprised to learn that the something was her divorced husband. Martha seldom spoke of him, or of the ten years she had spent with him. It was as though she feared if she touched any part of it, he would rise up out of the ground and snap at her. As it was he could sometimes be heard clear across the ocean, rumbling and growling, breathing out complaining letters and worried messengers, though what had stirred him up was not clear. Perhaps he was bored, thought Hartwell, who never wanted to meet the bastard, having grown fond of Martha, in his fussy, fatherly way. He was her superior at the U.S. cultural office, and saw her almost every day, to his pleasure.

The bastard himself Hartwell had also seen in a photograph that Martha had showed him, drawing it from her purse while lunching with him in a restaurant. But why carry his picture around? Hartwell wondered. Well, they had been talking of dogs the other day, she explained, with a little apologetic shrug and smile, and there was the dachshund she had been so fond of, there on the floor. But Hartwell, staring, was arrested by the man—that huge figure, sitting in the heavy chair with some sort of tapestry behind, the gross hands placed on the armrests, the shaggy head, and big, awkwardly tilted feet. Martha's husband! It made no sense to think about, for Martha was bright and cordial, neither slow nor light-headed, and she had a sheer look that Hartwell almost couldn't stand; he guessed it was what went with being vulnerable. "He looks German," protested Hartwell. She thought he meant the dog. "Dear old Jonesie," she said. Hartwell chuckled uneasily. "No, I meant him," he said. "Oh. Oh yes. Well, no, Gordon is American, but it's funny your saying that. He studied in Germany and his first wife was German." "What happened to her?" Martha tucked the photograph away. "She died. . . . I was Gordon's student," she added, as though this explained something.

Why did the man keep worrying her? Why did she let him do it? Hartwell did not know, but the fact was, it did go on.

But sometimes the large figure with the shaggy head left her alone and she would be fine, and then she would get a letter from a lawyer she'd never heard of, speaking of some small lacerating matter, or an envelope addressed in a black scrawl with nothing but a clipping inside on a political issue, every word like a needle stab, considering that he knew (and never agreed with) how she felt about things. And if one thought of all the papers he had gone shuffling through to find just the right degree of what he wanted! And sometimes some admirer of his would come to Rome and say he wasn't eating at all well and would she please reconsider. "He never ate well," she would answer. "Only large quantities of poor food." She thought of all the hours spent carefully stirring canned cream of mushroom soup. And yet—thinker, teacher, scholar, writer, financial expert, and heaven knew what else—he had been considered great and good, and these people were, she understood, his friends. She tried to be equable and kind, and give them the right things to drink—tea, or Cinzano, or scotch—and show them around the city. "But *he* never says he would be better off if I were there," she would make them admit. "He never says it to you, or me, or anyone." Then she would be unsteady for a week or two.

Nobody can change this, she decided; it will always be this way.

But she grasped George Hartwell's sympathy, and knew that when he gave her some commission outside Rome, it was really done as a favor and made her, at least, unreachable for a time.

"Do you want to go to Genoa?" he asked her. It was June.

He was sitting at his large friendly disorderly desk, in the corner office of the consulate, and he was round and cherublike, except for a tough scraggle of thin red hair. There was always a cigar stuck in the corner of his mouth. He scrambled around among manila folders. "Arriving in Genoa," he explained, "cultural exchange people, heading eventually for Rome. But in the meantime they've excuses for wanting to see Milano, Padova, Lago di Como, perhaps going on to Venice. Italian very weak, but learning. Guide with car would be great help."

"But who are they?" She always had a feeling of hope about moving toward total strangers, as if they would tell her something good and new, and she would go away with them forever. She took the files as he found them for her. "Coggins . . . what an odd name. Richard Coggins and wife Dorothy and daughter Jean."

"That's the ones. Some friend of the family's wrote Grace about them. We've got to do something a little extra for them, but it just so happens I have to go to Florence."

Martha smiled. George's wife Grace, out of an excess of niceness, was always getting them into things. She wanted everyone to be happy, she wanted things to "work out." And so it followed, since she herself was away in Sicily, that one wound up having to be helpful for a week or two to a family named Coggins. "Mr. Coggins is an expert on opera, George, no kidding. Did you know that? Look, it says so here."

"That we should be floating somebody here to lecture the Italians on opera," George Hartwell complained. "Any six waiters in any one of a hundred trattorie in Rome can go right into the sextet from *Lucia* for fifty lire each. Italian women scream arias during childbirth. What can we tell any Italian about opera?"

"I wonder," said Martha, "if they listen to us about anything."

"Martha! That's the remark we don't ever make!" But he laughed anyway, shuffling papers. "Here we are. The others make a little more sense. . . . James E. Wilbourne and wife Rita. No children. Economist . . . thesis brought out as book: *New Economic Patterns in . . .* et cetera. He won't stick with the group much, as is more interested in factories than art galleries."

"Maybe the worst of the Coggins' is their name."

"You'll go then?"

"Yes, I'll go."

"Atta girl."

But, certainly, she thought, moving through the sharp June shadows under the trees around the consulate, something will happen to change these plans—there will be a cable in the hall or someone will have come here. She entered her summer-still apartment through all the devious stairways, corridors, and *cortili* that led to it. "Sequestered," George Hartwell called her, as though knowing it was not the big terrace and the view alone she had considered in taking a place one needed maps and even a compass to reach. The sun and the traffic noises were all outside, beyond the windows. There was no cable, no telephone message, but—she almost laughed—a letter. She recognized the heavy black slant of the writing and slowly, the laugh fading, slit it open. To her surprise the envelope was empty. There was nothing in it at all. He had probably meant to put a clipping in; it was a natural mistake, she thought, but some sort of menace was what she felt, being permanently lodged in the mind of a person whose love had turned to rejection. "Forget it," Hartwell had advised her. "Everybody has something to forget." But, alas, she was intellectually as well as emotionally tenacious and she had, furthermore, her question to address to the sky: how can love, in the first place, turn into hate, and how can I, so trapped in hatred, not suffer for it?

In his apartment, the expensive, oak-paneled, high-ceilinged place in New York's upper Seventies, crusted with books and littered with ash trays, she had lived out a life of corners, and tiny chores had lengthened before her like shadows drawn out into a sun slant; she had worn sweaters that shrank in the back and colored blouses that faded or white ones that turned gray, had entertained noble feelings toward all his friends, and tried to get in step with the ponderous designs he put life to, like training a hippopotamus to jump through hoops. There had been the long rainy afternoons, the kindness of the porter, the illness of the dog, the thin slashing of the brass elevator doors, the walks in the park. She still felt small in doorways. Not wanting to spend a lot, he had had her watched by a cut-rate detective agency, whose agent she had not only discovered at it, but made friends with.

She crumpled the empty envelope and dropped it in the wastebasket, bringing herself up with a determined shake rather like a shudder.

2

Martha Ingram would always remember the first sight she had of her new Americans at the dock in Genoa. She got a chance to look them over before they saw her. She had to smile—it was so obviously "them." They stood together in clothes that had seen too much of the insides of suitcases and small metal closets in ship cabins; they were pale from getting up early after an almost sleepless night at sea, and the early breakfast after the boat had gone still, the worry over the luggage, would have made them almost sick. The voyage was already a memory; they waved halfheartedly, in a puzzled way, to a couple who, for ten days, must have seemed their most intimate friends. They formed their little huddle, their baggage piling slowly up around them, while the elder of the two men—Mr. Coggins, beyond a doubt—dealt out hundred-lire notes to the porters, all of whom said that wasn't enough. The Coggins girl's slip was too long; she was holding a tennis racket in a wooden press. She looked as if she had just got off the train for summer camp. Her mother had put on one white glove. The young man, Wilbourne, gloomy in a tropical-weight tan suit, seemed hung over. Was this Mrs. Wilbourne sprinting up from behind, her hand to her brow as if she had forgotten something? But it was somebody else, a dark girl who ran off crying, "Oh, Eleanor!" Mr. Coggins had graying hair that stood up in a two-week-old bristle. His lips were struggling with a language he believed he knew well. He understood opera, didn't he? *"Scusatemi, per favore. . . ."*

Martha hated to break this moment, for once they saw her, they would never be quite like this again. "Are you, by any chance, the Coggins'?" They were. How thrilled they were, how instantly relieved. They had been expecting her, but had not known where to look. It was all open and friendly beyond measure. Martha became exhilarated, and felt how really nice Americans were. So the group formed instantly and began to move forward together. "Taxi! Taxi!" It was a word everyone knew. . . .

Two weeks later George Hartwell rang them up. They had crossed Italy by then and had reached—he had guessed it—Venice. How was it going?

"Well, fine," Martha said. "It's mainly the Coggins'. Mrs. Wilbourne couldn't afford to come and stayed behind. She's flying out to Rome in a week or so. George, did you ever know an economist who didn't have money problems?"

He chuckled.

"Mr. Wilbourne doesn't stay with us much. He goes off to visit industries, though God knows what he can learn with sign language. It's churches and museums for the Coggins'—they're taking culture straight."

"Should I come up and join you with the other car?" His conference was over in Florence; he was feeling responsible and wondering what to do.

"We managed okay with the baggage rack. They've shipped nearly everything ahead." She felt obscurely annoyed at being found. "How did you know where we were?"

"I remembered that pensione, that little palace you like. . . ."

It was indeed, the pensione in Venice, a building like a private palace. It had once been some foreign embassy, and still kept its own walled campo, paved in smooth flagstones, ornamented with pots of flowers, boxed shrubs, and bougainvillea. The tall formal windows opened on a small outdoor restaurant. "You mean we get all this and two meals a day?" Mr. Coggins was incredulous. "And all for six thousand lire each," chanted Mrs. Coggins, who was by now a sort of chorus. That was the first day. Jim Wilbourne, angrily complaining about some overcharge on the launch from the station, joined them from Padova just in time for a drink before dinner, and they felt reunited, eating out in the open with the sound of water, by candlelight. They decided to stay on for a day or two.

One afternoon they went out to the Lido—all, that is, except Martha, who had decided she would spend the time by herself, revisiting one or two of the galleries. When she came out of Tintoretto's Scuola into the quiet campo where the broad shadow of a church fell coolly (had everyone in Venice gone to the Lido?), there in a sunlit angle, a man, with a leather briefcase but no apparent business, stood watching. The campo, the entire area, all of Venice, indeed, seemed entirely deserted. There had been no one else in the gallery but the ticket seller–no guide or guard–and even he seemed to have disappeared. The man with the briefcase held a lighted cigarette in his free hand, a loosely packed nazionale, no doubt, for the smoke came gushing out into the still air. When he saw Martha pause and look at him, he suddenly flung both arms wide and shouted, "*Signora, signora! Che vuol fa', che vuol fa'?*" "I don't know," Martha answered. "*Non so.*" "Something has gone wrong!" he shouted across the campo, waving the briefcase and the cigarette. "Somewhere in this world there has been a terrible mistake! *In questo mondo c'è stato un terribile errore!*"

Martha walked away to the nearest canal and took a gondola. Mad people show up all over Italy in the summer; they walk the streets saying exactly what they think, but this was not like that: it was only scirocco. The air was heavy. She remembered Tintoretto's contorted figures with some desire to relax and straighten them out, and the cry from the man with the briefcase, comic and rather awful at once, swept through and shook her.

Already the sky was beginning to haze over. On a clothesline hung behind an apartment building, a faded red cloth, like a curtain or a small sail, stirred languorously, as though breathing in the heat itself. The boat's upcurving metal prow speared free, swinging into the Grand Canal. Even there the traffic was light; the swell from a passing vaporetto broke darkly, rocking the gondola in a leaden way.

At dinner everyone was silent. Jim Wilbourne ate very little and that with his elbow propped beside his plate. Martha judged that the Coggins' bored him; they seemed another order of creature from himself. Some days before he had wanted to know what Italian kitchen appliances were like. The kind of apartment he wanted in Rome absorbed him.

Jean Coggins, who had sunburned the arches of both feet at the Lido, looked about to cry when her mother said sharply: "If you insist on having wine, you could at least try not to spill it." Mr. Coggins, whose brow was blistered, sent back his soup, which was cold, and got a second bowl, also cold.

To Martha the silence was welcome, for always before when gathered together, they had done nothing but ask her about the country–

politics, religion, economics, no end of things. She was glad they had at last run down, like clocks, and that they could find themselves after dinner and coffee out in the back courtyard because some fiddlers had happened to pass. The guests began to dance, first with one another, then with strangers, then back to known faces again. When the music turned to a frantic little waltz, Jim Wilbourne stumbled twice, laughed and apologized, and led Martha to a bench near the wall, where they were flanked on either side by stone jars of verbena.

"I'm so in love with that girl," he said.

Martha was startled. What girl? The waitress, one of the guests, who? There wasn't any girl but the Coggins girl, and this she couldn't believe. Yet she felt as the guide on a tour must feel on first noticing that no one is any longer paying attention to cathedrals, châteaux, battlefields, stained glass, or the monuments in the square.

Jim Wilbourne offered her a cigarette, which she took. He lighted it, and one for himself.

"Out at the Lido this afternoon," he went pleasantly on, "she got up to go in the surf. Her mother said, 'You're getting too fat, dear. Your suit is getting too small.' For once I could agree wholeheartedly with Mrs. Coggins."

So then it was Jean Coggins. "But she's only a kid," Martha protested.

"That's what I thought. I was ten days on that damn boat and that's what I thought too. Then I caught on that she only looks like a kid because her parents are along. She's nineteen, actually. And rather advanced," he dryly added.

"But when–?" Martha exclaimed. "I've never seen you near each other."

"That's strange," said Jim Wilbourne.

She almost laughed aloud to think how they had so quickly learned to walk through walls; she felt herself to be reasonably observant, quite alert, in fact. But she was also put out–she and George Hartwell were not really delighted to have Americans who leaped into *la dolce vita* the moment the boat docked–if not, in fact, the moment they embarked. She got up and walked to the wall where she stood looking over the edge into the narrow canal beneath. From under the white bridge a boat went slowly past, a couple curled inside; its motor was cut down to the last notch, and it barely purred through the water. Before Jim Wilbourne came to stand beside her, the boat had slipped into the shadows.

"Italy always has this romantic impact," Martha began. "You have to take into account that the scene, the atmosphere–"

"Generalizations," Jim Wilbourne teased her, quoting something she was fond of saying, "are to be avoided."

"No, it's true," she protested. "After a year or so here, one starts dreaming of hamburgers and milk shakes."

"Indeed?" He flicked his cigarette into the water and turned, his vision drawn back to where Jean Coggins was dancing with the proprietor's son, Alfredo, the boy who kept the desk. Her skirts were shorter, her heels higher, her hair, a shambles on her return from the beach, had been brushed and drawn back. She had put on weight, as her mother said, and she did, to Martha's surprise, look lovely.

Martha, who disliked feeling responsible for people, toyed with the idea of seeking the elder Coggins and hinting at what she knew, but there in the faraway shadows, around and around a big oleander pot, the Coggins' were dancing cheek to cheek. Richard Coggins accomplished a daring twirl; Mrs. Coggins smiled. The two grubby musicians, with accordion and fiddle, who had brought an empty fiasco and offered to play for wine and tips, had not even paused for breath for an hour. They could go on like this all evening.

Scirocco, Martha thought, deciding to blame everything on the weather.

She slipped away, walking inside the broad, dimly lit hall of the pensione. It looked shadowy and lovely there, its wide doors at either end thrown open to the heavy night. On the beamed ceiling reflections from water were always flickering, breathing, changing. Behind the desk a low light burned, and the proprietor, a tubby, shrewd-faced man, was bending over one of his folio-sized account books. He had told Martha that the pensione was owned by a Viennese lady, who came there unannounced twice a year. She might descend on him, like the angel Gabriel, he had said, at any moment. So he kept his nose to his figures, but now, as Martha went by on her thoughtful way upstairs, he looked up.

"Ah, signora," he said, "there's nothing to do about it. *Non c'è niente da fare.*" But what he meant, if anything, was not clear.

She heard the lapping of tiny waves from everywhere, and through a window saw the flowers against the wall, hanging half closed and dark as wine.

3

In Piazza San Marco where she went the morning after with some idea of keeping her skirts clear of any complications, Jim Wilbourne nevertheless appeared and spotted her. Through hundreds of tables and chairs, he wove as straight a line toward her as possible, sat down and ordered, of all things, *gelato*. He was wearing dark glasses as large as a pair of windshields, and he dropped off at once into a well of conversation–he must have enjoyed college, Martha thought. The scarcely concealed fascism of Italy troubled him; how were they ever to bring themselves out into democracy?

"Quite a number have jumped completely over democracy," Martha said.

"I simply cannot believe," he pursued, trying to light a cigarette with any number of little wax matches, until Martha gave him her lighter, "that these people are abstract enough to be good communists. Or Democrats either, for that matter. I think when the Marshall Plan came along they just wanted to eat, and here they are on our side."

"Oh, I really doubt they're so unaware as you think," Martha said. "The idea of the simple-hearted Italian–not even English tourists think that any more."

"I don't so much mean simple, as practical, shrewd, mainly a surface life. What would happen, say, if this city turned communist right now? Would one Venetian think of hauling the bones of St. Mark out of the cathedral and dumping them in the lagoon? I just can't see it."

"The Coggins' seem to like everything just the way it is," Martha laughed.

"Do you see that character as I do? As long as Richard Coggins can hear some *ragazzo* go by whistling *'O soave fanciulla,'* he's gone to paradise for the afternoon. The more ragged the *ragazzo* is, the better he likes it. I have two blind spots; want to know them? Opera and religious art. A million churches in this country and quite likely I'm not going to like a single one of them."

"So no wonder you keep escaping us."

"Oh, it's been pleasant enough; you've done your best to keep us happy. And then, there's daughter Jean–" He paused, adding, "Don't get me wrong," though she had no idea what that meant. By now he was eating through a mountain of ice cream, striped with caramel and chocolate, piled with whipped cream and speared with wafers.

"The Coggins' are going down to Rome tomorrow," he went on. "As you know they've got this meeting with Coggins' opposite number, somebody who's going to the States to tell us all about jazz."

"I ought to know about it," Martha said. "I went to enough trouble to set it up. Anyway, it's chamber music, not jazz."

"Okay, Mrs. Ingram. So you'll get me straightened out some day; keep at it. Anyway, I wondered if maybe you wouldn't stay on a day or so, with Jean and me. She thought it would be a good idea; we could all go to the Lido."

"That might be fun," said Martha.

"If you're worried about the Coggins'–well, don't. Him and his bloody opera plots. Ketchup all over the stage, women's heads bellowing out of sacks. Is he serious? Those people were born to be deceived."

"The real hitch for me is that I have a schedule back in Rome. I only made this trip to please my boss."

"It can't be all that important," he pursued, though it was obvious to her that by actually mentioning deception he had spoiled it all.

"Anyway," she pointed out gently, "in this weather the water will be no good at all for swimming. There's sure to be a lot of rain."

"How nice to know so much."

She maneuvered easily, but the fact was he puzzled her. Are they all turning out like this, she wondered, all of them back there? Yet he consistently gained her attention, if that was what he wanted; she had found him attractive from the start, though she had assumed he was accustomed to creating this sort of reaction, and would not have thought it remarkable if he noticed at all. As for herself, she wanted only to place a face value on him. Tanned, solid, tall, dressed even to his watchband with a sort of classical American sense of selection, he was like something hand-picked for export; if you looked behind his ear you might find something to that effect stamped there. He was very much the sort who showed up in ten years leading a group of congressmen by the nose and telling them what to look for and where, though when on home leave she might encounter him even before that, being interviewed on some TV show. It would be like him to leap out at me, right in a friend's living room, she thought. And when he had appeared in Venice a few evenings back, she had been looking toward the bridge he crossed to reach them and had seen him mount up angrily, suddenly, against the horizonless air. He gave her then, and fleetingly at other times as well, the impression of being seen in double, as people always do who carry their own image in their heads.

"How can you smoke and eat ice cream at once?" she asked him.

He stopped, both hands, with spoon and cigarette, in air. He looked from one to the other. "Funny. I didn't know I was." He dropped the cigarette at once, smashing it out carefully.

"I've been wondering how to tell you this," he said, still looking down, but straightening as he finished. "It just happens that I seem to know your former husband rather well."

The bright level surface between them on which she had, in her own way, been enjoying the odd sort of quarrel they had been having, tilted and she slid definitively, her heart plunging downward. So another one had arrived.

"Why didn't you say so before?" she asked him.

"It isn't so easy to say, especially if–"

"If you have a message," she filled in.

She sat looking out at the square. It had filled with tourists, mainly Germans, moving in a slow, solemn, counterclockwise procession, ponderous, disorderly, unattractive, as though under tribal orders to see everything. There were the pigeons, more mechanical still, with their wound-up motions, purple feet, and jewel-set eyes. And then there was a person, all but visible, right at home in Venice, moving diagonally across the great colonnaded ellipse of the piazza, head down, noticing no one, big shoulders hunched forward under his old tasteless tweed jacket, gray-black hair grizzled at the nape. He was going to the corner drugstore, somewhere near East 71st and Madison. The smell of a late New York summer–just a morning hint of fall–was moving with him, strong enough to dispel the scent of European cigarettes, the summer-creeping reek of the back canals. He would spread books on the counter, stir coffee without looking at it, clumsily allow the bit of lettuce to drop from his sandwich.

"Not so much a message," Jim Wilbourne said.

"You see, people are always turning up when I least expect them!" She longed now simply not to sound helpless.

"Oh, then," he said, in a relieved voice, "you must already know about the accident."

"Accident!" She started like a quiet, lovely insect into which someone has suddenly stabbed a pin; her wings quivered; her eyes were fixed.

"Oh my God, now I've done it!" She tried twice to speak but failed and the voice below the green mask soon continued: "I think he's all right now."

"Oh. . . . Then nothing serious happened–" She drew a shaky breath.

Jim Wilbourne glanced out across the square. "There was some doubt about his being able to walk, but I think–" He broke off again, tentative, mysteriously cold.

Martha stirred compulsively, as though to shake herself free of whatever net had fallen over her. In doing so, her knee struck the little table, rattling the cups and spoons. She remembered the letter on the table in Rome, and the emptiness of the envelope was now her own. "He was always a completely awful driver," she was presently able to continue. "Go on, now you've started. Tell me the rest."

Were they reading lines to each other? Nothing, even turning the table completely over, bringing three waiters rushing down upon them with long arguments about paying for the glassware, would have quite restored her bearings, or loosed her from this cold current into which he seemed deliberately to have plunged them both. "Tell me," she insisted.

His vision seemed, behind the glasses, to pass her own. "Oh, it wasn't a driving accident. But who should tell you this?–it's not my business to. He was out hunting with one of his patients, up in the Berkshires. I never thought that aspect of it made too much sense–well–to take a mental patient hunting, that is. Almost like an experiment, just to see if he'd do it to you on purpose. I never meant to get into all this. But since he is okay now, you naturally will be relieved to know–"

The entire piazza, thickening steadily in the closing weather, had become a total wet-gray illusion. "This isn't Gordon Ingram," Martha said. "It can't be."

"Gordon? No, Donald Ingram. The psychologist, you know. My wife studied with him at Barnard. Well, he does have an ex-wife in Italy. It was just that we were sure–"

Martha was really angry now. "I think you invented the whole thing!" She had not quite lost control. Sparing herself nothing, she had hoped, as though striking off a mask, to find something unequivocal and human facing her, to lose the sensation of conversing with a paper advertisement for shirts and whiskey.

"No, honestly. Quite sincerely, I promise you. It was just a natural mistake."

If there was a person back of the glasses, she had missed him completely. She was not going to succeed in confronting him with anything, for his voice, with as much sameness as a record, went on, "–a natural mistake."

Well, she supposed it was true. She sat looking down into the treacly dregs of espresso in her cup, into which a drop or two of the oppressive mist occasionally distilled and twinkled. She gathered up her bag, lighter, a couple of packages including a glass trinket and a book she had bought for a friend, and got up to leave.

Jim Wilbourne leaped to his feet. He was halted by the waiter, who had arisen from nowhere to demand payment. Now he was running after her. "Wait!" She turned. "If I don't see you . . . I may take the train down, to stop off in . . ."

Just as he reached her a whole family of German tourists walked straight into him, knocking off his green glasses. Martha had the startling impression that an entirely new face had leaped into place before her, in quick substitution for the one she had been across from at the table. It was even saying different things: his tone now openly challenged her: "So you won't?" "No." "Not for even a day?" "Exactly."

Their faces, contesting, seemed for an instant larger than life; yet she could remember, recalling the exchange, no further words than that, and the moment must have faded quickly, for in retrospect it seemed telescoped and distant in the vast sweep of San Marco. Jim Wilbourne was backing away as though in retreat, and Martha stood holding her packages while two pigeons at her feet plucked at the smashed bits of his glasses. There was no weakest blot of sun and she wandered out of the square into the narrow labyrinth of Venice where the lions had mildew on their whiskers and St. George slew the dragon on every passing well.

She had looked back once, in leaving the arcades, thinking she had left a camera on a chair, and had seen Jim Wilbourne with Jean Coggins, who must have been nearby all along. They were standing near the corner of the arcade, talking. The girl had a white scarf wrapped around her hair. The vision flickered, and was gone.

He would have been angry with me anyway, she told herself. The story was only an excuse, a pretext. But why should I have angered him?

She walked, moving sometimes with clumps and clots of people, at other times quite alone, beginning to settle and stabilize, to grow gentle once more after the turmoil, the anguish, which his outlandish mental leap at her had, like a depth charge, brought boiling up inside her. She took a certain view of herself: someone, not unusual, who had, with the total and deep sincerity of youth, made a mistake; now, the mistake paid for, agonizingly paid for, the only question was of finding a workable compromise with life. But now at this point did she have to learn that there was something in life which did not want her to have even that? The threat seemed distinctly to be hanging in the air, as thick as the threat of heavy weather.

I should have talked more with the man with the briefcase, she thought, for, far from being mad, he had got things exactly right. *Perchè in questo mondo c'è stato veramente un terribile errore*. Don't I really believe that Jim Wilbourne's *terribile errore* was deliberate? She had accused him of it, certainly, and she did believe it.

She had believed more than that, looking back. She had thought that he was simply stirring up the Jean Coggins romance to question her authority—but that was before she had actually seen the girl standing there.

Martha stopped and almost laughed aloud. She had been about to walk straight into a wall, an architectonic device painted upon it to suggest continuing depth where none existed. The laugh would have bounced back at her, perhaps from the false corridors, the steps and porticos and statuary of that very wall. Laughter was a healthy thought, nonetheless, which said that not so many things pertained to herself as she sometimes seemed determined to believe. And as she stood there a woman much older than herself, gray, but active and erect, walking with the easy long stride of Venetians, who are good at walking because they are always doing it, went past and entered a doorway, bearing a net of groceries—*la spesa*—in one hand. Just before she entered, she glanced up, and a cat uncurled itself from the column base near the entrance where it had been waiting, bounded past the woman's feet, and entered the door in one soft flowing motion. The door closed.

Martha recalled her apartment in Rome; how easily and comfortably it closed about her once she had got past the place where the messages waited and, beyond, found the *salotto* empty and free. How quietly then she took out her work and spread it on the table, opened the shutters out to the terrace in summer, or bent in winter to light the fresh fire the maid always left.

A new season lay ahead. Perhaps the messages would begin to dwindle now, and not so many couriers would show up; time perhaps had no other result but the dissolution of things that existed, and after this something new came on. Martha, if she never had anything worth calling a new life, would have settled simply for a new silence. It would happen, she believed, when Gordon Ingram finally went back totally to his friends, who would convince him that if his young failure of a second wife ever existed, she had had no right to. (And let it even be true, she thought; if it makes him content, why, I'll believe it too.) She thought then of Jim Wilbourne and Jean Coggins, off somewhere together in the city's rich labyrinth.

Asking the direction of the Grand Canal from a young woman who was eating chocolate, she went off in the way she was told.

4

Sometime after four it began to rain—the city, more than ever like a gray ghost ship, a hypnotic evocation, nodded into the thicker element. The rush and whisper of rain came from every distance. Inside, the air clung like cloth. The maids at the pensione hastened about closing the shutters; they set the restaurant up indoors and brought candles out to decorate the tables—Martha felt she was viewing a new stage-set, a change of scene. Like an opera almost, she thought, and at that moment, sure enough, here came the Coggins' skimming in together hand in hand through the rain. Now they were laughing together at the door and soon, from the desk, were appealing to her. "Have you seen Jean?"

She said she hadn't, but Jean herself came along not much later, walking alone through the rain. She had been sight-seeing in a palace, she said, and had got lost when she left it. "You go right upstairs and take a hot bath," Mrs. Coggins said.

Jean went by, making wet tracks and looking curiously at Martha, of whom she was somewhat in awe. Her foreign clothes, her long fair smoothly put-up hair, her intelligence, and near absence of make-up made her seem to Jean like a medieval lady in a painting. "I can't tell what she's thinking," she had complained to Jim Wilbourne. And he had said nothing at all.

The Coggins' called Martha aside and confided to her with shining eyes that they had experienced a most curious phenomenon since coming to Venice. They had been able to relive in great detail, vividly, their entire past lives. Martha, who could not think of anything worse, nodded, smiling. "How wonderful," she said. "Marvelous," they assured her.

In the heavy air Martha had all but dissolved, and went upstairs to take a nap. She left the two Coggins' murmuring below. Tomorrow they would all be in Rome; there would be the sun.

She slept and dreamed.

In the dream Gordon Ingram was standing along some country road, in New England, among heavy summer trees, and saying, "You see, I have been severely injured in a hunting accident. I cannot come there; please understand that otherwise I would." He looked very young, like the young man in photographs she had seen of him, taken long before they met, standing in the sort of hiking clothes he must have worn in walking over Europe in days, vacations, the like of which would never come again. She was reaching out her hand and saying, as in a formal note to someone, "I sincerely regret . . . I deeply regret. . . ." It seemed the first thing they had had to talk about in many years; the first time in many years that he had spoken to her in his natural voice. The rain-colored shadows collected and washed over the image and she half woke, then slept again, but could not summon up the dream. She remembered saying to herself, perhaps aloud, "What a strange city this is." For it lay like a great sleeping ear upon the water, resonant and intricate. All the while the rain poured vastly down and could be heard even while sleeping and dreaming, speaking one continuous voice.

In a half-daze she woke and dressed and went downstairs, and at the desk found a note for herself. Jim Wilbourne had just left; he had probably let in the ragged splash of water near the door. He had written a scribble to say that he would see them all in Rome. She crumpled the paper and dropped it in a wastebasket back of the desk. She tried to ring George Hartwell, but could not reach him; the line seemed muffled and gave her only a vague wavering sound. The operator, after a time, must have shut her off for the day. But she remembered that George had said once, one evening when he had drunk too much, that Americans never lose their experience abroad, they simply magnify it. "It's the old trick of grandfathers," he had said. "Before the fire they make little motions and big shadows dance on the wall. Europe is the wall the shadows dance on." His voice went with her for a step or two.

There was nothing to do till dinner and she went upstairs again. The smell of cigarettes hung stagnant in the upper hall and from somewhere a shutter banged in the shifting wind. She pursued stairways and long halls, passed alcoves and sudden windows. Everything was as dark as her dream had been when it faded. A lance had whistled past her ear, and the impression persisted that she moved in a house of death.

PART TWO

5

In Rome that fall she stopped herself just before telling a friend that her husband had been wounded in an accident. This was very odd, for the fall was bright and sane, and she was at the time nearly eclipsed in cleaning up a lot of George Hartwell's extra chores. The cultural effort had taken on new life that year; the lectures were well received, the social events congenial; pools, lakes, marshes of American good will were filling up everywhere, and all Italians, you would think at times, were eventually going to splash and mingle in them, and the world would never be the same again.

A letter from a lawyer came to Martha, suggesting a price for some property she had owned jointly with Gordon Ingram. It should have been settled long before; it was only since they had gone so happily into it—this small wooded crook of land beside a stream in New York State—that she could never bear to discuss it. But why wouldn't he write me about it? she wondered. Why get somebody else? She sat with the letter and realized something: that if he had had an accident it would have been about here that it happened, right on this bit of land. There were some rocks and a stream below a slope, screened by maple trees.

At last she wrote: "Dear Gordon: Do take the property outright. I do not want any money for it. Will sign whatever transfer is necessary. Martha."

But he could not stand brief notes, simple transactions, direct generosities. Her motives now would suspend him for days. When people dealt with him too quickly, he always suspected either that he had made them too good an offer, or that they were trying to shake away from him; and so, suspicious, obscurely grieved, he would begin to do what he called considering their own good; he would feel it his duty to make a massive re-evaluation; he would call all his friends. He would certainly call them all about Martha.

They had all discussed her to death anyway; for years she had interested them more, it seemed, than they interested themselves. They had split her up and eaten her, some an arm and some a leg and some the joints of her fingers.

Sitting at her desk on a Sunday morning, in sunlight, Martha pressed her palm to her brow. Should she mail the letter at all, or write to the lawyer instead, agreeing to everything, or write to her own lawyer to take it over? And must all life, finally defeated, turn itself over with a long expiring grateful sigh into the hands of lawyers? No, she thought with sudden force; I will keep it a personal matter if both of us have to be accidentally wounded. It is, after all, my life.

So in the end she wrote two letters, one to the lawyer and one to Gordon Ingram. Once, before she left the States for Italy, a year after her divorce, she had run squarely into him in New York, getting out of a taxi she had hailed, and before she could stop herself she had almost screamed, and that must have been terrible for him—poor Gordon. But she well knew that if she deceived herself by thinking she knew how he felt, she might act upon it, with sympathy, and trap herself, falling a victim of his pride.

It seemed to her in retrospect that while she debated her letter that Sunday morning, the sun went away; sensually, in recollection, she could almost feel it slipping from her hair, her cheek, her shoulder, and now Rome was deep in winter, with early dusks, blurred neon on the rush of shining streets. *Tramontana,* the wind from the mountains, struck bitterly, or heavy weather moved in from the sea; the great *campagna* around Rome became a dreary battlefield of contentious air, and one had to be sorry for the eager Americans, there for one year only, who now had to learn that a sunny, amiable, amusing, golden land had passed in one night into a dreary, damp, cold dungeon of a world where everybody was out to cheat them and none of them could get warm. Martha was used to it. She had been there several years and she liked it. Far stranger to her had been that sudden shift of weather in Venice, back in the summer. It had plunged her, like a trap door opening under her feet, into a well of thought she could not yet get out of. She must have been deeply in it the very day when, going home in an early dark after tea with friends, she had run into Jim Wilbourne.

She had seen the Wilbournes fairly often during the fall. Rita Wilbourne, though somewhat more flamboyant than Martha cared to think about—she wore chunky jewelry, bright green and corals, colored shoes—was energetic in getting to know people. She studied Italian, learned it quickly, and took up a hobby—she would make ceramics. It had been a Grand Idea and now it was beginning to be a Great Success. All one room of the Wilbourne apartment had become a studio. It exuded the smell of solvents and plasters.

There had been intermittent invitations. George and Grace Hartwell, the Wilbournes, and Martha Ingram often found that they had gravitated into the same corner at a party, or were ringing each other up to come over for supper on rainy Sundays. What did they talk about so much as the Coggins'?

Jean Coggins had a job in a glove shop on the Piazza di Spagna. About once a week, every young Italian in Rome made a point of coming in and buying gloves. Some did nothing but walk back and forth before the window for hours. The owner was having to expand.

Richard Coggins was the success of the entire cultural program. His Italian, once it quit rhyming like opera, was twice as fluent as anyone else's; he learned, he learned! He was invited—a great coup for the American image—to address the opera company in Milan. His lectures were packed and ended with cheers and cries. (Bravo! *Bis, bis!*) Oh, no one had ever furnished more party talk than the Coggins'. Yet there was something enviable about their success.

One night at the Wilbournes' apartment after dinner, Jim Wilbourne remarked: "Jean Coggins' effect on Italian men began to happen the minute the boat docked. It was spontaneous combustion. Do you remember Venice, Martha?"

Martha looked puzzled. She shook her head. The trouble was she remembered nothing but Venice; it was a puzzle which had never worked out for her; what exactly did he mean?

"There was some boy who kept the desk—Alfredo, his name was."

"Oh yes, the proprietor's son."

"What happened?" someone—Hartwell's wife—wanted to know.

"Well, they were hitting it off so well that she wanted me to persuade Martha—you must remember this, Martha—to stay on a day or so, so that her parents would let her stay too. The only catch was she didn't want me to mention Alfredo: it seems the Coggins' believe that Italian men are incorrigibly passionate or something. She nagged me until I promised to do it, but the only excuse I could think of was to say I was interested in her myself."

Everyone laughed. "So what happened?" they wanted to know.

"Well, I got nowhere with Martha. She got out of it very well."

"What did you say?" Hartwell asked her.

"I forget"–she let Jim Wilbourne finish his story.

"She said she'd like to stay on but she had some appointments or other–very grand she was."

Hartwell, after a hard week, had had a drink or two more than usual. He gave Martha a hug. "I love this girl."

"But I was in the dark myself," Martha protested. She soon followed Rita into the next room to look at her workshop.

"So she tried to be philosophic, which for a Coggins is something of a strain, to put it mildly. She went off in the rain with Alfredo, off in Venice somewhere, and called it a day."

"I wouldn't have thought these two colors would go at all," Martha said to Rita, who had joined her. "But you've made them work."

"Yes, but Italians are so bold with their colors. I think it must be something in the sunlight here–when there's any sun, of course." She picked up two sections, handle and basin, from an unfinished hors d'oeuvres dish. "You see, you wouldn't think that would do well, but I find the more I experiment–" Her bracelets jingled together as her hands moved. They were thin, quick, nervous hands with tinted nails. Grace Hartwell had told Martha that the Wilbournes were expecting a child. Why is George such a puritan? Martha wondered. You'd think I'd struck a blow for freedom by keeping lovers apart.

"Did you, by any chance," Martha asked Rita, "know a Professor Ingram at Barnard?"

"Oh yes, but not at Barnard. I went to Columbia. He teaches there occasionally, one semester every so often. Yes, I not only knew him, but we were sure for a time that you must be the former Mrs. Ingram. She's somewhere in Italy. It's odd your asking that."

"I'd just recalled when we were talking of Venice that Jim mentioned him to me there. And several other times," she lied, "people have assumed that he–I never met this person, of course."

"But beginning to feel you know him rather too well?"

"I also heard he had been in some sort of accident last summer. Did you know anything about that?"

"Oh, that must be another Ingram still. No, unless something happened just recently—"

The ceramics were laid out in a bare, chilly servant's room on a large makeshift table, strips of wallboard held up by a smaller table underneath and supported on either end by chairs. The effect was of a transferred American look, makeshift and practical, at no pains not to negate the parquet floor, a scrolled mirror now layered with cement dust. A small French escritoire had been pushed into a corner, and beside it, a gilded baroque angel holding a torch stood face to the wall. The room had probably been intended as a smoking or drawing room off the *salotto*. They had dined on frozen shrimp from the PX, and only in here with the ceramics was the odor escapable. Why would anyone buy frozen American shrimp in Italy? Martha had wanted to ask, but had not. It had been answered anyway, at dinner; Rita was afraid of the filth in the markets. But the markets were not filthy, Martha thought, murmuring how delicious it was.

"Hey, Martha!" Hartwell again.

"We're busy," Rita called.

"Information required," Grace Hartwell said.

"They always want you to tell them things, don't they?" said Rita, with a moment of woman's sympathy. "If I were you, I wouldn't."

Martha came to the doorway, her shawl tugged around her. Her hands felt cold. Hartwell was lighting his third cigar. Would he not, singlehanded, eventually drive out both shrimp and ceramics smell? "Martha, I thought scirocco was a wind. Jim here says it's not. He says in Venice it's nothing but heavy weather. Now you settle it."

"I believe it's an African wind," she said, "and causes storms all along the coasts, but sometimes the wind doesn't get as far as Venice, especially in the summer, so then you have heavy weather and rain."

Jim Wilbourne laughed. "You mean it is and it isn't."

"I guess that makes you both right," she agreed, and smiled.

All their faces were momentarily turned to her. There was some way, she realized, in which, in that moment, she drew them, the two men primarily, and because of the men, inevitably, the women as well. She would have as soon dropped from her the complex self that was for them, in separate ways, her force, dropped it off like a shawl on the threshold and walked away. But where? Toward other eyes, of course, who could look, be looked at, in a new and simpler way. Why not? The coil of her own being held her, and she could not; that was all.

Yet the possibility continued to tease her mind until the night she ran into Jim Wilbourne, down in the low Renaissance quarter of the city, in the windy, misty, December cold. In brushing past they recognized each other, and for some reason, startled, she slipped on an uneven paving stone so that he caught her back from falling. Then he asked her into a café and they had a drink together. She felt she was seeing him after a long absence.

He had changed somewhat; she noticed it at once. He was paler than in Venice, no longer seemed so well turned out; needed a better haircut, had a cold. He was complaining about Italian medicine; it was his wife's having a miscarriage only a week or so after their dinner party that had got them so sensitive to these matters. Martha thought how soon the bright young Americans began to look tarnished here. The Wilbournes had had some squabble with the landlord about their apartment. He had believed that Rita, who had begun to sell her ceramics, was obviously using the place for business purposes, so he drew up papers demanding either eviction or a larger rent. Martha had heard this through the grapevine, in the same way she had learned that there had been some disagreement with American friends about a car. All these were the familiar complications of Roman life, which only the Coggins' seemed to escape. *Their* landlord had dreamed of an opera career when young, and as a result brought them fresh cheeses from the country, goat's milk, ropes of sausages. The Wilbournes, stubbornly American, were running against the Italian grain, so of course everything was going wrong. Yet Jim Wilbourne did work hard; it was this that Hartwell always said, as though making up for something.

Jim Wilbourne asked her the name of the pensione where they had all stayed in Venice. A friend of his was going up. "But do you think they'd enjoy it this time of year?" she asked. "What's the matter, the weather?" The weather, obviously; she hardly needed, she thought, to nod. "I must be thinking of Verona." He frowned. "There was a big fireplace–?" She shook her head. "I don't think so."

The door of the café stuck on the way out; getting it to work, he gave her an odd smile. He walked along with her for about a block, then, saying something about somewhere he had to be, he turned abruptly and went back the other way.

She turned around in the cold misty street, looking after him. The street was long and narrow and completely deserted, the shop windows covered over with iron facings which had been bolted to the pavement. Almost involuntarily, she lifted her hand. "Wait!" She did not speak very loudly and it was a wonder he heard her at all. He did stop, however, and looked back.

She began to walk toward him, and presently he even came a step or two to meet her. She stood huddled in her dark coat. The damp got in everywhere. She shifted her feet on the cold wet stones. "It's a silly thing to ask—I keep meaning to mention it whenever I see you, then I always forget. Do you remember a conversation we had in Venice when you said that someone you knew named Ingram—you mistook him for my husband—had been shot in a hunting accident?"

"I had hoped you'd forgotten that. It was a hell of a conversation. The whole place was depressing: some start for a year in Europe." He did not exactly look at her, but past her in a manner so basically unsatisfactory to her she would have liked to complain about it. Then when he did look at her, her face, she realized, slanting up to him, must have become unconsciously strained. She laughed.

"I'm shivering in this cold. This is ridiculous, of course. I wouldn't have remembered it at all, but Rita mentioned it to me, not long ago—this same man, I mean. But what she said was that he never had any accident at all. Neither he nor anyone else she knew."

"Well?"

"Well, I simply wondered what the connection was. Why did you say it at all?"

"I must have got him confused with someone else."

"Oh, I see. Someone you know and she doesn't?"

He did not reply.

"Was that it?" she insisted.

"Lots of questions," he remarked, amusing himself, though he was not what she could call light about it. "I guess I just don't remember it so well as you."

"It was in San Marco, in Venice. You ran after me and broke your dark glasses and just after that Jean Coggins came there—to meet you."

Watching him was like looking up into a dark mirror, or trying to catch some definite figure embedded in glass. Yet his features were singularly without any motion at all. She had, as she had had before, the impression of a photographed face.

"Oh yes, Jean Coggins. . . ." She thought for a moment he would not continue. "She wanted you to stay on, she got me to ask you. I told you that," he added, impatiently. "In fact, I went to some trouble to tell you. As for her coming there, I don't remember that–I don't think it happened."

A Lambretta sputtered behind her, turning with a cough into the narrow, resounding street. The echoes clapped, climbing up to the high tile eaves above them. Pools of rain, surfaced in the uneven paving, seamed and splashed. Jim Wilbourne and Martha Ingram stepped back into a shallow alcove against an iron door, where large white letters were painted, advertising the name of the shop. The roar mounted with an innocent force and turmoil which seemed close to drowning them, then it passed, faded, turned a corner. They both stepped back into the street.

"All this seems to have got on your mind in some sort of way," Jim Wilbourne said. "Here, come on, I'll walk you home."

The damp chill had crept up to her ankles, but she did not stir, though he caught her elbow to urge her forward. Her private idea of him was beginning to form; namely, that he was a sort of habitual liar. He might, if this was correct, be incapable of telling the truth even when it would do him no shred of harm to do so, even when it might be better that way. Any exact nature of things he was called upon to reconstruct might seem always to escape him. Hartwell had called her in once about a mix-up which had involved Jim Wilbourne and she had said then that she thought he was absent-minded, but Hartwell protested, "That simply won't hold a thing like this." Then she said, "I don't think he would do anything to damage his work." They were, between them, she and Hartwell, aware of new Americans, newer than themselves, perhaps different, perhaps more nearly right, than they who had been "out here," "away from things" for longer. The feeling was that people, like models of humanity, might quickly become obsolete in some overruling set of American terms even now, beyond their knowledge or power, being drawn up; so their confidence grew weak before the solid advantage of the Wilbourne image. He was so definitely American-looking, while Hartwell had recently given in to shoes with pointed Italian toes which looked extremely odd on him, and Martha went habitually to Roman dressmakers and looked extremely well, though hardly Fifth Avenue. So with this thinking interchanged between them, Hartwell agreed not to make an issue of the Wilbourne default, and let the matter slide.

Martha said to Jim Wilbourne, "Naturally it got on my mind. It concerned me, didn't it?"

"Not at all. It concerned me, Jean Coggins, and a man you used to be married to."

She gave a laugh that did not sound altogether pleasant, even to herself. "A rather close relationship," she said. Rambling about in those half-dreams which Gordon Ingram's giant mahogany bed, like being lost on a limitless plateau with the same day's journey always in prospect, seemed both to encourage and deny, she had often thought the relationship could be a lot closer, yet now she regretted most the times that it had been. She would have liked to extinguish those times not only out of memory but out of time itself.

They began to walk off together in her direction. She protested against being any trouble to him, but he did not seem to hear her, and soon he was walking ahead at a rapid, nervous pace she found hard to keep up with in her thin shoes. His long legs and narrow heels were striking accurately down before her. The streets were narrow and dark and his raincoat went steadily on, as though its light color cut a path for them.

"Jean Coggins," he told her with his short hoarse laugh, "has a lot of boy friends but never gets to bed with any of them. We found this out from the maid whose sister works for the family of one of the boys. She's a great girl in topolinos, picnics, out among the tombs. She could probably make love in a sarcophagus. Her morals are well defined, but what if she never gets over it?"

"How do her parents get along with all this?" Martha asked.

"Her parents," said Jim Wilbourne, "are still in Venice, dancing around a flower pot."

This was not only funny, but true; Martha often saw them there herself.

He slowed his step, letting her catch up even with him, and for a moment caught her hand. "Why do I always talk to you about Jean Coggins?"

"It does get monotonous," she admitted.

"I can't think why I do it. She's comical. All the Coggins' are comical."

"You told me you loved her. You're probably still trying to get out of that."

"I don't know. It was the Italian boy–"

"Yes, I know. Alfredo."

"I remember now I told her to ask you herself, about staying on in Venice, but she didn't have the nerve. She found you awe-inspiring, your intelligence, authority, something–I don't know. As for me, I had some sort of strong feeling for you, right from the first. I imagined you felt the same, but then–" He broke off, but added, rather dryly, "Your attention was elsewhere. You seemed–enclosed."

She said nothing, walking, hearing their footfalls on the stones, and how sometimes the sound of them interlocked and sometimes not.

"I try not to think of myself at all," she ventured. And this was true; she would have put herself quite outside her own harsh, insistent desire for him, if this had been possible. As it was not, she meant simply to hold it aside.

"Well, you don't succeed," he said pleasantly. "Nobody does."

"You took that way of getting my attention by telling me that Gordon–that my husband–" Only to get that question out of the way! She felt she could get herself intellectually right, at least, and as for the rest– But striving with him to get it answered only drew her deeper in and her feeling mounted that it was no more possible to make him speak openly to her than to make an intelligent animal consent to converse.

"I kept trying to get out of it, once I started it," he reminded her. "But nothing seemed to work. I had some notion you were slipping away from me; you did it repeatedly–it was a question of whether anything on earth could reach you at all. On that peculiar day, the question seemed what you might call urgent."

"But even on a peculiar day," she argued, "to make up death like a parlor game–"

He stopped walking. "I didn't invent any death. You did–or seem to have."

It was true. Her heart filled up with dread. Not even her dream had mentioned death. The wildest leap of all had been her own.

"Oh, God!" she murmured. "Oh, my God!" She stood before him, her head turned severely aside. They had reached the top of her street, and from the far end there came, in the narrow silence, the trickle of a commonplace little fountain. The mist, shifting, prickled sharply against her cheek. Some minutes back, from high up among the roofs and terraces, a cat had mewed, trapped on a high ledge.

He drew her in, quickly, easily, against him. The motion for them both was accurate beyond measure, and the high tension between them broke up almost at once. At its sudden departure, she gasped sharply. His arm still tightly around her, he brought her to her doorway and leaned against it with her. A small boy went past without a glance, and then a girl in a swinging coat, who looked twice and then away. The street came back to them, constricted, gray-black, high and dim.

"You've made too much of a mystery of this," he said. "I wanted to see you before, but—well, obviously, it was difficult. And then how could I be certain what went on with you?"

"I don't know," she said, but rousing somewhat out of the muffled clamor of her senses, she thought to ask: "How did you know that anything went on?" to which he did not reply.

She thought of his various hesitances and evasions in terms of his life being elsewhere: how could he manage to get into hers without disturbing his own? The problem could have any degree of intensity for him. She fully intended to say this, when he said:

"There's nothing very unusual about all this that I can see. You've wanted him out of the way all along. You wanted me to get rid of him. You see that, don't you?"

And he had cast her, with one casual blow, straight into madness. She was back in her terrible private wood where the wind howled among the thorn trees; she was hearing the roar of the gun down by the stream, the crash of the autumn-garish leaves. She was racing to get there in time and the thorns tore her gown and her flesh. "Out of the way," "get rid of him"—these phrases were plainly and diabolically murderous, and she could not hear either one or echo it without a shudder. How could Jim Wilbourne speak with such an absence of horror? An accomplice speaks this way, she thought, brought too late into the action to have any but the most general notion of it, but once there, what way can be taken back to the time before him? With a staggering mental effort, nothing short of heroic, she closed down the lid on her chestful of bedlam, and said to him calmly:

"You must understand: hatred is too much for me. I can't face it; you have to believe that." He stirred, shifting her weight entirely against his arm and shoulder, but as he said nothing, she presently hurried on: "We would be here anyway, whether you had told me that miserable story in Venice or not. We'd still be here–I know that's true!"

This declaration was so swift and plain, it caught them in like all of truth, in one warm grasp, so that she felt it might never have ended, until he drew back to point out: "My darling, of all places in the world to make love! Do I break the door down? Haven't you got a key?"

She drew herself back, collecting the shreds and rags of what she had been thinking. Something was being ignored; she found it about the same time as she located the key. "But you do see what I mean to say." Her hand lay urgently on his arm. "It's important to me to know you understand."

"I understand it isn't true. You'd never have called me back tonight if it hadn't been for what you call my miserable story in Venice. And you know that, Martha, don't you?" He gave her a demanding shake. "Denying it–that's no good."

"I know, I know, but I–" The words rushed out at last like a confession. She felt a deep pang of relief and was unable to finish what she had begun by way of protest. She felt shaken and outdone. All her life she had longed for some world of clear and open truth, reasonable and calm, a warm, untroubled radiance (the sort of thing that Gordon Ingram wrote about so well), but though she thirsted like the dying for it, it never appeared to her and she wondered if every human being was not surrounded by some dark and passionate presence, opaque and confusing, its face not ever to be discerned without enormous cost. The rush of her emotion had thrown her fully against him, and she disengaged herself slowly. He let her go.

"I never meant to injure you," he said at last. "It's only that–well, I suppose in this case it matters, keeping straight on things."

Straight! She almost burst out laughing. Well, she thought somewhat wearily, all her rush toward him brought to a complete stop, she supposed he *had* gone to some high degree of concentrated effort to keep her straight. As for the straight of *him,* it was such another question, it made her dizzy to think about it. The truth about even so slight an episode as the Coggins girl alone would have quite likely baffled a detective force. And where, for that matter, had he been going tonight? In a return to her native aristocratic detachment, she could not bring herself to ask him things like this; perhaps it was because she did not really want to know.

She turned, finding her key in her bag, and tucking her hair up with one hand, unlatched the door. It was a small winter- and night-time door cut within the larger *portone,* and sprang easily back so that she stepped inside the dimly lit interior at once. She looked back reluctantly to observe him. He had not pressed in behind her but stood as she had left him. It was only that one arm was thrown out against the door. The crumpled sleeve of his coat, the white inch of cuff, the set of his hand, pressed into her senses like the bite of a relief. His gaze, meeting hers, did not implore her for anything. His face was simply present, and would be, she recognized, as it had been for a long time now, present and closely with her whether she shut it out or not. From somewhere she had gained the strength to take it now, deliberately, whenever the moment came, between her two hands.

She nodded, and bending sideways to avoid the low frame, he stepped inside. The closing door made a soft definitive thud, echoing strongly within, but only once, dully, in the narrow street outside. She mounted the long stairs, proceeded through corridors and turnings, archways and landings. She did not look back or speak, but moved quietly on ahead of him.

She had lived a year at least, she thought, since running into him in the Via de' Portoghesi.

PART THREE

6

George Hartwell got the news in Milano. By then it was summer, summer even in Rome, which he had left only two days ago to help maneuver the Milan office through a shake-up; and the weather finally pleased everyone. The old damp, closed medieval shrunken city, which had all but destroyed them, had evaporated in one hour of this glorious new season. And what could have happened in it that was not gone with it? he wondered, and read the letter once more.

On Sunday morning he was driving there. It's the least I can do for her, he thought, just in case. In case of what? The road flickered up, the sea appeared and melted away and crashed in again. In case, in case, he thought, and soon might even make a song of it, and go bellowing as operatically as Richard Coggins all along the sea road south, past Santa Margherita, Portofino, with Tarquinia ahead and Santa Marinella . . . the plains, the mountains, and the sea.

In some ways he wondered if it was a serious matter at all. Is any personal matter, he asked himself, a serious matter any longer? Isn't a personal matter simply a bug in the machine? Get rid of it as quickly as possible, or one of the rockets in your space capsule might jam. Push button C with all due reverence, for any other one will be your doom. The sea grew pink, then crimson, then a blue so deep and devastating he thought he would give up all considerations and sit out several days on a rock. Then life would change, if we would do that. If every other person, every other week . . .

A Lambretta roared up out of a curve, all but shaving the paint from his left front fender. He did not slacken speed, but drove on. He was not going to go and sit on any rock, ever, not even if they dropped the bomb next week.

Martha Ingram, all this time, was serenely alone upon her terrace, drying her long hair in the sun. Observant as a cat in the morning still, she had just seen far down in the little square below, where the fountain twinkled, the last courier come and go, a rich little white-haired lady from Connecticut, some cousin or friend (was it?) of Gordon Ingram's—Martha could not remember her name. The sun stood at ten and a large daytime moon floated in the sky; pale, full-blown as a flower, it seemed a contrivance of the imaginary sort, fragilely mounted for effect. Was it because she could not remember the name that she had not gone to the door? The name, actually, had been called to her attention no earlier than yesterday, when a note had come, written from the lady's hotel—the Grand, of course, nothing less. (Martha had often thought that Gordon Ingram was in Rome and staying at the Grand, which would have suited him so; they had large fronded palms in the lobby, and the steps which broke the interior floor between the reception area and the lounge were so long you could never find the end of them.) Martha wondered what she had done with that note—she didn't know.

Just now, through the beautiful weather, an hour earlier in the summer morning the Italian messenger from the embassy had come with a dispatch case for her: she was to add a stack of reports for Hartwell and take them in the next morning. Well aware of the season, the Italian, whose name was Roberto, was amiable and conversant and invited her for an afternoon at the beach. He had his sister's car, he said, by way of recommendation, and had recently visited the States. Martha agreed the beach would be nice; she had got together with him on several minor problems recently and had found him astute. He was, in a pleasant way, a sort of social spy; he could tell an *arrivato* a mile off, and he knew ways of isolating, or deflecting, people. If Hartwell had found some way of listening to someone like Roberto during the winter past, the Coggins' would not have leaped to such prominence in the cultural program that people now had the Americans all taped as opera lovers. So what Roberto was in turn going to want . . . questions like that flowed along easily with Roman life; they were what it was about. She thought of that gently sparkling sea and what a slow progress she had made toward it through heavy weather a year ago, back when it all began.

Going out, Roberto passed by the porter and the little lady in blue. Martha could hear by leaning over the terrace that the porter (whom she had bribed) was saying over and over: *"La Signora Ingram non c'è . . . la Signora Ingram è fuori Roma."* Roberto stopped by the fountain; turning swiftly, he seemed to stamp himself with a kind of ease on his native air. *"Si, si, c'è . . . la signora c'è . . . l'ho appena vista."* Then, catching some glance from the porter, he retreated. *"O, scusi . . . uno sbaglio. . . ."* He turned, a little gray Fiat, the sister's car, no doubt, his goal, but the little lady shot after him, quick as a rabbit. She caught his sleeve. "I am looking for Mrs. Ingram. She lives here. Now would you be so kind." *"Non parlo inglese, signora. Mi dispiace. . . ."* How quickly, Martha thought, they did solidify. She had always, from the first, had some knack of getting them on her side. But was it fair that poor little lady friends of the family should get the runaround? *Le prendono in giro,* Martha thought. They are leading her in a circle. A little more and she would go down and open the door, come what might.

She never saw any friends, messengers, from the States any more. She never read her mail. And when the little lady looked up, she ducked cleverly behind the parapet of the terrace, bringing her hair, which she had just shaken damp from the wet scarf to dry, down with her. She loved the warmth on the back of her neck, the sun's heat reaching to the roots of her hair, through the fabric of her dress. Who would leave it for a minute to descend three stone flights that still smelled like winter?

So the rich lady cousin went away in her fitted blue summer coat with the funny squat legs V-ing down from the broad behind into the tiny feet in their specially ordered shoes. What a world of shopping, the kind these ladies did, came back to Martha as she watched her go. And there was her loud English to the porter (the louder we speak the more chance we have), and then for the sweeter part, her brave attempt at Italian: *"Voglio parlare con la Signora Ingram, per cortesia."* It was as if someone had said that if the lady's duty lay in climbing a mountain at once, she would not even have stopped to change clothes.

The porter was not touched in the least. *"No, signora. La Signora Ingram non c'è. L'appartamento è vuoto."* They went on and on, their voices in counterpoint, echoing in the wide-open hallways below, now touching the fountain, now climbing to the terrace. If I could think of her name, Martha thought, I might weaken and let her in. Surely she has nothing to do with, knows nothing about, the property in New York State which they must have got me to sign something in regard to or they would not now be so determined to get me to sign something releasing it. You would think they had found a deposit of gold and diamonds six inches beneath the soil, though it is quite possible that I am holding up a real estate development. Who can tell what goes on back in that green dream across the Atlantic?

The porter kindly called a cab. Now he would earn two ways—the tip from the lady, and Martha's bribe. All he had to do was be as adamant as a barred door, which was his true nature anyway. The lady rode off in her hat of blue-dyed feathers with the tight veil, fitting sleekly as it had been carefully planned to do, over her white hair, her two million wrinkles. She held her neck up straight, giving orders to the driver, an indomitable little white duck.

If I could have thought of her name, I would have let her in, thought Martha, as the cab disappeared from the square. She wasn't as bad as the rest of them, I do remember that. Martha knew too, by the slight degree of feeling by which even mad people recognize character, as though fingers upon a fine string in the dark had discovered a knot in it, that the lady in blue was not indulging in ugly suspicions as to if and why lies had been told her. She was saying that she simply did not know. That was all.

Oh, mythical bird, vanishing American lady! She had been, Martha felt certain, the last courier.

Martha picked up her hairbrush and, drawing her chair close to the edge of the terrace, she began to brush her hair. The bells had begun to ring, and she had put her hair up when George Hartwell drew up in the square below, hot and rumpled and jaded, hitching up the handbrake sharply. So I was right to have the papers ready for him, Martha thought, but it wasn't especially the papers he had come there for. He tossed his hat aside and sat down in the sun.

He held out a letter to her, though it had come to him. "Your sister says you don't answer your mail," he told her, stirring the coffee she brought him. "She also wants you to know that Gordon Ingram is very sick. He is in New York Hospital."

"I haven't answered much mail recently," Martha admitted. "I've scarcely read my mail at all."

A long silence grew up between them. Hartwell's wife was in the States attending their son's graduation from prep school in Massachusetts. Everyone had begun to be displaced. The Wilbournes were gone, Jim to take a job on some new economic council for advising private industry, and Rita to open a ceramics shop, having shipped loads of material, not quite legally, through embassy channels. They had left their flat in a mess, having sneaked out unexpectedly three days early: Hartwell still had calls from the landlord. The parquet was ruined, the mirrors . . .

How was it that the sun seemed literally to warm one's heart? Hartwell now thought kindly of Martha Ingram's husband for the first time in his life. The poor old bastard, was what he thought. A man that age. Quite likely he's dying.

"So will you consider going there?" he asked her. "It can be arranged."

In the sun her hair shimmered like a fine web. Hartwell had once said about Martha Ingram when he was drunk, "Being from Springfield, Missouri, I am moved by women with grave gray eyes," which, as everyone told him, made no sense at all. It was a flight that failed. He had had some reference to his mother, aunt, some old magazine picture, or advertisement, maybe, showing a lady who wore her long hair up, face partly turned aside, serious and quiet. It was his way of worrying out loud. For his wife had speculated that there was undoubtedly a man in her life, but who? Hartwell used to think it over in the office alone and then wad paper up and hurl it at the wastebasket.

A slight movement just now of a curtain through one of the terrace windows made him think of Jim Wilbourne's even, somewhat longish, smoothly observant face, his nervous gesture of banging the heel of a resoled American shoe against a desk or chair leg when he talked, his cough and cigarettes and short hoarse laugh. Anybody, thought Hartwell, but Jim Wilbourne. Yet there she was, shining and fair, surfaced out of a long hard winter.

"Going there?" she repeated, as if he had mentioned a space ride. "It's nothing he's suggested. Don't tell me she said that."

"No," Hartwell admitted, "but look at it anyway. . . . You haven't even read it." She had taken it, but it was lying on her lap. When she moved, it slid to the terrace and she did not pick it up.

"But I know anyway," she said. "The last time I saw him was in Venice. He did not even look my way."

"Venice! Your husband was not in Venice," Hartwell corrected her, with a slightly chilly feeling.

She tucked one foot meditatively beneath her. "You see how crazy I am," she pointed out.

After some time, Hartwell said, "Intentionally crazy, I take it?"

"It's necessary," she finally replied.

At this Hartwell stopped drinking coffee, perhaps forever.

"What are you thinking?" she asked him.

"I think the weather is better," he said.

"That isn't what you think," she said gently, and gently too she went so far as to pick up the letter and place it—most untrustworthily—upon the table.

A small bell in a small church rang close by. It had a lovely clear sound and one actually looked about, expecting to see it, as though for a bird which had burst out singing.

"If only you could have got by without Wilbourne!" Hartwell cried, astonishing himself.

Martha built a pyramid out of burnt matches beside the milk pitcher. "He's gone. And anyway, what was it to you?"

"I didn't like him," said Hartwell arbitrarily. "This has happened before. It's nothing new. Those tall young men. . . ." It had happened all his life, in fact; he never having been one of them. At Harvard he had seen them, in the clothes of that day, older, of course, than himself, their strong easy step moving down corridors; and at Oxford, English tall with heavier bone structure, their big knees ruddy and tough in the blear cold. Now they were younger and would be younger still, but the story was still the same. "One expects such brilliance, and what happens? A moderately adequate work program, someone dear to me damaged"—she gave him a glance but did not stop him—"and now this headache of an apartment going on and on into the summer."

They had wrecked their apartment when they left, Jim and Rita Wilbourne. The parquet, the mirrors, the plumbing, the furniture. It was a vengeance on the landlord whose nature was infernal, and who had made their life a grating misery for the whole year. Now Hartwell had to listen to the landlord; he came once or twice a week to Hartwell's office; he would come tomorrow. *"Signor console, deve capire che sono un uomo giusto e gentile. . . .* You must understand I am a just and honorable man." The world was smeared and damaged, and Martha's craziness obsessed him, the more because she having completed herself he was in some ways crazier than she, else why would he let the landlord in for these interminable visits complaining of something which he could be said to be responsible for only in the vague sense of directing an American program in which Jim Wilbourne had, for a short time, taken part?

"You are linking me, George," she half-teased him, "to what the Wilbournes did to the landlord. Is that reasonable?"

"No, it isn't. It isn't reasonable at all. It just happens to be the truth, that's all. And anyway, you didn't see it–you didn't get the guided tour after they carried out the crime and ran away to Naples in the night. Carelessness is one thing, disorder left by people who aren't so tidy, something not at all nice about it, smelly maybe, but still human. But Rita and Jim Wilbourne had taken hammers, crowbars, scissors . . . !" He had begun, somewhat ludicrously, to shout.

Martha thought it was time somebody repaid a Roman landlord in kind, though anything short of crucifixion seemed genteel, but even to think of a Roman landlord seemed out of place in the timeless, non-bitterness of a Sunday morning full of sun.

"If he found that was the only way to get even," she said, "there may even have been some logic in it. I'm sure he got no more than even, and maybe no less. You forget he was an economist, so that might have something to do with the way he felt; I really don't pretend to know."

"I'm sure you would know more than I would," Hartwell said, somewhat recovering himself.

"I know he was the only one who could deal with Gordon Ingram–I do know that. But I never thought of him as smashing apartments up, though now that you mention it–"

The little church bell stopped ringing about then, and she wondered at Hartwell, this stupor of moral horror in his face, and predicted, the instant before he did it, that he would ask for a drink. She went and got it, drifting free and anchorless through her apartment, then going off to rearrange some flower pots, having no more ties than a mobile, invisibly suspended in the sun. Yet she was kind enough to reassure him. "If my judgment of him is worth anything, he seemed more quiet than not."

"Quietly murderous?" Hartwell murmured, and fell into the scotch with a sigh.

She had to recognize, for by turning her head she could even see what made a space for itself rather constantly in her mind–how the room just beyond the tall windows onto the terrace looked now. They would have both known a long chain of rooms like that from childhood on, known their quiet, with shadowy corners and silent chairs and pictures that look only at one another, ornaments of no earthly connection to anything one knows about or can remember, and known too the reason for their precise quality, even down to the slow wind of dust motes in the thin slant of winter sun, the cool rest the marble has in summer, and the small light of the lamps: the reason being that somebody has been got rid of in them. In spite of her, their thoughts, like profiles in a modern painting, merged and coalesced: she appeared as one of a long line of women who have rooms like this: invariably handsome, well dressed, detached, goalless, they have struck at life where it lived, unnaturally, because it grew unbearable.

He recalled from his long lost Missouri days, various women, their features indistinct, but their spirits clear to transparency, who lived in shady white houses with green latticework under the porch where the land sloped away. In varying degrees of poverty and wealth, they gave up their lives day by day, like sand running through a visible hourglass, to some trembling cross old father or invalid brother or failure of a husband or marvelously distorted and deeply loved child. But out and away from this monotony, they ranged far and wide among friends of the town, accepted, beloved, understood, praised. He saw them shift through that lost world with the sureness of angels, and though he said to himself it was lost, the thought occurred to him that it was perhaps only himself that was lost to it; for certainly it was there still: what made him think it wasn't? It was still there and going on, and repeating moreover its one relentlessly beautiful message, that you had to stand what you couldn't stand, or else you couldn't live at all. And for the first time it came to him that Martha Ingram did not, any longer, exist. He felt a pang of missing her, as though sometime back somebody had come in the office and told him the bad news and he had done all the decent things.

Whereupon she looked at him, reflectively, through the sun, and all the fabric of his fantasy crumbled. At least in the warm intelligent effigy of the flesh she was still there and still able to get through to him. She was all but pointing out to him that he didn't really know, how could he know just how it was? It was inhuman; it was monstrous —that was the first thing to know. Therefore, who was to say what she had or hadn't had the right to do about it?

7

As to whether or not she was really there any more, she could have said that she had simply become the winter past. Its positive motion against her, which seemed at times as blindly relentless as a natural force breaking up her own life, would always be with her. But it could not, unlike a natural force, ever be forgotten, for human faces had appeared in it and voices had cried to her, human motion had struck her down, and by these things, grasped at, sometimes only half understood, she had been changed for good, and could never escape them. It had been a definitive season.

But why George Hartwell now had to rush back into its devastating glooms and vapors, the flicker of its firelights, and quick gasps of its passions, so grotesquely lighted up in shadow play against the walls of his good and gentle heart—that she could not say. She did not really want to say. He seemed distant to her. She was fond of him. She could not have been any more or less than that if he had wanted her to, and he would never say so if he did, even, she supposed, to himself. She could, however, indulge him. He had his curiosity, so much a part of his affection—she could honor both by letting him in on things. She doubted if she would ever go so far as to say very much about the evening she had run into Jim Wilbourne on the Via de' Portoghesi, but in a way by just recalling it, it could be in some way shared by George Hartwell's openness in her direction, which she might have been leaning over to pat on the head, like a house pet. But then, of course, he would want to get past all that as hastily as possible, and on to the next thing, the next stone in her private torrent, and she guessed, looking back, that that would have been the Boston lawyer. In January, wasn't it?

Yes, she could share that with George. She could even tell him about it, for she would not forget a single detail of it, even down to the gray suit the lawyer was wearing. He was all gray, in fact, all over, even to his cuff links, hair, and tie, and his name was gray as well—Bartram Herbert. He was a close friend of Gordon Ingram's. She had known him for years.

He flew in in the afternoon, to Ciampino, just as his telegram had said he would. She did not meet the plane, and had even decided that she would leave the city for Naples, but unable to make herself do so, showed up exactly where he had asked her to, the Flora lobby near the Porta Pinciana. She even arrived on the exact hour, clasped his hand with a pale smile, and turned her chilly cheek for a token kiss. He took her down to have a drink with him in the bar. Next he ordered a cab to Ranieri's (had he reserved by cable, she wondered?), which is an old-fashioned Roman restaurant where the carpets sink deeply in and the soft chandeliers swing low and the waiters murmur in French, bending at Monsieur's elbow, and he said (this being the kind of place his voice was best adapted to), "Gordon feels some income should be set up from the land for you. It is on his conscience because you may remember that some of your parents' legacy went into the original purchase; it was not noted in the deed of sale and indeed could not be; this is only a matter of personal conscience, as I'm sure you must appreciate correctly."

She was wearing a stern black suit and noticed, in a discreet but enormous mirror in a heavy frame, how pale she looked, though perhaps it was only the lighting, how subdued she sat, almost clipped out with scissors. She watched the neat insertion of his pointed spoon in the melon he had discovered on the menu and was now enjoying, and longed to say, "But you and Gordon were directors in that trust company that failed in the crash—I heard all about it—and somehow you never got precisely ruined, though of course ruined was the word you used for yourself but it was never visible." But she did not. She wondered if it was not too easy to suspect dishonesty where people are really only loyally seconding one another's ideas, echoing one another's politics and views of humanity which sound despicable, only to prove their common ground of affection. Then she said, "I think the trouble with all these messages, these visitors and plans and letters and schemes, is that everyone is looking at things only as Gordon sees them." His glance was sheer genius. "Oh, not at all, my dear. If it's what you feel, why that's unfortunate, but certainly in Mrs. Herbert's—

Ruth's–view and my own, you and Gordon were simply too dissimilar to manage a happy arrangement." Dissimilar! She tried desperately to keep the word from clanging in her head. Had Gordon really poisoned the dog, as she suspected? she wanted to ask, for certainly the vet had told her so, clear and round, and he had said, If you think I will stoop to so much as answer this degrading nonsense. The dog was not poisoned, they are either confused or are deliberately telling you something to cover some mistake on their own part. There was, of course, another word like dissimilar: incompatible. "I have often wondered, however, granting the fact that no one can really say what causes such desperate conditions in a marriage that divorce is the only way out–I have often wondered what I did to turn all Gordon's friends against me. Why did you hate me so much?"

"It looked that way to you, did it?" He took a small sip of French wine. "I can see how it might. We all felt, you see–protective of Gordon. He has meant, through the years, so much." "So you wanted him back to yourselves?" "There was some sort of reaction." "There certainly was," Martha agreed. "I wanted to love you," she added. "I'm sure we made it difficult for you," he admitted. "I, for one, was somewhat conscious of it at the time. I tried, in some way, do you remember, to make amends." "I remember," she said, "that you took me down to see the fish pond." "So I did." He smiled. "And wasn't that pleasant for you?" "Yes," she said, "but it was scarcely more than decent. You never said anything to let me know you saw the difficulties I was half drowning in, with everyone else." "Well, but wouldn't that have been disloyal to Gordon?"

There was the thin sound of his spoon touching down on the plate and she said, "I suppose now that this bit of land is turning out to have some value I have not heard about."

"There is no attempt afoot to give you less than every cent that could possibly be due you."

"I did not mean there was," she said. Good God! she thought, how old he makes me feel. "I only meant that I have a reasonable interest in business."

"Well, then, you may as well know that the area is being opened up as suburban property–quite in the junior executive line; maybe you aren't familiar with the term."

"Oh yes."

"Has someone else got to you then?"

"Oh no, it's only that I guessed that I was being treated rather well for there not to be better than average sums involved." I shouldn't have said that, she thought. Of course, I make them angry; they don't like it, of course, they don't like it, and why do I do it? "Listen," she said intensely, "I'm sorry. I never meant to–"

"You must remember, my dear, that Gordon only got interested in finance through having to manage property you were left with. He saw what a sorry mess things were in where you and your sister were concerned and he so interested himself that he could now earn fifty thousand a year as a market analyst, that is, if he cared to. Your sister Annette says she never goes to bed without thanking God for Gordon Ingram."

In Martha's view her sister Annette was a near illiterate who would have gone on comparing prices of soap powders if she had a million dollars. She felt a blind white tumult stir inside, the intellectual frustration, of always being–she could only think deliberately, but how was one to know that?–misunderstood.

"I think it's wonderful how well he manages money, but that wasn't the point of what I was saying."

"Why don't we take our coffee elsewhere, if you're agreeable." In the *carrozza* he hailed for them in the narrow empty street, he conversed intelligently about the city, telling her in the course of some chance recollection several things she didn't know. And in the *carrozza* she experienced the tug of motion as one doesn't in a car, and the easy sway of the wheels, the creak of leather. He handed her down in a comfortable way. "Well, and what a pleasant thing to do!" Moving her toward a quiet café, "Shall we just have some coffee here?"

How charming they would all be, she thought, if only one could utterly surrender the right ever to disagree with them. She wished she could have sat in the handsome bar, all white rococo and gilt, and bring him out on some old story or other: reminiscence, that was what they loved, but she had desperately to try once more, for the bar was teeming with Italians: he was all she had of America here.

"I only wish that someone would admit that a man can be as wonderful as a saint to everyone in the world, but behave like a tyrant to one person."

He gave her a quiet gray look. "I cannot see anything tyrannical about Gordon wishing you to have your share of this property settlement."

"I only want to be forgotten," she said.

"Surely a rather singular wish."

It was right there on the table that she signed it. She remembered the crash of the gun down by the stream's edge. The ink flowed easily from the pen. It was only, she thought, a question of money. His hands in receiving documents were extremely adept.

"There will of course be other papers," he said. "They will reach you through the mail."

8

And all this time in the thick or cutting weather of that winter she had been blown adrift about the city, usually going to put in a social appearance somewhere that the Hartwells didn't have time for, and when George saw her as he did see her once, driving by in his little car—she was on the Veneto—it gave him the odd sensation that all was not well. As if to confirm it she stopped still and laughed. The sight was pleasant, but the idea worrying; she had told him something even back that far about the Boston lawyer, whom he had actually seen her having cocktails with at the Flora, but, in the days that followed the laugh, he fell to wondering what his responsibility was. He recalled the sudden break in her walking there by the high wall just past the embassy, and the giant twin baroque cupids playing with a basin into which a fountain gently spilled, and thought that if Martha was in New York she would be swelling some psychiatrist's income by now, a thing he withdrew himself from even considering. He sat meditating evenings before a Florentine fireplace covered with Della Robbia cherubs, a full-length angel or two which he called his dancing girls, and with sighs of joy sank his stone-chilled feet deeply into hot water poured into a copper pot which his wife had bought from a peasant in the Abruzzo and which was someday going to be filled to abundance with bronze chrysanthemums in some white American home among the flaming autumn hills, but right now . . . she poured another boiling kettle in. "I wish to heaven you would find out definitely once and for all that of course she does have a lover. Or even two or three. Or decide that you want her yourself. Just tell me please, so I don't have to overhear it at the opera." "It's too hot," he protested for the third time. "You don't have to scald me. And anyway, I hope she does have somebody if he's the right sort. I just don't want her jumping out of a top window of the

Colosseum, or off St. Peter's balcony, or even her own terrace, for Christ's sake. You know about the suicide we had in Germany." "But why should she–?" "I don't know, I can't tell. It's just a feeling I have."

An old bathrobe he had bought in Missouri to take with him to Oxford where it had been his heart's comfort and one sure joy was hugged round his shoulders, and cupids, winged but bodiless, alternating with rich purple clusters of grapes and gently prancing unicorns, looked down upon him from the low, beamed Rinascimento ceiling, justly famed. Their palazzo was listed in guidebooks and it seemed a shame that they could never remember once having been warm in it. His wife was bundled up in sweaters and an old ski jacket; she even sometimes wore gloves indoors in the damper weather, and George himself was turning into an alcoholic just from trying to get enough whiskey in himself to keep out the vicious mists. A glass of Bourbon sat beside him on the marble floor.

9

What George Hartwell now recognized that in those days he must have been fighting off was no more than what Martha herself had spent so long fighting off—that around one corner he was going to run headlong into Jim Wilbourne. He told himself he was afraid she had got mixed up with an Italian, though it might not in the long run perhaps mean very much—Italians generally left the American women they made love to, or so ran the prevailing superstition. The question of her divorce would have been in it from the first, thus practically guaranteeing she would get hurt. But then he worried too that it might be the English or the Americans, whom one counted on really to mean it, or so the legends went, and hence might get lulled into trusting too implicitly for anything. That might be more damaging in the long run.

"Who is it?" he came right out at lunch once and asked her. "Who is it, Martha?" But as he had not led up to this demand in any way, she assumed, quite naturally, that he was referring to somebody who had just passed their table and told him a name they both knew of a girl from Siena who used to work at the consulate but had had to return home to live with her aunt, but what was she now doing back in Rome. He said he didn't know.

The day was misty and the light blurred, lavender and close all day, dim as the smoke from the chestnut braziers, on the branched trees of the Villa Borghese where the gravel smashed damply under the thin soles of Roman shoes. The crowds flowed out, engulfing and persistent; a passing tram blocked out whatever one might have thought one saw. Hartwell gave up worrying; suicide seemed out—she looked invariably blooming. He had enough to bother him, what with new government directives which occasioned the reorganization of the entire staff (by a miracle he stabilized himself, Martha, and one or two others he wanted to keep upon the shaky scaffolding until it quieted down—these earth tremors left everybody panting). Then there was the thing of the ambassador's getting poison off the ceiling paint—*Ceiling paint?* No Roman ever believed this, just as no American ever doubted it. Solemn assurances eventually were rendered by a U.S. medical staff that the thing had actually taken place. The Romans howled. You could judge how close you came to being permanent here by how much you doubted it.

Martha forgot to come one evening and help Grace Hartwell out with the Coggins', who had to be invited somewhere occasionally; they had to be acknowledged or clamors went up from their admirers. George made a monstrous effort and kept them out of the festival plans now being talked in reference to Spoleto where no one who remotely resembled them would be included, a thing they would never have understood. Martha rang up late, excusing herself on the grounds of some trouble with her maid. Maid trouble was always a standard excuse among Americans, and though it seemed almost Italian to lie to close friends, Grace Hartwell accepted it not to risk upsetting George.

"You abandoned me, just the same," she told Martha. "And that girl now is into some trouble over her work permit."

"She never had one at all," said Martha, who knew the straight of the story. "She agreed to help at the shop or be allowed to hang around just to learn Italian. She wanted experience instead of money."

"I don't know how much experience she got," said Grace, "or for that matter had already, but the proprietor had a fight with his relatives who are all out of work and say she's taking food out of their mouths and now she's been reported somewhere. The Coggins' seem to have got her out of it just by having so many friends at the Istituto Musicale di Roma, but now she's out of work."

"Unemployment is on the rise," said Martha flippantly, making Grace cross.

"There is so little for young people in Rome," said Grace, "they don't know what to do with her. It seems all the young Italians—"

"They can always send her back," said Martha.

But seeing that she had made Grace Hartwell angry, an almost impossible feat, she invited Grace and Dorothy Coggins to tea at Babbington's on the Piazza di Spagna. They were joined by Rita Wilbourne, who had been at Grace's. Dorothy Coggins said she used to come here often before Jean left the glove shop, which was right across the street. Grace Hartwell gave full attention to Rita, who always looked tentative in Italy, rather like an ailing bird, but who, at least today, was subdued in what she wore, a navy dress and dark beret. Grace seemed to feel that given enough scones to eat she might actually be fixed in place in some way so far lacking. But Rita protested that she felt much better since some friends took her up to Switzerland, a civilized country.

Martha, who liked Grace and often used to confide in her, now felt herself so utterly bored she wondered if she could make it through to a second cup of tea, when suddenly, as if a signal had been given, they all found themselves deeply involved in talking about a new couple who had just come out from the States. They were soon examining these people in about every verbal way that exists, briskly, amiably, with enormous, almost profound curiosity, not at all unkindly, hoping for the best and not missing anything, from the two children's immediate cleverness with the language (they reminded Grace of *English* children. "Oh yes, you're right," Martha enthusiastically agreed. "It's their *socks!*") to the woman's new U.S. clothes and probable family background, somewhat superior, they thought, to the husband's, who had worn a huge Western hat (he taught in Texas) down the Via Nazionale and was trailed around by knots of people, some of whom believed him to be a famous movie director. This was really rather funny, when one considered that he was actually an authority on Virgil, though Grace said she did not know which was funnier, to consider an authority on Virgil in a cowboy hat on the Via Nazionale, or in Texas in any sort of headgear, and Dorothy Coggins said that Texas was getting way way up, culturally speaking; that remark only proved what an ancient Roman Grace was getting to be. And Rita said that Jim loathed Italian hats and would not have one. Martha did not recall he ever had a hat at all.

"Richard doesn't mind anything Italian," said Dorothy. "He's simply gone on the place. Jean has a modeling job now," she told Martha. "I thought at first I'd have to arrange for her to go home; she was running around too much, meeting too many of these boys who just hang around places. I don't know what they do. I can never understand. Their families are well off, I suppose, but still I— You got it for her, didn't you, Martha?" "Why, no," said Martha, "I don't think so." "She mentioned you to that designer—what's her name?—Rossi. The little elegant one on the Via Boncompagni, and you were just the right one for her to know. She had to lose fifteen pounds—she ate nothing but salami for ten days. They were to call you up and she was sure—" "They didn't, but it's all right." "She thinks you got it for her." "Well, I—" Martha suddenly knew nothing to say. It looked clever of Jean to go to that one shop and mention her; but it had been perhaps merely luck. It was the sort of haphazard luck the girl had. "She admires you so," said Dorothy Coggins, with housewifely openness. "She always did. It really is amazing," she added. "I can't see anything amazing about it," said Grace, with her generous laugh. They had all paused and were looking, with more admiration than not, at Martha, and Rita said, "What a lovely pin—I must borrow it sometime to copy it." It was something she had had forever. She felt silent and alone in a certain shared secrecy with the pin—its quiet upcurving taste enclosing amethysts—and though she said she would lend it to Rita sometime she had no intention of doing so.

The women sat together, in their best suits and hats, shoes damp from the streets, handbags beside them, at a corner table while the early dusk came on and the soupy traffic thickened outside. The ceiling was low, dark, and beamed in the English manner; the place a favorite haunt of the quieter English colony. The Brownings might have just gone out. Yet under the distant assurance of even that name lurked some grisly Renaissance tale. Martha found her gloves and asked for the check.

Afterward, she drove with Grace to carry Dorothy Coggins up the Gianicolo to the American Academy to meet her husband. They left Rita to catch a cab home. "It will be a blessing," said Dorothy as Grace fended through traffic, "if she has another baby as soon as she can; she's not going to be happy until she does. I know that from my own experience."

"Well, if she could just—" Grace Hartwell broke off, fighting traffic for dear life. She and Martha were quite solidified in not wanting to hear just what Dorothy's experience had been.

When she dropped Dorothy off, she drove around for a time among the quiet streets above the city, also above the weather, for up here it seemed clear and cold and glimpses of the city showed below them framed in a long reach of purple cloud.

"You didn't mind my bringing Rita?" she asked Martha.

"No," said Martha, and then she said, "I see a lot of Jim, you know."

"I thought something like that, this afternoon, I don't know why. I really cannot think why. I think it was when she asked you for that pin. Isn't that amazing? Well, I won't tell George."

"I know you won't," said Martha.

"I just hate seeing nice people get hurt," said Grace, somewhat shyly. She and George had fallen in love at a college dance. They had never, they did not need to tell you, loved anybody else but one another.

"I don't know who is supposed to be nice people," said Martha, with a little laugh.

Grace did not answer and Martha added, "I don't want, I honestly do not want to embarrass George in any way."

"Why, it's possible he won't ever hear about it at all. Unless everybody does. Or unless the marriage breaks up or something. Is that what you want to happen?"

Martha fell completely silent. This was the trouble with the run of women, considered as a tribe, with their husbands—George, Jim, and Richard—to talk about and other families to analyze. How they assembled all those alert, kind-tongued comparisons! How instantly they got through an enormous pot of tea and a platter of pastries! How they went right straight to the point, or what they considered to be the only point possible. To Martha it was not the point at all. The fact of her trusting Grace was the more remarkable in that she understood, even in advance, that they would from now on in some way be foreign to one another.

"I don't know that I want anything to happen," said Martha.

"Rita came over," said Grace, "to talk about—"

"Oh do stop it," said Martha, laughing, but somewhat put out as well. "You're trying to say it wasn't about me."

"You know, I honestly feel tired of it already," Grace said. She paused. "I'll think of it all as we were, as you and George and I always have been, all these years. I'm going to do that," she reiterated, and began to accelerate. Pulling her chin up sharply, a habit for preserving her chin line, and gripping the wheel with hands in worn pigskin gloves, she went swinging and swirling down the Gianicolo, past the high balustraded walls of those tall terra-cotta villas. She remained firm and skillful—a safe driver—her reddish-brown hair, streaked with gray, drawn up rather too tall from her wide freckled brow so forthrightly furrowed (like many people with warm, expressive faces, the thin skin texture of nice women, she was prematurely lined). But now, Martha noticed, her face looked strained as well.

"Confidences are a burden, I know," said Martha. "I'm sorry, Grace."

"It isn't keeping secrets I mind. You know that. No, it isn't that at all."

Martha did not ask her to define things further, for to encounter love of the innocent, protective sort which George and Grace Hartwell offered her and which she had in the past found so necessary and comforting seemed to her now somewhat like a risk, certainly an embarrassment, almost a sort of doom. Grace did not press any further observations upon her, did not kiss her when she was ready to get out of the car. She waved and smiled—there was something touching about it, a sort of gallantry, and Martha was sensitive to the exaggeration, the hint of selfishness, which this reaction contained. She did not blame Grace, but she read her accurately. She was protective of her husband, the sensitive area was here, and here also was written plainly that Martha was more of a help to George Hartwell than she herself had known. Somehow she thinks now I'm in bad faith and she in good, Martha saw. Does she think I can live for George Hartwell?

She took off her damp topcoat and the hat with which she had honored the tea and saw on the telephone pad a note saying that Signor Wilbourne had called.

10

"Martha?"

Whether at home or in the office, at whatever time of day, the name, her own, coming at her with the curious, semi-hoarse catch in it, seemed to fall through her hearing and onward, entering deep spaces within her. She listened as though she had never heard it before, and almost at times forgot to answer. Hurried, he was generally going on anyway to what he meant to tell her, the clatter of some bar in the background, he would be shifting whatever clutch of books or briefcase he had with him to unfold a scrap of paper and read an address. Then she would write it down. There were streets she'd never heard of, areas she did not know existed, bare-swept rooms at the tops of narrow stairs, the murmur of apartment life from some other floor or some distance back of this one, the sounds of the street. The wires of small electric stoves glowed across the dim twilights of these rooms, and if she reached them first, she would sit quietly waiting for him to come, drawing the heater close to warm her damp feet, wearing one of the plain tweed suits she wore to work, her scarf and coat hung up, her face bent seriously forward. She thought of nothing, nothing at all.

She would hear his footsteps on the stair striking, as his voice on the phone did, directly against her hearing, but when the door opened she would scarcely look up, if at all, and he on his part gave her scarcely more than a passing glance, turning almost at once to put his coat up. Yet the confrontation, as brief as that, was absolute and profound. It was far more ancient than Rome.

"Is it okay here? Is it all right?" To a listener, he might have been a landlord speaking. She sat with her hands quietly placed beside her. "It's like the others. There's nothing to say about it, is there?" "Well, it's never warm enough. Someday we'll . . ." "Do what?" "I don't know. Go right into the Excelsior, I guess. Say to hell with it." "But I like it here." "You're a *romana*."

His cheek, the high bone that crossed in a straight, horizontal line, pressed coldly against her own; it was damp from the outside air. His hands warmed momentarily beneath her jacket. His quick remarks, murmured at her, blurred off into her hearing–stones thrown in the sea. In the long upswing of her breath she forgot to answer, and tumbled back easily with him against the bed's length. "God, there's never enough time!" "Forget it." "Yes . . . I will . . . yes. . . ."

In these beginnings, she often marveled to know if she was being made love to or softly mauled by a panther, and that marveling itself could dwindle, vanishing into the twin bars of the electric fire, or the flicker of a white shirt upon a chair. She could reach the point of wondering at nothing.

Yet something–some word from without them both did come to her–either then or in recollection of those widely spaced-out little rooms hidden among the crooked roofs of Rome, where the mists curled by, and thought stood still and useless, desiccated, crumbling, and perishing; it was only a phrase: Run slowly, slowly, horses of the night. It fell through her consciousness as her own name had done, catching fire, mounting to incandescence, vanishing in a slow vast cloudy image silently among the gray skies.

Sometimes he gave her coarse Italian brandy to drink out of a bottle he might have found time to stop in a bar and buy; and she sometimes had thought of stuffing bread and cheese in her bag, but they were mainly almost without civility–there was never any glass for the brandy or any knife for the cheese, and if anyone had hung a picture or brought in a flower or two their consciousness of one another might have received, if not a killing blow, at least a heavy abrasion.

She asked him once why he did not simply come to her, but there was something about Rome he instinctively knew from the start and chose to sidestep. Ravenous for gossip, the Romans looked for it in certain chosen hunting fields–nothing would induce them to rummage around in the poorer quarters of Trastevere or wonder what went on out near San Lorenzo. And anyway–

And anyway, she understood. It was merely a question, perhaps, of furniture. The time or two he did stop by her place, ringing her up from a tobacco shop or restaurant nearby, they almost always disagreed about something. Disagreed was not quite the word; it was a surprise to her that she still found him, after everything that went on, somewhat difficult to talk to. She remembered the times in Venice and later in Rome that she had sparred with him, fighting at something intractable in his nature, and the thought of getting into that sort of thing any more made her draw back. She just didn't want to. Perhaps it was a surprise to him that she never asked him anything any more; she never tried to track him down. Did he miss that or didn't he? Did he ask himself? And if he had would he have known what to answer? He was busy—that was one thing, of course. Committees had been set up—there was a modest stir about economic planning on certain American lines proceeding at a level far below the top governmental rank, only in educational circles, but still— He thought of plunging off into field work, studying possibilities of industry in the south of Italy. "Then you might never come back," said Martha. "You mean to Rome?" "Oh no, I meant—it's a separate world." She did not think he would ever do it. "You don't think I'll ever do it, do you?" She seemed even to herself to have drifted away for a time, and finally murmured or thought she had said, "I don't know." She was tired herself, with mimeograph ink on her hands and a whole new library list to set up, and her brain gone numb at so much bandying about of phrases like "the American image abroad." "What did you say?" he asked her. "I said I don't know." She rallied. "It's a worth-while project, certainly." "Thank you, Mrs. Ingram." His tone stung her; she glanced up and tears came to her eyes. "I'm sorry," he said, with a certain stubborn slant on the words.

He had been leaning against her mantelpiece talking down to where she sat in the depths of a wing chair, sometimes toying with objects—small statuary, glass clusters, and paperweights—distributed on the marble surface. When he pulled her up against him by way of breaking off a conversation that had come to nothing, his elbow struck a china image to the floor. The apartment was rented furnished, only half such things were hers and this was not. He helped her clean the fragments and must have said a dozen times how much he regretted it, asking too, "What was it?" "A little saint, or maybe goddess . . . I don't know." "If you don't know, then maybe it wasn't so good, after all." She smiled at the compliment. "I wish we were back in some starved little room," she said, "where nothing can get broken." "So do I," he agreed, and left soon after.

Reflecting, she was not long in coming upon the truth the little rooms made plain: that they had struck a bargain that lay deeply below the level of ordinary speech; in fact, that in rising toward realization in the world where things were said, it only ran terrible risks of crippling and loss.

And yet one afternoon when the rain stopped and there was even a red streak of late sun in the clear simple street below, she felt gentle and happy and asked him to walk down in the street for just a little way. And then when he consented a dog trotted up and put its nose in her palm; it would have laid all of life at her feet like a bone. A cat purred near the open furnace of a pizzeria, which burned like a deep-set eye of fire in the stony non-color of a winter day, and a child ran out with bare arms into the cold, its mother following after, shouting "Pino! Pino!" and holding up a little coat. When they left the pizzeria, he lit a cigarette leaning against a damp wall and said, All right, all right, if she wanted to they would go away for the weekend somewhere. She looked up startled and gratified, as though at an unexpected gift. It had been somewhat offhandedly thrust at her and yet its true substance was with it.

11

They drove to the sea in what started out to be fine weather but thickened over damply. Nevertheless, he had been full of a run of recklessly funny talk and stories ever since he got off the tram and crossed the sunlit street to meet her, way out near the Laterano, and the mood persisted. The feeling between them was, though nobody had mentioned it, that they would never be back at all. They took turns driving.

Martha admired the artichoke fields warm in the new sun and recalled a peasant who had plowed up a whole Aphrodite in his field and didn't know what to do with her, for if he told anybody his little farm would be made an archaeological area; he wouldn't get to raise any more artichokes for a decade or two. So he and his family kept hiding the statue and every now and then someone would be smuggled in to have a go at wondering how much could be got for her in devious ways and the whole thing went on for a year or so, but in the end the farmer buried her again and let her rest in peace; he could never decide whom he could trust, for everybody had a different theory, told a different story, and offered him a different sum. He then went back to raising artichokes. "So every field I see I think of Aphrodite under it," said Martha. This was not true, but she did think of it now–the small compact mindless lovely head, the blank blind exalted eyes, deep in the dark earth. "Imagine finding Aphrodite and not knowing what to do with her," he said. He began to cough.

The racking of this particular cough had gone on for weeks now. He said he would never understand Martha for never being sick. The Wilbournes were always in the thick of illnesses; there had not only been Rita's miscarriage, which had afflicted him with a tenacious sort of despair, a sense of waste and reasonlessness, the worse for being almost totally abstract. What kind of home could be had in this city, in this entire country? (Here the sun, distinctly weakening, had about faded out; he seemed to be grasping for it.) The Italians didn't even have a word for home. *Casa.* It was where you hung your hat, and slept, and froze, and tried to keep from dying. Oh, Lord, thought Martha, getting weary of him. To her, Rome was a magnificent city in any weather and she moved in it easily with friends in four languages at least–she had not been Gordon Ingram's student for nothing. The city's elegant, bitter surfaces were hers naturally, as a result of his taste and judgment; and there were people about who knew this, in their own way of knowing, from the instant she stepped across the threshold of a *salotto*. She had luck, as well. She rented from a contessa in Padova, who counted her a friend; if she told all this to Jim Wilbourne he would class her with the Coggins' who had got invited to a *vendemmia* in Frascati a short time after they arrived.

At the sea they sat before a rough fire in the *albergo* (there were no other guests) and her mind wheeled slowly round him like a gull. It was going to dawn on him someday, she thought, how well she got along, how easily she got things, not the sort of things the Coggins' got, which nobody wanted, but the sort of things one coveted. She started out of this, startling herself; this was wrong, all wrong–he was better than that. He was self-amused, even in his furies, and never lost the thread of reason (this being one reason Italians preyed on him; the reason in a reasonless quarrel delighted them; they would probably have gone on fighting with him for a generation or so, if he had remained, for when the maid stole the case of economics texts on loan from the States and was forced to admit it, she returned to him books in the same case, weighed within an *etto* of the original weight, the books even being in English and some, she pointed out, having been printed in the States: they were mainly mystery novels, but included a leather-bound history of World War I dedicated to the Veterans of Foreign Wars–he found this appropriate). And even he would admit that what he needed most for his nerves in a country so uncivilized was an evening at the bowling alley, a stroll through a drugstore, a ride down the turnpike, an evening at the neighborhood movie house. These things were not as much a myth to Martha as might be thought to look at her, in her classic Roman grays and black, for Woolworth's and Radio City had once stabilized her more than human voices. He believed this, and the rain sprang up off the sea, lashing in ropes against the tall windows. Her heart sank. "It's so nice here in summer," she said faintly. His face had turned silent; in Italy he had acquired a touch of despair that she felt sorry for. He could make her feel responsible for the weather.

She never knew if he heard her at all. A shift of wind off the sea had blown one of the glass doors wide, and a maid rushed through to close it, but they scarcely noticed, if at all. They had reached the shore, an extremity of sorts, and had already discovered themselves on the other side of a wall, shut, enclosed, in the garden that everyone knows is there, where even the flowers are carnivorous and stir to avid life at the first footfall. He had caught her hand, near the cup, among the silver. She sat with her face half-turned aside, until her hand and arm reddened from the fire. She did not remember leaving the table and going upstairs.

The room where they stood for a time, clinging together a step from the closed door, was unlighted, dark, though on this troubled coast it seemed a darkness prepared and waiting with something like self-knowledge, to be discovered, mapped, explored, claimed, possessed, and changed for good, no inch of it left innocent of them, nothing she had ever felt to be alive not met and dealt with. They were radical and unhurried as if under imperial orders, and it seemed no one night could contain them; yet it managed to. As she fell asleep she heard the rain stop; it had outdistanced them by a little, as though some sort of race had been going quietly on.

The next morning there was a thin light on the sea which hung leaden and waveless below their windows, its breast burnishing slightly, convexly meeting the fall of the light, like a shield. She saw a bird on the window sill outside. Its feathers blew, ruffling in the wind, and once it shifted and looked in for a moment; she saw the tiny darting gleam of its regard.

The silver light held through the whole day. They drove far up the coast toward Pisa and she feared for a moment toward midday, voicelessly without decision as they seemed to be, they would come full circle at Genoa, where she had first seen him, in which case the sky would fall in broken masses of gray light. But the way is longer than it might be thought to be, and the slowly unwinding journey seemed perpetual, the fields and villages strict and sharply drawn with winter, the coast precipitous and wild, vanishing only to reappear; and their own speed on nearly deserted roads was deceptive—no matter what the speedometer said, they seemed adrift. They came on a fishing village and stayed there; she could never remember the name of it, but perhaps she never knew.

Where they were drifting, however, was not toward Genoa and the sky falling, nor to any mythical kingdom, but like thousands of others before and after them, it was only toward Sunday afternoon. He was sitting putting on his shoe in the pensione when the shoelace suddenly snapped in his narrow fingers, jarring him into a tension that had seemed to be gone forever; if there was anything he immediately returned himself to, after the ravishment of strange compelling voyages, it was order; he was wrenched by broken shoelaces, and it was to that slight thing she traced what he said when they were leaving: "It disturbs me to think I'm the one you aren't going to forget—yet it's true, I know it is."

His arms were around her; he was human and gentle; but she filled up instantly with panic—it was time he had let in on them, in one phrase. Had he meant to be so drastic as that? But it had always been there, she reasoned desperately, and though watching the abyss open without alarm is always something of a strain, she tried to manage it. Yet going down the stair she felt numb and scraped her wrist against a rough wall surface. Reaching the car ahead of him, she sat, looking at the surface of the harshly rubbed skin, which had shaved up in places like thinly rolled trimming of chalk, and the flecking of red beneath, the wonder of having blood at all at a moment when her ample, somewhat slow, slightly baroque body had just come to rest as finally as stone.

Miles later on the way back to Rome she asked him, "What about you? Are you going to forget it?" He glanced at her at once. "No." And repeated it: "No."

On that she would be able to stay permanently, she believed; it was her raft on the long, always outflowing tide of things, and once back in Rome could linger, not being obliged to be anywhere, in the bare strict narrow rented room, and ride the wake of his footsteps hurrying down toward the empty street, but one day she discovered on walking home alone that the rain had stopped for once, and traveling a broad street—Via Cola di Rienzo—that rose toward a high bridge above the Tiber, the sky grew gray and broad and flashed with light into which the *tramontana* came bitterly streaming, drawing even the wettest and deadest leaves up into it, and the whole yawning city beneath was resonant with air like wind entering an enormous bell. This is the center of the world, she thought, this city, with a certain pride, almost like a native might, or should have.

And passing through the post office, far across the gigantic enclosed hall of a thousand rendezvous, and small disbursements for postal money orders and electric bills and letters sent *posta aerea* to catch the urgent plane and the smell of ink and blotted bureaucratic forms and contraband cigarettes, she saw Gordon Ingram leaning on a heavy mahogany cane, the sort of thing he would either bring to Europe with him or find for himself the instant he arrived. His back was toward her, that heavy-shouldered bulk, and he was leaning down to write on a sheet of paper, but even while she watched, something must have gone wrong with the pen for he shook it twice, then threw it aside and walked away. The letter fluttered to the ground and she soon went there and picked it up but by that time a heel or two had marked it in walking past.

Yet she made out clearly, in handsome script, the best Italian: "*Sebbene* (whereas) . . . *tu m'abbia accusato di ció che ti piace chiamare inumanitá* (you have accused me of what it gives you satisfaction to call inhumanity, you must realize if you have any mentality at all, that this man in spite of his youth and attractiveness is far less human than anyone of my generation could possibly be, without the least doubt. He takes an interest in you because he must live in this way to know that he is alive at all, and his behavior is certain to disappoint a woman like yourself, such as I have taught you to be, in such a manner as to make you wish that it could never be said by anyone including yourself that you were ever in any contact with him. You know that whatever else you may say or think, I have never lied to you—this you cannot deny—I have never once lied to you, whereas you have done nothing but pride yourself on your continual lying as though it were some sort of accomplishment, an art you had mastered so well you could use it carelessly (*pensarci*—"))

She went home holding the letter in one hand and reached the apartment with the heel of one shoe in the other, limping, because she had twisted the heel off in the irregular paving of the piazzetta below. She had spent the morning helping George Hartwell draw up a new lecture program, and there had been the interview with the priest who wanted to start a liberal newspaper in a small town near Bari. At last anyway, she had a letter, a direct word. She hung up her umbrella, coat, and scarf, but dripped still, a limping trail into the big *salotto,* which, awaiting her in the quiet, looked utterly vacant, as disinhabited as if it were rented out afresh every three months, and she thought, He can't have written this; he is dead. Nobody is ever coming here again.

She fell face downward on the couch and slept, half-recalling and half-dreaming–which, she did not know, and why, she did not know, though the whole held no horror for her whatsoever any more than some familiar common object might–the story of a man who shot and wounded a she-wolf on his way home through the woods at twilight, and coming home, found his wife dead on the couch, a trail of blood leading inward from the door. She was awakened by a banging shutter.

She went out to the terrace and saw that the clouds had cleared before the wind and were racing in long streamers like swift ships, and that a moon, so deeply cold it would always do to think of whenever cold was mentioned, raced without motion. The city beneath it lay like a waste, mysterious, empty discovery, cold and vaulted beneath it, channeling the wind. It came to her for the first time to wonder, standing out on her empty, winter-disarrayed terrace, if a cold like that might not be life's truest definition, since there was so much of it.

And certain cold images of herself were breaking in upon her now, as though she had waked up in a thunder-ridden night and had seen an image of herself in the mirror, an image that in the jagged and sudden flash seemed to leap unnaturally close. What am I doing? Am I asleep sitting straight up? A thousand times she had said to life in the person of a bird, brilliant and wise in the cage of a friend, or a passing dog (just as she had said to Gordon Ingram), I forgive you everything, please forgive me too, but getting no answer from either, her mind went on discriminating. She had not been Gordon Ingram's student for nothing and she longed to discuss it with him:

If life unreels from an original intuition, what if that intuition was only accident, what if it was impulse, a blind leap in the dark? An accident must be capable of being either a mistake or a stroke of luck, depending on what it is in relation to whom it happens to. So what do you think of this one, since you were the victim of it? Before you are quite gone, forever and ever, answer that for me at least.

But he was silent; Gordon Ingram was always silent.

Jim Wilbourne, however, told her many things about himself and (she had not been Gordon Ingram's student for nothing) none of them were supremely interesting things; she listened but was not utterly arrested, sometimes she half-listened. So he said, "Listen, Martha—listen," and she did stop the car (it being her turn to drive) coming back from the sea in the wet sea-heavy night, and she did try to listen, but traffic sprang up from everywhere—there was a confluence of roads and they all led to Rome, a glare and snarl and recklessness in the rain and dark, and someone shouted, *"Stupida! Ma guarda! Guarda!"* They poured past her like the hastening streams of the damned. She turned her face to him and he was talking, haltingly; he fell almost at once into platitudes and she wondered that the person whose face she encountered in the depths of her dreams had nothing more remarkable to say than this.

It did not escape him. He wanted to return everything to its original clear potential, to say that love, like life, is not remarkable, it is as common as bread; but every contact between the two of them was not common; it was remarkable; he was stopped before he started. "I'm listening; I'm listening," she said.

"It's the way you're listening."

"Don't let that matter to you," she said gently, kindly, for the shadow of some nature far beyond anything that had happened to her occasionally came to her. "I live in a mirror, at the bottom of a mirror somewhere."

"I think we both do; it's why we make love so well."

"There must be some way to stop it . . . to go back to where we might have been, to change. I always wanted to think of it differently. You remember I told you—"

"Yes, I remember." He urged her to drive on; the stop was dangerous, and presently said out of a long sequence of thought not told to her: "I simply can't ever believe there's any way back from anything." The force of the statement reached her, and she sensed it as distantly related to fury. He had made another jump, she realized, and now there was no turning back from that either. She had finally, like any other woman, to hold on the best way she could.

PART FOUR

12

Coming up from the winter's recollections was what she and George Hartwell had to do every so often, to keep from drowning.

They were still on the terrace, and it was still Sunday morning, a healing timelessness of sun, though Hartwell went on gnawing at things he drew up out of fathomless reservoirs.

"And did you know," he was saying, "and did you fully realize, that Wilbourne got me to recommend him for an Italian government grant? He was going to study the economic picture south of Naples—the self-sacrificing servant of his times, he was harkening to duty's voice, he was going to leave the world a better place. Then what did he do but turn around and use that very grant as a lever to land his fat job back in the States."

"I'm not surprised," said Martha.

"But think what a hell of a position it put me in," Hartwell complained.

"Well, why did you let him talk you into it?"

"I thought you wanted him here. I thought you—"

"You thought *I* did it?"

"Something like that."

"It wasn't my idea," she said. "It was only that he did talk about it. I suppose, for a time, he considered staying on; he may even have believed that he meant to."

"But you said you weren't surprised."

"I wasn't . . . no . . . when he changed his mind, you mean? No, I wasn't too surprised. He only existed in relation to Gordon." There had always been the three of them, she thought; they had got stuck in the same frame forever.

"You mean destructively, of course," George Hartwell grumbled.

He wondered what portion of the service they had reached in Mass, for though not a Catholic, he could hope that it was some deep and serious portion which could bite him up whole and take elaborate care to lift him back out of this pit he had blundered into on a fine Sunday morning.

"Did you see a little white-haired American lady on your way in?" Martha asked. "She was wearing a blue feather hat with a close veil over her hair and face, and a matching blue coat. She was bowlegged."

"Martha," said Hartwell, "aren't you going to spare me anything?"

He had begun to laugh. The whole thing was crazy, and probably had been all along. There wasn't any little old lady in blue. That was one certain fact. It was something to tie to. It enabled him to keep on laughing.

But there had been no laughter for him at all from any source on that February day back in the winter when the phone rang in his office and the voice said:

"This is Gordon Ingram, Mr. Hartwell; may I see you for a short time?"

"Where are you? Where are you?" was all he could think of to say; that and "Yes, Albergo Nazionale . . . of course, right away."

To his amazement a chill like a streak of ice had run down his spine; he went out in no time, breaking three appointments, grabbing a cab rather than take the car. Had the man already called his wife? Did she know? If so, she was likely driving blindly away somewhere, fodder for the next highway crash, or more deliberately, walking straight off into the Tiber would do just as well. He felt himself in the grip of fates and furies. In the dank, gusty February day, every step seemed bringing him nearer to the moment when statues speak and old loves appear.

Albergo Nazionale ran inward from a discreet doorway. The rugs were heavy and the décor firm. He searched among the sofas, the coffee tables, the escritoires, the alcoves, and bronze gods taming horses, for a shape ponderous and vast, a heavy thigh and a foot like an elephant's, and toward the last he was spinning like a top and had whirled upon the desk clerk, saying, "I'm looking for a Signor Ingram, *un professore americano*." But before he could get that out altogether, a hand touched his sleeve, and it was only Robert Inman, English and slight with sandy hair severely thinned, a classmate at Balliol. "I say,

George, I've tried this makes three times to stop you, can't have changed so much as all that, you know." It could not have been Robert Inman who had telephoned, yet it had been. There was no Ingram on the register.

George Hartwell lived through a weak scotch in an armchair which threatened to swallow him whole, so small was he already in addition to feeling unreal, extended a dinner invitation, reviewed old histories, and afterward, still in bleary weather, he walked up to the Campidoglio and stood looking through a heavy iron grill at something he had remembered wondering at before, back in his early days in Rome, the enormous hand from the statue of an emperor, standing among other shards in the barred recess. It was the dumbness of the detached gesture, there forever, suggesting not so much the body it was broken from as the sky it was lifted toward—one could be certain all through the centuries of similar skies. And with very little trouble he could find which step Gibbon was probably sitting on when he thought of *Decline and Fall,* but why do it unless perhaps he wanted to plant him down on the cold stone and catch pneumonia? And what indeed did he have to think of that was a match for Gibbon? He had to realize that in missing three appointments at least—two of which had to do with Italian cultural organizations interested in co-operating with American exchange programs—he had not done a good thing and that now he would have to dictate letters explaining that his son was in an accident and that he had thought for a time of flying home. Anyway, it was too late now.

He walked a bit and in passing near the post office saw the Wilbourne car, which was now fairly well known in Rome because so much had got stolen off it at one time or another, and certain quarrels had centered about it as it had once been jointly owned with another couple who complained that the Wilbournes (though the car was in their possession each time it was rifled) insisted that the expense of each misfortune be shared and shared alike. The body was a sort of dirty cream which Hartwell did not like, possibly because he did not like the Wilbournes, so why be called upon to stop and wait and why, when Jim Wilbourne appeared alone, ask him into the German beer hall nearby to share a stein and bend his ear about this odd thing—this misunderstood telephone call—as if by talking about it, it would be just odd and nothing more. And it seemed, too, that only by talking could he say that from the first he had felt a concern for Martha, that she had stirred his sympathies from the first and he had learned her story a little at a time. This, too, he judged, was only a way of talking about people for once, instead of programs, programs—one built up a kind of ravenous appetite for individuals, for the old-time town life he, back in Missouri, had had once and called the past. He was winding up by saying, "Of course, don't repeat any of this to Martha," and there was a certain kind of pause hanging in the air and Jim Wilbourne carefully lit a cigarette behind his hands, worrying the match five or six times before it went out, and Hartwell thought, Oh, God, Oh, my God, having caught it on one side now I'm catching it on the other. I didn't know and yet I must have known.

He also thought: She is not this important to me, for all this about her to happen in one afternoon.

Neurotic to the last notch, she had dragged him into her exile's paranoia as into a whirlpool. He foresaw the time when the only individuals would be neurotics. They were the only people who still had the nerve to demand an answer. He doubted if Jim Wilbourne was neurotic or that he would qualify as an individual, but he without a doubt had a sort of nerve balance that so obviously related him to women it seemed in the most general sense to be a specific of blessing, like rain or sun, and why shouldn't she, in common with everybody else, have sun and rain? Who was to rule her out of golden shores? But with her there would always be more to it than that. Hartwell had blundered into this picture and now he wanted out.

"Did you ever know this guy?" Jim Wilbourne asked.

"Who, her husband? Well, only by reputation. He was at one time a leading American philosopher, or that was the direction he took early on. There were a couple of books . . . some theories of goodness, relating action to idealism . . . something like that. I remember one of them excited me. I read half of it standing in the college library one afternoon. . . ." One long-ago fall afternoon at Harvard. What reaches out of nowhere to touch and claim us? At a certain age, on a certain sort of afternoon, it may be any book we pick out from a shelf. "But perhaps you've read it too."

"Oh, Lord, no. I read practically nothing out of my field. I know that's not a good thing. It makes me laugh to think—I'd laid all sort of plans for doing some catching up on reading in Italy, after I learned the language, of course." He ended by coughing badly.

"You have learned it," Hartwell said, complimenting effort.

"Damned near killed me. It was a hell of a lot of work."

"You're telling me." Hartwell gulped his way into a second beer.

At the end of the encounter, catching a cab back to the office, refusing a ride, Hartwell felt outdone and silly. He envied Jim Wilbourne his cool intelligence, his quick judgments, his refusal to drink too much. I am the world's most useless citizen, he thought, an impractical cultural product, a detached hand reaching out, certainly changing nothing, not even touching anything. I am the emperor of Rome–I shall be stabbed in a corridor.

He longed for his own warm table and his wife's brown eyes, under whose regard he had so often reassembled his soul.

13

"There was always something rather depressing to me," said Hartwell with a laugh, "about all those damn ceramics. She kept on turning them out as if her life depended on it, and every one of them was in the worst possible taste."

"She knew the market back in the States," Martha said kindly. "I think that's what she had in mind."

"It's no wonder the Italians preyed on them. There was something about some chickens."

"The landlord's cousins kept some chickens out on the terrace next door, which was disturbing," Martha related, "and then when the Wilbournes got an order through the *condominio* to remove the chickens, they put some ducks there instead. The Wilbournes killed and ate the ducks. That was not as bad, however, as the fight over the electric bill."

"Oh, Lord," said Hartwell. "Even we had one of those. Martha, you never had a fight with Italians in your life."

"Never," said Martha, "but then I never tried setting up a business."

"I'm frankly glad as hell they're gone," said Hartwell. "If she started a business," he went on, unwisely, "it was probably out of desperation. She never seemed very well. If a vote of sympathy was taken, she'd get mine."

They had taken Rita Wilbourne for a drive one day to Tivoli—he and his wife—and had discovered near there in the low mountains a meadow full of flowers. It was as close to a miracle as they could have hoped for, for it was misty when they left Rome and raining when they returned, but here she grew excited and jumped out of the car and walked out into the sun. Hartwell and his wife Grace sat in the car and spoke of her; she was unhappy, displaced in life, and alone far too much.

She had walked on away from them, here and there, in a brightly striped raincoat, always with her back to them, so that it was easy to imagine she might be crying. She talked about too many different things. Grace Hartwell worried about her. "Men like Jim Wilbourne are difficult," she said. "They're bitter, for one thing. I dislike bitter men–they are nothing but a drain." Yet when Rita came back to the car she had not been crying at all that Hartwell could see. She had found some bits of mosaic to copy in the bramble-covered remains of something–a villa, a bath, a tower–a whole acanthus leaf done in marble; her eyes were flat, bright, almost black; she was like a wound-up doll. She said it was marvelous to see the sun; she said it was wonderful to find a meadow full of flowers; she said it was quite unusual to find a whole acanthus leaf in marble. Who was she to demand George Hartwell's fealty? She was an American girl who happened to be walking across a meadow near Tivoli; she thought automatically of what she could do with what she found there. Martha Ingram hardly heard him when he spoke of sympathizing with her; she correctly judged that he was attacking Jim Wilbourne.

"What have you got against Jim? I doubt his being so bad as you think. There was nothing whatever bad about him, in an extraordinary sense."

"Yes," said Hartwell, "but who do you think is? Always excepting Gordon Ingram, of course?"

She fell silent; he wondered if he had got to her. Self-appointed and meddlesome, she could certainly call him, but he would stop her if it killed him, he thought, and it probably would. It was then she flashed at him with sudden definition, like an explosion of tinder:

"But I love them both. Haven't you understood that was the reason for it all?"

And the one to be stopped was himself.

He sat and mopped his brow as though in a period of truce, by himself, at least, much needed.

So they finally turned to business, having worn each other out.

The papers came out of her desk and he was leaning close to the shadow of the terrace wall to glance at some notes she could and did explain from memory–one thing clearly emerging from all this, like a negative from a slow developer, was how excellent she was; she seemed to have got up one morning and put her work on like a new dress. People were always calling George Hartwell up to tell him in assorted languages how lucky he was to have her, how lucky the United States of America was to have her, and in truth he himself had to marvel at how intelligently she could appear at varied distances in the conversation of *salotti, terrazzi, giardini*. He thought she would grow the torch of liberty out of her hand any day now, or at least show up photographed in some sleek expensive magazine, a model of the career woman abroad. She might even eclipse him: had he thought of that? He thought of it now, and decided that it did not supremely matter. In view of his long ambitious years, what a surprising thing, right now, to learn this about himself. Grace in leaving had been brimful of talk about their son, graduating at home, the solemn black mortarboard procession stretching and contracting, winding beneath green elms, every sun splotch another sort of hope and promise; the twin tears in Grace's eyes meant grandchildren beyond a doubt. Even when packing to leave, her son's future was infinitely exploding within her. She at some unknown hour had acquiesced to something: the shift in women's ambitions–true augur of the world. It was known to all, George realized, how much he drank, and Martha now was fetching him another, moving in and out among the azaleas. The truth at last emerges (he took the glass); but it had been there, relentlessly forming all this while.

"But what if the poor old bastard wants you, needs you? What if he dies?"

"I've been there already," she said, remembering how they had got the land away from her where it had all happened, she had signed the papers at Colonna's on the Piazza del Popolo and heard how the gun's roar faded along with the crash of the leaves.

"That isn't good enough!" said Hartwell, but her gray regard upon him was simply accidental, like meeting the eyes in a painting.

So there was no way around her.

I'll go myself, thought Hartwell, halfway down the scotch. In the name of humanity somebody had to, and it seemed, for one sustained, sustaining moment, that he actually would. He would go out of the apartment, reach his car, drive to the nearest telephone, call the airport for space on the first plane to New York. He could smell the seared asphalt of a New York summer, could see soot lingering on window sills in the coarse sunlight, feel the lean of the cab turning into the hospital drive, every building in an island aspect, turning freely. An afternoon of dying. . . . A strange face in the door's dwindling square, rising above the muted murmur of a hospital at twilight: "I have come from your wife. You must understand she would come if she could, but she cannot. You must understand that she loves you, she said so: I heard her say so. She has been unavoidably detained . . . restrained? . . . stained? . . . maimed?"

Then he knew it was time to go. He picked up all the documents, and put the last swallow down. The stairs were below. "Lunch with me this week." "Poor George, I think I upset you."

Poor George (he kept hearing it). Poor George, poor George, poor George. . . .

PART FIVE

14

But she had never said Poor Jim, though he too had gone down that very stairway as shaken as he had ever been in his life or ever would be. Their parting had torn at him desperately–she saw it; it was visible. And all this on the first day of sun.

"Love . . . love . . . love . . ." The word kept striking over and again like some gigantic showpiece of a clock promptly, voraciously, at work to mark midnight, though actually it was noon. Returning to her was what he kept talking about. "Yes, yes, I'll always be here," she replied.

But his total motion once begun carried him rapidly down and away, *cortile* and fountain, stairway and hidden turning–the illusion was dropping off like a play he had been in, when, at the last flight's turning, he came to an abrupt halt and stood confronting someone who had just come through the open *portone* and was now looking about for mailboxes or buzzers, a fresh-faced young man whose clear candid eyes had not yet known what stamped a line between the brows.

He was wearing a tropical-weight suit which would have been too optimistic yesterday, but was exactly right today. Second-year university, just arrived this morning, Jim Wilbourne thought, holding to the banister. The young man seemed to have brought the sun. Jim Wilbourne, fresh air from the *portone* fanning his winter-pale cheek, thought for the first time in months of shirts that never got really white, and suits that got stained at the cleaners, of maids that stole not only books but rifled drawers for socks and handkerchiefs, of rooms that never got warm enough, and martinis that never got cold enough, and bills unfairly rendered, of the landlord's endless complaints and self-delighting rages, the doctor's prescriptions that never worked, the waste of life itself to say nothing of fine economic theory. He coughed —by now a habit—and saw, as if it belonged to someone else, his hand at rest on the stone banister, the fingers stained from smoking, the cuff faintly gray, distinctly frayed. He felt battered, and shabby and old, and here was someone to block not only the flow of his grief, but the motion of his salvaging operation, that was to say, the direction of his return; for every step now was bringing him physically closer to the land he had had to come abroad to discover, the land where things rest on solid ground and reasons may be had upon request and business is conducted in the expected manner. It all meant more than he had ever suspected it did.

"Could you possibly tell me—you are an American, aren't you—I don't speak much Italian, none at all, in fact—maybe you even know who I'm looking for—does a Mrs. Ingram live here?"

"She isn't here just now, at least I don't think so. Come to think of it, she's out of the city, at least for the time being."

He grasped at remembering how she felt about it—about these people who kept coming. She did not like it; he knew that much. But a boy like this one, anybody on earth would want to see a boy like that. He retreated from her particular complexities, the subtly ramified turnings were a sharp renewal of pain, the whats and whys he could of course if necessary deal in had always been basically outside his character, foreign to him, in the way a clear effective answer was not foreign whether it was true or not.

"Very odd. I got her address just before leaving from the States."

"When was that?"

"Oh—ten days ago."

"Well then that explains it. She's only left a couple of weeks back, or so I understand."

He ran on down the stairs. The boy fell in step with him and they went out together. The fountain at the corner played with the simple delight of a child. "You see, I have this package, rather valuable, I think. I would have telephoned, but didn't know the language well enough—the idea scared me off. Now I've gone and rented this car to go to Naples in, that scares me too, but I guess I'll make it. I just wonder what to do with the package."

"Mail it—why not? Care of the consulate. She works there. Your hotel would do it, insured, everything."

"Did you know her well then? You see, I'm her nephew, by marriage, that is. When I was a boy, younger than now at least, she used to–"

"Listen, it's too bad you and I can't have a coffee or something, but I happen to be going to catch a plane."

They shook hands and parted. He had begun to feel that another moment's delay would have mired him there forever, that he had snatched back to himself in a desperate motion his very life. Walking rapidly, he turned a corner.

He went into a bar for coffee and was standing, leaning his elbow on the smooth surface and stirring when somebody said, "Hi, Jim!" and he looked up and there was Jean Coggins. She was eating a croissant and gave him a big grin, whiskery with crumbs. He laughed in some way he had not laughed for a year. "What d'you know?" he asked her. As usual, she didn't know anything back of yesterday. "I was going down to Capri yesterday but it rained. It even hailed! And that storm last night! Now look at it. Wouldn't it kill you?" "It shouldn't be allowed." He paid for her bill and his and while doing so wondered if at any time during the entire year in Italy she had ever actually paid for anything. She skimmed along beside him for a short way, going on like a little talking dog; he soon lost track of what she was saying; she always bored him–everything named Coggins bored him, but she was at least fresh and pretty. Walking, he flung an arm around her. "I heard from Alfredo," she said, "you remember in Venice?" "I remember something about some stamps," he said. She giggled.

(Because that day they got back from the Lido, with Martha out somewhere, or so the proprietor said, and the weather getting dim, the air covered with a closing sort of brightness, she had tried to buy stamps at the desk, feeling herself all salty in the turns of her head and creases of her arms, but the proprietor said he was out of stamps and Jim Wilbourne, going up the stairway, heard her, though he was already a flight up and half across the lobby, and he said, "I've got some stamps, so just stop by number something and I'll let you have them," but when she went and scratched at the door and thought he said Come in he was asleep–she must have known they weren't talking entirely about stamps, yet when he woke up, scarcely knowing in the air's heaviness, the languor the surf had brought on and the boat ride back, the lingering salt smell, exactly where he was, and saw her, he could not remember who she was, but said at once, "My God, you've got the whitest teeth I ever saw," and pulled her down under his arm. But she didn't want to. She liked fighting, scuffling, maybe it was what she felt like, maybe it was because he was what she told him right out, an Older Man, which made him laugh though on the street that day coming out of the bar, almost exactly a year later, it wouldn't have been funny one bit, not one little bit; and then she had bitten him too, which was what he got for mentioning her teeth. Otherwise, she might not have thought about it. He had cuffed her. "Let's stay on," she said, "I love this place. All across Italy and couldn't even swim. That old lake was slimy. Anyway I'm in love with the boy at the desk. Get them to let us stay." "You mean get rid of your parents," he said, "that's what you're driving at. Or is it her too?" "You mean Martha? Well, she makes me feel dumb, but she's okay." She came up on one elbow, in sudden inspiration. "She likes you." "Oh, stop it." "I know." "How do you know?" "I just know. I always know. I can tell." "But maybe it's you that I–" "But it's Alfredo that I–" "Alfredo? Who's that?" "You don't ever listen. The boy at the desk." She had squirmed out from under and run off, snatching up a whole block of stamps off the table–he actually had had some stamps, though this surprised him, and later in the pensione walking around restless as a big animal in the lowering weather, he had heard her talking, chattering away to the boy who kept the desk, sure enough, right halfway down on the service stairs, and the little maids stepped over and around them with a smile: "*Ti voglio bene, non ti amo; dimmi, dimmi–Ti voglio bene.*" One way to learn the language. He thumbed an ancient German magazine, restless in an alcove, and saw Martha Ingram go by; she had come in and quietly bathed and dressed, he supposed, her hair was gleaming, damp, and freshly up, her scent floated in the darkening corridor, she did not see him, rounding the stairs unconsciously in the cloud of her own particular silence. Some guy had given her one hell of a time. He thought of following her, to talk, to what? He flipped the magazine aside; his thoughts roved, constricted in dark hallways. . . .)

"I've got his picture, want to see?" "I don't have time, honey." Next she would be getting his advice. She loved getting advice about herself. He told her good-by, taking a sharp turn away. Would he ever see her again? The thought hardly brushed him.

(Would she ever see him again? The thought did not brush her at all. What did pass through her mind–erroneously, anyone but Jean

Coggins would have thought–she did not know a word like that–was a memory of one day she was in Rossi's, the fashion shop where she worked on the Via Boncompagni, and had just taken 10,000 lire from the till–and not for the first time–to lend to a *ragazzo* who took pictures on the Via Veneto and was always a little bit behind though he kept a nice *seicento.* She would have put it back before the lunch hour was over at four, but the signora found it gone and was about to fire her, though she denied having done it except as a loan to her mother's *donna di servizio,* who had forgotten money for the shopping and had passed by on the way to the market. She would bring it right back from home. She faded off toward the back of the shop, for the signora was waggling her head darkly, and working away in an undertone. *Figurati!* And while she was in the back, way back where the brocade curtains and satin wallpaper faded out completely and there were only the brown-wrapped packages of stuffs, *tessuti,* stacked up in corners of a bare room with a gas jet and a little espresso machine, and snips and threads strewn about the floor, she heard a voice outside and it was Martha Ingram and the signora was saying with great *gentilezza,* "O, signora, the American girl you sent me, the Signorina Co-gins . . ." and then she heard, in the level quiet poised educated voice, almost like a murmur: "Oh no, there was some mistake about that. I never sent her to you, signora, there was some mistake. . . . However, *nondimeno.* . . . I am sure she is very good . . . *È una brava ragazza, sono sicura.* . . ." And then there was something about some gloves. *Addio,* she thought, in Italian. *Adesso comincia la musica* . . . now the music will really begin. She thought of running out the back door. She liked working up near the Veneto, where it was fun. And then the Signora Rossi herself appeared in her trim black dress with her nails all beautifully *madreperla* and her gold Florentine snake bracelet with the garnet eyes and her sleek jet hair scrolled to the side and her eyes that were always asking how many mila lire, and she twitched at the curtain and said, "Signorina Co-gins, you are a liar–it is always *la stessa cosa.* . . . You have given the money to that *paparazzo,* and the money was not even yours, but mine. It would have been *gentile* indeed if you had first asked me if *I–io, io*–had had some debt or other to pay. *Davvero.* But then I do not drive you out to Frascati in a *seicento*–not often, do I? No, not at all. But as for using the name of Signora Ingram, *mia cliente,* to come into *mia casa di moda* . . ."

It went on and on like this, a ruffling stream of Italian, unending; as though she had stuck her head in a fountain, it went pouring past her ears. And then she remembered, out of her scolded-child exterior, that pensione in Venice, and Jim Wilbourne this time, rather than Alfredo—the dim concept of the faceless three of them—him and her and Martha Ingram—afloat within those rain-darkening corridors and stairways. She remembered tumbling on the damp bed and how he was taller than she and that made her restless in some indefinable way, so she said what was true: "She likes you." "Oh, stop it." "I know." "How do you know?" "I just know, I always know, I can tell." For the truth was she was not at all a liar: she was far more honest than anybody she knew. It was the signora who had said all along, just because she said she knew Martha Ingram, that she had been sent there by Martha Ingram, who was close to the ambassador, and the signora could tell more lies while selling a new gown than Jean Coggins had ever told in her life, and another truth she knew was that Martha Ingram was bound to come in and "tell on her" someday to the signora. It had been a certainty, a hateful certainty, because women like Martha would always fasten to one man at a time. She remembered her awe of Martha Ingram, her even wishing in some minor way to be like her. And then she saw it all, in a flash; perhaps, like that, she turned all the way into her own grown-up self, and would never want to be like anybody else again, for she suddenly pushed out of the corner where a tatter of frayed curtain concealed a dreary little delivery entrance from even being glimpsed by accident by anyone in the elegant *negozio*, started up and flung herself full height, baring her teeth like a fox, and spit out at the signora: *"Che vuole? Non sono una donna di servizio.* I am not a servant. *Faccio come voglio* . . . I will do as I like. *Faccio come mi pare* . . . I will do as I please. *Che vuole?"*

There was a sudden silence, rather like somebody had died, and the street door to the *negozio* could be heard to open. Signora Rossi broke into a laugh, at first an honest laugh—possibly the only one she had ever given—shading immediately into a ripple of pleasant amusement of the elegant *padrona* at her pretty little *assistente;* she turned on her narrow black stiletto heels and having touched her hair, folded her hands in that certain pleasing way, and moved toward the door.)

When Jim Wilbourne reached his own apartment, there at the head of the first flight of steps which ran down into the open courtyard, the landlord was lurking, paunchy and greasy-haired with a long straight nose and tiny whistle-sized mouth, a walking theater of everything that had been done to him by the Wilbournes and all he could do in return because of it; here was the demon, the one soul who proved that inferno did exist, at least in Italy. Jim Wilbourne felt the back of his neck actually stiffen at the sight of Signor Micozzi in his white linen suit. The demon's energy, like the devastating continuous inexhaustible energy of Italy, was always fresh and ready for the fray; the time was always now. "Jesus, another round," Jim Wilbourne thought; "will I die before I leave this place?" Smoking, saying nothing, he climbed the stair to within two steps of the waiting figure which had bought that new white suit, it would seem, especially to quarrel in. The two of them, on perfect eye level, stared at one another. Jim Wilbourne dropped his cigarette, stepped on it, and walked deliberately past. His hand was on the bolt when the first words fell in all the smear of their mock courtesy:

"*Scusi un momento,* Signor Wilbourne, *per cortesia.*"

For a moment, at the door, they ran through the paces of their usual nasty exchange. It was all he could do to keep from striking physically; in Italy that would have involved him so deeply he would never be free; Italy was the original tar baby; he knew that; getting out was the thing now; he had a sense of salvage and rescue, of swimming the ocean.

"*Scusi, scusi!*"

"*Prego!*"

They were shouting by now, their mutual contempt oozing wretchedly out of every word. He stepped inside and slammed the door.

His wife poked her head into the corridor. She was working; she was always working. Thin, in a pair of knee-length slacks of the sort nobody at all in Italy wore, which hung awkwardly, showing how much weight she'd lost in one nagging illness after another, her dark hair lank and flat, lying close to her head, framing like two heavy pencil lines her sharp face and great flat eyes: "All that bastard had to do was stand a few inches to the left when he passed the window, and I would have dropped this right on him," she said. She pointed to a ceramic umbrella stand she had made herself. It must have weighed seventy pounds at least. Her voice, slightly hoarse by nature with a ready tough fundamental coarseness in everything she observed when they were alone (she was never much "like herself" with other people), was a sort of life to him. He could not even remember life without it. "They called from the university about some survey on Neapolitan family management. It was due last week. I called your office but nobody answered." "I was there all morning but nobody rang." A world of old quarrels hung in shadowy phalanxes between every word of an exchange like this one, but both of them wearied to pour enough energy into any one of them to make it live. He stood in the doorway of her studio where she had even hung up a Van Gogh reproduction—the whole place looked American now. The Italian furniture had acquired the aspect of having been bought in a Third Avenue junk shop. "The dear old telephone system," she said, turning away, the corner of her mouth bitten in. He picked up the paper and stood reading it, leaning against a gilded chest of drawers, pushing at the dark hair above his ear with restless fingers. How would she have picked it up, he wondered, the umbrella stand? She would doubtless have managed. It was then the phone started ringing. "If that's the landlord—" he said. He knew it was. It was a favorite trick of Signor Micozzi's, when the door slammed in his face, to circle down to the bar on the corner and ring upstairs, continuing the argument without the loss of a syllable. Martha Ingram would never get into this sort of mess— The thought wrote itself off the page. He crashed the paper to the floor. His wife whirled around and saw the way he looked. "Now, Jim, please—!"

"Look, you realize how much deposit he took on this place? Three hundred and fifty dollars. If he so much as hesitates about giving it back." "That's what he came for! Of course, he hesitates. He's never had the slightest intention of giving it back." "All right. Okay. He's in for a surprise or two." "But not to him, not to him! Don't you touch him!" She suddenly began to sob without crying, a grating desperate sound, biting out between the jerks of her breath, "If you touch him we'll never get out of here, we'll be here forever in this country, this horrible place, I'll die, I'll die here!" She leaped at him, latching on to his arm with both hands, and she had grown so light and he had grown so angry that when he lifted his arm she came up with it, right off the floor, as handy as a monkey. They both began to laugh—it was ludicrous, and it must have been soon after that they started figuring things out.

Her cry was over; she had even combed her hair. Then she began to bully and mock and dare him slightly; as totally disenchanted as ever, she had begun to be herself again. In some ways he listened, in others he didn't have to; most of all he was drawn back to where he was a few streets after he departed from Jean Coggins for all eternity, when, abruptly halting in a little crooked alley all alone, at some equidistance—mentally speaking, at least—between Martha and his wife, he gave over to wonder; for the first time, astringent and hard with himself, he allowed it to happen, he allowed the wonder to operate; fully, beautifully, he watched it curve and break in a clean magnificent wave.

What had he taken there, what had he conquered, so much as a city—a white, ample, ripe city, with towers, streets, parks, treasures? One bold leap of the imagination back there in Venice (the sort of thing he had always wanted to do but had never brought off quite so perfectly) had taken him soaring across the stale and turgid moat of her surrounding experience, had landed him at her very gates. It had been all blindly impulsive, perhaps cruel; but one thing had to be said for it—it had worked.

But there was something he knew and this was it: he could never have created her, and a thousand times, in turning her head, or putting on a glove, she had silently, unconsciously, praised whoever had put her together, ironically, the object of their merciless destruction—Jesus, what a trap! He rebelled at the whole godawful picture: it wasn't true. Love did not have to refer to anybody; that could all be changed in five minutes of wanting to. He had only to tell her, say so, absolutely— For an instant his mind crazed over like shattered glass, and it was some time before he hauled himself together, as though after another blind charge, this time at a wall, the first of many. Was it there or later, he allowed himself—briefly, but he did allow it—a moment's wonder at himself, recognizing a young man not even thirty and what he had challenged, taken, known. He knew in what sense he was the possessor still, and in what sense no matter when he left he would always be.

(About here he came to a corner, and frowning, leaned against a wall. Grace Hartwell saw him; she was coming down from the dressmaker, hurrying home to pack.)

He was clearly aware of the many ways in which his Italian year wore the aspect of failure, of an advance halted, his professional best like chariot wheels miring in the mud, nothing, in short, to be proud of.

He walked on, at last, with a dogged, almost classical, stubbornness. This was what it had worn down to. He would live beyond himself again; he would, in future, be again gleaming and new, set right like a fine mechanism; he had to go to the States for that. But in this hour, blazed at by a sudden foreign sun, he presented to himself neither mystery nor brilliance, any more than he did to his wife or the landlord, in whose terms he did not even despise to live, if only his energy held out till the shores of Italy dropped behind him forever. But Martha too had been Italy–a city, his own, sinking forever. There was the wall again, blank and mocking. He could go crashing into it again, over and over and over, as many times as he wanted to.

15

It was George Hartwell who got the full force of the Wilbourne departure after they had left Rome earlier than they had said they were going to, in the night. Now every day or so, the landlord, Signor Micozzi, called Hartwell and "Yes," he said, *"Va bene,"* he said, and *"Grazie, signor console, molto gentile, sissignore,"* said Signor Micozzi.

Hartwell gave Signor Micozzi appointments when no one else could get one, while the important people went across the hall to see Martha; he swiveled back in his chair and listened and listened . . . his mind wandered, sometimes he dozed, he could pick up the refrain whenever he cared to. *"Gente cattiva, quei* Wilbourne. *Cosa potevo fare . . . cosa? Sono assolutamente senza . . ."*

"Ma Signor Micozzi, lei ha già ricevuto il deposito, non è vero?"

"Si, ma questo, signor console, non deve pensare che il deposito è abbastanza per questo . . . hanno rotto tutto! . . . Tutto è rovinato!"

One day soon now, he was going to haul himself together. One has to wake oneself; one cannot go on forever, unraveling the waste, the inconsequential portions of a dream that was not even one's own. So one day soon now he was going to stop it. He was going to say, like any tourist in the market, *Quanto allora?* He might even write a check. It was his American conscience, that was it. . . .

Poor George Hartwell, there was one success he had had. Everyone assured him of it—the Coggins', of course. He could take pride in them; who would have thought that Italians would let any American tell them about opera?

He left Martha's doorway. The sun struck him a glorious blow and the little fountain pulsed from white to green in the new season.

Ah, yes, the Coggins'. *Veni, vidi, vici.*

He looked for his car and found it. Dorothy, Richard, and Jean.

They had gone off triumphantly to take the boat at Genoa, had been waved off at the station by contingents of Roman friends, leaving time to go by Venice and revisit that same pensione, having sent on ahead to the boat crate upon crate of tourist junk, a whole case of country wines (a gift from the landlord, by now a lifelong friend). There were also a package of citations and awards from a dozen appreciative music companies, autographed photos of half the singers in Italy, and 90 per cent of all the chocolate in Perugia, which had been showered upon Jean by admirers from Trastavere to the Parioli, from Milan to Palermo. Perhaps at this moment, she was talking to Alfredo again in the pensione, giggling at his soft Venetian accent, all in a palazzo set on waters crackling in the brilliant light, or strolling about the garden, hearing a motorboat churn past. Waiting for Sunday dinner in the central hallways, with one or two of the same old guests and the proprietor with his head in the books . . . waiting for Sunday dinner. It was a Western tradition, a binding point for the whole world. And why not? In his vision of Venice, for a moment, Martha Ingram and all her long mad vision stood redeemed. But not for long. Jim Wilbourne was never far enough away; his head turned slowly, his regard scorched slowly across the scene; as though the Coggins' had been in an eighteenth-century engraving deployed in each pleasant detail about their Venetian casa, the edges curled, the loosely woven paper bent backward, the images distorted, changed—one turned away.

Hartwell at last got home and opened windows in an empty flat, fetched bread and cheese from the kitchen, fought steadily against the need for whiskey, and sat down to unlock the dispatch case. His wife, so easily evoked, crossed the ocean at his nod to stand at his elbow and remark with her warm wit that along with all those dispatches, briefings, summaries, minutes, and memoranda from the embassy, he might possibly draw out a poison toad, a severed hand, some small memento of Martha Ingram.

But he did not.

The reports she had done for him were smooth and crisp, brilliant, unblemished. Their cutting edge was razor-keen, their substance unrolled like bolts of silk. There was nothing to add, nothing to take away. It was sinister, and he did not want to think about it alone. But he had to. Who has been destroyed in this as much as me? he wondered. Gordon Ingram is not alone. No, it was against George Hartwell's present and fond breast that the hurled spear struck.

Knowing this, he could not stand it any longer.

Getting up, slamming out, he got into his car and went nosing about the streets again. The Grand Hotel, a Sunday vision also, elegance and the Grand Tour, too little exercise, every wish granted, marmalade for tea, and if you're willing to pay extra, tours can be arranged through the— He had charged halfway across the lobby before he stopped to think, to enquire.

"A little *signora americana* in blue, *sissignore*. She is there, *eccola là.*"

And there she was. He saw her. She was real. Martha was not that crazy.

She was over in a far corner before some enormous windows reaching to the ceiling, canopied with drawn satin portiers, and she was not alone. The Italian floor cleaner who had mopped and dusted the lobby there for at least ten years but had never once before this moment sat down in one of the sofas was now beside her. She had gone upstairs, and using her dictionary (as Hartwell was later to hear) had written down the message which she had to give to someone, and now she was reading it off. A piece of light blue letter paper trembled in her little crooked hand.

"Ho un amico che sta morendo . . . I have a friend who is dying. *Questa mattina ho ricevuto la notizia* . . . only this morning I received the news."

"O signora!" cried the floor cleaner. *"Mi dispiace* . . . I am so sorry!" He leaned toward her; his small-featured Latin face wrung instantly with pity. He also had lost friends.

"Mio amico era sempre buono . . . è buono . . . buono. . . ."

It was then that George Hartwell appeared. The floor cleaner sprang to his feet. *"S'accomodi* . . . sit down," said Hartwell. *"In nome di Dio."*

There was no one really around. The bright day was subdued to the décor of the great outdated windows, which made a humble group of them. And really, thought Hartwell, I've got no business here, what am I doing with these two people? Once I had a little kingdom here. It is stolen, it is gone. Should I tell them? Would they cry?

He sat and listened.

Now the sentiment, the inaccuracy, of the usual human statement was among them; irresistibly as weeds in a great ruin, it was springing up everywhere around what was being said of Gordon Ingram. His books, his wisdom, his circle of friends, his great heart, his sad life. . . . Hartwell was translating everything to the floor cleaner, who had forgotten that he was a floor cleaner. He was, above all, a human being, and he accordingly began to weep.

George Hartwell told the lady in blue that Martha Ingram was out of town.

16

On a day that now seemed long, long ago, had seemed long ago, in fact, almost the precipitate instant its final event occurred, she had gone out of her apartment, which Jim Wilbourne had been in for an hour or so, for the last time. It was a matter of consideration to them both to give him time to get well away before she went out behind him, leaving rooms she could not for the moment bear to be alone in. She did not know that he had been delayed on the stair. She saw him, however, come out of the bar with Jean Coggins, laughing with her over something; she stepped back, almost from the curb into the street which at that point was narrow, damp, still in winter shadow; and then a car passed and she looked up in time to see Gordon Ingram's nephew driving by. She never doubted that was who it was. He had grown a lot, that was all. He did not see her; the car nosed into a turning which led away from her, away, she realized too late, icily, from her apartment. He had been there already; he had gone. From out of sight, in the chilly labyrinth where the sun would slowly seep in now and warm and dry and mellow through the long summer months, she heard Jean Coggins laugh. The boy had grown so much; she used to give him books and read to him: what college was he in, would no one tell her? She had stopped still–after her first futile steps, begun too late, of running after the car–in a small empty square. The direction of the car pulled against the direction of the laugh, in an exact mathematical pivot, herself being the central point of strain, and in this counterweight, she felt her life tear almost audibly, like ripping silk. She leaned against a wall and looked out on the little empty space, an opening in the city. The sun brought out the smell of cigarettes, but no one was about; only dumb high doorways and shadows sliced at a clear, straight angle across a field of sun.

He was driven away from me, she thought: Jim Wilbourne did it; I know that it is true. I am no more than that meeting point of shadow and sun. It is everything there is I need to know, that I am that and that is me.

It was the complex of herself that her spirit in one motion abandoned; those intricate structures, having come to their own completion, were no longer habitable. She saw them crumble, sink, and go under forever. And here was what was left: a line of dark across a field of sun.

When the small package arrived for Martha—a strand of pearls which had belonged to an aunt who had left them to her in memory of—she hardly read the letter, which was not from Gordon Ingram but from the nephew who was now in Greece. The lettering on the package had been done by Gordon Ingram. There was no message inside. She went carefully, in a gentle way, downstairs and laid the strand in the crevice of the palazzo wall, like an offering to life. She felt as a spirit might, rather clever, at being able to move an object or leave a footprint. Some Italian would be telling the story for many years, waving the pearls aloft. *"Dal cielo! Dal cielo! Son cadute dal cielo!"*

George Hartwell's saying to the lady in blue that Martha was out of town was no lie; perhaps he was incapable of telling one. She was driving to the sea to meet Roberto there, possibly the sister and the sister's husband, possibly not, the plans were generous, promising, and vague. She more and more arranged to do things alone, a curious tendency, for loneliness once had been a torment, whereas now she regarded almost everything her eyes fell on with an equal sense of companionship; her compatibility was with the world. The equality of it all could of course be in some purely intellectual, non-nervous way disturbing. Things were not really equal, nor were people; one explanation might be that she simply did not care very deeply about anything, the emotional target she had once plainly furnished had disappeared. Was this another name for freedom? Freedom was certainly what it felt like. She bent with complete compassion, fleshless, invisible and absent, above the rapidly vanishing mortality of Gordon Ingram, at the same time she swung happily, even giddily (there went that streak again, the necessary madness), around the Colosseum, where the fresh glittering traffic, like a flight of gulls, joyous in the sunlight, seemed to float and lilt, fearless of collision. Children's bones and women's skulls had been dug up there and conjectures could be easily formed about what sort of undemocratic accidents had overtaken these fine people, but now the old ruin stood noble and ornamental to Rome, and views of it were precious to those apartments which overlooked it.

Faceless and nameless, the throng rushed on; they always had and would forever, as long as the city stood.

It was not Gordon Ingram who had died, nor was it Jim Wilbourne who was absent. It was herself, she thought. I am gone, she thought; they have taken me with them; I shall never return.

If only George Hartwell could understand that, he would know better about things, he could even bear them. But then, she saw, he might be compelled to trace a similar path in his own life; for knowing it arose merely, perhaps only, from being it. Let him be spared, she thought; let him be his poor human soul forever.

She was of those whom life had held a captive and in freeing herself she had met dissolution, and was a friend now to any landscape, a companion to cloud and sky.

PART III

1965–1971

THE ABSENCE

Her husband having gone away on his long visit, Bonnie Richards settled down to a stack of books. They were all about science, about which she knew little, and designed for the popular reader. She was alone in the house except for the dog, who took to looking at her curiously. She thought he only missed his master and wanted to ask about him, but nonetheless his large, beseeching eyes could be disquieting. She read the science books at night and became more disquieted than ever. Matter was made of atoms, as she already knew, but the behavior and organization of these small active objects were extremely uncertain. No one knew just what matter was. No instrument was delicate enough to observe atoms without making a grave impact, which altered their habits. They thus enjoyed an unbreakable privacy. Some scientists had seriously conjectured that particles within atoms were not compelled to behave as they did but could choose what they felt like doing. All conclusions seemed open to doubt.

Space she had to quit reading about, early on. It was unthinkably gigantic, yet finite, was exploding outward, had already burst at points. There was no up or down; we were like creatures placed on the round surface of an expanding balloon, and all she had remembered from high school geometry, which had to do with flat surfaces, was no use, because nothing was flat. The moon used to be so near the earth that tides three miles high went shooting up to meet it, out in the Pacific. It was difficult not to see this awesome spectacle, in the mind's eye. When she took the dog walking in the evening, she avoided looking at the sky. Mystery books were out, for the ones she liked always unfolded in creaky old houses where dogs started barking for no reason. Her house was not old, but occasionally it creaked at night.

Bonnie was not a visitor of neighbors; most of the Richards' friends were scattered out. They had her come to dinner or for drinks, and once she drank too much and skinned her knee on the front steps when she came home. The hall light had burned out and the dog was asleep under the bed in the guest room. There was a peculiar smell in the basement, like an oil leak, but no oil was visible.

Days, she went to the grocery, and once she went to the ballet, standing at intermission in the thickly carpeted foyer, feeling elegant and somewhat mysterious in her black pumps and gray silk. Another afternoon, she went to the movies in the rain, where, wearing her old raincoat, flat heels, and a scarf, she began to feel as she had back in college. She got the house painter to come and redecorate the living room, and had such a fine time with him over coffee that she stayed in love with him for two days. He was aware of this, it was obvious, when he came the next time. She was trying to reason her way either out of it or into it, when his ladder slipped (he had grown somewhat nervous) and he broke a large window. By the time the details of repairing it were ironed out, she was simply impatient with him. He was ignorant, and when they went to the hardware store to have new glass cut, he tried to explain to her, on observing some bad reproductions of modern painting, that there was really nothing to Picasso.

The weather grew warmer, and she took out her dissatisfaction on the flower beds, planting salvia and portulaca, lobelia and marigolds, weeding the day lilies and wrecking her hands. Her husband wrote that he was having a splendid time and that his parents' health had improved since his arrival. She went to the library on quite a warm day—the warmest so far—and read for a time before large windows opening on a small park, where red cannas, freshly set out, were beginning to unscroll. Birds splashed in a rough ornamental crater filled with water. Sometimes, when they tilted up for their steep ascent, water fell from their serrated wing tips in splashes bright as mercury. She did not know what she was reading.

It was coming over her gradually what she wished to be—something she had never consciously thought of before. She wished to be a person, a being, who appeared and disappeared. She should have liked, conveniently, to have the power to disappear even from herself, to put herself away like something folded in a drawer, or simply not to be when there was nothing to be for. If not in a drawer, then better still to go outward as a color, soft and pleasing, or to be a bird's wing, or the water that the bird splashed in. She might even arrange to exist, to be in the regard, the very glance, of her husband or of those dear to her when they most or least looked for her–emerging into rooms or from around corners, coming toward them with a piece of news or a cup of coffee. The conception had started, she now realized, some time ago, back in the winter, when, coming in out of a sub-zero night, she had drawn herself close against her husband in bed and shivered for such a long time he said she should turn back into a rib, which was what wives had come from originally. She had rather fancied the idea, for her husband had a fine, practical way of carrying his body–shoulders, head, skin, bones, and all–in a manner rapid yet controlled, with a good deal of vitality and the definite promise of good things unfolding before him as he went along. He was invariably warm. She couldn't be better disposed of than in this fashion.

The next day, the dog ran off but was eventually brought back home by a small girl named Doris, whose family had been living three doors down, in an apartment in one wing of a widow's house. Bonnie invited Doris in and gave her some cookies as a reward. Doris sat down quite amiably and talked away, eating cookies. She expressed a liking for "Batman" and "The Man from U.N.C.L.E.," and said she wanted to become a dancer in shows and night clubs. It seemed unlikely at the moment that she was very promising material for this career, being mousy and rather fat, but she said it so matter-of-factly that Bonnie was persuaded she would go straight to the goal, even becoming lithe and blond and beautiful at the appropriate moment. Every day thereafter, Doris came to look at TV, since her family did not have a set. One day, her mother came for her. She said it was time for Doris to come to dinner, and asked Bonnie as a special favor if she would cash a check for ten dollars, because she had to run to the grocery, and the grocer was notoriously reluctant to cash checks. Bonnie had one of her moments of definitely appearing, and gave the money quite happily. She heard herself already telling her husband, "They are not especially nice people, but I let the girl come to pass the time. I'll just say I'm busy or something if she begins to make it a habit."

Two days later, she went by the bank to cash the check. She then learned that Doris's family had moved away in the night, having given a number of worthless checks like her own before departing. The child herself had distributed some of them, though whether or not aware of what she was doing was not known. Nobody knew where they had gone.

That night, Bonnie did not sleep at all. Nothing has happened, she kept telling herself. What's ten dollars? Why is a bird's wing waterproof? What is an atom up to? How did the moon get as high as it is? What is the dog trying to say? If the smell in the basement is not oil, then what is it? What do I myself think of Batman? The dog whimpered, and jumped on the bed and lay close to her, and though she had never allowed this before, she let him stay.

Her husband materialized exactly on schedule, through the doors into the waiting room at the airport, which sprang open magically, even royally, when he approached them.

"Is everything O.K.?" she asked.

"Fine, fine, everything's fine. Nobody was seriously sick after all. You should have come. Why are you pale, why are you crying? Come on, let's get a drink."

He was walking rapidly, bag in one hand, hustling her along. He looked brown and happy. All her reasons for things came back. They sat down together in the airport bar. It was bright and friendly, the music familiar and gay.

"The neighbor's child writes checks that bounce," she told him, which was not quite true. She was laughing. "Oh, it's a long story. I'll tell you about it." And she told him.

"I don't see anything so long about it," he said. "And anyway, what's ten dollars?"

"I wondered that, too," she said.

THE DAY BEFORE

When I started to school, my grandfather and the old maid next door and her two old bachelor brothers took a great interest in the event, so important in my life, and tried to do everything they could think of for me. One bought me a lunch basket; another planned just what should be put in it, and Miss Charlene Thomas, the old maid, made me a book satchel out of green linen with my initial embroidered on it in gold thread. Somebody even went uptown to the drugstore where the school books were sold and got me a new primer to replace an old one, still perfectly good, which had belonged to my cousin. And there was a pencil box, also green, with gilt lettering saying PENCILS, containing: three long yellow Ticonderoga pencils, an eraser–one end for ink, the other for lead–a pen staff, two nibs, and a tiny steel pencil sharpener. My grandfather laid the oblong box across his knees, unsnapped the cover, and carefully using the sharpener he began to sharpen the pencils. After doing one of them and dusting off his trousers, he took out his pen knife, which had a bone handle, and sharpened the other two in the manner which he preferred. Then he closed up the box and handed it to me. I put it in the satchel along with the primer.

Mr. Dave Thomas, one of the two bachelor brothers of Miss Charlene, having made a special trip uptown in the August heat, came in to say that copy books were not yet on sale as they had not arrived, but could be bought for a nickel from the teachers on opening day. "Here's a nickel right now," said Mr. Dave, digging in his trousers pocket. "*I'll* give her one," said my grandfather. I was spoiled to death, but I did not know it. Miss Charlene was baking ginger cakes to go in my lunch basket. I went around saying that I hated to go to school because I would have to put shoes on, but everybody including the cook laughed at such a flagrant lie. I had been dying to start to school for over a year.

My grandfather said that the entire family was smart and that I would make good grades, too. My mother said she did not think I would have any trouble the first year because I already knew how to read a little (I had, in fact, already read through the primer). "After that, I don't know," she said. I wondered if she meant that I would fail the second grade. This did not fill me with any alarm, any more than hearing that somebody had died, but made me feel rather cautious. Mr. Ed, Mr. Dave's brother, called me all the way over across the calf lot to his house to show me how to open a new book. I stood by his chair, one bare foot on top the other, watching him while he spread the pages out flat, first from the center, then taking up a few at a time on either side and smoothing them out in a steady firm way, slowly, so as not to crack the spine, and so on until all were done. It was a matter, he said (so they all said), of having respect for books. He said that I should do it a second time, now that he had showed me how. "Make sure your hands are clean," he said, "then we can go eat some cold watermelon." I remember still the smell of that particular book, the new pages, the binding, the glue, and the print as combining to make a book smell—a particular thing. The pencil box had another smell altogether, as did the new linen of the satchel. My brown shoes were new also, a brand called Buster Brown. I did not like the name, for it was invariably printed above a picture of a little round-faced boy with straight bangs and square-cut hair who was smiling as though he was never anything but cheerful. I did not know what I looked like especially, but I knew I did not look like that, nor did I want to. I asked to be allowed to wear new tennis shoes to school, and if not new ones, then old ones. My mother said I could not wear tennis shoes of any description to school and when I said I wanted to go barefoot then, she said I was crazy. I told my grandfather but he only said I had to mind her. I felt that he would have let me do as I liked and was only saying what he had to. I felt that my parents were never as intelligent as my grandfather, Mr. Dave, Mr. Ed, and Miss Charlene.

After dinner that day it was very hot and when everybody lay down and quit fanning themselves with funeral parlor fans because they had fallen sound asleep, some with the fans laid across their chests or stomachs and some snoring, the two Airedales that belonged to Mr. Dave had running fits. If a relative was visiting, or any stranger to our road, which was a street that didn't go anywhere except to us and the Thomas house, they were liable to get scared to death by those Airedales because the way they sometimes tore around in hot weather it looked as if they had gone mad. It was something about the heat that affected their brains and made them start running. It all happened silently; they would just come boiling out of nowhere, frothing at the mouth, going like two balls of fire, first around Miss Charlene's house, then up and down the calf lot between their house and ours, then all around our house, finally tearing out toward the field in front of the house, where, down among the cotton and the corn, they would wear it all out like the tail of a tornado. Eventually the foliage would stop shaking and after a long while they would come dragging themselves out again, heads down and tongues lolling, going back to where they belonged. They would crawl under the house and sleep for hours. We had got used to their acting this way, and though it was best, we agreed, to keep out of their way, they did not scare us. The Negro children used to watch them more closely than anybody did, saying, "Hoo, boy, look a-yonder." White people had sunstrokes or heat strokes or heat exhaustion–I did not ever learn quite what the difference in these conditions was, and don't know yet. Dogs had running fits instead.

The Airedales were named Pet and Beauty, and only Mr. Dave, who owned them, could tell them apart. He took their fits as being a sort of illness, and as he loved them, he worried about them. He gave them buttermilk out of dishes on the floor and got them to take cobalt blue medicine out of a spoon, holding their jaws wide with his thumb, pouring in the medicine, then clamping the jaws shut tight. It must have tasted awful, for the dogs always resisted swallowing and tried to fight free, their paws clawing the ground, heads lashing around to get away and eyes rolling white and terrible. They could jump straight up and fight like wild ponies, but he always brought them down, holding on like a vise and finally, just when it seemed they weren't ever going to, they would give up and swallow. Then it was all over. I never knew if the medicine did them any good or not.

They had one of their fits that very afternoon, the day before school started. We had a friend of my aunt's from out in the country who had stopped by and been persuaded to stay for dinner and she saw them out her window and woke everybody up out of their nap. "Those dogs!" she cried. "Just look at those dogs!" "It's all right!" my father hollered from down the hall. "They've just got running fits, Miss Fannie," my mother cried. "It's not rabies," she added. "At least they don't bark," said my grandfather, who was angry because she had waked him up. He didn't care much for her anyway and said she had Indian blood.

I don't know what I thought school was going to be like. It was right up the road, only about twenty minutes' walk, just a little too far to come home for dinner, and I had passed the building and campus all my life, since I could remember. My brother had gone there, and all my cousins, and still were recognizable when they returned home from it. But to me, in my imagination beforehand, it was a blur, in the atmosphere of which my mind faltered, went blank, and came to with no clear picture whatsoever.

After I got there it was all clear enough, but strange to the last degree. I might as well have been in another state or even among Yankees, whom I had heard about but never seen. I could see our house from the edge of the campus, but it seemed to me I was observing it from the moon. There were many children there, playing on the seesaws, sliding down the sliding board, drinking at the water fountains, talking and running and lining up to file inside to the classrooms. All of them seemed to know each other. I myself did not recognize any of them except occasionally one of the older ones who went to our tiny Sunday School. They stopped and said, "Hey," and I said, "Hey." One said, "I didn't know you were starting to school." And I said, "Yes I am." I went up to a child in my grade and said that I lived down that street there and pointed. "I know it," she answered. She had white-blond hair, pale blue eyes, and very fair skin, and did not look at me when she spoke. The way she said "I know it" gave me to understand that she probably knew just about everything. I have seen sophisticated people since, and at that time I did not, of course, know the word, but she was, and always remained in my mind, its definition. I did not want to go away and stand by myself again, so I said, "I live next door to Miss Charlene Thomas and Mr. Dave and Mr. Ed Thomas." "I know it," she said again, still not looking at me. After a time she said, "They feed their old dogs out of Havilland china." It was my turn to say I know it, because I certainly had seen it happen often enough. But I said nothing at all.

I had often lingered for long minutes before the glass-front china cabinet on its tiny carved bowed legs, the glass, not flat, but swelling smoothly forward like a sheet in the wind, and marveled to see all the odd-shaped matching dishes—"Syllabub cups," Miss Charlene said, when I asked her. "Bone dishes," she said, "for when you eat fish." There were tiny cups and large cups, sauce bowls and gravy boats, and even a set of salt holders, no bigger than a man's thumb, each as carefully painted as a platter. It was known to me that this china, like the house itself and all the fine things in it, the rosewood my mother admired, the rose taffeta draperies and gilt mirrors, had belonged to the aunt of the three Thomases, a certain Miss Bedford, dead before I was born, who had been highly educated, brilliant in conversation, and whose parrot could quote Shakespeare. I did not find the words to tell any of this to the girl who knew everything. The reason I did not was because, no more than I knew how to do what she so easily accomplished in regard to the dogs' being fed out of Havilland china—which had often been held up to the light for me and shown to be transparent as an eggshell—I did not know what value to give to what I knew, what my ears had heard, eyes had seen, hands had handled, nor was there anything I could say about it. I did not think the child was what my grandfather meant by being smart, but I did know that she made me feel dumb. I retreated and was alone again, but a day is a long time when you are six and you cannot sit opening and closing your new pencil box forever. So I went up to other children and things of the same sort continued to happen. In the classroom I did as I was told, and it was easy. I must have realized by the end of the week that I would never fail the second or any other grade. So everything would be all right.

From then on, life changed in a certain way I could not define, and at home in the afternoons and on weekends I did not feel the same. I missed something but did not know what it was. I knew if I lived to be a thousand I would never do anything but accept it if an old man fed his dogs out of the best china or if a parrot could quote Shakespeare. At home when I looked up, I saw the same faces; even the dogs were the same, named the same, though they, as was usual, had stopped having fits once the nights got cooler. Everybody, every single person, was just the same. Yet I was losing them; they were fading before my eyes. You can go somewhere, anywhere you want—any day now you can go to the moon—but you can't ever quite come back. Having gone up a road and entered a building at an appointed hour, there was no way to come back out of it and feel the same about my grandfather, ginger cakes, or a new book satchel. This was the big surprise, and I had no power over it.

Life is important right down to the last crevice and corner. The tumult of a tree limb against the stormy early morning February sky will tell you forever about the poetry, the tough non-sad, non-guilty struggle of nature. It is important the way ants go one behind the other, hurrying to get there, up and down the white-painted front-porch post. The nasty flash and crack of lightning, striking a tall young tree, is something you have got to see to know about. Nothing can change it; it is just itself.

So nothing changed, nothing and nobody, and yet having once started to lose them a little, I couldn't make the stream run backward, I lost them completely in the end. The little guilt, the little sadness I felt sometimes: was it because I hadn't really wanted them enough, held on tightly enough, had not, in other words, loved them?

They are, by now, nearly every one dead and buried—dogs, parrot, people, and all. The furniture was all either given away or inherited by cousins from far away, the house bought by somebody and chopped up into apartments; none of this can really be dwelt on or thought of as grievous: that is an easy way out.

For long before anybody died, or any animal, I was walking in a separate world; our questions and answers, visits and exchanges no more communicated what they had once than if we were already spirits and flesh and could walk right through each other without knowing it.

Years later, only a few months ago, when home for a visit, I was invited to play bridge with some friends and on the coffee table saw a box of blue milk glass, carved with a golden dragon across the lid, quite beautiful. "That came out of the old Thomas house," my friend said. She had got it in a devious way, which she related, but had never been able to open it. I picked it up, not remembering it, and without even thinking I moved my finger at once to the hidden catch, and the box flew open. It wasn't chance; I must have once been shown how it worked, and something in me was keeping an instinctive faith with what it knew. Had they never been lost then at all? I wondered. A great hidden world shimmered for a moment, grew almost visible, just beyond the breaking point of knowledge. Had nothing perhaps ever been lost by that great silent guardian within?

THE BUFORDS

There were the windows, high, well above the ground, large, full of sky. There were the child's eyes, settled back mid-distance in the empty room. There was the emptiness, the drowsiness of Miss Jackson's own head, tired from tackling the major problems of little people all day long, from untangling their hair ribbons, their shoelaces, their grammar, their arithmetic, their handwriting, their thoughts. Now there was the silence.

The big, clumsy building was full of silence, stoves cooling off, great boxy rooms growing cool from the floor up, cold settling around her ankles. Miss Jackson sat there two or three afternoons a week, after everybody else had gone, generally with a Buford or because of a Buford: It was agreed she had the worst grade this year, because there were Bufords in it. She read a sentence in a theme four times through. Was it really saying something about a toad-frog? Her brain was so weary–it was Thursday, late in the week–she began to think of chipmunks, instead. Suddenly her mouth began to twitch; she couldn't stand it any longer; she burst out laughing.

"Dora Mae, *what* are you doing?"

The truth was that Dora Mae was not doing anything. She was just a Buford. When she was around, you eventually laughed. Miss Jackson could never resist; but then, neither could anyone. Dora Mae, being a Buford, did not return her laugh. The Bufords never laughed unless they wanted to. She drew the book she was supposed to be studying, but wasn't, slowly downward on the desk; her chin was resting on it and came gradually down with it. She continued to stare at

Miss Jackson with eyes almost as big as the windows, blue, clear, and loaded with Buford nonsense. She gave Miss Jackson the tiniest imaginable smile.

Miss Jackson continued to laugh. If someone else had been the teacher, she herself would have to be corrected, possibly kept in. It always turned out this way. Miss Jackson dried her eyes. "Sit up straight, Dora Mae," she said.

Once this very child had actually sewed through her own finger, meddling with a sewing machine the high school home-economics girls had left open upstairs. Another time, at recess, she had jumped up and down on a Sears Roebuck catalogue in the dressing room behind the stage, creating such a thunder nobody could think what was happening. She had also shot pieces of broken brick with her brother's slingshot at the walls of the gym, where they were having a 4-H Club meeting. "Head, Heart, Hands, and Health," the signs said. They were inside repeating a pledge about these four things and singing, "To the knights in the days of old, Keeping watch on the mountain height, Came a vision of Holy Grail, And a voice through the waiting night." Some of the chunks of brick, really quite large, came flying through the window.

Dora Mae, of course, had terrible brothers, the Buford boys, and a reputation to live up to—was that it? No, she was just bad, the older teachers in the higher grades would say at recess, sitting on the steps in warm weather or crossing the street for a Coke at the little cabin-size sandwich shop.

"I've got two years before I get Dora Mae," said Miss Martingale.

"Just think," said Mrs. Henry, "I've got four Bufords in my upstairs study hall. At once."

"I've had them already, all but one," said Miss Carlisle. "I've just about graduated."

"I wish they weren't so funny," said Miss Jackson, and then they all began to laugh. They couldn't finish their Cokes for laughing.

Among the exploits of Dora Mae's brothers, there always came to mind the spring day one of them brought a horse inside the school house just before closing bell, leading it with a twist of wire fastened about its lower lip and releasing it to wander right into study hall alone while the principal, Mr. Blackstone, was dozing at his desk.

The thing was, in school, everybody's mind was likely to wander, and the minute it did wander, something would be done to you by a

Buford, and you would never forget it. The world you were dozing on came back with a whoosh and a bang; but it was not the same world you had dozed away from, nor was it the one you intended to wake up to or even imagined to be there. Something crazy was the matter with it: a naked horse, unattended, was walking between the rows of seats; or (another day altogether) a little girl was holding her reader up in the air between her feet, her head and shoulders having vanished below desk level, perhaps forever. Had there actually been some strange accident? Were you dreaming? Or were things meant to be this way? That was the part that just for a minute could scare you.

The Bufords lived in a large, sprawled-out, friendly house down a road nobody lived on but them. The grass was never completely cut, and in the fall the leaves never got raked. Somebody once set fire to a sagebrush pasture near their house–one of *them* had done it, doubtless –and the house was threatened, and there were Bufords up all night, stamping the earth and scraping sparks out of the charred fence posts and throwing water into chicken wallows, just in case the fire started again.

When any of the teachers went there to call, as they occasionally had to do, so that the family wouldn't get mad at the extraordinary punishment meted out to one of the children at school–Mr. Blackstone once was driven to give Billy Buford a public whipping with a buggy whip–or (another reason) to try to inform the family just how far the children were going with their devilment and to implore moral support, at least, in doing something about it–when you went there, they all came out and greeted you. They made you sit in a worn wicker rocking chair and ran to get you something–iced tea or lemonade or a Coke, cake, tea cakes, or anything they had.

Then they began to shout and holler and say how glad they were you'd come. They began to say, "Now tell the truth! Tell the truth, now! Ain't Billy Buford the worse boy you ever saw?" . . . "Did you ever see anybody as crazy as that Pete? Now tell me! Now tell the truth!" . . . "Confidentially, Miss Jackson, what on earth are we ever going to do with Dora Mae?"

And Dora Mae would sit and look at you, the whole time. She would sit on a little stool and put her chin on her hands and stare, and then you would say, "I just don't know, Mrs. Buford." And they would all look at you cautiously in their own Buford way, and then in the silence, when you couldn't, couldn't be serious, one of them would say, very quietly, "Ain't you ever going to eat your cake?"

It was like that.

There had once been something about a skunk that had upset not just the school but the whole town and that would not do to think about, just as it didn't do any good, either, to speculate on what might or could or was about to happen on this or any future Halloween.

Was it spring or fall? Dreaming, herself, in the lonely classroom with Dora Mae, Miss Jackson thought of chipmunks and skunks and toad-frogs, words written into themes on ruled paper, the lines of paper passing gradually across her brow and into her brain, until the fine ruling would eventually print itself there. Someday, if they opened her brain, they would find a child's theme inside. Even now she could often scarcely think of herself with any degree of certainty. Was she in love, was she falling in love, or getting restless and disappointed with whomever she knew, or did she want somebody new, or was she recalling somebody gone? Or: Had someone right come along, and she had said all right, she'd quit teaching and marry him, and now had it materialized or had it fallen through, or what?

Children! The Bufords existed in a haze of children and old people: old aunts, old cousins, grandfathers, friends and relatives by marriage of cousins, deceased uncles, family doctors gone alcoholic, people who never had a chance. What did they live on? Oh, enough of them knew how to make enough for everyone to feel encouraged. Enough of them were clever about money, and everybody liked them, except the unfortunate few who had to try to discipline them. A schoolteacher, for instance, was a sort of challenge. A teacher hung in their minds like the deep, softly pulsing, furry throat in the collective mind of a hound pack. They hardly thought of a teacher as human, you had to suppose. You could get your feelings hurt sadly if you left yourself open to them.

"Dora Mae, let's go," Miss Jackson suddenly said, way too early.

She had recalled that she had a date, but whether it was a spring date (with warm twilight air seeping into the car, filling the street and even entering the stale movie foyer—more excitement in the season than was left for her in this particular person) or whether it was a fall date (when the smell of her new dress brought out sharply by the gas heater she had to turn on in the late afternoon, carried with it the interest of somebody new and the lightness all beginnings have)—which it was, she had to think to say. At this moment, she had forgotten whether she was even glad or not. It was better to be going out with somebody than not; it gave a certain air, for one thing, to supper at the boardinghouse.

Even the regulars, the uptown widows and working wives and the old couples and the ancient widower who came to eat there, held themselves somewhat straighter and took some degree of pride in the matter of Miss Jackson's going out, as going out suggested a progress of sorts and put a tone of freshness and prettiness on things. It was a subject to tease and be festive about; the lady who ran the boardinghouse might even bring candles to light the table. In letting Dora Mae Buford out early, Miss Jackson was responding to that festiveness; she thought of the reprieve as a little present.

She recalled what she had told a young man last year, or maybe the year before, just as they were leaving the movies after a day similar to this one, when she had had to keep another Buford in, how she had described the Bufords to him, so that she got him to laugh about them, too, and how between them they had decided there was no reason, no reason on earth, for Bufords to go to school at all. They would be exactly the same whether they went to school or not. Nothing you told them soaked in; they were born knowing everything they knew; they never changed; the only people they really listened to were other Bufords.

"But I do sometimes wonder," Miss Jackson had said, trying hard to find a foothold that had to do with "problems," "personality," "psychology," "adjustment," all those things she had taken up in detail at teachers' college in Nashville and thought must have a small degree of truth in them—"I wonder if some people don't just feel obligated to be bad."

"There's something in that," the young man had answered. (He had said this often, come to think of it: a good answer to everything.)

Now the child trudged along beside Miss Jackson across the campus. Miss Jackson looked down affectionately; she wanted a child of her own someday—though hardly, she thought (and almost giggled), one like this. It went along on chunky legs and was shaped like cutout paper-doll children you folded the tabs back to change dresses for. Its face was round, its brow raggedly fringed with yellow bangs. Its hands were plump—meddlesome, you'd say on sight. It wore scuffed brown shoes and navy-blue socks and a print dress and carried an old nubby red sweater slung over its books.

"Aren't you cold, Dora Mae?" said Miss Jackson, still in her mood of affection and fun.

"No, ma'am," said Dora Mae, who could and did answer directly at times. "I'm just tired of school."

Well, so am I sometimes, Miss Jackson thought, going home to bathe and dress in her best dress, and then go to the boardinghouse with the other teachers, where, waiting on the porch, if it was warm enough or in the hall if it was not, sitting or standing with hands at rest against the nice material of her frock, she would already be well over the line into her most private domain.

"I don't really like him all that much," she would have confided already–it was what she always said. "I just feel better, you know, when somebody wants to take me somewhere." All the teachers agreed that this was so; they were the same, they said.

What Miss Jackson did not say was that she enjoyed being Lelia. This was her secret, and when she went out, this was what happened: she turned into Lelia, from the time she was dressing in the afternoon until after midnight, when she got in. The next morning, she would be Miss Jackson again.

If it was a weekday.

And if it wasn't a weekday, then she might still feel like Miss Jackson, even on weekends, for they had given her a Sunday School class to teach whenever she stayed in town. If she went home, back fifty miles to the little town she was born in, she had to go to church there, too, and everybody uptown called her "Leel," a nickname. At home they called her "Sister," only it sounded more like Sustah. But Lelia was her name and what she wanted to be; it was what she said was her name to whatever man she met who asked to take her somewhere.

One day soon after she had kept Dora Mae Buford after school, she went back into the classroom from recess quite late, having been delayed at a faculty meeting, and Dora Mae was writing "LELIA-JACKSONLELIAJACKSONLELIAJACKSONLELIAJACKSON" over and over in capital letters on the blackboard. She had filled one board and had started on another, going like crazy. All the students were laughing at her.

It became clear to Miss Jackson later, when she had time to think about it, that the reason she became so angry at Dora Mae was that the child, like some diabolical spirit, had seemed to know exactly what her sensitive point was and had gone straight to it, with the purpose of ridiculing her, of exposing and summarizing her secret self in all its foolish yearning.

But at the moment she did not think anything. She experienced a flash of white-faced, passionate temper and struck the chalk from the child's hand. "Erase that board!" she ordered. A marvel she hadn't knocked her down, except that Dora Mae was as solid as a stump, and hitting her, Miss Jackson had almost sprained her wrist.

Dora Mae was shocked half to death, and the room was deadly still for the rest of the morning. Miss Jackson, so gentle and firm (though likely to get worried), had never before struck anyone.

Soon Dora Mae's mother came to see Miss Jackson, after school. She sat down in the empty classroom, a rather tall, dark woman with a narrow face full of slanted wrinkles and eyes so dark as to be almost pitch black, with no discernible white area to them. Miss Jackson looked steadfastly down at her hands.

Mrs. Buford put a large, worn, bulging black purse on the desk before her, and though she did not even remove her coat, the room seemed hers. She did not mean it that way, for she spoke in the most respectful tone, but it was true. "It's really just one thing I wanted to know, Miss Jackson. Your first name is Lelia, ain't it?"

Miss Jackson said that it was.

"So what I mean is, when Dora Mae wrote what she did on the blackboard there, it wasn't nothing like a lie or something dirty, was it?"

"No," said Miss Jackson. "Not at all."

"Well, I guess that's about all I wanted to make sure of."

Miss Jackson did not say anything, and Mrs. Buford finally inquired whether she had not been late coming back to the room that day, when Dora Mae was found writing on the board. Miss Jackson agreed that this was true.

"Churen are not going to sit absolutely still if you don't come back from recess," said Mrs. Buford. "You got to be there to say, 'Now y'all get out your book and turn to page so-and-so.' If you don't they're bound to get into something. You realize that? Well, good! Dora Mae's nothing but a little old scrap. That's all she is."

"Well, I know," said Miss Jackson, feeling very bad.

At this point, Mrs. Buford, alone without any of her children around her, must have got to thinking about them all in terms of Dora Mae; she began to cry.

Miss Jackson understood. She had seen them all, her entire class, heads bent at her command, pencils marching forward across their tablets, and her heart had filled with pity and love.

Mrs. Buford brushed her tears away. "You never meant it for a minute. Anybody can get aggravated, don't you know? You think I can't? I can and do!" She put her handkerchief back in her purse and, straightening her coat, stood up to go. "So, I'm just going right straight and say you're sorry about it and you never meant it."

"Oh," said Miss Jackson, all of a sudden, "but I did mean it. It's true I'm sorry. But I did mean it." Her statement, softly made, threw a barrier across Mrs. Buford's path, like bars through the slots in a fence gap.

Mrs. Buford sat back down. "Miss Jackson, just what have we been sitting here deciding?"

"I don't know," said Miss Jackson, wondering herself. "Nothing that I know of."

"Nothing! You call that nothing?"

"Call what nothing?"

"Why, everything you just got through saying."

"But what do you think I said?" Miss Jackson felt she would honestly like to know. There followed a long silence, in which Miss Jackson, whose room this after all was, felt impelled to stand up. "It's not a good thing to lose your temper. But everyone does sometimes, including me."

Mrs. Buford rose also. "Underneath all that fooling around, them kids of mine is pure gold." Drawn to full height, Mrs. Buford became about twice as tall as Miss Jackson.

"I know! I know that! But you say yourselves—" began Miss Jackson. She started to tremble. Of all the teachers in the school, she was the youngest, and she had the most overcrowding in her room. "Mrs. Buford," she begged, "do please forget about it. Go on home. Please, please go home!"

"You pore child," said Mrs. Buford, with no effort still continuing and even expanding her own authority. "I just never in my life," she added, and left the room.

She proceeded across the campus the way all her dozen or so children went, down toward their lonely road—a good, strong, sincere woman, whose right shoulder sagged lower than the left and who did not look back. From the window, Miss Jackson watched her go.

Uptown a lady gossip was soon to tell her that she was known to have struck a child in a fit of temper and also to have turned out the child's mother when she came to talk about it. Miss Jackson wearily agreed that this was true. She could feel no great surprise, though her sense of despair deepened when one of the Buford boys, Evan, older and long out of school, got to worrying her—calling up at night, running his car behind her on the sidewalk uptown. It seemed there were no lengths he wouldn't go to, no trouble he wouldn't make for her.

When the dove season started, he dropped her. He'd a little rather shoot doves than me, she thought, sitting on the edge of the bed in her room, avoiding the mirror, which said she must be five years older. It's my whole life that's being erased, she thought, mindful that Dora Mae and two of her brothers, in spite of all she could do, were inexorably failing the fourth grade. She got up her Sunday School lesson, washed her hair, went to bed, and fell asleep disconsolate. . . .

Before school was out, the Bufords invited Miss Jackson for Sunday dinner. Once the invitation had come—which pleased her about as much as if it had been extended by a tribe of Indians, but which she had to accept or be thought of as a coward—it seemed inevitable to her that they would do this. It carried out to a T their devious and deceptively simple-looking method of pleasing themselves, and of course what she might feel about it didn't matter. But here she was dressing for them, trying to look her best.

The dinner turned out to be a feast. She judged it was no different from their usual Sunday meal—three kinds of meat and a dozen spring vegetables, hot rolls, jams, pickles, peaches, and rich cakes, freshly baked and iced.

The house looked in the airiest sort of order, with hand-crocheted white doilies sprinkled about on the tables and chairs. The whole yard was shaggy with flowers and blooming shrubs; the children all were clean and neatly dressed, with shoes on as well, and the dogs were turned firmly out of doors.

She was placed near Mr. Tom Buford, the father of them all, a tall, spare man with thick white hair and a face burned brick-brown from constant exposure. He plied her ceaselessly with food, more than she could have eaten in a week, and smiled the gentle smile Miss Jackson by now knew so well.

Halfway down the opposite side of the table was Evan Buford, she at last recognized, that terrible one, wearing a spotless white shirt, shaved and spruce, with brown busy hands, looking bland and even handsome. If he remembered all those times he had got her to the phone at one and two and three in the morning, he wasn't letting on. ("Thought you'd be up grading papers, Miss Jackson! Falling down on the job?" . . . "Your family live in Tupelo? Well, the whole town got blown away in a tornado! This afternoon!") Once, in hunting clothes, his dirt-smeared, unshaven face distorted by the rush of rain on his muddy windshield, he had pursued her from the post office all the way home, almost nudging her off the sidewalk with his front fender, his wheels spewing water from the puddles all over her stockings and raincoat, while she walked resolutely on, pretending not to notice.

From way down at the foot of the table, about half a mile away, Dora Mae sat sighting at her steadily through a water glass, her eyes like the magnified eyes of insects.

"'Possum hunting!" Mr. Tom Buford was saying, carving chicken and ham with a knife a foot long, which Miss Jackson sometimes had literally to dodge. "That's where we all went last night. Way up on the ridge. You like 'possum, Miss Jackson?"

"I never had any," Miss Jackson said.

Right from dinner they all went to the back yard to see the 'possum, which had been put in a cage of chicken wire around the base of a small pecan tree. It was now hanging upside down by its tail from a limb. She felt for its helpless, unappetizing shapelessness, grizzly gray, with a long snout, its sensitive eyes shut tight, its tender black petal-like ears alone perceiving, with what terror none could know though she could guess, the presence of its captors.

"Don't smell very good, does it?" Billy Buford said. "You like it, Miss Jackson? Give it to you, you want it." He picked up a stick to punch it with.

She shook her head. "Oh, I'd just let it go back to the woods. I feel sorry for it."

The whole family turned from the creature to her and examined her as if she were crazy. Billy Buford even dropped the stick. There followed one of those long, risky silences.

As they started to go inside, Evan Buford lounged along at her elbow. He separated her out like a heifer from the herd and cornered her before a fence of climbing roses. He leaned his arm against a fence post, blocking any possible escape, and looked down at her with wide, speculative, bright brown eyes. She remembered his laughing mouth behind the car wheel that chill, rainy day, careening after her. Oh, they never got through, she desperately realized. Once they had you, they held on—if they didn't eat you up, they kept you for a pet.

"Now, Miss Jackson, how come you to fail those kids?"

Miss Jackson dug her heels in hard. "I didn't fail them. They failed themselves. Like you might fail to hit a squirrel, for instance."

"Well, now. You mean they weren't good enough. Well, I be darned." He jerked his head. "That's a real good answer."

So at last, after years of trying hard, she had got something across to a Buford, some one little thing that was true. Maybe it had never happened before. It would seem she had stopped him cold. It would seem he even admired her.

"Missed it like a squirrel!" he marveled. "The whole fourth grade They must be mighty dumb," he reflected, walking along with her toward the house.

"No, they just don't listen," said Miss Jackson.

"Don't listen," he said after her with care, as though to prove that he, at least, did. "You get ready to go, I'll drive you to town, Miss Jackson. Your name is Lelia, ain't it?"

She looked up gratefully. "That's right," she said.

JUDITH KANE

It must have been Thursday when I first came to Mrs. Holloway's and certainly it was June. It had to be Thursday because the first three days of the week I was busy working for that professor, typing his thesis notes, checking his sources, and keeping his office in order. It wasn't Friday because I wanted to settle in my new quarters before the weekend, when somebody might ask me to the movies or a party or something. I know absolutely that it was June, because that was when the summer term began at the university. Since my dormitory had closed for lack of students to stay in it, I had to find somewhere off campus to stay.

A Thursday in June. Sometime in the late 'thirties. Money was all-important. A dollar was a dollar. The professor I worked for was paying me, and by working hard on my own I could get a couple of courses ticked off and my family wouldn't have to keep me in school quite so long. Times were hard and everyone had to work to get ahead. My education had to be given me somehow, but I must understand that because of it my sisters were going around in hand-me-down clothes, the house needed a coat of paint, and the fence was falling down. I knew it all, in all its earnest truth and rightness, and had willingly put my nineteen-year-old girl-shoulder to the wheel where it belonged; yet I was sulky, too. In those pre-war days, going to summer school was something between a reformatory sentence and having to get a job as a waitress.

Having paid the cab, I stood on the curb for a good long minute or so in my limp dirndl skirt and white blouse, dirty from moving things out of the dormitory closet, with suitcases beside me on the grass along with grocery store cartons filled with odds and ends, coat hangers tied together by the hooks, my old rag doll, and patchwork pillows stuffed around some books on the English Renaissance. It was afternoon and the sun was straight in my eyes as I shielded my face with one hand and looked at the house I was coming to take a room in, a large three-story white frame house with verandas and balconies, turret and shade tree, holes neatly bored in every step to let the rain water through, and wrought-iron foot scraper clamped to the floor right by the fresh hemp door mat. Mrs. Holloway's house on Knowlton Place.

The maid let me in, helping me get everything upstairs, trudging good-naturedly with me time after time through the hot front yard into the cooler interior where I was cheered by a renewed vision of built-in columned fireplace with mirror set above, glassed-in bookcases in dark-stained oak, dark-bannistered staircase with a creaking step or two, and a cool pitcher of lemonade set out on the landing. I had remembered all this from the time I came to see the room and take it; now I found it all the same. I sat on the bed in my small front room before unpacking, comforted by the hominess of Mrs. Holloway's. A breeze blew through the windows, which overlooked the street. It touched my hot brow and damp hair.

It's better than the dormitory, I thought. *There could be worse places, even if I don't want to go to summer school.*

A door must have closed in the hallway behind me, but I didn't hear it. My own door was open, and I felt a presence behind me and turned around with a start.

"Just moved in?"

Looks like it, I would have cracked to anybody I knew. Instead, I nodded politely, then did a real double take. The girl who was standing there was somebody I knew and had known for a long time. She didn't know me at all. The only reason I knew her was the same reason everybody knew her; she was so beautiful, tall and put together like a Greek statue, with corn-silk hair brushed back and hanging or drawn up in a swirl behind. The boys all talked about her for obvious reasons, admiring her and wishing they had a chance to date her and all; and the girls all wanted to look like her. Now, there she stood, at closer range than I had ever seen her, in a loose blue housecoat, just out of the shower, with the air of someone who had been in this house a long time.

"Judith Kane!" I said. "I didn't know you lived here."

"I thought I was going to be alone all summer," she said. "Everybody left but me."

"You just about will be," I said, "except on weekends. I've got so much work to do I expect I may even have to sleep in the library."

"I used to work there," she said, "after I graduated."

"What do you do now?" I asked, after telling her my name and who I worked for. I was hardly conscious of what words I was using, her looks were so astonishing. I know all this about how they say Southern girls are so pretty and how they come pouring out of little towns and from way up in the hills to get elected Miss Pickle Queen and Miss Watermelon Queen, Miss Centennial Year, Miss America, Maid of Cotton, Miss Universe, and so on. All true, but not all that interesting. Nothing of this related to Judith Kane. She wasn't cute or pretty, her measurements weren't for contests or advertising copy, but for aesthetics; she was, simply, a creation.

"Do?" she repeated. "Not much of anything, I guess. That's just the trouble. Welcome, anyway. I'd help you unpack but don't have time."

The reason she didn't have time was because she had a date. I soon heard the front door close and by going to the window to look could see her go off across the street with a lean, sandy-haired guy, who moved out beside her to where a blue-green Pontiac convertible stood shimmering beside the curb. The doors went *chunk* and *chunk* and the car accelerated silently like a lioness which has sighted the prey. Judith's white shoes, her lime-green summer dress and scrolled-up hair, made me feel the way I looked, tired and unattractive. I had sat brooding the whole time she was dressing. Whoever came to take me somewhere, any fool could plainly see, was bound to get interested in her. I felt I had no looks or clothes or any asset to hold a candle to hers. Personally speaking, the prospects of this summer didn't give me a lot to rave about.

But, as the days went by, I saw I had been hasty, at least as regards Judith Kane.

Judith was twenty-four, that was the first thing to cheer me. Though to admit to being that old seemed a shame, she evidently didn't mind, for Mrs. Holloway knew it and told me. "Not that it's any of my business," she said, giving me my mail. "All I wonder is what's she still doing around here, not going to school or anything." The boys who came around sometimes on weekends to take me to the movies seemed able to survive the sight of her after all. One said she was a knockout all right, and let it go at that; another said he'd heard she was expensive. She was friendly with them in a harmless, open way, and might run up from the basement in an old skirt with a scarf around her head and some warm ironing over her arm, making no effort to please anybody. She told me once in passing that boys without money were of no interest to her. I guess the boy with that Pontiac must have had financial resources, all right. Seen close to, I found him not so much attractive as well turned-out. The possession of the right articles meant a lot to him—you could tell that by the way he opened the car door—and Judith said he had good taste. Once he brought her a bottle of champagne and they sat down on Mrs. Holloway's front porch in the swing drinking it. She poured out some in a fruit juice glass from the kitchen and ran upstairs to give it to me. "It's champagne," she said. "Take some." I was under a reading lamp, bent over a book with my hair in pins. *This is not the way to drink champagne,* I thought, and finished it off like Alka-Seltzer. The boy's name was Grant Exum, I now remember, and somebody in summer school mentioned him one day, again in connection with his car, which was the fanciest thing around, and further said that he wanted to marry Judith Kane, but his parents wouldn't let him marry anybody till he finished law school. "Money families," whoever was telling this remarked, "are always bossy. Po' folks are a whole lot easier." The memory drifts back after so many years: sitting out gossiping in a group on the library steps, with sun glossing the empty summer campus, far and wide.

I then concluded that Judith stayed around on account of Grant Exum, holding a job downtown in a small branch library which, with summer hours, took up scarcely half her time. It could not have paid her very much or interested her very much. In the afternoons I came in from work, toiling up the stairs to my room. She would generally have been home for an hour or so, and would be reading out in the corridor, where a breeze drew, smoking a cigarette with her hair up, or sometimes sipping some of Mrs. Holloway's lemonade. She seldom said anything, and often never even looked up: it was rather like passing a garden statue, and it became disconcerting only when she did speak. To hear "Hi, there" or "How's it going?" was almost as startling as her first appearance had been. She read T. S. Eliot, Auden,

Mann, Proust—a lot of highbrow things—with concentration, paying that close sort of attention that does not seem to have enjoyment or future conversation anywhere in mind, the matter being more urgent than that. I was in literature, too, but might as well have been analyzing Tennessee rain water for all she would care to talk to me about. But I finally came to realize, the first couple of weeks having gone by like this, that Judith Kane's life, like her extraordinary looks, was no more to me than Mrs. Holloway's, or the house which had somehow managed to absorb both of them into it; for, if the downstairs with its starched antimacassars and glass-front bookshelves and sanded-glass ornaments belonged to Mrs. Holloway, the upstairs—white-curtained, smooth, simple, immaculate, and quiet—had long been Judith's and hers was the rocking chair that I, finding it empty in the hallway, dropped into one afternoon when I arrived home early from work.

The heat was severe that summer. I watched the white curtains swell and thought that I was tired thinking of anything that came out of books or went into them. I thought I would be glad to think of nothing, for one whole year at least. But all I had ahead were a few free weeks in August and September before the round began again. And there was still some of July and August yet to go.

I heard Judith come in, stop for the mail, and start upstairs, and I lingered, rocking and comfortable in the afternoon breeze, before getting up to go to my room and give her favorite place to her, as obviously I had no business there. But rounding the landing and seeing me, she made a gesture that indicated I should stay where I was, and as a further surprise, sat down on the edge of the cot Mrs. Holloway kept out in the hallway and offered me a cigarette, lighting one for herself. She had on a white linen dress with sea horses worked on the front in dark brilliant thread. I never saw a dress like it, before or since.

"Do you want to hear a story?" she began. "I feel I've just got to tell somebody, I don't know why. It happened last spring—you won't tell? That's a stupid thing to ask. What I mean is, if you tell, get it right and don't make it sound silly."

The remark revealed nothing so much as how she thought of me—not me so much personally, I believed, as girls of my average sort—but being curious, I decided not to object. At that point I would have listened to anyone's story, to anything at all that didn't come out of a book.

It had happened one early morning back in the spring, before I had moved in. There were only some elderly ladies across from her, now graduated from a teachers' college nearby and gone back to wherever they came from, no one in the front rooms but an occasional overnight guest. Judith had been standing in her own room at the window looking down on the little garden of the tall brown house next door, wearing nothing and brushing her hair. It was then she felt suddenly drawn, compelled, to look up instead of down and saw in the attic window above a young man leaning close to the glass and watching her. He was sprawled face down on a bed or bunk and his face wore the expression of one who breathes the air of paradise. She had the distinct feeling that he was exactly where he always spent this hour of the morning, had been there not once, not twice or a dozen times, but morning after morning for perhaps a year, perhaps for the entire three years she had lived there.

"But do you always," I asked her, "stand there without any clothes on and brush your hair? Even in the winter?"

"I guess I do, quite a lot. Yes, I hadn't thought of it so much—but I did for a long time make a habit of it. I don't go near that window now, and as he saw me look up that time he hasn't been back either—at least, I've never seen him. I've not seen him even on this street again since that day."

"Well, who is he?" I asked her. "Did you recognize him?"

To me this all seemed rather funny and I almost laughed, but at this point she became terribly serious and tried twice to go on but her voice, so much in control ordinarily that it seemed a cool comment on anything that could possibly be brought up, like a water sprinkler passing over a lawn, faded out twice when she tried to speak. She essayed another cigarette, but her hands shook so violently, she had to give up.

"I saw him today." She finally got it out. Her anguish at this point was so intense it got across to me something of the force the experience had had for her. I began to feel uneasily that I might have done better to stick to books.

"I've got to tell somebody," she went on. "I've felt for months that I was losing my mind. I couldn't see myself in a psychiatrist's office; in the first place, can't afford it. I began to see that boy's face everywhere

—car hops, movie ushers, students on the bus, taxi drivers—for a while, every face could make me look at it at a certain distance, but once the distance lessened and it wouldn't be that face, after all, I would get a sick dizzy feeling, and wild . . . wild!" She laughed. "There was a shoe clerk once. . . . But it's no use remembering them all. A lot of stupid pickups, when they noticed. Somebody to get rid of."

"But," I said, though I hesitated to become practical, "wouldn't it have been simple just to go next door and ask who the boy was—or maybe get somebody to do it for you?"

She hardly heard me, remarking after a long silence, "I did go there once. Nobody was in, but the door was open. So I went all the way upstairs, up to the attic. There's only that one room plus a nightmarish kind of storage place, trunks and old pictures, a box full of tennis stuff, a rack of old dresses and suits. He isn't there any more, nobody is. Nobody saw me. I went there and came back here and then wondered if I dreamed it all. I wondered if I was dreaming when I came back and was actually still up in that attic. And next I wondered if I were both places and could look down at myself, in my own room."

"Good Lord," I said, and saw there wasn't any end to thoughts like that. "But you saw him. You said you met him today."

"He crossed the street by the grill and I was coming out, so we met."

"Then what happened?"

"His name is Yancey Clements. He teaches swimming and gym at the Y. On weekends he keeps the desk there. Sometimes he works at a high school gym over in the east of the city. He used to be a paper boy."

At the end of this recital, I broke out laughing, but she did not hear me laugh. She had turned pale and her make-up seemed to be too strong for her face. Crazy as it all might sound to me, it had succeeded in stirring her as ordinary things did not.

"So did you talk to him?" I asked.

"Oh, he knew right away why I stopped him. I felt he understood everything in a minute, even before I spoke or got across the street with him. He said he'd moved from that house. I think he decided to move the day I looked up. Then he said he wouldn't see me."

"So that finishes that," I said.

"It doesn't finish anything. Why do you think that? I begged him. Indeed I did. Finally, he gave in. He's going to have a drink with me, tonight, and we'll talk, something will happen to break it up for me. I've got to break it up, you see. It's got into everything."

She had wandered nervously about the cot, and had reached the pair of windows through which the breeze was now blowing more strongly. The white sheer curtains, standing out, blew around her, and she looked hectic and for the first time I thought this house could not really contain her, a big friendly old comfortable innocent house like this. She was threatening it already, and had been for a long time.

Singular though it was, I for some reason did not mention this conversation to anyone for a time, nor did I receive any further confidence from Judith. I did not for one thing, see her, even in passing. At the weekend she went off early with the law student in the Pontiac and did not reappear till Monday.

When I finally talked about her, it was to a graduate student named Scott Crawford—older even than twenty-four, I guess—who worked near me in the library and sometimes asked me over to the grill for coffee, or across from the campus to a café for a beer. This time, evening being nearly on us, it was across the street we went, and that was how I happened to come out with it all. It would have been surprising if I hadn't, though, for I had been confiding just about everything I had on my mind to Scott Crawford, for about a year now, and he talked a lot to me too, seeming to enjoy it, for we used to laugh a lot together.

"So what happened when she saw him?" he asked me.

"Well, I don't know yet," I said.

"It's funny your telling me," he said.

"Well," I said, "I knew you knew her slightly."

"Slightly! What gave you that impression? I used to go with her."

"I didn't know that."

"I was never so in love in my life."

"I didn't know that either," I said.

"I know you didn't, or you wouldn't have mentioned her current problem, I don't think. At least, not in the way you did, like a curious thing. It is a curious thing. But once you understand her tendencies, then it gets pretty clear. She broke everything off with me. Reason? She couldn't see herself as a professor's wife in some pokey little college town. She has this idea about herself, about her own image. Being intelligent and looking like that, I guess you think it's just a happy miracle. Well, maybe it ought to be a happy miracle, but how is she not to realize it? And realizing it, how is she not to ask herself the main question: What's good enough? What's great enough? What could possibly be good or great enough for Judith Kane? Not that she'd come right out with it, nothing blunt or corny. But if she doesn't say it to herself, she's letting the mirror say it, forty times a day. Do I think she was right to give me up? Sure, I think she was right. I agree with her."

I had to grin a little because he said this last in the self-amused way he had, half-bitterness, half-gaiety, that made him engaging and showed his intelligence to me much more than the doctor's dissertation he was slaving over, trying to get it done before school was out, so he could qualify for a higher salary somewhere. I would probably never read it anyway. Scott Crawford smoked a pipe and carried masses of stuff around with him, to stoke it and clean it and light it and so on. He worked on this pipe as hard as some men work on cars. Picking all his junk off the table took about five minutes at the least, and during all this time he thought steadily on about the state of affairs at Mrs. Holloway's.

I, meantime, thought on about him, about what I knew of him, that is. He lived near the East Campus, two blocks over toward the park, in an apartment with thin walls and sprung furniture. His wife was rather pretty but had begun to look tired of the life there. Her heart was set on having a house someday. He sometimes asked a few of us over to have a beer and talk about things. The baby had cried with a heat rash the last time I was there. That was June, I remembered, thinking it must by now be about melted away like a snail, but he said it was all right. That he was attractive, everyone agreed; though that he was completely unconcerned about it, all could see. He was respected by the faculty, and I once overheard a professor say that he had a classical, unsentimental mind. He spoke with a harsh, backcountry R, almost like a Yankee, and this gave a clean, intellectual turn to his speech, and drew the kind of attention to it that clarity always commands.

That night, when we got out on the street where the evening was still coming slowly on through the lingering heat from pavement and grass, I could sense the direction of his thoughts, like seeing the segment of a path. "No good will come of it," he said, and shook himself together for going back to the library and getting down to his grind. As we approached a parting of ways within the library foyer, he threw an arm around me. "Look, honey, you find out what happened, hear?"

I didn't say I would or wouldn't, just ran up the steps away from him, wishing I'd never mentioned Judith Kane. Had she confided in me because she had learned somehow that I knew Scott Crawford? I wondered. Whether the answer was yes or no, I just was not going to go into it any further, just as I was not going to conclude that Scott had married his wife Ruth on the rebound, or let it interest me in the least that he was never going to be really happy now. Having been so terribly, gorgeously, deeply in love with Judith. What business was it of mine? I had wasted time over there talking and would have to work till ten instead of nine. I ran down the hall to plunge into a mass of stacked-up carbons on onionskin with footnotes two thirds the way up every page, and ran smack into my professor, who had come back over for a book.

"What's the matter with you?" he asked.

"Nothing," I said, breathing beer upon him, without a doubt.

"Must be good," he said, an automatic phrase. He never really noticed anything that wasn't down in print.

What he was working on was a treatise on Hawthorne's ideas of good and evil. He kept me working along with him to verify footnotes and I had to wade through a lot of old musty New England sermons, too, copying out parts that might have some bearing on his train of thought. The odd thing was that this man seemed so mild and inattentive—he could never get my name straight—I wondered if he ever would have thought there was any such thing as good and evil if he hadn't come across the words in books. Ideas did excite him, though. He once came in just bursting with something which had come to him while walking past the grill, namely, that the great white squid in *Moby Dick* might have been deliberately used by Melville to symbolize love and goodness, just as the white whale was nemesis and evil. He was heatedly explaining this to me, and I couldn't help but think what his wife had to listen to while cooking supper. "A squid?" I said. "You mean those awful things like octopuses?" It sort of took the wind out of his sails, putting it that way.

I chose to ignore Scott Crawford's request to check up on Judith Kane. Wouldn't that have made me more of a go-between than ever? I didn't want to be one.

Then one late middle of the night I woke and couldn't sleep, the heat was so intense and not a breath of air was stirring. The sheet stuck to my back, and I could hear the tap drip from the kitchen downstairs, and somewhere way off a motor grinding, trying to start on a rundown battery. I got up to run water over my wrists and put a wet cloth on the back of my neck and do all the other little things they cheerfully advise in the newspaper columns when you're stifling to death, and when I went through the hall past the cot and rocking chair there sat Judith, smoking.

"Sit down," she said. "We'll whisper. Have a cigarette."

"It's not only too hot to smoke; it's too hot to breathe," I said.

"True," she said, lighting a fresh one off the stub.

"So what happened?" I asked her. "Did you see the gym teacher?"

"He didn't come. I looked him up the next day at the Y and he just got angry. He said he didn't come because he didn't want to."

"So he was just a peeper and starer, after all," I said. Why couldn't she stop it?

"I don't believe it," she answered at once, with the quickness of anger, or fear. "I don't believe that for a minute."

"But isn't he a lot younger than–" I paused, "younger than we are?"

"Oh, sure." She laughed in a hushed clear way, and seemed in such a perfectly good humor with herself I couldn't think but that another person was suffering like this somewhere and she was describing it all. "I wasn't considering matrimony," she said. "He knows how I feel; he knows it all. He just doesn't care. He saw me as I am, and he does not care. It's all I can hear, all the time. A voice inside, on a record as big as the moon. Would you like to live like that?"

"I'd stop it," I said. "Shut it off."

"How?"

"Just do it," I said. "Do it anyway."

"I can't," she said. "I just can't."

She did look, even in the dark, terribly thin. She had begun to look like a *Vogue* model. I asked then if she still had her job–she said she had given it up. I wondered what she was living on, but guessed she hadn't eaten anything in days and did nothing but smoke, read, and drink lemonade. The law student had called about a million times, but she never would come to the phone, and even he had given up. She made me think there must be times when the world is separated from yourself with something like a wall of glass that you cannot find a foothold on, and what if the key to the one gate in it is in the possession of something which calls itself Yancey Clements and works at the Y?

"Just to talk to him would make me feel better," she said, in a calmer tone. "He won't even do that. I'm a mass of neuroses," she laughed, "and everything I do or think is in a world by itself and can't get out."

"Maybe you ought to just try going out and eating a lot of good food," I suggested. "Starting with breakfast in the morning."

She seemed to give me up, and snuffing out her final cigarette, wadding the pack for hurling in the wastebasket, she started back to her room. "What's it to you?" she asked, good-humoredly, as always. "What should it be to you?"

Her door closed, and I had never once mentioned Scott Crawford. I had clammed up dead to the world around his name.

The next morning Mrs. Holloway stopped me at the door. She wanted to know what on earth was the matter with Judith. Was she sick? If so, why not see a doctor? She had taken her chance, when Judith was in the bath one day, to peek into that room, and could hardly see anything through smoke so thick it looked like a gambling house. There were choked ash trays islanded around and shoals of books, and the bed looked to have had a wild cat in it. I said I didn't know anything about it, I was always working. But I had heard the mounting anxiety in her voice and knew her mild, widowed world was being shaken, trembling like a great big web that's all carefully worked out to hold in every part. Next thing the house would shake, for they'd be at each other in some final way.

After lunch I went over to the Y and asked for Yancey Clements. They said he wasn't working there right now but was out doing some sort of gym teaching or other in a high school in the east of the city. That was how I happened to be on the bus in the early afternoon heat riding to a strange part of town where they had, miraculously, tiny friendly houses with small front yards, small plots of flowers, windows open, radios going. How nice, I kept thinking. How nice it is.

The high school, a large, dark brick building, was summer-empty. From the gym, way out in the back wing, I heard somebody bouncing a basketball. There was the usual acrid smell, the deep thumbed-book smells, chalk, blackboards, erasers, and floor polish smells, but all breathed over and subdued by summer, and back near the gym door, overriding everything, were the sweat smells of basketball uniforms, along with the sound of the ball spanking harder and harder in the silence of the building. I was sure the boy with the basketball would turn out to be Yancey Clements, but I was wrong.

He was only a stringy high school boy in a moth-eaten red jersey and blue trunks too big for him, whamming the ball at the floor as though he'd never done another thing in his life. I thought I would have to go and take the ball away from him to get his attention, but he finally looked up. "I'm looking for Yancey Clements," I said, or shouted, over the sound of the ball. "Is he here, or not?" The boy jerked his head. Then Yancey himself stepped out of a small dark doorway that led back of the stands into the lockers, beyond a doubt.

I knew right away this really was Yancey because I had seen him, I now realized, from time to time at the hamburger place near the Y. He must have just showered and dressed because he had on a pair of old cotton trousers and a clean white shirt. He was blond with a shock of hair that came up like a rooster's comb, and he had a very funny face, with protuberant teeth that crossed each other in front, a high bridged nose, and gray-blue eyes. He was absolutely humorless and he came straight to me before I could speak and said, "Don't think I don't know why you're here."

Good Lord, I thought, *he thinks I'm after him, too.*

"Listen, you come over with me," he said. "I was just going for a Coke."

We crossed the street, which was empty, and sat down in the drugstore. He ordered Cokes for both of us, and when they came he stuck a pair of straws in his bottle, and then did the same for me, in the manner of one making an enormous concession, and behaving like a gentleman if it killed him. "I prefer a glass with ice in it," I almost said, but not wanting to throw him into a rage, I let it go.

"That girl is nuts," he said. "I don't care about seeing her. I told her that. I just don't care. She's beautiful, but she's nuts. Look at the trouble I've gone to. You think I like living over here? I couldn't stay over there and have her hanging around, that's a positive fact."

"But look," I said, "I'm sure she'd be different from what you think if you'd only talk to her. She might be reasonable and very sweet, and get over it all just over a Coke in the drugstore—like this, for instance. What harm would there be in trying? She laughs about it all herself," I added.

"Oh, she does?"

"You did start it," I said. "And now she feels awful. If only you were a little kind—"

"Kind!" He bit his lip stubbornly; he was nervous and tough, and no one should have said "kind" to him.

I rode back on the bus; I was the only person on it besides the bus driver and a colored maid who rode only four stops, and looked out the window the whole time, daydreaming. It was when we got on the long hill going from one side of the city to the other (and what with very little traffic at that hour of the afternoon, the bus went flying along, reeling, bounding and rattling over the rough uneven brick and asphalt) that all the colored beads began to fall off my hat. It was an old hat, and I had found it in the college office where I worked, having left it there after church last Easter. It was the only hat I owned; I had had it since high school. It was navy blue straw with a bunch of large vari-colored glass beads sewed on the band, and it went with everything and was never out of style and showed no age at all except that I had often in moments of stress reached up and twisted the wire which threaded the beads together, and I must undoubtedly have twisted it several times that day or else the wire had about died of old age, because every time the bus hit another bump in the road another bead fell off on the floor. They made a terrible racket rolling and tumbling around, and as the hill was steep, several rolled all the way down the aisle and up around the driver's feet. He stopped the bus at the bottom of the hill. "Listen, miss," he said, "do you want these things?"

"Well, no, I guess not," I said. It just seemed like too much trouble; and besides, how would I get them back on? He began to pick them up anyway.

"I thought at first you were throwing them," he said. "There were some kids in here, throwing some marbles the other day. One or two people tripped up on them. Them things," he said, "are worse'n banana peel, and if you think of old people and all . . ."

"I wasn't throwing anything," I said. "It was an accident."

That night I saw Scott Crawford, or rather he saw me. He came all the way over to my office in the library where I had to work that evening to make up for the afternoon.

"How is Judith?" he asked me. We had gone out to sit on the steps of the library by then, and it was a calm, full late summer night, so rich and sweet it wouldn't do to think too much about it. There were the low mountains outside the city, covered with heavy late summer green, and the long roads that went tilting through them, winding on forever.

"I don't want to hear about it any more," I said. "I don't want to talk about it. I've done the best I could." I told him about Yancey Clements.

"She's run up a blind alley and won't believe it," he said. "Can't you understand it? That minute she looked up and saw him watching, blank as a mirror, but as if a mirror could look back, admire, finally possess. . . ."

He had clenched his hand beside me in the dark and before I knew it, I had grasped it, trying to get the fingers open and relaxed. "I wish I'd never mentioned her," I said. "We always had such a good time till she got into everything. Why don't you just stop it?"

"Stop it?" He did unclench his hand, take mine, and give it an affectionate squeeze, which went through me deep and clear. But it was only affection; that was all. "Stop it how? How?"

She was almost present then, his thought of her had summoned her before us both, alive in the strong disaster of her looks, which his intelligence and wit and everything I admired about him could only multiply until she had wrapped him up in a million ways and drawn him endlessly down. She, too, he was saying, with fine logic, had fallen for herself; it was not Yancey Clements she wanted, only that the lightning stroke of his look had thrown her off-balance, maybe for good and all.

"If you don't stop it," I said, "it's just going to go on down forever, like the bottomless pit. Isn't it?"

At long last, he agreed. "You're right. I'm going to let it go." He got up and walked away, vanished into the night among the thick tree shadows. I wanted to run after him, had wanted to maybe for months now, but all this of Judith had trapped and denied my own feelings for him. They rose now, swept over me and fell; my heart ran after him, but I never moved at all. The words I might have said had all been taken.

He came to the house the next afternoon. I was upstairs working so did not see him on the street, and he must have just walked in without knocking, because no one challenged him or went to the door. I heard his first step down below and knew what had happened. The whole house knew it too, that ramified abode of women, women, women, over the long years. Turret to basement, it had needed this for a long time, that stride in the hall, that step on the stairs. Out in the upstairs corridor, I heard him blundering, trying one door after another, saying "Judith? Judith?" Then he found her. "Who?" she said, and then with a low cry, filled with surprise, opening toward joy, "Scott? Oh, Scott!" She must have risen then, out of her ruins, to go to him. I heard her stumble, fall and get up, or be lifted up by him.

Judith came to my room after he left. It was just at twilight. The spell was broken; as if to prove it, there had even been some rain. She had emerged at last, with new purpose, to bathe and dress, had put up her hair, got make-up on, stained her shoes fresh as chalk, and slipped into the lime-green dress, which hung on her limbs like a nightgown or a robe.

"You did it," she said, reflectively. "It was all because you talked to him about me, wasn't it? But one thing," she continued, leaning in the doorway. "One thing. You've got to understand it. I didn't know you knew him."

"It's a lie," I said. "A lie! You must have known, you had to know! You used me to make him come back. You can't deny it!"

She shook her lovely head; it was gaunt and rapacious now as some tall white bird, one with a great latent wingspread for long flight. Where would she lead him to, where would she drop him when she moved furiously on to some other high perch, to astonish and confound whoever found her there? My heart filled up with dread. For him, I guess; that was where the dread started, but it had a way of spreading: it was more than just for him.

"Don't look at me like that," she said, raising her hand uneasily to touch her hair. "Why are you looking that way?"

"How could he do it, come here, come to you, when he knows about Yancey Clements? You were ready to crawl to that awful boy, that peeper, that vile, stupid, no-account. . . ." I couldn't go on. But the questions forced themselves up anyway, kept rising to my lips. "Are they so much alike to you, you can't tell the difference? How could you want them both? How could you?"

Her head had snapped back, and her features strained to the force of my innocent words, as though I were striking her. I saw this, and stopped. In the silence (in which she could have turned and walked away but did not), I saw suddenly appear before my eyes identical streaks of tears from the corners of her eyes downward.

"I don't know," she whispered at last. "Oh, believe me, I don't know why."

I turned back to my work table, on which papers and books had been scrambled about and ink spilled, a great mess. "It's his most important time," I said. "Right at the end. Exams and all."

"You cared for him, didn't you?"

"Yes, but I . . ." I nodded, and with a strong, releasing sigh that shook me, confessed it. "Yes."

She melted from the threshold, vanished. She had taken that from me, too, I realized, had come for it and easily taken it, my one privacy. She had had to have it, and so had demanded it.

She went out shortly after, going toward whatever place he had said; bone-thin and swift, moving–inexorable, indifferent, and sublime –toward him, as he desired. I watched through the window till I could no longer see her, and only the empty street was there, lit by street lights.

WISTERIA

Charles Webley rather liked his hostess, though he imagined a lot of people didn't. She talked too much, for one thing, but then you didn't have to listen. Her voice was pleasing and made a soothing ripple of sound which broke in occasional laughter. At the moment she didn't mean to be taken seriously. She was hefty, to put it mildly, way too big by English standards. But, he thought, lazily tolerant, she was not overbearing, no Brünnehilde she, and one could always be reminded of the jolly Dutch women, in popular conception at least, with their butter-colored hair cut short and their rotund, softly elephantine, white limbs. But Evaline's hair, in the years since they had met, must have gone from blond to gray, or why would she have got it stiffly done up in what she probably thought of as silver gilt, but which looked to him like new aluminum? How, charitably, was he to picture her in Dutch clogs and a peaked cap now that her waistline had vanished? She was at present all baled up in Roman silks. He gave a short explosive laugh.

"Thought you'd like that, Charles." She had just wound up a little story, no word of which had reached him.

He wandered out into the garden. The apartment was on the ground floor, unusual in Rome, with a wisteria vine thickly roofing the terrace. Blooms like bunches of pale grapes hung down and grazed his tall head. One cluster, so disturbed, suddenly shed all its blossoms upon him. Lavender flowers fell from his head to his shoulders and scattered on the paving about his feet; and one final petal, letting go like the rest, landed in his martini. He stood regarding it, trying to grasp, hold on to, the surprising moment, generous and fragrant, which had created a sharp start in his breast, resembling love. He looked up for someone to share it with.

"Do you prefer flowers to lemon peel?"

The woman–not young, not old, thin, rather sallow, with large brown eyes, nondescript dark hair, a plain navy dress–was not the right one for that moment, nor had she said the right thing. She did not in any way amplify that tender instant, the heart of it, when the wisteria petal had actually touched the chill surface of the gin.

"I don't think that ever happened to me before," he said.

"I never saw it happen to anybody before."

"At my age you have to be careful about saying what's never happened. At your age you don't have to."

Her eyes acknowledged his compliment. "How long have you known Evaline?"

Wrong again, he thought, but saw the reason: she was shy, and knowing that, he had to answer, no matter how much questions like this bored him.

"Ages. I knew her first husband; the only one, I mean. We were in school together, kept crossing paths."

"What's he like?"

"Good sort. Pleasant." He got impatient. "Hell, what's anyone like?"

One of the doors opening out on the garden filled up to two thirds of its height and all its breadth, as Evaline herself emerged upon them.

"So glad you met Dorothy, Charles. She paints, you know. Would never tell you, so how could you know? I've one of her things in the guest room. You've got to see it before you go."

"Indeed I must."

The girl averted her face. There was a kind of subdued distaste in it, an aversion to being patronized, he supposed. If the painting had been put in the salon, instead of stuck away out of sight . . . As it was, why mention it at all? He experienced a sudden, genuine feeling for this girl after all. He could read her, as clear as anything. The maid was elsewhere, so Evaline herself was taking their glasses.

"So grand to see Charles again. Such a surprise when you rang. It really did give me a lift; you've no idea."

He agreed, and in a way really meant it. Whatever mix-ups and misunderstandings there had been in the past, back when she lived in

London, why remember them now? Why give any importance, at this late date, to the ins and outs of it all? Old friends were best because they didn't matter so much any more; it was all coasting from now on out, and there was downright comfort in the thought.

"I was lucky to find you in. I think of you Romans being always in motion, especially from May on. The mountains or the sea. Going off somewhere interesting."

"He's being absurd," Evaline explained to Dorothy. "No, if you must know, I'm here nearly all the time these days. You'll get out of me all the reasons why." She thus reminded him, as she turned away for the drinks, that he had invited her to dine with him that evening, so getting himself asked to one of her little cocktail gatherings beforehand. Evaline being charming and parceled out at one of her own parties was one thing; Evaline as she would shortly be across a narrow table from him, pouring out her various troubles, complexes, illnesses, labyrinthine relationships, was another. He couldn't count on just happening to laugh when she finished being witty, just happening to cloud over when the theme was tragic; that would be pushing his luck. No, he would have to listen.

"Listen," he said urgently to the girl. The pace of the chatter had stepped up in the room behind. The knots of guests were now mainly standing, except for a jet-haired Roman girl settled in an armchair with men hovering about her on hassocks and smaller chairs. Soon they would finish this round and take a notion to disperse, gather up hats and purses, go scattering out into the open.

"Listen." He caught the girl by the elbow and steered her aside, out of the central area of the garden, back turned toward the company. He noticed how light she was and how maneuverable. Her head turned to him with a sort of serene attentiveness, and he remembered the quiet fall of the blossoms.

"Do you know Evaline well?" It was a similar question to her own, but she had been making conversation; he was not.

"I've known her off and on for years. Five in all, I guess." She added, "She's been very kind to me."

"Oh, stop it." He almost snapped. "What I mean is, do you see her alone, and if so, does she confide in you? She must. She confides in everyone."

The girl nodded. "I've noticed that. A few times–yes, I would say she's been confidential." She risked something. "I don't like so much confidence."

"I know, I know. Italian lovers, money problems, quarrels, defections of friends . . ." Now he had got her with him, and she actually grinned. He continued, "Has she mentioned her husband?"

"Well, often—yes, I'd say very often, but always rather distantly. I long ago decided he must have been a myth."

"I'm having dinner with her, right after this, taking her out somewhere. Does she know? I keep asking myself. Does she know he's dead?"

"Good Lord, no! At least, I think not."

"Why?"

"Well, she'd have said. She'd have called up everybody, right away."

"I assumed she would have been told. But then he did marry again, and Rome is a long way off." He walked away with the girl at his elbow; they had really drifted now, apart from the gathering. "I came early to this party, for just that reason, to mention it, offer condolences, whatever people do. She never seemed aware of it. No opening of any kind. Yet it happened over a month ago, in London." He stared down at his feet in deep preoccupation, a business habit. "Well," he demanded of her, "what would you conclude?"

"I think that everybody must have thought that someone else had told her."

"Just as I have. Is that what you mean?"

"Yes. Just as you have."

They turned to find Evaline before them once more, their fresh drinks hospitably extended in either hand. "Here you are, you two." She was beaming upon them, but implicit in the smile was the knowledge that he was safely landed as her escort for the evening. The restaurant she would suggest was already selected. It would be nice to be seen with him. She could afford to pretend to Dorothy that, seeing the two of them alone out there, she had assumed a flirtation was in progress. Charles Webley and Dorothy dutifully took their glasses.

The predictable moment arrived. The guests were flowing out to say their good-bys, remarking on the wisteria, a choice conversation piece, and Evaline, full of a loving glow on its behalf, told the history of how it had been planted there, what narrow escapes it had had, what she had done to make it flourish and flower.

"They bloom twice, you know. Oh yes, indeed. Early, and late."

She saw she had gained the center of the party and was holding it. To make the most of it, she nudged the last phrase into a double meaning, as though it referred to women, to all women, herself especially. She then touched her hand to the gathered silks above her heart.

The party caught the idea and laughed gaily, as she had meant them to, and Charles Webley and the girl Dorothy involuntarily struck glances. All was said, framed and frozen, in that instant's communication, and as one they turned off in opposite ways.

A BAD COLD

The grated window overlooked a not very busy street, full this noon with weakened sunlight. He stood looking out of it to avoid looking at his two children, who kept coming in and out of the living room. He could not stand to look at them because, as he often remarked to his wife, "Each of those children is actually smoking forty cigarettes a day, the air pollution is so bad. Do you realize it? It's been medically ascertained that everybody in this city is doing that, just by breathing. You don't even have to light a match. You don't even have to think of tobacco. Since I learned that, every time I see them they seem to be chain-smoking." This impression was especially bad by daylight; at night, smoking himself, with enough to drink inside his head, he forgot it. Anyway, at night you seldom got the full impact of air pollution, because you did not have to see the sunlight being diluted by it. Now he was at home with a cold, and he further imagined that the air pollution was making the cold worse.

He did not want anything but soup. If some was already open, he would take that. His son, Henry, stood by the refrigerator door, having just put out one of those invisible cigarettes, and asked what he was looking for.

"Some soup," he said. "Leftover will do."

"It's in that," said Henry, pointing to a small covered dish.

"Get away from me," said his father. "I've got this awful cold."

"It's past time for catching it," said Henry, and began to swing on the chrome door handle. "Mother said so."

"That doesn't make it true," he said.

"Oh yes, it does," said Henry.

Henry was a stout soul. When he asserted something of a sincere emotional nature, his father never argued.

"Yesterday a balloon flew by the window," said Henry.

"What color was it?" he asked.

"Brown."

"I never heard of a brown balloon."

Henry did not reply. He had been right about the location of the soup, which was leftover vegetable alphabet. His father dumped it in a small saucepan and flicked on the gas. He stirred it so it wouldn't stick. In a minute, he began to smell it, the first smell in two days.

The phone rang in the hall. He heard his wife come out of the far recesses of the apartment, from a small back room she had fitted out as an office, and hasten toward it. It was much nearer to him, and he would have reached it first, but the soup was beginning to boil. He had to watch it or turn it off. So she completed her dash, catching up the receiver just after the third ring.

She had been back there typing. Every few days, she got little packages of dictated tapes to type, brought to the door by messenger. This occupation was paid for by the typed word and earned her a substantial sum each month. No sound of this ever came to the children or to him. The tape was unpackaged and fitted into a smart gray-and-blue metal tape recorder made in West Germany. It talked directly into her ears through tiny wired earphones. Even her electric typewriter was almost soundless, and could never be heard through the door. This highly insulated and completely impersonal arrangement worked two ways. She could not be disturbed by the usual humdrum, unextraordinary sounds the children made, but could hear them shouting if they were in some crisis that needed her attention. She could also hear the doorbell or the telephone.

She needn't have run, he thought. Probably she forgot I'm here. He switched off the gas under the soup and heard her say, "I'm awfully sorry . . . Yes, I know. . . . It's just that Pete's at home sick."

"Who was that?" he shouted at once. "Your lover?"

She did not answer, but hurried back down the hall, heels going clack-clack, and clacked shut the door. She's paying me no attention, he thought, and decided to torment her. He went in after her with the soup in a cup, eating it with a teaspoon. Having closed the door, he began to gnaw at her neck. He said he wanted to make love.

She shut off the tape recorder, switched off the typewriter, and took the little earphones out one at a time. They were different colors, for left and right ear. "You what?" she asked.

He repeated it, and she replied, "That's what I thought you said." They looked rather tipsily at one another. "At high noon, with the children every which way?"

"It would be better for them than all that mechanical world you keep on dealing with. And don't tell me I have a bad cold. Anyway, colds always make me feel sexy. They dull certain senses and sharpen others. I feel definitely like reclining luxuriously. And not alone!" He growled the words in a sidelong, wolfish fashion.

She broke out laughing.

"Besides," he said, "the children are both busy smoking. They have to get through their two packs a day."

"They are not," she said. "They want their lunch, I bet. What have you got in that cup?"

"Vegetable alphabet soup. Who was that on the phone?"

"Mavis."

"In town again? But she just left for that trip."

"It didn't work out. Bermuda isn't very warm. She was disappointed and came back. Bad weather, to boot."

"I think it was your lover. Otherwise, why did you make a break for the phone with me only three feet away from it?"

"I forgot you were here. It was reflex action. You're never at home."

"But that's the first thing you said. You didn't forget at all. 'Pete's home,' you said. 'Pete's home!' Why, pray, would Pete being home keep you from talking to Mavis about the weather in Bermuda?"

"I didn't have time to talk to her, that's all. If you hadn't been here, I would have said–well, something else. Like 'Mavis, I'd love to talk, but I have to call you back. I have a whole set of company promotion-announcement letters to type up, plus letters regretfully accepting the resignation of–oh, of people nobody knows.'"

He glared at her. "I don't believe it. Men get their regular secretaries to do work like that."

"I sometimes get work like this when they're short-staffed. I work for an agency. I told you a hundred times."

"I don't believe it this time. Let me hear. Put the little anodes in my ears."

"Oh, stop it. You're just acting dreadful. I do have to finish things today."

"If you won't let me hear what's on those tapes and you won't let me answer the telephone and you won't let me make love to you, what can I do?"

"You can finish your soup. It must be getting cold."

"I think it is your lover who writes passionate letters to you, has them tape-recorded, and sends them to you by messenger. He is wealthy. The messenger is his servant in disguise. You sit back here with the typewriter, all hooked up to that thing, pretending to type up routine letters, and all the time your soul is drinking from fresh fountains. Every few days he sends you more."

"When do I meet him?"

"Not often. You can let several weeks go by: You like it this way. He objects. He calls on the phone at noon. It is his words you lust for. This whole setup is completely phony. You take money from him not because you want it but to make me think that you are really working. If I am not right, why won't you let me answer the telephone, why won't you let me play the tape recorder?"

"You are trying your best to give me that cold," she said. "You have been from the first sneeze."

"No one can catch a cold after the incubation period. Henry said so."

"Henry can be wrong."

"In this case he isn't. Where is Phyllis?"

"Sewing. On that funny miniature electric sewing machine you gave her for Christmas."

"What does she make?"

"Different things for dolls. She's fascinated with it now, but I guess she'll soon get tired of it. Do you know, Pete, you can go to stores to get supplies for that little machine—all sorts of tiny parts, little patterns for doll dresses. It's all worked out, down to the last detail."

He took the rest of his soup and sat on the day bed, first carefully moving aside the sheets of neatly typed letters. "I wonder why I'm happy," he said.

"You're happily married. You have two fine children, who are healthy and well cared for. You have a good job, which interests you. You have a quick mind, which invents amusing things, so you're never bored. You know, you're never really boring, Pete. I mean, even when you are boring, it still has something coming up in it, something interesting is cooking in what you say."

"That isn't why I'm happy. The other day, when I was getting this cold, I was walking down in the West Forties somewhere, because I had to go over three blocks to another drugstore to get some 4-Way Cold Tablets, because the one I went to first was out of them. On the way, I passed a sort of run-down seafood restaurant, and there were some run-down lobsters in the window. At first I thought they were made of red wax, like artificial flowers, and then I thought, Holy cow, they're real but stone dead, and who would go in that place wanting ptomaine poison in addition to a bad cold? And then I saw one move. Just a little groping movement with one poor old claw. God, it was sad. Do you know why it was especially sad to me? Because I knew what the lobster was saying. Whether the lobster knew it or not, whether anybody would pass and think of it or not, I knew. It was saying, 'Where is my world? Oh, where is my world, my own true world?' Over and over. On and on. How can I think about that poor damned lobster and still be happy?"

She came right out and told him. "O.K., I'll tell you. You're happy because of me."

"And why are *you* happy? Don't think I don't know. It's because of what comes out of that machine."

Exasperated, she snatched up a handful of equipment; red, black, and pink plastic wires dangled in an abstract pattern from her fingers. "Do you actually want to hear what is really on those tapes? Do you? Just listen, then. Go right ahead!"

"Of course I won't. Do you take me for an eavesdropper, a keyhole watcher, a happiness killer? Do you think I'm destructive?"

Hunched over his cup and spoon, he devoured the last of the soup, smiling through a provoking haze of headache, sore throat, bleared eyesight, and severe nasal congestion.

PRESENTS

The beagle trotted down the quiet white path. When a squirrel jumped high up in a bare oak tree, he did not notice; when a blue jay floated past he did not turn his head. His tail was high, his gait steady, and he looked responsible for something. Sandy, the minute he came out of the wood to where she was sitting with her first cousin down by the lily pond, knew exactly the way in which he had been coming toward them. The beagle was serious and had no time for animals and birds. It was Christmas and he had come to see about the children. What if they had taken their shoes off? It was warm, but not that warm. They might be sitting on the damp ground, which could lead to a bad cold and missing school. They had had too much excitement and could be struck by crazy ideas at the best of times. If no one now remembered that school was going to resume, the beagle remembered. Somebody had to think of these things.

The two little girls were sitting on an ornamental stone bench, and though it was cold, they did not have their coats on. The beagle jumped up on the bench and sat down between them. He made a show of indifference, yawning a bit when Sandy's cousin Linda reached out and patted him. It was clear that he belonged to Sandy, for they did not notice one another at all.

At least, the adults, back at the house, would have said that he was Sandy's dog. The truth was, of course, that Sandy belonged to him. He never lay at her door or rambled along glued to her heels as a boy's dog will do. At night before the fire when she tried to romp with him, he always at once scrambled away. He growled, yelped if his ears were so much as touched, all but fiercely closed his teeth upon her, and pulling entirely free, shook his rumpled coat together. He was not amused. She was beneath his dignity; who did she think she was? He went off to the kitchen to see about his supper. But at times he lay near her with his head fixed between his white forepaws. He sat at her feet when she was studying. He chose his own length of time to start waiting for school to be out.

The two little girls sighed. Everything was over now. It had been building up all through the year, or at least ever since summer, when, having nothing else to do, somebody might say on a hot afternoon (holding their skirts up before the electric fan), "What you going to want for Christmas?" Since November, it had been definitely in the air, and since Thanksgiving it had been almost unbearable. At school there had been all the paper cutouts to do and paste in windows, songs and programs and readings in the textbooks. At church they had the pageant to practice for, Christmas carols to sing, and Sunday School lessons about little baby Jesus. At home it was on the radio and the TV all the time, and it hid in the far backs of closets and was spread out on beds in chilly guest rooms, so that every door you might open somebody would say "Can't come in here, you'll see your present!" And if you drove way back in the country to pick up a quilt from an ancient colored woman, she would stand on the porch and the last thing she would say was: "Christmas comin', gonna snow." Everybody promised you snow, but it wouldn't snow. You could go out at night in the yard and shiver, squint your eyes out staring up at the crystal sky, imagine you felt one flake graze your cheek, but still it wouldn't snow. It would, however, be Christmas. Inch at a time, creeping closer day by day, the time would come. Now it had ended in a burst of tinsel, angel hair, lights, ribbon. Too much, far too much. Too long awaited, far too long, and gone in a flash. This accounted for the stillness. This accounted for the three of them sitting together down by the lily pond on a stone bench with nothing much to say.

"Did you get everything you wanted?" Linda asked. There had been about a million presents. The question was, in all the furore, if you could even remember what you wanted. Everyone went "Oh!" and "Look, just look!" "What'd you do it for?"

"Well, no, I didn't," said Sandy, just remembering. "There was one thing."

"What was it?" Linda pursued. Sated with gifts, tired from fitful dreams of the night before, from getting up early, shouting "Christmas gift!" being hugged by everybody, gorging on turkey, cranberries, candied sweet potatoes, ambrosia, fruitcake, and a hundred hot biscuits, the children found it simpler, not as far beyond the range of the appetite, to think of what they didn't get than what they did.

"I don't know," said Sandy, and hooked her fingers through the beagle's collar. "I can't remember."

Yet it had been most important at the time she was making out lists and wishing. This had all happened before; there was always something you didn't get. Either it cost too much, or the stores were all sold out, or the line discontinued, or they said she was too old, or too young, or they decided it was in bad taste. If you kept on begging maybe you got it anyway, like the brightly striped dress in the store window, which never looked right no matter how many people worked on it, or the rabbit's fur muff which not only kept her hands warm during church and held her Sunday School book, but also looked, as her mother had warned her, ridiculous. Whatever it had been this year, however, she hadn't campaigned for it hard enough; maybe she hadn't cared. Or maybe—this was the hard part—she knew in advance that something was liable to be the matter with it, turning it to no value in others' eyes, and so, eventually, in her own. So by now it—whatever it was—might as well be a shooting star over the cedar tree at night for whoever might be up and wishing. And in the way of stars it might just as well come swooping back her way sometime ages from now, maybe sooner. "I can't remember," she repeated, and like that, even the desire to left her.

"Mama got her silver dresser set," said Linda.

"I know it," Sandy said.

"It was gorgeous," Linda mused.

"Sure was," said Sandy, but she wasn't thinking of it, or of anything.

Quiet took a deeper hold; the ground looked swept on purpose. The sunshine had no color, it felt like Sunday without church. Could you be wide awake and asleep, both at once? Sandy was.

The dry brown winter leaves—sliver-shaped leaves from some kind of oak—lay carpeted over the paving about the lily pond which had no lilies in it. Everybody had done their best all day and now turned into such good people: even the Negroes, sitting out back, had something nice to say to you if you went by. The beagle jumped down from the bench and trotted off into the woods. He came back with an old shoe sole in his mouth. He gave it to Sandy, laid it down in front of her. It was time to go.

The little girls began to walk home. Sandy did not see Linda very often. Linda lived twenty miles away, in a bigger town. She imitated her mother, which seemed to Sandy an odd thing to do. Sandy felt there must be a part of the world where all little girls imitated their mothers, but it was not a part that made her very curious. She was happier with the dog than that could ever make her. With no right to any idea of what Christmas was or wasn't (though he seemed caught up on it, the whole time), he trotted ahead of them, complete in some kind of knowledge.

When they got to the house, they found their mothers sitting in the front swing, just as they themselves had been sitting by the lily pond. The young women were in a good humor, for they liked each other, in spite of being in-laws, and they said, "Look, he's bringing them back. Did you ever?" they said.

The whole day was the quiet color of the field gate which no one had ever painted, and many hands had worn smooth. Far out in the field, a flight of crows, thick as a black cloud, tilted to rest in a bare pecan tree, so that it seemed suddenly to have grown a treeful of coal-black leaves.

The two young mothers were talking of their husbands. "But then you know Jerry was always unselfish like that," said Linda's mother. "He'd give you his last cent."

"Just like Bob," said Sandy's mother.

"I think they could be brothers, even though they aren't any kin."

"I know it," said Sandy's mother. "They're just alike in so many ways. What have you got in your hand?" she said to Sandy.

"It's an old shoe sole," said Sandy. "The beagle brought it to me."

"The silly old dog," said Linda, suddenly wicked. "The ugly old hound dog."

"He's not silly," said Sandy. "He's not ugly." She had felt a start of anger which did not recede when Linda squirmed into the swing between her mother and Sandy's mother. The beagle accompanied Sandy into the house. Now they were out in the sun parlor where everybody sat.

"I never thought I'd see the day," said Aunt Jennie, "when a dog would be allowed inside this house." She leaned down to look the beagle in the eye. "You sassy little thing," she said.

"They worship one another," said Sandy's grandmother. "You know *he* was a Christmas present."

"I know he was. Cutest thing I ever saw. Don't you remember trying to keep him quiet on that Christmas Eve night, so she wouldn't guess? We smothered him in blankets. We put five alarm clocks in with him."

Sandy's brother Hernan came in. He was cramming a fistful of fruitcake in his mouth. "Sandy, there's a girl off at school that brought her horse with her. You ought to see him. She rides him every afternoon. Real pretty bay."

Hernan went to a military school. There was a girls' finishing school across the road from the boys' school.

"Reckon you want to take the beagle off to college with you?" said Sandy's granddaddy, coming up out of the newspaper. It seemed Granddaddy could arrange everything.

"Law, the beagle will be dead and gone by then," Aunt Jennie said. She thought everyone would be dead and gone sooner than they ever were, except those who had accidents and were removed before you could think about it.

"Some dogs live to be twelve or thirteen years old," said Sandy's grandmother.

"I knew a horse once that lived to be thirty-five years old," said her grandfather. "I certainly did," he said, and put the paper entirely aside to think it over. That particular horse's face came back to him now; you could tell.

"Turtles live to be five hundred!" cried Hernan, as though in triumph.

What were they saying? What did they mean?

Sandy eventually got all the way to the back porch, all the way out with the Negroes. "Thank you, ma'am, for the handkerchuffs, Sandy," said Elvira. "I meants to get you a present, but I didn't have no money."

"What was you gonna git her, Mama?" said Tommie, Elvira's boy, after a long time. He was sitting out on the steps, and when he said this he was making fun, just like Elvira. You gave presents to Negroes; they never gave presents to you.

Sandy went down the steps and sat down on the very bottom step with her back to Tommie, who was sitting up near the door, and to Elvira, who was sitting in a straight chair on the screen porch, taking her ease now all the dinner was finally over with and the dishwasher going. Elvira's husband Charlie had long ago eaten his big turkey dinner and gone home.

"A pair of pink socks, for Easter," said Elvira, comfortably, still making it up. "Easter the next thing."

"You ain't going to get me nothing," said Sandy, right out, talking without grammar, the way you did to Negroes.

"That's right," said Elvira, amiably. "I sho ain't."

Cold truth was what they had spoken.

The beagle, having stopped to lick up some onion dressing from the kitchen floor, pushed through the back door and came to sit down beside Sandy. He curled his tail around him neatly and looked out at the dun-colored winter yard and the mild bare sky. She held the shoe sole in her lap.

All Sandy's presents—the ones from the tree—were stacked in her room inside the house. She would go look at them some time later and be glad, she guessed, but just now all she wanted was to rest her hand on the smooth brown and white head. Far beyond horses and turtles he would endure, no matter what they said.

ON THE GULF

Mary Dee went out in the heat in the early afternoon and began to swing. Back and forth, back and forth, sitting with her skirt around her, flying open and shut. It was something to do.

Semmes, their old colored woman, came out and said, "Don't swing so high, Dee-dee. It worries your mama."

"She's on the other side," said Mary Dee, swooping past.

There was a daytime moon. When she went her highest, her tennis shoes rested on it.

"Them folks coming from N'Orlens. You know how your mama is about company."

"Wears her out," said Mary Dee, and getting tired, her hair damp and hot, she let the cat die. It died slow as anything, then she was scarcely moving over the bare place in the grass where you pushed, and then she turned around until the ropes wound tightly around each other, going higher and higher. She let herself go, spinning. She did that three times.

"Your head swimming, I bet," said Semmes. She was sitting down now, a little way off, in a lawn chair.

"Whyn't you go to the pool?" Semmes asked.

"It's too late. Time I get there."

"Ain't no more than three-thirty."

"Ain't you got to cook?"

"Certainly I do. Got to start in."

"Who's coming?" Mary Dee asked, the first she'd thought to wonder. At the table when there was company she sat and said, "Yes, ma'am," and "No, ma'am"; her mother liked it that way.

"Them Meades," said Semmes. "Comes every summer. Eats like horses."

"It's cool out here; over there it's hot," Mary Dee said.

"Ain't that entirely. They counts on my dinner, Dee-dee." She looked toward the house. It was two-story, red brick, old, with a big side yard where they were. It was afternoon-still. Way up in the live oak, even the Spanish moss looked as sound asleep at that hour as a dog would be. "Any minute now, Miss Annie going to get out of that bed and start straightening up."

"When I grow up I'm not going to worry any." Mary Dee started spinning the other way.

"One time them Meades come and got into rain crossing the Pearl. Rain like brickbats; hail big as eggs. I'd a-turnt back, been me. No, sir! Car dented all over the roof with hail. Hail that big around. Chunks big enough to put in the highballs, which they did. Frozen solid."

Mary Dee stopped. "How'd they get it?"

"It skips, don't you know. Goes bouncing along. Put their hand out the car window and caught it. That's how. Blamming on the roof of the car. Them Meades inside, scared and laughing both. I ain't so struck on them Meades."

"Mama's not either. I heard her say so. Twice. 'I just can't stand them another year.' That's what she said."

"They keep on coming," said Semmes. "It's got to be regular."

"What you going to have?"

"Crawfish bisque, stuffed hen, pickled peaches, biscuits, cauliflower, beets, tomatoes, rice and beans on the side, strawberry chill with macaroons. Chicory."

"Same as ever," said Mary Dee.

"Between here and Florida, ain't no cook good as me," said Semmes.

"And we got you," said Mary Dee, complacently, repeating what she'd heard.

"Got to take me home, though," Semmes gloated. "Got to go get me. Even if I move a hundred miles. I ain't walking nowhere. Not before I die."

"When you die? Where you think you can walk to when you die?"

"Lord knows," said Semmes. "He tell me, chile."

"I'm eight years old," said Mary Dee, not knowing exactly what she meant, and ran into the house.

Semmes scratched in her ear with a straw, and presently, smoothing out her dress, she got up and walked over to the fish pond. She turned one or two of the lawn chairs straight on the paving around the water, brushing them free of twigs and droppings. Gulls were the worst. Sometimes, when stiff weather came on, rain hanging in dark splotches way out on the gulf, the gulls sailed in to refugee. Once they ate the goldfish. The glass-top table needed polishing. That was Miss Annie's job. Mister Lawrence could dip trash from the pool. The car would ease in through the gate. Soon they would all be out here, getting drunk and acting crazy about one another, with Dee-dee in a big prissy sash and white socks, passing canapés. A goldfish, biggest in the pool, came above the surface and looked Semmes in the eye.

Semmes had a familiar spirit she often spoke with, something she'd got many years ago, at just about Mary Dee's age. She'd been to the nuns' school and nothing she had learned there discouraged her from having this spirit around, though in one way or other, what with so many things happening, wars and elections and everything, times different, she never talked about it. Every now and then she picked up a piece of colored glass, a sort of blue glass, apt to be iridescent, some shells, some little rock, and just going along, whenever she took a notion, she threw these things aside, and maybe the spirit got them. Did it eat them? How would she know what it did?

"Organdy's scratchy," said Mary Dee, upstairs and complaining.

"It's a beautiful dress," said her mother. "Even Daddy noticed."

"I wore it Sunday."

"Semmes can press it. Just take it in the kitchen, hang it on the chair. I haven't got time."

"Mama, why do we have to have the Meades?"

Her mother, filing her nails, fresh from her bath, sitting in a loose cotton robe and slippers, legs crossed, eyes lowered, flashed her a look and smiled. "Don't you say that in front of them, monkey."

"But why do we?"

"They brag on things out here. We went to their open house once, after the Sugar Bowl. They have this lovely old house with original floorboards a yard wide. Then they call up and say Come to Antoine's, but we never can." She threw the file aside. "*I* don't know. Daddy says that too. I just don't know. I declare I don't."

"So much to *do,*" said Mary Dee, who did not have to do anything but march into the kitchen with her dress. She sat in the chaise longue and let it comfortably engulf her. She looked out at the sky. From here you could see the water. Two gulls were sailing so far up they looked carefully shaped and thin, like the scalloped edges of a pillow case. They passed across the daytime moon. "First it's over yonder, now it's over here," said Mary Dee.

"What is, precious?"

"The moon."

"Don't bite your nails," said her mother.

"'A girl is known,'" said Mary Dee, quoting–she had felt guilt for a moment, then she joked it away–"'by her hands, her skin, her carriage, and her hair. We cannot all be beautiful.'"

"You're getting too smart," said her mother. "Who's going to tell you things if I don't? Someday you'll be glad to know all that."

"Have the Meades got any children?"

"Just that brother that always comes."

"He caught the hail, I bet," said Mary Dee.

"That was the silliest thing," said her mother. "They should have gone straight back. Right into that black cloud."

"Daddy said Come hell or high water."

"Daddy said that but you ought not to."

A wonderful odor, spicy and rich, began to come up from below. They both looked toward the direction of it, as though it could not only be seen but could look back.

"That bisque," her mother murmured, biting her lip with hunger and pride, a combination not so rare in that household.

Mary Dee jumped up suddenly. She had not gone swimming at the pool that day, but the feeling of swimming came strongly over her, out of habit, so she ran and dived straight into the bed, kicking her brown legs and flailing her arms until exhausted.

"Them old Meades." Now she was mimicking Semmes. "I wish they's gone already."

Her mother shot her a glance, even sharper than before. "Don't you know better than to carry on like that? What are you trying to grow up to be? That's what I'd like to know! Stop listening to us! Stop hearing anything we say!"

SHARON

Uncle Hernan, my mother's brother (his full name was Hernando de Soto Wirth), lived right near us—a little way down the road, if you took the road; across the pasture, if you didn't—in a house surrounded by thick privet hedge, taller than a man riding by on a mule could see over. He had live oaks around the house, and I don't remember ever going there without hearing the whisper of dry fallen leaves beneath my step on the ground. Sometimes there would be a good many Negroes about the house and yard, for Uncle Hernan worked a good deal of land, and there was always a great slamming of screen doors—people looking for something they couldn't find and hollering about where they'd looked or thought for somebody else to look, or just saying, "What'd you say?" "Huh?" "I said, 'What'd you *say?*' "—or maybe a wrangling noise of a whole clutch of colored children playing off down near the gully. But in spite of all these things, even with all of them going on at one and the same time, Uncle Hernan's place was a still place. That was how it knew itself: it kept its own stillness. When I remember that stillness, I hear again the little resistant veins of a dry oak leaf unlacing beneath my bare foot, so that the sound seems to be heard in the foot's flesh itself.

As a general rule, however, I wasn't barefoot, for Uncle Hernan was a gentleman, and I came to him when I was sent for, to eat dinner, cleaned up, in a fresh dress, and wearing shoes. "Send the child over on Thursday," he would say. Dinner was what we ate in the middle of the day—our big meal. Mama would look me over before I went—ears and nails and mosquito bites—and brush my hair, glancing at the clock. "Tell Uncle Hernan hello for me," she would say, letting me out the side door.

"Marilee?" she would say, when I got halfway to the side gate.

"Ma'am?"

"You look mighty sweet."

"Sweet" was a big word with all of them; I guess they got it from so many flowers and from the night air in South Mississippi, almost all seasons. And maybe I did really look that way when going to Uncle Hernan's.

I would cross a shoulder of pasture, which was stubbled with bitterweed and white with glare under the high sun, go through a slit in the hedge, which towered over me, and wriggle through a gap in the fence. This gap was no haphazard thing but was arranged, the posts placed in such a way that dogs and people could go through but cows couldn't, for Uncle Hernan was a good farmer and not one to leave baggy places in his fences from people crawling over them. He built a gap instead. As I went by, the dogs that were sprawled around dozing under the trees would look up and grin at me, giving a thump or two with their tails in the dust, too lazy to get up and speak. I would go up the steps and stand outside the door and call, looking into the shadowy depths of the hall, like a reflection of itself seen in water. I had always to make my presence known just this way; this was a house that expected behavior. It was simple enough, one-story, with a square front porch, small by Southern standards, opening out from the central doorway. Two stout pillars supported the low classical triangle of white-painted wood, roofed in shingle. The house had been built back before the Civil War. Uncle Hernan and Mama and others who had died or moved away had been brought up here, but they were anxious to let you know right away that they were not pretentious people but had come to Mississippi to continue being what they'd always been—good farming people who didn't consider themselves better or worse than anybody else. Yet somebody, I realized fairly early on, had desired a façade like a Greek temple, though maybe the motive back of the desire had been missing and a prevailing style had been copied without any thought for its effect.

Uncle Hernan, however, was not one of those who protested in this vein any more, if he ever had. He lived the democratic way and had friends in every walk of life, but Sharon—that was the name of the house—had had its heyday once, and he had loved it. It had been livened with more airs and graces than anybody would have patience to listen to, if I knew them all to tell. That was when Uncle Hernan's pretty young wife was there. Mama said that Uncle Hernan used to say that the bright and morning star had come to Sharon. It all sounded very Biblical and right; also, he called her his Wild Irish Rose. She was from Tennessee and brought wagonloads of stuff with her when she came, including a small rosewood piano. Every tasseled, brocaded, gold-leafed, or pearl-inlaid thing in Sharon, you knew at once, had come from Tennessee with Aunt Eileen. At the long windows, for instance, she had put draperies that fastened back with big bronze hooks, the size of a baby's arm bent back, and ending in a lily. Even those lilies were French—the fleur-de-lis. All this was in the best parlor, where nobody ever went very much any more, where the piano was, covered with the tasseled green-and-white throw, and the stern gold-framed portraits (those belonged to our family). It was not that the parlor was closed or that there was anything wrong with going into it. I sometimes got to play in there, and looked at everything to my heart's content. It was just that there was no reason to use it any more. The room opposite, across the hall, was a parlor, too, full of Uncle Hernan's books, and with his big old plantation desk, and his round table, where he sat near the window. The Negroes had worn a path to the window, coming there to ask him things. So life went on here now, in the plain parlor rather than the elegant one, and had since Aunt Eileen died.

She had not lived there very long, only about three or four years, it seems, or anyway not more than five, when she got sick one spring day —the result, they said at first, of having done too much out in the yard. But she didn't get better; one thing led to another, all during the hottest summer Mama said she could ever remember. In September, their hopes flagged, and in the winter she died. This was all before I could remember. Her portrait did not hang in the best parlor with the other, old ones, but there was a daguerreotype of her in a modest oval gold frame hanging in the plain parlor. She had a small face, with her hair done in the soft upswept fashion of the times, and enormous eyes that looked a little of everything—fearful, shy, proud, wistful, happy, adoring, amused, as though she had just looked at Uncle Hernan. She wasn't the angel you might think. Especially when she was sick, she'd make them all jump like grease in a hot skillet, Uncle Hernan said, but he would say it smiling, for everything he felt about her was sheer affection. He was a strong, intelligent man; he had understood her but he had loved her, all the time.

Uncle Hernan never forgot that he'd asked me to dinner, or on which day. He would come to let me in himself. He always put on the same coat, no matter how hot it was—a rumpled white linen coat, faded yellow. He was a large, almost portly man, with a fleshy face, basically light in color but splashed with sunburn, liver spots, and freckles, and usually marked with the line of his hatband. He had untidy, graying, shaggy hair and a tobacco-stained mustache, but he kept his hands and nails scrupulously clean—a matter of pride. I was a little bit afraid of Uncle Hernan. Though I loved to come there, I was careful to do things always the same way, waiting to sit down until I was told, staying interested in whatever he told me, saying, "Yes, thank you, Uncle Hernan," and "No, thank you, Uncle Hernan," when we were at the table. He was fond of me and liked having me, but I was not his heart of hearts, so I had to be careful.

Melissa waited on us. Melissa had originally come there from Tennessee with Aunt Eileen, as her personal maid, so I had got it early through my head that she was not like the rest of the Negroes around home, any more than Aunt Eileen's tasseled, rosewood, pearl-inlaid, gold-leafed, and brocaded possessions were like the plain Wirth house had been before she got there. Melissa talked in a different style from other Negroes; for instance, she said "I'm not" instead of "I ain't" or "I isn't" (which they said when trying to be proper). She even said "He doesn't," which was more than Mama would do very often. It wasn't that she put on airs or was ambitious. But we all stood in awe of her, a little. You never know for sure when you come into a Negro house, whether you are crossing the threshold of a rightful king or queen, and I felt this way about Melissa's house. It was just Uncle Hernan's cook's cabin, but I felt awkward in it. It was so much her own domain, and there was no set of manners to go by. She had turned scraps of silk and satin into clever doilies for tables and cushion covers and had briar-stitched a spread for her bed with rich dark pieces bound with a scarlet thread; you could tell she had copied all her tastes from Aunt Eileen. The time I discovered that I really liked Melissa was when she came to our house once, the winter Mama had pneumonia. She came and stayed, to help out. She wore a white starched uniform, so then I learned that Melissa, all along, had been a nurse. It seemed that when Aunt Eileen was about to get married,

Eileen's father, seeing that Uncle Hernan lived in the wilds of Mississippi, had taken Melissa and had her trained carefully in practical nursing. I guess he thought we didn't have doctors, or if we had we had no roads for them to go and come on; anyway, he wasn't taking any chances. After Mama passed the danger period, Melissa spent a lot of time reading aloud to me. I would sit in her lap by the hour and listen and listen, happy, until one day I went in to see how Mama was and she said, "I wouldn't ask Melissa to read to me too long at the time, Marilee."

"She likes to read," I said.

"I know," she said, "but I'm afraid you'll get to smell like a Negro."

Now that she mentioned it, I realized that I had liked the way Melissa smelled. I wanted to argue, but she looked weak and cross, the way sick people do, so I just said, "Yes, ma'am," and went away.

It is a mighty asset in life to be a good cook, and Melissa never spared to set the best before me when I came to Uncle Hernan's to dinner. If it was fried chicken, the crust would be golden, and as dry as popcorn, with the thinnest skim of glistening fat between the crust and the meat. If it was roast duck or turkey or hen, it would come to the table brown, gushing steam that smelled of all it was stuffed with. There were always hot biscuits–she made tiny hot biscuits, the size of a nickel three inches high–and side dishes of peach pickle, souse, chopped pepper relish, green-tomato pickle, wild-plum jelly, and blackberry jam. There were iced tea and buttermilk both, with peaches and dumplings for dessert and maybe homemade ice cream–so cold it hurt your forehead to eat it–and coconut cake.

Such food as that may have been the main excuse for having me to dinner, but Uncle Hernan also relished our conversations. After dinner, I would sit with him in the plain parlor–he with his small cup of black chicory coffee before him, and I facing him in a chair that rocked on a stand–telling him whatever he asked me to. About Mama and Daddy, first; then school–who taught me and what they said and all about their side remarks and friends and general behavior. Then we'd go into his part, which took the form of hunting stories, recollections about friends, or stories about his brother, Uncle Rex, who now lived several miles away, or about books I ought to be reading. He would enter right into those books he favored as though they were a continuation of life around us. *Les Misérables* was a great favorite of his, not so much because of the poverty and suffering it depicted but because in spite of all that Valjean was a man, he said, and one you came little at a time to see in his full stature. His stature increased, he would say, and always put his hand down low and raised it up as high as it would go. I guess he was not so widely read as he seemed to me at that time to be, but he knew what he liked and why, and thought that knowing character was the main reason for reading anything. One day, he took a small gold box from his pocket and sniffed deftly, with his hand going to each nostril in turn. When I stared at him, startled into wonder, my look in turn startled him. His hand forgot to move downward and our eyes met in a lonely, simple way, such as had not happened before.

Then he smiled. "Snuff," he said. He snapped the box to and held it out. "You want to see? Don't open it, now. You'll sneeze." I took the box in my hand and turned it—golden, with a small raised cage of worked gold above the lid. I thought at once I had come on another of Aunt Eileen's tracks, but he said, "I picked that up in New Orleans a year or so back," and here I had another facet of Uncle Hernan—a stroll past shops in that strange city I had never seen, a pause before a window, a decision to enter and buy, cane hooked over his forearm. The world was large; I was small. He let me out the front door. "You're getting to be a big girl," said Melissa, from halfway back down the hall. "I'm soon going to have to say 'Miss Marilee.'"

The one thing I could never do was to go over to Uncle Hernan's without being asked. This was laid down to me, firmly and sternly. It became, of course, the apple in the garden. One summer afternoon when I was alone and bored, getting too big, they said, to play with Melissa's children anymore, I begged Mama to let me go over there. She denied me twice, and threatened to whip me if I asked again, and when Daddy got in from the field she got him to talk to me. They were both sterner and more serious than I ever remembered them being, and made sure I got it straight. I said to Mama, being very argumentative, "You just don't like Melissa." She looked like I had slapped her. She turned white and left the room, but not without a glance at Daddy. I knew he was commissioned to deal with me (he knew it, too), but I also knew that he was not going to treat me as badly as Mama would have if he hadn't been there. He sent me to my room and hoped for the best. There I felt very sorry for myself and told myself I didn't know why I was being treated so harshly, sent to bed in a cold room with no supper, all for making such an innocent remark. I said I would stay in my room till I died, and they'd be sorry, Mama especially. I pictured the sad words that would certainly be exchanged.

Mama relented well before I came to this tragic end. In fact, she came in the room after about an hour. She never could stand any kind of unhappiness for long, and after urging me to come and get supper (I wouldn't reply) she brought me a glass of milk and lighted a little fire to take the chill off the room. But, sweet or not, she was a feline at heart, and at a certain kind of threat her claws came out, ready for blood. She was never nice to Melissa. I overheard them once talking at the kitchen door. Uncle Hernan had sent some plums over and when Mama said, "How are you, Melissa?" in her most grudging and offhand way, Melissa told her. She stood outside the steps, not touching the railing–they had reached their hands out to the farthest limit to give and receive the bucket, and Mama had by now closed the screen door between them–and told her. She had a boil on her leg, she said; no amount of poultices seemed to draw it out and it hurt her all the way up to her hip. She had also been feeling very discouraged in her heart lately, but maybe this was due to the boil.

"I don't see why you don't go on back to Tennessee," Mama said, cold as ice. "You know you ought to, now, don't you?"

"No, ma'am," Melissa answered her politely, "I don't know that I ought to. I promised Miss Eileen I'd stay and care for Sharon."

"You aren't fooling anybody," Mama said. "If Miss Eileen–"

"Good morning, Marilee," said Melissa sweetly.

I said, "Morning, Melissa," and Mama, who hadn't noticed me, whirled around and left without another word.

The day came when I crossed over. Wrong or not, I went to Sharon when nobody had asked me. Mama was away to a church meeting, and Daddy had been called down in the pasture about some cows that had got out. It was late September, still and golden; school hadn't been started very long. I went over barefoot and looked in the window of the plain parlor, but nobody was there, so I circled round to the other side, stopping to pet and silence a dog who looked at me and half barked, then half whined. I looked through the window of the fine parlor, and there they both happened to be, Uncle Hernan and Melissa, talking together and smiling. I could see their lips move, though not hear them, for in my wrongdoing and disobedience I was frightened of being caught, and the blood was pounding in my ears.

Melissa looked pretty, and her white teeth flashed with her smiling in her creamy brown face. But it was Uncle Hernan, with the lift of his arm toward her, seated as he was in a large chair with a high back that finished in carved wood above his head, whose gesture went to my heart. That motion, so much a part of him whom I loved, was for her and controlled her, as it had, I knew now, hundreds of times. She came close and they leaned together; he gathered her surely in. She gave him her strength and he drank it; they became one another.

I had forgotten even to tremble and do not remember yet how I reached home from Sharon again. I only remember finding myself in my own room, seated on the edge of my narrow bed, hands folded in my lap, hearing the wrangle of Melissa's children out in the gully playing–they were beating some iron on an old washtub–and presently how her voice shouted out at them from across the back yard at Uncle Hernan's. She had four, and though they could all look nice on Sunday, they were perfect little devils during the week, Mama complained, and Melissa often got so mad she half beat the hide off them. I felt differently about them now. Their awful racket seemed a part of me–near and powerful, realer than itself, like their living blood. That blood was ours, mingling and twining with the other. Mama could kick like a mule, fight like a wildcat in a sack, but she would never get it out. It was there for good.

THE FINDER

Dalton was a pleasant town—still is. Lots of shade trees on residential streets, lots of shrubs in all the front yards, ferns in tubs put outside in the summer, birdbaths well attended, and screen side porches with familiar voices going on through the twilight. Crêpe myrtle lined the uptown streets. The old horse troughs on the square were seen by some in authority to be quite fine, so they were never removed but ran with water even after the last mule had died and the last wagon of the dozens that used to creak into town on Saturday from out in the country had fallen apart in somebody's barn or had been chopped up for kindling. So even on the hottest summer day the persistent murmur of water could be heard through still moments, and the lacy shade of crêpe myrtle lay traced on the sidewalks, on the heads of passing ladies, and on the shoulders of shirt-sleeved men.

There were several strong families in the town, and Gavin Anderson belonged to one of these. In the 1930s, there must have been seven or eight branches of the original Anderson parent stem living in and around there, in addition to others who had been taken North or into cities, according to the professions they picked or the men they married, but all of the Andersons had "kept up" and they came back from time to time. No matter where they went, they always said they felt as if they were living right there in Dalton on the Waukahatchie, where all the good picnics were held, down on the sandbar. Since most of the Andersons were from a little distance alike and since nearly all of them were full of the same cordial sayings and the same way of chuckling with forbearance over what they couldn't help, making it funny if possible, it was hard to remember which of them were dead and which had been more recently born. Not that they lacked personality, but only that together they were like one continuous entity, a long table of a family, rather than a history in which the people might be thought of as different shapes and sizes of beads on a string. And the way they talked of one another—with such clarity and wit about the ones who had passed away—you would think the dead were still right there about to come in any minute.

Gavin Anderson was not different from his family in any discernible way. Looking at him, a stranger would never have guessed what there was about him. It must have started just as a game when he was little, out in the sandpile with all of them. Perhaps somebody had said, "I lost my favorite agate. Now, where is it?" and Gavin's eyes might have been closed just from shutting out the sun as it came too strongly through the cedar limbs, or closed to keep cedar twigs from dropping into them, and maybe the question "Now, where is it?" hadn't been asked of anybody in particular; but lying there with his bright, healthy, tan-colored Anderson hair, dry as spun glass, in the remains of a sand castle, and one short practical Anderson hand thrown over his eyes, Gavin suddenly sat up and said, "It's rolled back behind the kindling box in the kitchen. I saw it there." Or if it was a letter that was lost, he would say, "You left it in the ninth-grade history book." Or if it was a book somebody had borrowed, he would say, "It's on Miss Jamie Whittaker's library shelf; she's put it up with her own by mistake." It got to be noticed he was always right. It was further noticed by an old-maid aunt, who had a sharp ear for picking up the flaws and lapses in what was said to her, that when he said he saw something, he had not, in the ordinary sense, seen it at all. Thereupon she questioned him all one afternoon, announced to the family at supper that it was right uncanny, and returned before day the next morning to a town near Jackson where she had taught Latin for twenty-three years. She herself was known to have second sight, and could generally be counted on "to get a feeling" a few days in advance of a death or disaster. Nobody paid much attention to her discovery about Gavin, as it was a busy fall and too much work to do. None of the Andersons were ever spoiled, because there were too many of them. Still, nothing was ever quite forgotten, either.

When Gavin's gift came to general attention, it was over the incident of the seed-pearl star pin that his father, Robert Anderson, had given to his mother and that had been lost so soon they suspected a servant of taking it. They did not want to suspect anybody, of course, and especially not Lulu, who was such a good cook. It was then that Gavin said right where it was—his mother, in her excitement, having hidden it even from herself. Lulu always said that the Lord spared her through that child. She announced this several times, coming once into the living room, and another time out of the kitchen into the dining room while they were eating. She never mentioned any gratitude to Gavin, and when the story was told in later years Gavin would add this observation with the particular little chuckle of the Andersons.

The story stuck. Even in Gavin's young manhood, somebody uptown would stop to ask him about it. "Was that really true about your mama's pin?" they would ask. He shrugged it off: "Should have gone on the stage, I guess. There was somebody up at the Orpheum in Memphis just the other day. Did you see it in the paper? I missed my chance for ever amounting to anything." But by then he was in his rugged, handsome stage and courting the girl he loved. All the Andersons married for love, and they always loved the right kind. One of the girls married a pharmacist who turned to dope and lost his license, but she stuck to him and he finally got over it. Her character was unbeatable; everyone was proud but none surprised.

It was soon after Gavin turned the insurance agency over to his brother and took the local hardware store over from his father—one of the many Anderson interests—and was every day now up on the town square, the father of two fine children, member of the Kiwanis Club, deacon in the church, with a boat on the lake for fishing every day in the summer with his boys, that the stories about him revived. Every once in so often, somebody would come to see him from out in the country or from a neighboring town, and it got to be known that a peculiar kind of worried look, like a bird dog uncertain of the scent, foretold the sort of errand they were on. Sometimes, too, a letter would arrive. He would get a thick packet, and inside, ink- or pencil-written on lined sheets or on cheap-grade blue stationery from the back counters in dusty drugstores, the entire story would come out in every detail. Something was lost: "Where is it? . . . Where is it? I feel like I just got to know—" Gavin's clerk and the bookkeeper would see him glance through page after page, refold the letter hastily, stuff it in his back pocket, and begin at once to do something else, some kind of straightening up he'd never think of otherwise.

One day in autumn, Gavin made a long-distance call to a neighboring town—a call he did not mention. He closed up the store and drove to that town, thirty miles away. He told his wife he had bank business in that part of the country; he didn't say exactly where. She had "a place" in that direction—something she had inherited. He always saw to it for her. She trusted him so much she never was quite sure where it was, and wouldn't have known how to find it if she had tried. Her name was Ethel. He got in the car and drove.

The minister was watching for his car to enter town, and had already reached the silent weekday church grounds before Gavin could cut off the motor. To reach the minister's study they first had to walk through the church itself. They unlocked the door, opened it, and Gavin stepped into the vestibule and encountered smells he had always, from time immemorial, associated with "religion." Hymnbooks, Sunday School literature, the pulpit Bible, the uncertain cleanliness of aging congregations, the starch of little girls' dresses, the felt in the organ stops, the smell of sunlight filtered by panes of stained glass discoloring the musty maroon carpet. Here there had been flowers sometime recently. He saw some white petals near the stove in passing, and coal dust left scanty by a broom's motion. He passed, following a step or two behind the gray brushed head of the minister—a man he remembered from the time when he had held the pulpit at Dalton but whom he had not seen in twenty-odd years. Dandruff flecked the good brown shoulders of his suit.

"All you all O.K.?" Gavin asked him.

The minister did not turn to answer. "Can't complain. Mrs. Cooper, though, 's got nothing to brag about."

"Serious?"

"Oh no. Hope not."

The door to the Sunday School annex stuck. The minister had to push, then rap the base with his toe. Back there it was cold. Gavin remembered his boyhood. Church-cold. Wasn't it always? Voices returned to him—the all-his-life voices. From last Sunday, from thirty years ago: ". . . not enough money to heat the auditorium, much less the Sunday School annex" . . . "They're only back there a little while; can't they keep their coats on?" And they did, hunched in uncomfortable chairs, sniveling with cold. And voices from those Sunday School classes: "Yes'm, He meant you had to have faith." . . . "Did He mean faith changes things?" Long pause. Somebody had to answer.

If nobody answered, there might not be any more Sunday School. There had to be more Sunday School. "Oh, yes'm. That is, it might." "Always?" "It might and it might not, I guess." "Does God answer prayer?" "Yes'm, He does." "You mean God does what I tell Him to?" "Guess He don't always. Don't for me." Laughter. "Well, now, to tell you the truth, Billy, He doesn't for me either." "Sometimes He does, don't He?" "Yes, sometimes He does. So . . . can you summarize?" "Can I what?" "Can you tell me what we've just decided?" Long pause. "Well, uh . . . we decided sometimes He does and sometimes He don't." "There might be a better way to put it. I'd say . . ." The bell rang, a tinkle from the hallway, and the superintendent entered and asked for the collection. The teacher gave it, an envelope already counted and recorded. "We'll be right there. I just want to leave you with this thought for the day. God always answers prayer. Sometimes He says yes, sometimes He says no. And the third answer, we didn't have time to get to. It is this: Wait. Remember that—all week. Now you can go." They would be gone already; there had been a shoving and creaking of chairs from the minute the bell rang.

A country man, a Southern man, a small-town man, not given to book knowledge—he read for entertainment—Gavin Anderson did not recall these things critically. He had a moment's self-doubt—himself and his religion, what did they have to do with one another? If he had once respected, been so impressed by this minister—this Mr. Cooper with the direct sympathies and the earnest plain speech, who could also field in baseball and hit a home run, who had a way of expressing great truths simply and a way of carrying within himself plainly the love of God—why had he waited twenty-odd years to look him up? Gavin noted that what had stirred a boy of twelve and convinced him of deep truth was almost nothing but a memory to a man of thirty-five. Still, he had come there about something.

They entered the study. The minister snapped on an electric heater. "Bought it myself," he explained. "I come over here to get my sermons up. Couldn't live with a cold all winter. It'll just take a minute to heat up." Theological texts, green-black and red, stood in bookcases covered by protective glass panels.

"Let me take your hat. Have a seat. Now." The minister was back of his desk. Gavin Anderson could not see through the frosted windows. The smell of the electric heat seeped into the room.

"Your family all all right? You've married, I understand? Who was it? Don't tell me—that little old Davis girl."

"You've got some memory."

"She O.K.?"

"Yes, oh yes—she is. Two boys. All fine. You thought I'd come about somebody being sick." His bemusement vanished. The Anderson charm, always there to save, made a swift return. He smiled warmly.

The minister glowed with relief. "I was just 'fraid it might be—"

"No. Nothing about illness. No, you'd never guess." He laughed his genial uptown chuckle. "It's something worries me. . . . You may not remember; no reason why you should. You might, though. It's right unusual—I don't recall outside the show-business circuit ever hearing of such a thing, and even that might be a fake. Well, to refresh your mind, I always had this certain gift."

"You weren't the one could find things?" The minister broke out laughing.

You'd think I rode all the way over here to have a tea party, Gavin thought. He was very nearly angry. "It ain't funny, Mr. Cooper. I mean, it's true. I really can. I could then and I can still. I'm telling you the truth, Mr. Cooper. There's a world of people in this state that know about me, and when they lose something they write to me. Recently it's got worse. It's never going to stop. I realized that about six months ago. I got three letters in one day—one from way off in Texas somewhere. It's a gift. I can't give it back. Every time I get a letter, I hesitate to open it. Because I don't like to practice it. I think it's a sin."

"Every good gift and every perfect gift is from above," said Mr. Cooper.

"I thought about that, too."

They were silent. What did I ever see in him? thought Gavin Anderson. "It might be the Devil's gift," he suggested.

"Why, I know your family, Gavin. Everybody knows the Andersons. Nothing you folks have got 's ever been near the Devil."

"It's mighty nice of you to say that," said Gavin. "You've helped me a whole lot."

But really the minister had not told him anything. He thought, I went all the way over there to say out loud what I thought myself.

It was later said in Dalton that Gavin Anderson had gone to see a minister and the minister had told him to give up his finding gift, it was a sin. But this had not happened, as Gavin knew. He let it go as truth, but it was not true. So sometimes still he opened the letters. Sometimes he didn't.

Then it was the day of the thunderstorm—a spring day when the sky got black as pitch around about noon. The tree leaves, which were just coming out, turned an incandescent green in the shift of light; they seemed to be burning with green fire. Just back of the square, a wall of velvet black hung flat as a curtain. The girl who came in to keep books half a day twice a week took off an hour early. "Go on," said Gavin Anderson. "I'll stay here. If you run, you can make it." She was out already, going headlong for her car. There was a short warning jab of lightning. The phone rang. It was the clerk's mother. She had been ailing all winter and now she was scared, up on that hill by herself. "Go on home, Percy," said Gavin Anderson. "Yo' mama sounds like it's blowing up Judgment Day." "What about you?" Percy Howell inquired. "Oh, I'll either lock up or stick it out. You're 'bout as safe one place as another." He called home, but no one answered. He had just replaced the receiver and stretched to switch a light on as the dark intensified when the phone rang a second time. He reached his hand toward it, but light snapped and thunder exploded simultaneously within the boxed area of the store. Fire leaped from the black mouth of the phone. He felt himself hurled aside, and lost consciousness for a moment or two—or was it longer? A livid turmoil of air stood at the door, loftier than flame. Rain like a white wall was now in swift advance. Not only leaves but the limbs themselves cross-whipped in crazy ways. He had been thinking of his family when the phone had rung and gone dead; now his thought, like an interrupted current, resumed. Where were they? Why, in his own vision, couldn't he find them? It had never occurred to him before; he had never yet tried to find a person, nor had he ever been asked to.

Then he was hastening to close the door, which had blown wide, and the woman shot through half screaming, a scared rabbit of the storm. It wasn't the bookkeeper back. He never thought it was.

The wild smell of the whole spring rushed terrible and vivid through the door, into his face and nostrils, charged with new life, white and cold. Then he slammed it. She stood in mid-floor, drenched, her face screwed up and her hands to her ears while thunder shook at the walls and ceiling, banged against the high transom.

She opened her eyes just long enough to say, "It's a tornado," then shut them tight again.

He'd never seen her before. The protection he felt toward his family, wherever they were, extended suddenly to her. Alone there, he might not have done anything to make himself safer. "Come here," he said.

He led her with him by the hand—she was not tall, and her hand was like a little wood-wet wild paw, trembling—to the back of the store and, opening a rough wooden door, went down some steps into a storage room, half underground, that his father had built during the Depression for storing potatoes. The walls were earthen and the whole hardly man-high, but as a storm pit he could see it functioning, unless debris fell in to bury them. "Sit down."

He crouched down himself and pulled her down. Drawing herself close to him, she waited in childlike terror, eyes, he could dimly make out, still shut up tight and one hand to her ear, the other hand clutching his hand. "Oh!" and "Oh!" she sobbed, and "Jesus, Jesus!" No woman in his own family said that. She wasn't from around here.

Some minutes later, gently putting her aside, he opened the door. Store air came into the earthen-smelling dark, and with it the steady beat of rain. "Come on," he said. He shook her. "It's O.K. now."

She opened her eyes—they were large and blue—and pushed her dark hair into place. She smiled, climbed the steps after him, and stood before him in the back area of the store among the crates of stock—a small full-breasted woman in her thirties, smartly dressed in black linen with a wide shiny belt, more than a hint of good living about her. She smoothed her hair a second time. "I've always been like that—storms scare me to death."

"Well, that was a bad one," he said, forgiving her. He gestured toward the store, but she took his hand first and turned it.

"I scratched you." She touched the red marks of her nails—there were three of them, one deeper than the rest.

"I see," he said.

He got out a chair for her and offered her a Coke—all he had. They sat together. The rain still lashed, swaying above the town and countryside. The tree limbs blew freely, and some were broken. The rain sluiced against the store windows and closed doors, but there was something domestic and ample about it now.

"You just passing through?" he asked. "You're not from around here."

But she said what he already suspected. She had been looking for a Gavin Anderson, because she had lost something.

It was nothing ordinary. Her grandmother had had it from a man who had died, and some had said he was the real grandfather–here a little laugh–but never mind. The stone was large, and valuable. She had written to Gavin Anderson two weeks ago, but had got no reply. She had the air of a small woman who tried things. If there was a finder to be found, she found him.

"You didn't get my letter."

"I often don't open those letters any more."

"You mean too many people worry you?"

"Something like that."

"You know, I thought that. I really did imagine it."

"I think–" He stopped. His innermost thoughts, his long struggle. Why give it all away, suddenly, to her? Yet he almost had.

"So I thought if I came and told you that it was special, a special case . . ."

"Everybody's case is special," he said. "Some little girl's pencil box is as important to her as a ruby ring is to you."

"How did you know it was a ruby?"

"I didn't know it. Of course I didn't."

He brought matches–store matches to light her cigarette. The rain beat steadily before the door, on the town square, on the town. As the smoke rose, he closed his eyes. He saw the ring. It had fallen in the crevice of some old, dark, broad-boarded floors. A piece of string and the head of a thumbtack lay beside it. The corner of a rug lay over it. He thought, She must have taken it off at night and didn't know she dropped it, going to bed after a party. It lay there in the dark, canted to the side, square-cut, wine red. A little more and he thought he might have seen the silver evening sandals she had probably removed, the stockings fallen beside them. But he opened his eyes. Through the smoke, she was half smiling at him. Now that the danger had come and gone, she looked blue-eyed and young, just out of high school.

He told her where to find the ring.

It was that very evening, after ten, she tried to reach him, but the lines were still down from the storm. She told him this the next morning, excited on the phone, not five minutes after service was resumed. "Right where you said! Can you imagine?"

"Listen," he said. "Please listen. I'm so glad. Yes, I really am, but you've got to listen. I don't want you to tell anybody." For suddenly, vast as an army, scattered out all over the South, maybe all over the country, the numerous connections a woman like that would have stirred to shadowy life in his consciousness. My God, I'll have to explain, he thought, and said, "Listen, are you at home? Will you be at home this evening—afternoon, I mean? Sometime around two or three o'clock?"

"Come to a party tomorrow night! Why don't you? Are you free?"

He was free, but he hesitated. A party was another thing entirely.

"It's nothing fancy," she went on. "Just cocktails and dinner. We'll have a drink or two, then eat. Some friends from Birmingham are bringing me a horse."

"Well, yes, ma'am," he found himself saying. "We'll try. It's sort of far for a party, but maybe we can make it." He hung up.

She would go around saying to everybody, "He has this gift, the most remarkable thing, you can't *ima*-gine, honey!" and her eyes, no longer clear blue and just out of high school, would burn overbright from alcohol. He wouldn't see her—not the way she seemed in the store just with him. And he would be the traveling magician, the oddity led by the wrist. Then he knew the truth about his fears, too—or were they hopes? Even if she did tell that world of people she knew, to them it would just be another of her stories about the backwoods. Most of them wouldn't even believe it. They'd tell the story maybe, but nobody would come look him up. They wouldn't, after an hour, be able to think of his name. And she—after a week or so, would she be able to?

He did not go to the party.

He went to see her instead. He was in that part of the state one afternoon. He got to the town and asked the way from a filling-station attendant. It was out of town, off a side road, over a cattle gap, through a pretty stretch of woods. The fences were all painted white. The house was at the end of a tree-lined path, quite a walk from the car, but the gate to let cars through was closed. He should have telephoned from town. He walked up the path. The trees, though oak, were not imposing, but small instead and rather twisted, as though storm-battered at an early age. And the house, even as it drew closer, was smaller than he had been expecting. It was white with a deep front porch, made private with thickset square pillars and a large bed of azaleas, past their prime. It was hard to get azaleas to bloom in that part of the state. The porch had a swing and white-painted iron furniture with comfortably padded green cushions. There were white-painted iron tables with glass tops, and lamps of wrought iron—all as it should be. No one there. Where was she? Should he stand, like the country man he was, and call? If he called, should he say Mrs. Beris or Naomi? Naomi Beris. It was an odd name. He ascended the front steps and knocked on one of the hollow white pillars. "Anybody home?"

There was a stir from within and a boy came out, tall, in his late teens, with wavy blond hair, wearing beige corduroys and beige suède shoes. The corduroy and suède went with the azaleas in the yard and the shadowy, waxed, thick-carpeted look of the hall. It went with the horses that Gavin Anderson already knew were out back, and would have known about even if she had not mentioned the horse she was getting from Birmingham.

"I'm looking for Mrs. Beris. Is she home?"

"She ought to be back pretty soon." The boy half turned to go inside. "Sit down, if you want to wait." He nodded toward the porch furniture. That was good enough, thought Gavin, feeling himself correctly defined. From a distance, the cattle gap rumbled.

She came in her car through the gate he had thought locked (it was automatic) and, parking in the side yard, got out and started toward the front porch. She was wearing short gloves and a dark cotton dress and carrying, along with her bag, a brown parcel. Near the steps, she paused and, shielding her eyes with one gloved hand, said, "Who is it? Now, don't tell me. It's Mr. Anderson!"

She had a drawling voice that only Southerners who have been away and come to know themselves in another context unconsciously cultivate.

"I was over here on business; just happened to be," he said.

Out back, she had the horses—two of them, a black and a bay. There was a white-fenced area for exercise and mounting, and a building with an open walkway through the middle, two stalls on one side and a tack- and feed-storage room on the other. The horses were small, to scale with everything there, to scale with herself. Perhaps she had a small fortune, Gavin thought. A Negro man who spoke to her pleasantly was cleaning the walkway, humming at his work. Gavin thought maybe the ruby that he had seen only in his vision was the only outsize thing she possessed. He did not ask to see it but, enchanted, listened and watched without seeming to.

"It's mighty pretty here," he said.

"It'd be a shame to part with it, now, wouldn't it?" she asked.

"You going to?"

"What can a lone woman do? My son's here, but after he finishes university he won't want to live here. There's nothing here for him."

"It looks like quite a lot here to me," said Gavin.

"Well, you know. . . . It's sweet of you to say so."

"I didn't know you were a lone woman."

"Divorced," she said. "I could face parting with the house, though it's been in the family a long time. But I couldn't sell a house with a ruby in it, now, could I?" He saw the ridiculous side of it. "Well, now," she pressed on, making him laugh more than ever, "how would you feel?"

She gave him a gin drink in a silver cup, fresh mint amidst the ice, and placed a small hand damp from the sweated silver into his as he stood on the steps, taking his leave.

He didn't get back to Dalton till after dark. He told his wife, Ethel, that he'd been up northeast of there to another county to see about some property he might invest in. It was the property, he said, in the ensuing weeks, that took him back up there, time and again. He asked her not to mention it.

"I think you know somebody up there," his wife said one evening. The boys had gone to a school program. It was autumn, the first cold snap. "I don't think you've bought any property up there at all. Anyway, there's plenty of property around here. So I don't believe it."

She was brushing her bobbed hair at the dresser. She had firm shoulders, had played basketball in school that year the girls' team was so attractive they used to get invited everywhere, and all the men turned out for miles around to whistle at their legs. She had short, strong, capable hands, the nails always breaking from housework, and knuckles a little large, a perennial cooking burn somewhere—but still attractive. The gas heater hissed in the room.

Gavin didn't answer her. There was no precedent, as far as he knew, for any Anderson's knowing at this point what to say.

"I just think you're trying to tell me not to go through with it about that property," he said at last. "I've been having some doubts myself. I bet you had a dream."

"I don't have to dream. You think I'm dumb? O.K., I never said anything. That's the way I'm going to act, from now on."

It was the year of the Anderson reunion—the year the Anderson grandmother was ninety-five, the year an Anderson daughter (Gavin's cousin) had twins, the year the Lord spared an Anderson grandson (Gavin's nephew) in a traffic accident in which four were killed and two cars demolished (the boy himself was pitched into a blackberry thicket and woke up not even scratched by briars), the year Gavin's son's calf won the state-wide blue ribbon, a year of prosperity in which (everybody hoped) there wouldn't be another German war. The reunion was down on the creek, in Indian summer, and a special moon appeared—a swollen oval at the horizon, so orange, so huge, so mysteriously brushed across with one thin black cloud, that one of the aunts kept saying over and over, "If it wasn't so pretty, it'd be downright scary." The night was warm. The Waukahatchie Creek curled near the bluff opposite the bar, running shallow after a dry fall over ribbed sand. The sandbar lay white beneath the moon, which had risen, grown smaller and radiant. Dozens of children, far and wide, knew just what they wanted to play, and down the path from the house, which wound through the willows, the women came tripping with plates of trimmed sandwiches, platters of fried chicken, bowls of potato salad, warmers full of rolls. Gavin sat with his brothers, harmonizing. They sang about the moon—a dozen moon songs—and clapping came up from the women near the tables. Ethel appeared, a ribbon in her hair, looking like a girl. "Thought you weren't coming," Gavin called to her. She'd had a headache earlier. "Changed my mind," she said, going by. The table spread, they lighted lanterns—somebody, got fancy and prosperous, had bought fashionable glass-shielded hurricane lamps, now sparkling grandly above the food. ("Where'd they come from?" one of the brothers asked. "Harriet," another answered. "Oh," said the first. You had to be one of them to get all there was in this.)

Now the brothers, five in all, were sent up to the house, and the grandmother was carried down in her rocker among them. When they appeared in her room, she was sitting straight and silent, dressed and ready. When she saw them, she broke into tears. "Wonderful boys," she kept saying. "Wonderful, wonderful boys." "Hush, now. Hush, now," they told her. And lightly they bore her down, among the willows.

On the way home, long after midnight, Ethel said, "Why wouldn't you find that bowl for them?" It was a silver bowl she meant. The family had all contributed to give it to the grandmother. Simple, engraved and beautiful, it was to sit on her dresser, a daily offering till she died.

"It wasn't lost," he said. "They were teasing."

"They weren't, either. I saw Marvin. He was just about crazy. So was Pat."

"Well, I didn't b'lieve it. I thought they were kidding. Anyway, you know I don't like to."

"Not even for Gran's birthday!"

"But they found it."

"But they really thought it was lost. It was just in George's car, but he went in for some ice and they didn't know it. But you wouldn't."

"I'm not on the midway. You can't just buy a ticket and have the show commence."

"Seems like if you ever did it in your life you would then. Wasn't your heart just so full with all the Andersons there? It's what you got up and said." This was undercutting of the worst kind—flat country-style.

"Yes, it was. I meant it all. Just like I said."

"You meant it when you said it, that's for sure."

He had got tired. Yet the reunion had finally reached him. His heart, though reluctant at first, had finally filled at that clear spring. The evening had said all the Andersons meant to each other—an eternal table, from the creation onward forever. Now it was plain to him that a tree does not choose to be struck by lightning, and that a plain man—even one who can find a ruby ring and who in consequence is given wine by candlelight and dark nakedness on fine linen—is a plain man still. But who, he thought, knew this better than Ethel? So how could she talk as she had? Well, the answer to that was plain also. He knew how she could, and why.

Next day, he tried all day to write the letter. For two weeks, he stuck strictly around Dalton, and every day he tried to write. At last, he made a phone call.

"I haven't been over," he said. "Listen, I don't think I can any more. You must have guessed that."

"Guessed? No. No, I didn't guess anything."

The conversation locked them in, close as a last embrace, and down, down they sank with it, till, touching bottom at last, they reversed and rose slowly toward the common light. "Just so long as you know how I feel," he was saying. "That I wanted to. Listen. Would you mind if we both came over? Ethel and me. I just want you to meet her." He hesitated. "I want you both to see." It was a crazy idea, but what he felt like. How did you act? How was an Anderson to know? What did it matter as long as Naomi understood?

"Gavin," said the brave, clear, sophisticated voice over the uncertain connection, "I understand perfectly. Y'all come ahead."

When he let himself out of the drugstore phone booth, a daze fell on him. What had he done? What was he blotting out? Whatever the answers, it was too late to stop. The plan, once agreed to, ticked on like a wound clock.

Ethel rode all the way that Sunday with her pretty face fixed on the road, back straight, her bag and gloves neat in her lap. It was a cool, dusty, early December day.

"How do you do?" said Naomi Beris. She was standing at the top of the steps, in a dress of thin white wool with a gold chain at the neck. "Sit down," she said. Her son came out and offered them Cokes on ice. Everything was Sunday-quiet. The cattle gap rumbled. "Who on earth?" Naomi said. A car appeared, green, larger and newer than average for those days. It paused to allow the gate to open and drew into the side yard beside Naomi's. A man got out. He was heavy-set, gray-haired, and florid-faced, dressed in khaki and high-laced riding boots, a worn riding coat over a whipcord shirt.

"Mr. Slatton's from Columbus," said Naomi. "He came about the horses. I guess that's right, isn't it, Abe?"

"Are the horses sick?" Ethel asked. Mr. Slatton, certainly not a veterinarian, gave no sign he had heard her.

"No," said Naomi. "I have to sell them eventually, and they show up best before the winter sets in. I didn't mention that, Abe," she said to Slatton. "You see how clever I am."

"Shouldn't mention it now." He did not look at her or at the guests.

He drank nothing, not even Coke, and stared out at the avenue of trees.

She was wearing the ruby. Gavin had never seen it before. He had asked her once, and she had said it was in the bank vault; she said the insurance was too expensive to keep up. Now it was just as he had envisioned it. Square-cut, dark as wine, it further shrank her small hand, which rested peacefully on the fine white fabric above her lap. It drank the light, inexhaustibly.

"That's the most beautiful ring," said Ethel, who had never heard of it.

Naomi said, "There's a story about it. My great-grandmother lived in an old house that burned. It was near the Natchez Trace, about a mile over yonder. The road is all fallen in now. Not many people even know that's what it was. This man used to come down it, always going to Jackson and then back to somewhere in Tennessee. He would stop by a spring we had. He was a terrible man—clothes made out of skins, probably smelled like bear grease, nothing to recommend him. My grandmother was a young girl, not but fifteen or sixteen. But he wanted to see her, so he always stopped. He used to wait on his horse in the woods till she went down to the spring to bring some water up for dinner so it would be cool for the table. And how many times he waited and how many times she had to run away from him nobody knew. Who knew if she *didn't* run away from him? Nobody would answer that. He carried a pack and a small blanket roll behind his saddle.

"One day he came through, and he'd had a fight with some men either the day before or the night before. He'd slipped away from them in the early morning. There was blood on him, so my grandmother said. He told her he would come back if he could. Meantime, he unstrapped the rolled blanket from the cantle and gave it to her. He'd come back for it, he said, if he could; if not, it was hers. And he said he trusted her.

"At the house, she unwrapped it—not a blanket but a dirty shawl such as Indians wore against the wind. Was that all he had to sleep in, or did he stay in inns? It was a small roll of things—a pewter cup, a blue glass bottle that smelled like corn whiskey, and then the ruby. She almost missed it; it was tied up in a rag. And he never came back. She married, or was married to, a Pontotoc boy, soon after. Too soon after, was what they said. So here we are still—and here's the ruby."

All of them were silent.

The man, Abe Slatton, gave no sign that he had listened to her. He had not once looked at her during the story. Finally, still staring out at the line of oak trees, he said, "You got the blood of that *ter*-rible man flowin' in yo' veins."

"Pete wouldn't be home," she said, nodding toward her son, "but the whole Georgia Tech team came down with flu. They had to cancel the Auburn game."

"Everybody's got it there, too," said Pete.

"Do you-all go to the games?" Naomi asked.

"We go to the high school games," said Ethel. "Our boy is on the team. It keeps us pretty busy, I guess."

Gavin and Ethel Anderson left soon after.

"That man was the rudest thing I ever saw," said Ethel. "He never even said good-by, glad I met you. Nothing. You didn't talk about the property," she added, sly as a fox.

"I told her on the phone I'd decided against it," he said.

"You believe all that about that ring?" she asked, ten miles farther on.

"I don't know."

"I wonder," said Ethel, "if it's even real."

Back in those days, all the roads in Mississippi, with two exceptions, were either dirt or gravel. The road from Naomi Beris's back to Dalton was sixty winding miles, thick-piled with gravel in the center and along the edges, roiling with dust if another car came by. They stopped in a drab little town–a chain of storefronts facing a railroad track, a few houses scattered up rutted roads along broken sidewalks–and had a sandwich in a café.

"Thank you for taking me, Gavin," said Ethel. She was looking at him tenderly, tears in the wide brown eyes that belonged to him; her slyness and undercutting, he knew, were gone. And she wouldn't talk, wouldn't "tell." Things were righted. He was fit once more to bear a grandmother in a rocking chair, feather-light among five strong men, down to the white sandbar. He could sing once more to the moon. What did he need with a wild witch who had blown up out of a thunderstorm, who writhed like a cat, spitting words out that belonged on the walls of a john? What had she wanted with him? A summer had been enough for both of them.

They came out of the restaurant and got into the car. At a curve in the road, the little town vanished like a thought of itself, something that had never been. Now they faced west, drawn straight into a fiery sun, at first so fierce and blinding through the dust that they had to stop until the worst of the glare had muted. It faded beautifully, from a flaming cauldron to blood to wine to deep red velvet, and sank straight ahead of them, removing its deep tinge almost at once from the sky.

His gift was flawed now. It would be like something from boyhood, put aside in a closet. Was he glad or sorry? He didn't know. Driving the harsh gravel, he felt numb somewhere, and placed one hand to his shoulder. Wet blood still thickly stained the dirty leather of his shirt, and the girl with the bucket of spring water, whose waist and lips he knew, reached up to take the rolled shawl, bound with leather strings. The horse shifted beneath him, and her hands, desperate with love, clung along his thigh, which was that of a horseman in his prime, powerful and bold.

INSTRUMENT OF DESTRUCTION

I think that someday I am going to come home and not have to hear anything about the little boy next door. But that may be because he has killed my aunt or she has stopped being a lady long enough to kill him. Of course, what he's been doing in the yard is a shame. He's ruined all the flower beds with his tricycle and now he's starting on the shrubs, breaking the thinner fronds out of the center of the spirea to plait into whips and ropes, and removing blossoms from the crêpe myrtle. Nobody can catch him. He waits till my aunt does her shopping, goes to the grocery, or uptown, or to a church meeting, or to the nursing home.

The reason my aunt doesn't like to make an issue about the boy next door is that she was so glad when he and his folks moved in. They have class and good taste and breeding; they come from an excellent family she has some connection with, down in Columbus, Mississippi, a very aristocratic town. Before they came she had nobody but the most ordinary neighbors, people of no interest to her. One woman—the one on the other side of her still—she really does not like and goes to some pains to avoid. The reason she gives is that the woman looks punished by life. True, the woman's husband is down-at-the-heels, has a low-paying job (night copy-desk editor at the newspaper), sleeps all day, looks unshaven, probably drinks too much, and never speaks. His wife's face reflects all this. Well, of course, it does, I tell her. But my aunt can't agree, can't see things this way.

She has had terrible misfortunes about Uncle Paul's illness, being alone, no one to lean on, yet she keeps everything up to a certain mark. The yard is taken care of: a man comes once a week to clip, weed, and mow. Her dresses are always fresh-looking and smart, her gloves when she goes out are white as snow. Her table is set with the best linen and china, every meal. She feels that life has to reach a certain standard daily, has to be pretty and fresh, or it isn't worth calling life. She was beginning to get discouraged, to feel herself islanded in a world that didn't understand her feelings–I obviously do nothing to suit her, trailing out to class daily at the university in skirts and blouses she wouldn't be caught dead in, and going around with what she would call the dregs of humanity if she would come right out and say so.

Then the McAllisters moved in.

Her heart lifted–I could tell–even before she met them, because the painters came and took the horrible gray trim off the house next door with neat applications of white. The windows got removed and painted as well, and new screens installed. Suddenly there were no cobwebs and the panes were glossy clear. Next the porch got freshly done and touches of iron were covered in black enamel. It went on like that. One afternoon, vans arrived, and shining antiques were lifted out from dim, churchlike interiors padded with green quilted hangings, and were transferred smoothly within, not a scratch on the lot, so far as we could tell. Chests came passing after. It was late afternoon with my aunt in the rocker and me in the swing, out on the front porch. "Don't let's look," said my aunt and we both began to laugh, because we both were drinking it all in, from sheer curiosity. Those chests would have draperies in them, we agreed, and linens and silver. Then came packing boxes, lightly borne: china and ornaments, we bet. The rugs followed, bound with lengths of grass rope and bending supple and velvety in the middle. And last of all, on another day, the people came. We'd seen them before, as buyers and directors of workmen. But that day the car–a dark Buick–stopped in the drive with finality and out came the man, the woman, and the boy, and in they went, and the door closed fast.

I have to hand it to my aunt in a lot of ways. If her sort of standards interested me (they don't), I guess I would want to behave just the way she did. She did not, for one thing, try to talk to the new neighbors over the hedge or across the fence in the back yard. She did not send over a cake or some cookies, with a coy welcome-to-our-street note tucked inside. She did not–God forbid–go to "call." As a matter of fact, she did not seem to notice the new family at all. She came and went in her fresh summer outfits and her snow-white gloves. One day, up at the corner (our street slopes down hill) she ran into the woman next door and she was about to pass with a nod but the woman spoke to her and thus she–my aunt–found herself stopped, greeted, even welcomed, in a way, and asked about things. What did one do about cleaning women, gardeners, groceries, etc.? Wouldn't it be nice to break the ice and get better acquainted? The new family did not know Tennessee at all. They were from Columbus, Mississippi. My aunt let go the name of a family there, an exceptionally good family. Like a charming bird released from its cage, the name circled the heads of those two ladies twice and thrice before it shot singing into the bright blue sky. In a day or so my aunt was invited over for a drink.

That weekend she was happier, more content with life, than I had seen her in a long time. The difference was in her eyes and face, in her walk and her voice, everywhere. They had asked all about her. She had told them about Uncle Paul and about me, her niece at the university, and how she'd never had children. They had understood her, it seemed. They had liked her. The little boy was so sweet, she told me. He had got some paints as a present and had brought them to show her.

The next week she had a better chance than ever to see the paints–they were all over the sidewalk. I saw them myself.

"Listen, Auntie," I said, "don't worry. It just means he subscribes to *Mad* magazine. That's where he's copied all that."

"I think he's an awful little midget," she said. "They're pretending he's a little boy."

But she kept on accepting when they asked her over for a drink and one warm lovely twilight, she had them, too, out in her garden. (They had got a sitter for the little boy.) Then, being so continually understood by them and so personally treated, she had them to a dinner with a couple of old friends. She loved to give small parties when Uncle Paul was there with her and now it all came back, the first she'd given since he went to the nursing home: she was both sad and excited. But being sociable at heart, her excitement won out and the dinner was a huge success. (The McAllisters, again, left the child with the baby-sitter.)

I myself am not interested in much social life; it seems to me a waste of time. I know when I graduate I will go on to graduate school in one of the sciences, that I will always know people in groups, we will always like music and books together, sex will be (already is) a pairing off among us, we will do cooking that is interesting and good. Married apartment living or small house living around campuses or research centers is what I see in my future. It is good enough. I don't care much where I live as long as it is humanly habitable. This is me. From about the time I got interested in high school chemistry and physics, I have been like this. I went to live with my aunt because my folks knew she needed money (she lives near the campus). But of course I haven't been any real help to her at all. We don't exchange confidences or ideas or anything. I have long dark hair and go around in sandals till my feet just about freeze. If she thinks I'm going to change, she is mistaken. This is me.

Little at a time, my aunt gave the McAllisters their whole social life in her city. She launched them. Otherwise they wouldn't have known the right people at all. This is what my aunt says, and she may be right. They had her to dinner soon with Mr. McAllister's boss (unimpressive, she said) and his wife (a bore, from a boring family she used to know in the church), and they also asked the couple she had introduced them to. Soon they were going to her church and she was leading them up to people there who had been friends of hers and Uncle Paul's and they were delighted with them all. She let them use her willingly because she had been longing for her own kind near her, people who understood her in a deep way. That was why she didn't raise too big a row when the little boy broke down the back fence. The McAllisters said he was an imaginative child and was always playing games in which something became something else. The fence was one wall of a fort, for instance, and was attacked and taken. Then the sidewalk was like a concrete tablet for drawing on and my aunt's flowers were enemy children from another planet and her crêpe myrtle blossoms were a secret poison to be cooked in with Irish stew and fed to a visiting Indian chief who was treacherous and meant to attack in the night.

"Do you tell Uncle Paul all this?" I ask my aunt.

"Of course not," she says, "what can he do? I told him about the McAllisters, of course. He's glad I'm so happy with them."

I wonder if she really is. I think she worries. How can she end the trouble with that child? What can she do? I think the child is crazy. He doesn't bother any other house or property but hers. From her front gate he murmurs ugly words, conducts (as long as anybody will listen) a bad dialogue with passers-by. My aunt is afraid of making issues, of telling the whole truth. She is afraid not only of losing the McAllisters but also of losing something else which the McAllisters by recognizing have increased her faith in: that is, her own self-image, her own belief in her unfailing charm and courtesy. So she can't take any steps at all, and something terrible will happen.

Her new friendship, which had opened up so beautifully and which she had given her all to with such whole-hearted skill, is not what she had hoped for. I see she is looking strained again and lonelier than before. I could say I dreamed she was tied to a stake in an Indian village while a child raced round her on a tricycle with a feather stuck through a band around its brow, whooping. But I didn't dream that.

He has started cutting the bark off her trees. He has a knife and removes the bark skillfully, in long strips.

I come home unexpectedly. That day I have a headache from too much formaldehyde in the lab plus my worst day of the month. My aunt is away at the nursing home. The child is working away on her pretty young maple. I walk across the lawn.

"Listen, Buster," I say. "You can get away with that with everybody but me. Now you put up that knife and get the hell on home, *comprenez?*"

He goes into a rage, no kidding. The knife slashes me twice before I can knock him winding, which I do. I'm pretty strong, not bad at tennis, and angry. Shocked, too, from the blood actually starting up out of my arm. I just plain clobber him. Then (it's raining and cold) I am racing in for a tourniquet to save my own life and the child is yelling to wake the dead. I am tearing up a cup towel in my aunt's kitchen and calling a cab to get myself to the hospital out-patient emergency entrance. That little bastard nearly killed me. By the time they stitch me up I'm about passed out but faint thoughts murmur something about the mess in my aunt's kitchen, blood all over the floor and for all I know dripped through the hall, over rugs and tables, staining walk and doorway.

Once a month I make the effort to go out with my aunt to see Uncle Paul. A man with naturally dark skin, he has kept his color better than most people would with what he's got and though emaciated he still has his keen glance. He doesn't make you feel sorry for him. I never knew him very well. I don't know him now.

He sits and plays checkers with some of the patients in the sun parlor every day and sometimes bridge, which amuses him more. He reads. I guess he must have been fun to talk to once and in love with her and all that. She must have loved his wiriness, attractive in a man, and loved the thin blade of his cheekbone pressed to hers. Now they've had their love, at least, and they hold hands. When I'm not there they may cry a little, but with me present they make an occasion of the visit, something they charmingly measure up to. I'm not worth it, I want to say. No. No, not that. Nobody is worth it, I want to say. Yet they are going to do it. They go right ahead, light and conversational, pretending the abyss isn't there.

"What happened to your arm?" Uncle Paul asks me.

How far can I go? I don't want to worry him. "An accident," I say.

"She was cutting a cantaloupe," my aunt says, "with that knife—oh, you remember those knives I had to have, handmade with hickory handles, from way out in the country. You always warned me."

"Get those things too sharp, you've got more than a knife," Uncle Paul says. "You've got an instrument of destruction." He laughs. "Is it okay now?"

"Sure," I say.

"Mighty glad you're with Mary," he tells me. He always says that.

"She's great," I say. I like him.

"Sure she is."

He asks about the McAllisters and she says they're fine.

But relations have certainly cooled with the McAllisters since the day their little boy slashed into me. They don't telephone any more. I feel they're going to have to look back on knowing my aunt as an incident of their first year in the new town. Among the other families on the street, those people my aunt doesn't care to know, the word has got round that the boy has calmed down quite a bit since I knocked hell out of him. My aunt would have a great chance now, if she'd make the slightest effort, to make some real human relationships on that street. They all know all about her, and some are there, mysterious among them, like everywhere, who can hold things up—sustainers in time of need.

But she doesn't want them. She wants friends like the McAllisters are, or would have been, if they hadn't given birth to that awful child.

GO SOUTH IN THE WINTER

Mrs. Landis came out into the morning sun of the West Indies in bathing suit and robe, seeking her beach chair before the Caribe Hilton in San Juan. She arranged her possessions around her, book and beach bag containing her cap, cosmetics, and wallet, then draped her towel on the back of the chair, and having smeared herself with sun-protective lotion, opened her book and began to read. She soon became sleepy (at the same time as her husband a thousand miles to the north was sleepy also: he suffered from a mild hangover and was disinclined to tackle his income tax). Sun drowsiness was Mrs. Landis' reason, and she welcomed it; she liked to doze in sunlight.

A wrangle of voices stirred her from her mood and she looked up. The young Jewish couple she had conversed with the day before were back, complete with baby in sun bonnet. Each time they turned the baby loose it came to her. Sandy, it clambered over her knees, pushed her book out of her hands, examined her face at close range, and seizing her hair by the fistful, shook her with real force.

"Sonia!"

Both parents called to her, and the young mother rose to fetch her, detaching her from Mrs. Landis a finger at a time. "She doesn't hurt, let her play," Mrs. Landis protested, laughing.

"She's got Mrs. Landis mixed up with her grandmother, I think. Don't you think so, George?" The young mother swung the baby free. "It's absolutely clear."

"Must be: they look alike," her husband agreed. He piled sand for the baby, who wanted strenuously to go back to Mrs. Landis and now began to cry.

"Did you see the show last night, Mrs. Landis?" the girl asked. She was dark, interested, relaxed, plump, her hair screwed up behind to keep her neck bare for sunning and swimming, a large floppy native straw hat set forward on her brow.

"The dancing? Just the beginning. I went up early."

"They were good, you know."

"Yeah, you shoulda stayed," the young man said.

The baby continued to wail and struggle to return to Mrs. Landis. The father held it, like an animal in harness, by the cross straps of its cotton sun suit.

"I'm here alone," said Mrs. Landis, "so that makes it—"

Here the baby's crying grew strident with demand, and the young couple turned to consult each other. "You'd better take her in," the wife agreed. The young man got up and carried the child toward the water. Halfway there she noticed the sea and leaned toward it, jumping to get to it faster.

What was I going to say? Mrs. Landis wondered. "That makes it . . ." What? She didn't know. Makes it difficult to be alone at floor shows? In former years she had tried conversations with various strangers—couples, other loners—and sometimes these had worked out pleasantly. Why didn't she want to do that now? On the other hand, why should she?

The reasons for doing anything were lacking for her, she reflected, at this particular period of her life. But after all, she'd come there just to drift, to do nothing she didn't feel inclined to do. She idly recalled the middle-aged divorcé she had some years back allowed to talk his way into her bed. She watched the gulls drift, turn, flap wings, soar, and drift again. On an arm of the beach, far out, the palms blew. The young father was floating his baby in the sea. It flailed arms and legs, making wild splashes, yelping with glee. What a violent child! Mrs. Landis thought, and at the same instant was startled as it leaped so high that, momentarily free of the water, it seemed magnified by a trick of vision into something larger than life, the painting of a baby, huge on a master canvas which contained, as minor objects, trees, sea, and clouds.

Mrs. Landis wondered if she would be feeling less detached if she were at home. She liked to play bridge but if deprived of the pleasure she would not have missed it much. Volunteer duty at the hospital did not utterly absorb her. She knew that her husband, though retirement had left him with little to say, still needed her. Her children telephoned and visited; her grandchildren wrote; her friends were faithful; and people who got to know her usually liked and admired her.

Arranging her hair where the baby had pulled it down, she rubbed lotion on her back and along the underside of her arms and legs. Then flattening the chair and balancing her body so as not to tip over, she turned to lie on her face.

Behind her, the young family were talking, the father having returned with the dripping child fresh from the sea; they were spreading down large beach towels for her to play on. Now they were switching on a transistor radio; Mrs. Landis heard the spiel of selected news items from the States and abroad which would be repeated in more or less the same form all day until around five o'clock, when new releases would be substituted. There went the latest Presidential primary, next came the Middle East, now a new White House appointment, then the latest in scandal and corruption. Mrs. Landis half-dozed.

She thought of her children, thought of her oldest boy when he was four or five and how she had found she could talk to him, converse with him, as one might to an adult, and how this discovery had been a great delight. In her memory they were walking, the two of them, along a road in Vermont. The fresh June green of maple and beech trees shadowed them; roadside bushes mingled with wild white and yellow flowers. The boy walked ahead of her, talking eagerly. His thoughts came out the instant he had them, no self-consciousness to stop or deflect them: what a joy this was! Near the top of a hill, rain overtook them from behind, a tough sudden downpour with a sharp wind. An empty house stood just off the road, so they climbed a fence and ran for it. Here they sheltered, under a porch roof half-fallen in. Lilacs overgrown and unpruned bloomed among the ruins. First lashed about and drenched, the branches then stood still and poured out fragrance; soon the sun came out again. Her son had talked constantly until halfway through the storm when he had finished all he had to say, then closed his mouth in that sudden serious way he was all his life to retain, though that one day it seemed to crystallize forever in her heart's thought of him. Was it the baby clambering about on her which had brought back all this treasure, at once warm yet inaccessible?

She had almost fallen asleep. Behind her, the news went on—most of it now from New York. An art gallery theft, a prediction of snow, the mayor's latest national pronouncement, a city commissioner's death, killed in a traffic accident coming from Kennedy Airport. His name was Landis. Landis. They said it three times, each with a blur of words between. Landis.

Mrs. Landis, who had never before heard of the man who had died, sat straight up. Tears streamed out from underneath her dark glasses, poured down through the lotion on her face. Her hand moved helplessly to conceal or stop them. The young couple had sat up to look at her. They were people who missed nothing. She had seen them only once, the day before, yet her name had been produced the minute they saw her. Now they had caught the thread at once, and were looking at her with alarm.

"Not what you think," she wanted to reassure them, but all she managed actually to say was: "My son . . . oh no!"

"Oh no!" the young wife echoed. "To hear it on the radio!"

The young man said nothing. He came forward at once, straightening from his knees up. Though apparently about to rise, he seemed, like a figure in a ritual, to be kneeling to her, arms outstretched.

"No, don't," said Mrs. Landis. She groped, gathering up book, beach bag, and towel and walked unsteadily away, leaving them behind. Halfway to the hotel, the young man caught up with her.

"Do you want anybody? Need anything? Can I—?"

"No . . . please, I—" She stumbled on and he stopped and turned back.

It had all happened in the sun, she thought. The strong, almighty sun—everywhere at once, beneficent, fierce, impersonal—what they'd come to find. She had not thought of it as a presence until she left it, felt it slip from her as she entered the hotel terraces. In her room she finished crying, bathed her face and showered, and stood at last in a fresh linen dress, overlooking the whole scene from her balcony: the beach, the palms waving, and the young couples taking their children down by either hand to go into the sea.

Late in the afternoon she sought out the two who had seen her cry.

She sat down and talked to them in a charming, open way, confessing everything.

"I happened to be dreaming about my son when he was a boy, then this news came in the middle of it about a man completely unrelated. Dreaming, but not dreaming . . . can you understand?"

"It tripped the switch," the young man said.

"We've been worried about you all day, Mrs. Landis," his wife said gravely.

"Thank you for being so kind," Mrs. Landis said. She was laughing, a woman sometimes foolish, but now restored to the smooth, safe surfaces. She said that she would come that night, to watch the dancing.

A KISS AT THE DOOR

When I was a child I sat on a high stool and watched my cousin Félice cooking. She kneaded dough for rolls or rolled out biscuits on a slab of marble. The stool brought my head to about a level with her shoulder. She was a tiny woman, though, and when out on the street in her brown coat was as small as a thrush. Her intense, honest face was innocent of make-up. Did she have enemies, did she have faults, had she ever been in love? So far as I know she was a friend to all and none. She was poor, as her father's firm had once lost money in a bad business deal. Though it was not his fault (so the family story went, anyway), he undertook to pay off the great debts. When he died, worn out, Cousin Félice took up the struggle. She worked all her life, buying only such clothes as were necessary to "look nice" at work and at church. Wasn't this boring? It may have been. Her house stood on the corner of a distinguished street in the big town. My family used to leave me there when they came in from the country for shopping or doctors. I don't remember anything she ever said. I assumed that all nice cousins looked like her and that she never had even once worn a stocking with a run in it and that her purse and gloves, worn though they might be, were of genuine leather. I think of her now when baking bread, as I do once in a great while.

What to knead it on? A marble slab would be ideal.

As we never conversed much on days when I was left with her, and as I was just the same extremely aware of her in every finely trained detail (nothing about her was accidental or rebellious) it seemed that I was not so much there to visit as to take an imprint, something that my mother and aunts—with their prospering husbands and heads full of sale ads and ideas about redecorating and new clothes and parties, bent on going everybody back home one better—valued but could not impart, for they had no necessity for staying spiritually still in one attitude.

I was of all children easiest in the world to influence. If they had left me in a convent I would have come out walking like a nun trailing imaginary robes about my shoes for days on end; if by mistake a thief had been engaged to look after me, I would have longed to get in the ten-cent store back home in order to practice my shoplifting. As it was, I became not so much an imitator or disciple of Cousin Félice, as some little cutout figure placed in smaller outline within herself. I besought my mother for a small brown morocco purse similar to hers and would comb my hair back in a manner much too old for me. Then I forgot: Cousin Félice went out of my head altogether once other and nearer stores and doctors were discovered by the acquisitive female world that my father and uncles slaved daily, all their lives, to supply.

Why does she now return? Is it because of the bread?

Placed in a warm place, the bread rises, doubles in size.

I have myself just about doubled, and Cousin Félice now exists, as regards myself, like a dim outline within me, for she herself would, if alive, come up no higher on me in my kitchen than I, sitting on a stool, once did in hers. And as she is one with the invisible host of the dead, she must exist to me as a shadowy self within, in dim outline and motion with me, at such times as my memory evokes her.

The surprise is, she isn't all that proud of being thought of. She won't stay. She leaves me almost as soon as she materializes. Who am I to have called her out? It is her disappearance which makes me ask this and other questions.

Did she ever love me? Did she ever love anybody? Did any of us ever know? Did she even want me to be left there with her on Saturdays, her one free day? Wasn't she just putting up with it for the family's sake? Wasn't she, for that matter, putting up with all of life for the family's sake, for the sake principally of that one bad business deal her father got mixed up in? Where on earth would she have been if he hadn't made that one mistake? It's what kept her from being considered just another old maid, wasn't it? Anyway, now she is impatient to be gone. I am not worth the trouble I am putting her to, even to remember her. She will tell me that, as easy as rolling out biscuits and cutting them out with a sharp tin cutter, none overlapping, each neatly defined, for the family will be in soon to eat supper. They have said they can't stay, but she will say it's already done; so laughing, and bursting with Southern compliments about any and everything, they will take off their hats and whisper behind her back that what they'd really like to take off are their shoes and their corsets. Over the food and the hot biscuits, they will say how wonderful she is. Later, she will stand at the door and say "Good-by" and "Come back when you can!" Before I go—last one out—she will kneel down to kiss me on the cheek.

It's all in order, that's what it is. It's why she hates to be bothered, to be called up to whatever strange city I happen to be in, because that's not where she's meant to be.

There was a small damp garden—what we called a back yard—back of her house, with a flagstone walk and an iron sundial in a circular flagstone area. She would let me go out there and sit on a stone bench. Once she came with me and sat by me, leaning forward, her hand heels pressed to the stone on either side, her legs crossed, talking briskly about something. She had an eager voice and wore a gold watch, loose on her wrist. Was there anything wrong about her? Nothing.

Of course, she'd had a boy friend. Somebody she had talked to at parties in the big houses where friends of her family lived and to which alone she was allowed to accept invitations, though if any from elsewhere were issued to her, we do not know from where and when. She was not shy with him, that lost face, that tall or slight form, dark or blond or brown. She talked with the eager voice and wore white (or maybe blue taffeta or maroon velvet) in a simple way, a gold ornament on a chain hanging below the square-cut neck. Why didn't she marry him? Had the shame, the shameful day and the ruined business and the house shuttered till late afternoon, and the family pew empty at church and the friends wondering whether or not to call, what attitude to take, and the talks with this one and that one in the established community and the haggard decision of honor, the mother sick in bed behind a screen—had all that interposed to ruin her happiness, like a sort of last-minute rescue by the U.S. cavalry or Sir Lancelot in reverse, leaving the father a Christ-figure, ruined but exalted in her heart, before whom the young man, losing solidity, melted? Or had the simple drive in the first place never been strong enough? Would she ever have wanted to marry anybody?

The truth is: there isn't any way to know. You can eat the biscuits, and the biscuits are good. For the rest, if she knows she won't tell you.

But she does know something she doesn't have to mention, and that one thing is forever—it sustains her.

She knew what burden she took on herself. Others knew it; they know it still. The burden became her identity. This is why she is restless with me and is leaving. She knows I am about to question her. The question? That's plain. To think it is to shout it—and she hears.

WAS IT WORTH IT?

She can't answer. She seems to be saying she never thought anybody would ask her that. She doesn't want to hear it. She is scared. Then, even at a distance, she rights herself, a diminished self, with terrible effort. She can and does ask me right back: What else could I do?

I know what I would have done and I boldly face her with it. I would have declared that that debt was no fault of mine. I would have let the guilt flee to haunt those tombs it belonged with in the first place. I would have sold the old house for something fresh, practical, and pretty. What money I could make I would have spent on life. Life. Life! The words die on my tongue. She is offering me supper. I am taking it.

But she is angry now, really angry. There is red in her cheeks, which, though they still retain a fine soft texture, burst in small red veins in a hot kitchen or under emotional stress into which I have now plunged her by suggesting that she chose the life she lived and might have chosen otherwise. There was no choice, is what she wants me to believe, what she herself has not ever had to tell herself, it was as belief so deep within her. Why bother her? Because I have to know one thing.

Cousin Félice, were you human?

I was, I was! she is crying. I am, I am! I felt hatred, knew rebellion. I was afraid in dark old rooms, knew the dry ache of dying desire. But I came out and it was spring. Jonquils were blooming. The air was warm. And you? And you?

Her little hand is in mine, feet urgent beside me, voice eager, as I monstrous, not deigning an answer, walk fast in a foreign city.

PART IV

1972–1977

A CHRISTIAN EDUCATION

It was a Sunday like no other, for we were there alone for the first time. I hadn't started to school yet, and he had finished it so long ago it must have been like a dream of something that was meant to happen but had never really come about, for I can remember no story of school that he ever told me, and to think of him as sitting in a class equal with others is as beyond me now as it was then. I cannot imagine it. He read a lot and might conceivably have had a tutor—that I can imagine, in his plantation world.

But this was a town he'd finally come to, to stay with his daughter in his old age, she being also my mother. I was the only one free to be with him all the time and the same went for his being with me—we baby-sat one another.

But that word wasn't known then.

A great many things were known, however; among them, I always had to go to Sunday School.

It was an absolute that the whole world was meant to be part of the church, and if my grandfather seldom went, it was a puzzle no one tried to solve. Sermons were a fate I had only recently got big enough to be included in, but Sunday School classes had had me enrolled in them since I could be led through the door and placed on a tiny red chair, feet not even at that low height connecting to the floor. It was always cold at the church; even in summer, it was cool inside. We were given pictures to color and Bible verses to memorize, and at the end a colored card with a picture of Moses or Jesus or somebody else from the Bible, exotically bearded and robed.

Today I might not be going to Sunday School, and my regret was only for the card. I wondered what it would be like. There was no one to bring it to me. My mother and father were not even in town. They had got into the car right after breakfast and had driven away to a neighboring town. An aunt by marriage had died and they were going to the funeral. I was too little to go to funerals, my mother said.

After they left I sat on the rug near my grandfather. He was asleep in his chair before the fire, snoring. Presently his snoring woke him up. He cut himself some tobacco and put it in his mouth. "Are you going to Sunday School?" he asked me. "I can't go there by myself," I said. "Nobody said I had to take you," he remarked, more to himself than to me. It wasn't the first time I knew we were in the same boat, he and I, we had to do what they said, being outside the main scale of life where things really happened, but by the same token we didn't have to do what they didn't say. Somewhere along the line, however, my grandfather had earned rights I didn't have. Not having to attend church was one; also, he had his own money and didn't have to ask for any.

He looked out the window.

"It's going to be a pretty day," he said.

How we found ourselves on the road downtown on Sunday morning, I don't remember. It was as far to get to town as it was to get to church, though in the opposite direction, and we both must have known that, but didn't remark upon it as we went along. My grandfather walked to town every day except Sunday, when it was considered a sin to go there, for the drugstore was open and the barbershop, too, on occasions, if the weather was fair; and the filling station was open. My parents thought that the drugstore had to be open but should sell drugs only, and that filling stations and barbershops shouldn't be open at all. There should be a way to telephone the filling station in case you had to have gas for emergency use. This was all worked out between them. I had often heard them talk about it. No one should go to town on Sunday, they said, for it encouraged the error of the ones who kept their places open.

My grandfather was a very tall man; I had to reach up to hold his hand while walking. He wore dark blue and dark gray herringbone suits, and the coat flap was a long way up, the gold watch chain almost out of sight. I could see his walking cane moving opposite me, briskly swung with the rhythm of his stride: it was my companion. Along the way it occurred to me that we were terribly excited, that the familiar way looked new and different, as though a haze which had hung over everything had been whipped away all at once, like a scarf. I was also having more fun than I'd ever had before.

When he came to the barbershop, my grandfather stepped inside and spoke to the barber and to all who happened to be hanging around, brought out by the sunshine. They spoke about politics, the crops, and the weather. The barber who always cut my hair came over and looked to see if I needed another trim and my grandfather said he didn't think so, but I might need a good brushing; they'd left so soon after breakfast it was a wonder I was dressed. Somebody who'd come in after us said, "Funeral in Grenada, ain't it?" which was the first anybody had mentioned it, but I knew they hadn't needed to say anything, that everybody knew about my parents' departure and why and where. Things were aways known about, I saw, but not cared about too much either. The barber's strong arms, fleecy with reddish hair, swung me up into his big chair where I loved to be. He brushed my hair, then combed it. The great mirrors sparkled and everything was fine.

We presently moved on to the drugstore. The druggist, a small, crippled man, hobbled toward us, grinning to see us, and he and my grandfather talked for quite some time. Finally my grandfather said, "Give the child a strawberry cone," and so I had it, miraculous, and the world of which it was the center expanded about it with gracious, silent delight. It was a thing too wondrous actually to have eaten, and I do not remember eating it. It was only after we at last reached home and I entered the house, which smelled like my parents' clothes and their things, that I knew what they would think of what we had done and I became filled with anxiety and other dark feelings.

Then the car was coming up the drive and they were alighting in a post-funeral manner, full of heavy feelings and reminiscence and inclined not to speak in an ordinary way. When my mother put dinner in order, we sat around the table not saying very much.

"Did the fire hold out all right?" she asked my grandfather.

"Oh, it was warm," he said. "Didn't need much." He ate quietly and so did I.

In the afternoons on Sunday we all sat around looking at the paper.

My mother had doubts about this, but we all indulged the desire anyway. After the ordeal of dressing up, of Sunday School and the long service and dinner, it seemed almost a debauchery to be able to pitch into those large crackling sheets, especially the funny papers, which were garish with color and loud with exclamation points, question marks, shouting, and all sorts of misdeeds. My grandfather had got sleepy before the fire and retired to his room while my mother and father had climbed out of their graveside feelings enough to talk a little and joke with one another.

"What did you all do?" my mother asked me. "How did you pass the time while we were gone?"

"We walked downtown," I said, for I had been laughing at something they had said to one another and wanted to share the morning's happiness with them without telling any more or letting any real trouble in. But my mother was on it, quicker than anything.

"You didn't go in the drugstore, did you?"

I looked up. Why did she have to ask? It wasn't in my scheme of thinking about things that she would ever do so. My father was looking at me now, too.

"Yes, ma'am," I slowly said. "But not for long," I added.

"You didn't get an ice cream cone, did you?"

And they both were looking. My face must have had astonishment on it as well as guilt. Not even I could have imagined them going this far. Why, on the day of a funeral, should they care if anybody bought an ice cream cone?

"Did you?" my father asked.

The thing to know is that my parents really believed everything they said they believed. They believed that awful punishments were meted out to those who did not remember the Sabbath was holy. They believed about a million other things. They were terribly honest about it.

Much later on, my mother went into my grandfather's room. I was silently behind her, and I heard her speak to him.

"She says you took her to town while we were gone and got an ice cream."

He had waked up and was reading by his lamp. At first he seemed not to hear; at last, he put his book face down in his lap and looked up. "I did," he said lightly.

A silence fell between them. Finally she turned and went away.

This, so far as I know, was all.

Because of the incident, that certain immunity of spirit my grandfather possessed was passed on to me. It came, I think, out of the precise way in which he put his book down on his lap to answer. There was a lifetime in the gesture, distilled, and I have been a good part of that long, growing up to all its meaning.

After this, though all went on as before, there was nothing much my parents could finally do about the church and me. They could lock the barn door, but the bright horse of freedom was already loose in my world. Down the hill, across the creek, in the next pasture–where? Somewhere, certainly: that much was proved; and all was different for its being so.

MR. McMILLAN

There are few sights more pleasant than a girl and a man dining happily together, and those two over in the corner were laughing as well that night, not too loudly but not softly either, because something was really funny, you had to suppose. In the courtyard restaurant out in the soft New Orleans September air, people spaced out among banana plants, lanterns, candlelight, palm trees, and a fish pool, turned from various distances and smiled.

Aline could soon be seen wiping her eyes on the big white napkin. It was an old habit, a tendency to cry when she laughed too much, and one which her whole family, she supposed, shared, for she could remember them all sitting through one perpetual summer after another in shorts and sandals on their screen porch, talking and telling things, and every once in a while bursting into such laughter that for a time no world would have been big enough to laugh in. So they would cry, great rolling salt tears as big as moth balls.

The man Aline was dining with apparently had no such family characteristic. He just quieted and refilled her wineglass.

"Good God," he said. "Incest, suicide, insanity, cancer, murder, divorce. Is that the best, really the best, you can do? I thought every Mississippi family had at least one idiot, two rapists, and a good criminal lawyer."

"I've only described my immediate family," she said. Whereupon they were both almost plunged back into merriment again, but the main course was set before them, a sizzling mass of flounder and shrimp.

"Of course," she said, lifting her fork, "I *love* them all."

"Well," he said soberly, "they sound very lovable."

She noticed he was doing very well with her, if that's what he wanted, and evidently he did. From now on they would have a note, a tone, to return to; they could share a knowledge that life was funny and serious both at once, the way, to her, it really was.

He had wired her up home, up in Mississippi, from Chicago. In the old days, the wire would have been called up or run up from the station and everybody in town would have known what was in it before it reached her. But now that the new exchanges had been put in, the message had been telephoned out to her impersonally from a point some thirty miles away. She had told her family it had been about her research at the university, that one of the department assistants was sick and a report was due right after Labor Day. She didn't want to talk about him, the young man she'd met three months ago at a convention in Indiana. If she laid it to her work, which was taking her eight years to train for, having to do with disease-carrying parasites in South American countries, they merely nodded. They never asked her anything about it, even when she had seen the light of what she could really do in the world and what she loved, and had determined to make for it, like a swimmer choosing a distant goal. Full of enthusiasm, with a fellowship promised her after graduation, she had come home and tried to explain. One by one she saw those faces, so like her own, turn glum, and dollar signs, as if in comic strips, appeared to grow on their eyeballs. As stuffed with money as piggy banks, they appeared for the first time to show how they'd earned it, by letting it be a prime motive in everything. Why hadn't she married as any pretty girl should? She would be further from it, now, with every year that passed. And she wouldn't even be earning. It did not matter how her face was glowing. She might as well have announced to them that she was going into anything, from Aristotelian philosophy to codifying puberty rites among African tribes. It was all the same to them. "We just don't know anything about it," was what they had said when she (a girl: imagine!) had determined on a science major. It was what they said now when she wanted to go further—a good answer, she supposed, for next to everything. On the second day they had started complaining; she could expect nothing, they had decided, beyond that fellowship, since it was so grand and pleased her so. On the third, they having got together again, she was the butt of ridicule, needled at table, ignored in hallways. She'd no old uncle or cousin or aunt out in the country to go and talk to, for heart's ease and understanding: they had died. But the uncle had left her a small wooded acreage near town. She had wanted to turn it into a town park someday, but needing money, she went secretly and mortgaged it, and, check in hand, heartsick, young, dashed, determining on the train not to think about it, to get that stricken look off her face, she had returned to New Orleans. No need to go home at all, she thought, unless they needed her.

But she did go back, from time to time. She would get to feeling bad about them and then, as two years had gone and thanks to no one up there she was actually making it, with her glow about it all intact as well, she would get to feeling something else. Her very capacity to pull through must have come, in some way, from them. If not, how could she love them still? They had wrecked her little piece of land: it was an accident. The lumber company they had contracted to cut timber off their own property had assumed hers part of theirs. When they'd noticed, they said, it was too late. Timber lost, the man who'd lent against her mortgage wanted out, and worst of all, the beautiful glade was spoiled for the next fifty years. Who had cared enough to keep things straight? When she thought of it, she would knot her fists, nails digging at her palms, wondering: What went with our laughter? Why don't we laugh any more? And big family-size tears would roll off into her pillow.

She believed in self-knowledge, even though trying to find it in the bosom of a Mississippi family was like trying to find some object lost in a gigantic attic, when you really didn't know what you were looking for. Why look at all? she wondered. Most of her traits she'd learned away from them. One was how not to talk all the time. She now retired into silence. It was he who got to talking then, and kept it up, interesting enough, witty enough, certainly happy to be with her, straight on through coffee and dessert and cigarette and out to his car and into the French Quarter where everybody on earth was walking around, even a group of Scots in kilts playing bagpipes. They got pushed apart time and again on the narrow streets.

"I think people must be wilder down here," he observed. "Of course, in Chicago when you feel wild you go out and shoot to kill. But for the reasons you have to read the papers, then you don't know."

"I'm sure that nobody you know shoots anybody," she kindly said.

"Hate to disappoint you. Some of my best friends–"

A couple of bars, a couple of drinks later, the evening began to drift around them like the river, broad and lazy; they drove around the park and then out to the lake, watching swans and colored fountains.

"Why are you living in that ruin?" he asked her, walking along the lake and angling kisses at her, now and then.

"I'm not. I came back a day early to see you and just went there. I didn't want Ann and Helen to know you were here, I guess. Those are the girls I–"

"Oh, I remember. They come out in hair curlers, dragging on cigarettes. You'd think you were still in college."

"They do make me feel that way. I stay there because it's cheap. I really can't afford anything different." She hesitated. "Do you have to save?"

"No, I guess I've always been lucky." A breeze blew. He wound his arm around her waist. She walked along a parapet, holding to his shoulder. "Money's never worried me," he confessed.

"When I came back here after the family wouldn't see why I wanted this career, I stayed a few days at what you call that old ruin. It really isn't a ruin, just an old pile of a Victorian residence. Somebody turned it into a hotel. Well, you saw the entrance hall, that great big stairway, so you know what it's like all over."

"That Moorish pin-up on the landing, stripped to the waist and holding a lamp–God, how can you stand it?"

"I just went there at first because it was near Tulane."

"Then you got sentimental about it. Couldn't wait to get back."

"No, it wasn't that." They were in the car again and she straightened up, drawing herself free of his arms, sitting away from him, arranging her hair. The gentle haze of alcohol was fading. She said: "I just go there because of Mr. McMillan."

"Mr. McMillan? So there is somebody you like."

"Nothing like that–not a boy friend."

"What then?" He was smiling, both within and without, asking himself, Am I sliding into a lifetime of listening to stories? He must not have felt it such a hardship, this being the third time he'd found himself all the way down here for no other reason than Aline. He'd marked her first as a pretty, still face in a knot of rattling Southerners at the Indianapolis convention, one face in a crowded hotel lobby. What was there about it? A strain pushing up beneath a calm surface

—anxiety? desire?—hinted at what might be interesting about her, what tugged his attention to her.

"Mr. McMillan came from up in Mississippi, too, like me. I never saw him. He had had a whole life in some little town, married this girl everybody expected him to marry as her life would have been ruined, she'd have been nothing but an old maid, if he hadn't, sent two children through school, cared for both parents till they died, cared for her—loved her, too, I guess—till she died, and then quietly having given all his life up to sixty-odd to doing just what everybody thought he ought to do and being all the time sincere—loving instead of hating, you know—he just calmly came down here and took a room for a night or so at that old hotel and never left."

"Then he must be there still. Or did he die?"

"Yes, he died, just about the time I came myself, though nobody would have mentioned that to a new guest. They had found him one morning after he died in his sleep, and they set about getting a doctor, telephoning up to that town to find out his children's names and notifying them, finding an undertaker—oh, they did everything without stint. And then the son and the son's wife came down on the train and went back with the coffin, northward, but nobody followed—just didn't go, somehow. If the ones left who had known him all along spoke of him, I don't know what they said. I came in and didn't know anything had happened, though the first day, once I looked back on it, there had been some sort of commotion, people talking in the TV lounge and others being called aside when they came in from work, into the little office where the switchboard is—it must have been a butler's pantry back in the old days—and at night a going up and down steps and a knock at certain doors. But I remembered all this later like something that happened while I dreamed. I wouldn't have noticed that one of the guests had gone for a day or so.

"I knew when he reappeared only by coincidence, because in the middle of a hot, still September afternoon I had come into that cool old hallway, spacious and dim as a church but freed of everything like duty and being holy. I had got to the desk and was looking around for somebody to ask for the key and for whatever mail or calls there'd been, when the lady who sometimes keeps the desk came out of the switchboard room and looked straight past me, her look went like a bullet, and I saw something like shock or strain on her face, but not either one—you'd have to call it recognition. I turned and there stood an elderly gentleman with nearly white hair whom I'd got glimpses of when I first arrived. He had the air of a traveler returned from a mission and he carried something the size of a box of candy under his arm. He held it out to her. 'It's him,' he said. She looked at it and nodded. It was such a singular thing, so intense. They really didn't know I was there, were so taken up they couldn't be conscious of anything beyond their own knowing. 'It's Mr. McMillan,' he said."

"In the box?"

Aline nodded.

"Cremated?"

She nodded again.

"Ashes to ashes," he remarked, looking out over Lake Pontchartrain, the night having swung close to its deeper hours, noting the distant lights of fishing boats, lonely, solitary with the knowledge of work continued in the forgetfulness of everybody else.

"He didn't return to dust or ashes either, not in the long run. Listen. He had let them bury him up there, let them do the whole thing. Then they read the will and found the envelope attached to the will and the letter inside saying what he really wanted. So then they called down to New Orleans, to the hotel. Mr. McMillan had been in the war. Scarcely under the age limit, at the time–thirty-eight or thirty-nine–he could have got out of it without even trying to, but he insisted he wanted to go. He went to Hawaii–Pearl Harbor–on something called Eastern reconnaissance, which meant, in his case anyway, that he traveled from the Pearl Harbor army base across to ships and took messages from the Army to the Navy and vice versa about what each knew that the other didn't. He covered the bay over and over, never knowing what information he carried or what effect it had on anybody, what lives were saved or lost because of it, or what file it finally wound up in. But he got to know the bay and he got to know the islands, and he loved it all apparently, though he never talked much about it. Being older than most veterans, he never hung around with buddies when he came home, or joined any of the groups, but when he died, he had quietly decided, he wanted his ashes scattered on that water. It was only a case of finding somebody who would do it for him, as nobody in that little town or in the family would have known what to make of such a request and would have probably decided right away that he was crazy for even asking it, but he asked them to notify the hotel and said that somebody there would take the envelope containing his request and the money for the trip. He didn't specify who it would be, not even man or woman. He just knew somebody would. And they did. Would you say it was just for a free ticket to Hawaii?"

"No, I wouldn't say that. Neither would you. He'd found his own sort, the people he wanted to do things for him, and then they did it. I guess all of life is worth that."

The dark had really come down on them. She could barely see his face.

"Up there where the family was, they didn't seem to care any more, once the funeral was over. It just became something after the fact, everything being settled for them when they had transferred the property and paid the undertaker. I guess after everything, every single thing, and every person is served, then you can have what you really want."

"You sound bitter," he said. "Why look at the world like that?"

"From failing, like he did. In a way I envied him. They got through doing all the things about his death that they expected of themselves. Then they saw the will and the letter inside, and the stranger. So they let him be dug up and carted off and burned to ashes and carried away like that–in a little box. And they didn't care. They didn't care at all." She was laughing.

"Don't laugh like that. It's late; you're tired."

Well, that was true, she thought, letting herself be drawn closely in, giving in to the all but strange face whose exact features up to the very reappearance of him that afternoon she could not recall. Mysteriously, his outline took firm life against her; even stranger, it seemed entirely right that it should do so–should be as it was, and more, should be all it intended to be. What is flesh and blood, she wondered, but what it seems right to be close to?

But when she shut her eyes at last, she heard in her head the silken wash and fall of Hawaiian water, and the night breeze that lay against her cheek was of that climate.

I, MAUREEN

On the sunny fall afternoon, I (Maureen) saw the girl sitting in the oval-shaped park near the St. Lawrence River. She was sitting on green grass, bent lovingly, as though eternally, over her guitar. They are always like that, absorbed, hair falling past their faces, whether boys or girls: there seems little difference between them: they share the tender absorption of mother with child. The whole outside world regards them, forms a hushed circle about them.

I, Maureen, perceived this while driving by on an errand for Mr. Massimo.

I used to live out there, on what in Montreal we call the Lakeshore. I did nothing right then, so returning to that scene is painful: I sought relief from the memories of five years ago by letting the girl with the guitar—bending to it, framed in grass, the blue river flowing by—redeem my memories, redeem me, I could only hope, also. Me, Maureen, stung with the identity of bad memories.

Everything any woman in her right mind could want—that was my life. Denis Partham's wife, and not even very pretty or classy: I never had anything resembling looks or background. I was a bit run-down looking, all my life. From the age of two, I looked run-down. People used to say right out to me: "You've just had luck, that's all." But Denis said the luck was his. He really thought that, for years and years. Until the day I thought he was dead. After that he had to face it that luck can run out, even for a Partham.

We had a house on the river and it was beautiful, right on the water. It was in Baie d'Urfé, one of the old townships, and you can describe it for yourself, if you so desire. There can be rugs of any texture, draperies of any fabric, paneling both painted and stained, shelves to put books in, cupboards to fill with china and linen. The choice of every upholstery sample or kitchen tile was a top-level decision; the struggle for perfection had a life-and-death quality about it. If my interest was not wholly taken up in all this, if I was play-acting, I did not know it. Are people when measuring and weighing and pondering names for a crown prince, serious? I was expecting the prince; that was why the Parthams gave us the house. Sure enough, the baby was a boy. Two years and another one arrived, a girl. (Isn't Nature great? She belongs to the Parthams.)

In the winter we had cocktails before dinner in a spacious room overlooking the frozen lake, watching the snow drift slowly down, seeing the skaters stroking outward. We had sherry between church services and Sunday lunch. Then the ice boats raced past, silent, fast as dreams.

Our children were beautiful, like children drawn with a pencil over and again in many attitudes, all pure, among many Canadian settings. Denis was handsome, a well-built man, younger than I, with dark hair and a strong, genuine smile. In his world, I was the only dowdy creature. Yet he loved me, heart and soul. And why? I used to sit in a big chair in a corner of the library hunched up like a crow, and wonder this. In summer I sat on the terraces, and there, too, I wondered.

All I knew was that aged twenty-five, a plain, single girl, I had come to the Parthams' big stone house high in Westmount with some friends. It was late, a gathering after a local play. A woman who worked at the library with me had a younger sister in the play and had asked me to come. One of the Parthams was in it, too, so we all got invited up for drinks. Somebody graciously learned that I was living way out in N.D.G., that area of the unnumbered middle class, and Denis, who had been talking to me about the library, offered to drive me home. When we reached the house, he turned off the motor, then the lights, and turning to me began to kiss me hungrily. He had fallen silent along the way, and I had felt he was going to do something like this. I simply judged that he was a rich boy out for more sexual experience, seeking it outside his own class, the way privileged people often do. Yet he was moved and excited way beyond the average: so I put him down as a boy with problems, and squirmed my way out of his arms and his Oldsmobile as best I could. Next day he telephoned me at the library, longing to see me again. He was that way from then on.

He said he could never change. Through all our dates, then through season after season, year after year, I saw how his voice would take on a different note when he saw me, how his eyes would light up. I knew his touch, his sexual currents, his eager kisses, his talk, his thoughts, his tastes. At some point, we got married. But the marriage, I helplessly realized, had taken place already, in the moment he had seen me in the corner of one of the many Partham living rooms in their great stone house, me (Maureen), completely out of place. Before I knew it, he had enveloped me all over, encased me like a strong vine. My family could believe my good fortune no more than I could. It was too good to last, but it did; too good to be true, but it was. We had, in addition to the Lakeshore house at Baie d'Urfé, an apartment on Drummond Street in Montreal, servants, two cars, wonderful friends, a marvelous life.

Then, one summer day, it happened. It could never unhappen.

Denis was out sailing and in passing under a bridge, the metal mast of the boat struck a live wire. His hand was on the mast and the voltage knocked him down. When they brought him in they had rolled him onto the sail and were carrying him by four improvised corners, like somebody asleep in a hammock. His head was turned to one side. Everyone on our lawn and dock seemed to know from the minute the boat appeared, unexpectedly returned, that something terrible had happened. We crowded forward together, all the family and friends not sailing, left behind on the lawns to swim, sun, play, or talk, and though I was among the first, I felt just as one of them, not special. I saw his face turned to one side, looking (the eyes shut and the skin discolored blue and red) like a face drowned through a rift in ice. I thought he was dead, and so did we all, even, I later learned, those who were carrying him. They laid him on the lawn and someone said: "Stay back," while another, running from the moment the boat touched the dock, was already at the telephone. But by that time there were arms around me, to hold me back from rushing to him. They encountered no forward force. I was in retreat already, running backward from the moment, into another world which had been waiting for me for some time. All they did was hasten me into it. My fierce sprinting backward plus the force of their normal human attention—that of trying to keep a wife from hurling herself with all the velocity of human passion toward her husband, so unexpectedly served up before her as (so it seemed) a corpse—outdid possibility. But we leave the earth with difficulty, and I wasn't up to that. I fell backward, sprawling awkwardly; I lay observing the bluest of July skies in which white clouds had filled in giant areas at good distances from the sun. Sky, cloud, and sun completed me, while ambulances wailed and bore away whomever they would.

Denis did not die; he recovered nicely. All life resumed as before.

A month later I made my first attempt at suicide.

It was finally to one of the psychiatrists I saw that I recounted how all of this had started, from a minor event, meaningless *to all but me.* (To me alone the world had spoken.)

I had been sunbathing on the pier a week or so before Denis's accident when two of the children whose parents owned a neighboring property began to throw things into the water. I could see them—two skinny boys on the neighboring pier—and know that while they pretended to be hurling rocks and bottles straight out into the lake, they were in reality curving them closer into land, striking near our docking area. I was thinking of getting up to shout at them when it happened. A bit of blue-green glass arching into the sun's rays, caught and trapped an angle of that light, refracting it to me. It struck, a match for lightning. My vision simply for a moment was by this brilliance extinguished; and in the plunge of darkness that ensued I could only see the glass rock reverse its course and speed toward me. It entered my truest self, my consciousness, reverberating with silent brilliance. From that point I date my new beginning. It was a nothing point, an illusion, but an illusion that had happened to me, if there is such a thing. . . .

"If there is such a thing," the doctor repeated.

"If there is such a thing," I said again, sounding, I knew, totally mad.

Doctors wait for something to be said that fits a pattern they have learned to be true, just as teachers wait for you to write English or French. If you wrote a new and unknown language they wouldn't know what to do with you—you would fail.

"It explains to me," I went on, realizing I was taking the risk of being consigned to the asylum at Verdun for an indefinite period, "why I ran backward instead of forward when I thought Denis was dead. I want my own world. I have been there once. I want to return. If I can't, I might as well be dead."

"Your attempts to take your own life might be thought of as efforts to join your husband, whom you believed to have reached death," the doctor suggested. He had a thick European accent, and an odd name, Miracorte. God knows where he was from.

I said nothing.

One day I left home. I had done this before but they had always come for me, tranquilized me, hospitalized me, removed things from me that might be handy ways of self-destruction, talked to me, loved me, nurtured me back to being what they wanted me to be–somebody, in other words, like themselves. This time they didn't come. A doctor came, a new one, younger than the first. He asked from the intercom system in the apartment building in East Montreal which I had fled to, taking the first furnished place I could find, whether he could see me. I let him in.

He was plain English-Canadian from Regina, named Johnson.

"Everyone is a little schizoid," he said. They had told me that, told me and told me that. "You choose the other side of the coin, the other side of yourself. You have to have it. If you don't have it, you will die. Don't you know that some people drink themselves into it, others hit drugs, some run off to the bush, some kill or steal or turn into religious freaks? You're a mild case, comparatively speaking. All you want is to be with it, calmly, like a lover."

I was crying before I knew it, tears of relief. He was the first to consent to my line of feeling. Why had it been so hard, why were they all reluctant to do so? We allow people to mouth platitudes to us one after another, and agree to them blandly, knowing they aren't true, just because there's no bite to them, no danger. The truth is always dangerous, so in agreeing to what I felt, he was letting me in for danger. But it was all that was left to try.

"There's a bank account for you at this address." He gave me the chequebook and the deposit slip. "If you need more, call me. Your husband has agreed to this plan."

I took the chequebook silently, but was vowing already that I would never use it. I was going to get a job.

The young doctor sat frowning, eyes on the floor.

"Denis feels awful," I said, reading his thoughts aloud. "This has made him suffer."

"I didn't say that," Dr. Johnson said. "It makes you suffer to stay with him. Maybe—well, maybe he can get through better without you than you can with him."

From then on I was on my own, escaping into the mystery that is East Montreal, a fish thrown barely alive back into water. Not that I had ever lived there. But to Westmount families who own houses in Baie d'Urfé, East Montreal presents even more of an opaque surface than N.D.G. It is thought to be French, and this is so, but it is also Greek, Italian, Oriental, and immigrant Jewish. I was poor, unattractive as ever; I ached for my children and the sound of Denis's voice, his love, everything I had known. I went through an agony of missing what I could have, all back, and whole as ever, just by picking up the phone, just by taking a taxi and saying, "Take me home."

But when I gave in (and I did give in every time the world clicked over and I saw things right side up instead of upside down), odd consequences resulted. I would call a number but strange voices out of unknown businesses or residences would answer, or someone among the Partham friends would say hello, and I would begin to talk about myself—me, *me,* ME—relating imagined insults, or telling stories that were only partly true, and though I knew I was doing this, though my mind stood by like a chance pedestrian at the scene of an accident, interested, but a little sickened, with other things to do, still my voice, never lacking for a word, went on. Once I took a taxi home with all my possessions loaded inside, but directed the driver to the wrong turning, overshot the mark and wound up at the wrong driveway. The people who came out the door knew me; oh, this was horrible; I crouched down out of sight and shouted, "Go back, go back! Take me home!" (The meaning of home had shifted, the world had flipped once more.)

Again I came on the bus in the middle of a fine afternoon, calm and right within myself, to "talk things over," sanely to prepare for my return to the family. I found no one there, the house open, the living room empty. I sat down to wait. At a still center, waiting for loved ones' faces to appear through a radiance of outer sunlight, I stared too hard at nothing, closed my eyes and heard it from the beginning: a silent scream, waxing unbearably. I had come to put out my arms, to say, I have failed to love, but now I know this. I love you, I love you all. What was there in this to make the world shrink back, flee, recede, rock with agony to its fair horizons? I could bear it no longer, and so fled. I ran past one of them, one of the Partham women (my mother-in-law, sister-in-law, aunt-in-law, a cousin?—they look alike, all of them) coming in from the garden in her white work gloves with shears in hand, a flat of cut flowers on her arm. *She* must have screamed also, I saw her mouth make the picture of a scream, but that is unimportant except to her. For if she was Denis's mother she must have wanted to scream ever since I had first walked into her presence, hand in hand with Denis, and then there I was back again, crazy and fleeing with a bruised forehead all purple and gold (in my haste to reach them I had slammed into a door).

My journey back on one rattling bus after another, threading streets under an overcast sky, seemed longer than I could have imagined. I wondered then and since if I had dreamed that journey, if I would not presently wake up in the dark room where my resolution had taken place at 3 A.M. (the hour of weakness and resolve), if the whole matter of getting up, dressing, taking the taxi, were not all a dream of the soul's motion upon deciding, while I myself, like a chained dog, lay still held to sleep and darkness. On the other hand, I wondered whether I had made that same decision and that same trip not once or twice but twenty or thirty times, as though the split side of myself were carrying on a life it would not tell me about. Denis had a brother who was a physicist and used to talk about a "black hole in space," where matter collapses of its own gravity, ceases to exist in any form that we know of as existence. Yet some existence must continue. Was this myself, turned inside-out like a sleeve, whirled counterclockwise to a vacuum point, when I disappeared would I (Maureen) know it? Confusion thickened in my head.

I thought I saw Denis at the end of a snowy street in East Montreal near Dorchester Boulevard, a child holding to either hand, and so sprang up my fantasy that they often came to watch silently from somewhere just to see me pass, but often as I thought I glimpsed them, I never hastened to close the distance and find the answer.

"You prefer the fantasy to the reality," Dr. Johnson said.

"What made me the way I am? Why have I caused all this?"

"Becoming is difficult."

"Becoming what?"

"Your alter ego. Your other self."

"You've said it a hundred times."

"So what?"

"It makes no sense, my other self. None whatever."

"You feel it's irrational?"

We both fell silent and looked down as if this self had fallen like an object between us on the floor.

"No one is wholly rational," Dr. Johnson said.

I still sat looking. Rational or not, could it live, poor thing? If I nudged it with my toe, would it move?

"Basically, you are happier now," he told me.

"I am lonely," I said. The words fell out, without my knowing it. Perhaps the self on the floor had spoken.

"You like it, or you wouldn't be," he said at once.

I was surprised by this last remark and returned home with something like an inner smile. For the first time in months I thought of buying something new and pretty and I looked in shop windows along the way. I stopped in a drugstore and got a lipstick. That night I washed my hair. Sitting out on my balcony, watching the people drift by, smoking, the way I always like to do, I put a blanket over my still damp head, for it was only March, and the world was still iced, crusted in decaying snow. I sat like a squaw woman, but inside I felt a little stir of green feeling. I would be happy in this world I'd come to, not just an exile, a maverick that had jumped the fence. I would feel like a woman again.

A woman invisible, floating softly through a June day, I went to church when my daughter was confirmed. I sat far in the back in the dim church, St. James on Bishop Street. Seeing her so beautiful, I felt exalted, meaning all the hymns, all the words. But as I was leaving I heard a murmuring behind me and my name spoken. Then a curate was chasing me, calling out my name. I knew him from the old days, didn't I? Wasn't he the one I'd asked to dinner and sherry and tea? He meant everything that was good; he wanted to grasp my hand and speak to me, about forgiveness, love, peace, the whole catalogue. But who stood back of him? Not the kingdom, the power, and the glory, but Parthams, Parthams, and Parthams. I ran like the wind. The air blew white in my face, white as my daughter's communion dress, white as a bridal veil. I stopped at last to gasp it down. No footsteps sounded from behind. I was safe once more. Running backward, I had broken records: forward, I'm unbeatable. This was the grim joke I told myself, skulking home.

"It was a big risk," Dr. Johnson warned me. "How did you even know about the service?"

"A maid I used to have. She told me."

"The trouble I've gone to. . . . Don't you realize they want to commit you? If they succeed, you may never get out again."

"Nobody could keep me from seeing her," I said. "Not on that day."

"To them you're a demon in the sacred place." He was smiling, but I heard it solemnly. Maybe they were right.

Such, anyway, were my forays into enemy land.

But some were also made to me, in my new country. For I saw them, at times, and at others I thought I saw them, shadows at twilight on the edge of their forest, or real creatures venturing out and toward me; it was often impossible to tell which.

Carole Partham really came, graceful and hesitant, deerlike, and I let her come, perceiving that it was not curiosity or prying that brought her over, but an inner need to break away, to copy me, in some measure.

There she was one twilight, waiting in the pizza restaurant near my entrance. Carole was born a Partham, but her husband was Jim O'Brien, a broker. He was away in Europe, she said. Now's your big chance, she had doubtless told herself.

A smart-looking girl, up to the latest in clothes, a luxury woman, wearing suède with a lynx collar, tall brown rain boots, brushed brown hair.

"Come in," I urged her, getting her out of that place where, dressed like that, she was making them nervous. "I'm safe to be with. You can see my place."

Then she was sitting, smoking, loosening her coat, eyes coasting about here and there, from floor to wall to ceiling. My apartment wasn't much to see. I would have set the dogs on her—dogs of my inner rages—if I hadn't seen her realness. Instead I saw it well: she was frightened. Happy or not? She didn't know. What does life mean? There was panic in the question, if you asked it often enough. She had no answer and her husband was away for quite some time.

"Come work here for a month," I advised. "You can get a job, or loaf, or think, or see what happens."

But her eyes were restless; they stopped at closed drawers, probed at closet doors. Sex! Oh, certainly, I thought. Oh, naturally. I remembered Jim O'Brien with his ready talk and his toothy grin flashing over an ever-present, ever-tilted tumbler of martini on the rocks, and the glitter and swagger in his stroll from guest to guest, his intimate flattering talk, and now I knew what I had thought all along: who would marry Jim O'Brien but a woman with a childhood terror still behind the door? And now she'd done it, how could she escape?

"Don't tell them where you are," I advised. "I can find a room for you maybe. Somewhere near if you want me to. You can see I've no space here."

"Oh, I didn't want—"

"Just tell them you've gone away. What about Florida? You can say that."

Helpless, the eyes roved.

"I've no one here," I told her. "No lover, no friend. I work in a photographer's studio. That's all there is to know. You'll see it at the corner. My boss is Mr. Massimo. He owns it. There's nothing to know."

After a long silence, she said, looking down at herself, "These clothes are wrong."

"Who cares? Just face it that nobody cares."

"Nobody cares? Nobody *cares?*" She kept repeating this. It was what she couldn't swallow, had got hung up on, I guess, all by herself. I had hit it by accident.

"I mean," I said, "nobody over *here* cares. Over there . . . I don't know about that."

"Nobody . . . nobody. . . ." Her voice now had gone flat. She got up to go, headed for the terrace window rather than the door, fell through the glass, stumbled over the terrace railing, her fashionable boots flailing the air, skirts sliding up to her neck. . . . But, no, this didn't happen. That wasn't the end of Carole. She went out the door, like anybody else.

She did move to the street for a time; I forget for how long. She brought plain old clothes and tied her head in a scarf. She worked some afternoons for a kind, arthritic Frenchman with white hair who ran a magazine shop. There was also the dark young man who stared down daily from a window four floors up; he descended to trail her home, offering to carry her grocery sack. How nice this tableau looked and how charming it would have been if only his I.Q. had been half-way average. He was once a doorman, I understood, but had kept falling asleep on his feet, like a horse.

She got drunk on resin-tasting wine one night in a Greek restaurant and lured eleven Greek waiters into a cheap hotel room. How sweet and eager and passionate they had seemed! They milled around—or so I was told—not knowing what to do. A humiliation to end all mental nymphomania: Carole escaped unmolested.

She had found a room with a woman whose mother had died and who baby-sat for pin money. On long evenings when she didn't baby-sit she told Carole the story of her life. Otherwise, Carole read, and drank, and told herself the story of her own life. She was happy in the butcher shop once and sat madonna-like with the butcher's cat purring in her lap, but the butcher's Spanish wife did not like her and kicked the cat to say so. Mr. Massimo pondered about her. "How did you know her?" he asked. "She once knew my sister," is all I answered.

Old clothes or not, Carole did one thing she didn't intend: she gave out the indefinable air of class. Surely, the street began to say, she was the forerunner of an "in" group which would soon discover us and then we would all make money and turn into background to be glanced at. So some thought. But when I saw her, knowing better, I saw a host of other women—pretty, cared-for women—walking silently with her, rank on rank, women for whom nothing will ever quite add up. Every day, I guess, she wrote down her same old problems, in different combinations, and every day she got the same sum.

Suddenly, one day, she was before me. "My month is up. It's been a wonderful experience."

"I'm glad you thought so."

We both sat smoking thoughtfully, occasionally glancing at each other. I knew her room had been rifled twice by thieves and that she could not sleep at night when the baby-sitter baby-sat. The faces of those Greek waiters would, I imagine, press on her memory forever. If the world is one, what was the great secret to make those faces accessible to her own self? The answer had escaped her.

"It's been a great experience," she repeated, smiling brightly, her mouth like painted wood, like a wound.

A voice, another voice, in that same room is talking . . . Vinnie Partham and her husband Charles? It can't be.

". . . I knew it was safe to see you again when Carole confessed that she had and you were all right. Carole's gone into social work, she got over her crisis whatever it was, and now we're thinking it's time you got through with yours, for you may not be able even to imagine how desolate Denis still is, Maureen. Can you, can you?

"We thought for a long time the problem was sexual but then we decided you were out to destroy us and then we thought your mental condition would make you incapable of anything at all by way of job or friends. But all our theories are wrong, I guess."

On she goes, with Charles dozing in his chair after the manner of British detectives in the movies, who look dumb but are actually intelligent and wide awake, solving the perfect crime, the difference being that Charles really is both half-asleep and stupid and has never been known to solve anything at all. Vinnie knows it. The phrases have started looping out of her mouth like a backward spaghetti-eating process. Luminous cords reach up and twine with others, grow into patterns of thought. The patterns are dollar signs. I see them forming.

"With Denis having no heart for the estate affairs, what chance have Charles and I for the consideration he's always extended us? And if you think who, out of a perfect grab bag of women now getting interested, he might actually take it in his head to marry—"

Something dawns on me. Vinnie Partham is never going to stop talking!

I stare at her and stare, feeling cross-eyed with wonder and helpless and hypnotized, like someone watching a force in nature take its course. What can I do? She'll be there forever.

"I'm tired, Vinnie," I tell her. "I'm terribly tired."

They melt away, her mouth is moving still. . . . Did I dream them? Do women still wear long beads? Can it really be they wanted me back for nothing but money? No, money is their name for something else. That chill place, that flaw in the world fabric, that rift in the Partham world about the size of Grand Canyon—they keep trying to fill it, trying to fill it, on and on, throwing everything in to fill it up. It was why Denis wanted me.

Oh, my poor children! Could they ever grow up to look like Aunt Vinnie and Uncle Charles?

At the thought of them, so impossibly beautiful, so possibly doomed, noises like cymbals crash in my ears, my eyes blur and stream. If my visitors were there I could not see them.

But they must be gone, I think, squinting around the room, if they were there at all. If they were ever alive at all . . . if they were ever anywhere.

Through all this, night was coming on; and summer—that, too, was coming on. Vinnie and Charles were dreams. But love is real.

I first saw Michel when he came to the photographer's shop for some application-size pictures. He was thin and ravaged, frowning, worried, *pressé*. I had learned to do routine requests as Mr. Massimo was often away taking wedding pictures or attending occasions such as christenings and retirements. Mr. Massimo thrived on these events, which included fancy food and lots to drink and dressed-up women. It was when Michel and I got in the semi-dark of the photographing room together that I received his full impact. I stirred about among the electrical cords, the lamp stands; I wielded the heavy-headed camera into focus; I directed his chin to lift, then found him in the lenses, dark and straight. Indian blood? I snapped the shutter.

He said he was new in the neighborhood, lived up the street, and would come back next day to see the proofs.

But I passed him again, not an hour later, on my way home. He was sitting outdoors at the pizza parlor talking volubly to the street cleaner who had stopped there for a beer. He saw me pass, go in my building, and I felt his regard in my senses.

Who was he? What would he do?

Something revolutionary was what I felt to be in his bones. Political? Then he would be making contacts and arguing for the liberation of the province.

I was wrong. No passion for Quebec but the rent of an empty barbershop was what had brought him there, one on the lower floor of a small building with a tree in front. He was going to put in one of those shops that sold hippie costumes, Indian shirts, long skirts, built-up shoes, some papier-mâché decorators' items, and some artwork. This would incidentally give him a chance to show some of his own artwork, which had failed to interest the uptown galleries. He was going to leave the barber chairs and mirrors, using them all as décor, props, for the things he sold.

He told me all this when he came to see the photographs. Mr. Massimo had gone to a reunion of retired hockey players. Michel looked over the proofs and selected one. He wanted it enlarged, a glossy finish he could reproduce to make ads for his shop. He was telling me how in some detail and I thought that a little more would find him back in Mr. Massimo's darkroom, doing it for himself.

"I hope your business works," I said.

The day before, skirting about among the photographic equipment, we had entangled face to face among some electrical cords, which we had methodically to unplug and unwind to find release from a near embrace. Now, he turned from a scrutiny of his own face to a minute examination of my own.

"If you hope so, then you think it could. *Vous le croyez,* eh?"

"*Moi? J'en sais pas, moi.* What does it matter?"

His elbow skidded on the desk. His face beetled into my own. It was his eyes that were compelling, better than good, making an importance out of themselves, out of my opinions, out of me.

"Your thinking so . . . why, that's strong. You have power. *Vous êtes formidable.* That's it, madame. *C'est ça.*"

A tilt of the head, an inch or two more, and our mouths, once more, might have closed together. My own was dry and thirsty, it woke to tell me so.

He straightened, gathered up his pictures, and neatly withdrew. His step left the doorway empty. I filled the order blank carefully.

It had turned much warmer and after work now I sat on the balcony with the windows open behind me and what I had to call curtains even stirred a bit, a dreamy lift of white in a dusk-softened room. I was moved to put a Mozart record on. I remembered that Mozart had died a pauper and been carried by cart to the outskirts of Vienna in winter and dumped in a hole. To me, that made the music tenderer still. Michel! From the day I'd seen him a private tower had begun to rise about me; its walls were high and strong. I might gnaw toast and jam and gulp coffee standing in my closet-sized kitchen, wriggle into the same old skirt, blouse, sweater, and leather coat (now put away), and walk to work, a drab, square-set, middle-aged woman going past at an accustomed time, but, within myself, a princess came to life and she leaned from high-set window sills. Did Michel know, she kept on asking, as she studied the horizon and admired the blue sky.

He passed the shop twice, once for his enlargement, once to talk; he went by daily on the street. A stir went up about his footsteps. He would change us all. At the very least, I reasoned, he kept my mind off the divorce papers.

One night there was a shouting in the street and a clang of fire engines. I rushed to the balcony and saw where it was: Michel's, up on the corner. A moment later I heard his voice from the shadows, down in the street below, and I hurried to let him in, climbed back with him unseen, opened my door to him for the first time.

He had caught my hands, holding them together in his own, in a grasp warm with life. His explanations blundered out . . . coming back from somewhere, tired, smoking in bed, fell asleep, the stuff collected for the shop catching fire. "But if they know I'm back, that I set the fire, then the shop will never open. Nobody saw me. Nobody. Will you let me stay? Will you?"

"Smoking in bed, that's crazy."

"Correct." He leaned wearily toward me, smiling, sallow cheekbone sharp against my cheek, then holding closer, his mouth searching, and mine searching, too, finding and holding. The will to have him there was present already: it was he who'd set the tower up, and furnished it, for this very thing, for his refuge. But for such enfoldment as we found, the binding of my thought was needed, the total silent agreement that a man and woman make, a matched pattern for love. The heart of his gamble was there. He won it.

Left alone while I worked, Michel sat in the corner and read all day.

"What do you do when you're not reading?" I would ask, coming in from work.

"Je pense."

"A quoi?"

"A toi."

"Tu pense à toi. Et tu le sais bien, toi." I was putting down my bag, I was emptying my grocery sack, but always I was turning to him. And I was moving to him. And he to me.

There was talk on the street of the fire, how the whole house had almost caught, and about the strange absence of Michel, whose inflammable junk had caused it all, but for whom nobody had an address or a telephone number.

One day I came from work and the tower stood empty. I knew it before I opened the door; Michel was gone. Through empty space I moved at last to the balcony and there up the street a taxi was pulling up before the rooming house. Out stepped Michel, as though home from a long journey, even carrying a suitcase! For the first time, it seemed, he was discovering his charred quarters, calling out the building superintendent, raising a commotion on the steps for all to hear. Quarreling, shouting, and multiple stories—they went on till nightfall.

Michel tried, at least, to collect the insurance on damages to his property. I never knew for certain if it worked. He said that it did, but he seldom told the truth. It was not his nature. If the fire was accidental, he escaped without a damage suit. But if he did it on purpose, hoping for insurance money to buy a better class of junk, and counting in advance on me to shelter him, then he was a fool to take so much risk. But why begin to care? Liar, cheat, thief, and lover—he stays unchanged and unexplaining. We have never had it out, or made it up, or parted. The tower is dissolving as his presence fades from it, leaves as water drying from a fabric, thread by thread. It floats invisible, but at least undestroyed. I felt this even after his shop opened—even after a dark young girl with long hair and painted eyes came to work there.

He comes and goes. Summer is over. *C'est ça.*

To think the Parthams ever let go is a serious mistake.

I recall a winter night now, lost in driving snow. There is a madness of snow, snow everywhere, teeming, shifting, lofty as curtains in the dream of a mad opera composer, cosmic, yet intimate as a white thread caught in an eyelash. The buses stall on Côte des Neiges: there is a moaning impotence among them, clouds of exhaust and a dimming of their interior lights as they strain to ascend the long hill, but some already have given up and stand dull and bulky, like great animals in herd awaiting some imminent extinction. The passengers file from them. I toil upward from Sherbrooke through a deepening tunnel, going toward the hospital. My son's name has become the sound of my heart. The receptionist directs me to a certain floor.

I think of everyone inside as infinitely small because of the loftiness of the night outside, its mad whiteness, chaotic motion, insatiable teeming. The hospital is a toy with lights, set on the mountain, a bump like a sty. The night will go on forever, it seems to be saying; it will if it wants to and it wants to and it will. So I (human) am small beneath this lofty whim. Perhaps I think like this to minimize the dull yet painful edge of guilt. My son may die; I abandoned him years ago. Yet he wants to see me, and they have thought that he should be permitted to. And I have thought, Why think it is good of them, nobody is that bad? and Why think it is good of me either, no mother is that cold? (But they might have been, and so might I.) Under realms of snow I progress at snail pace, at bug size, proving that great emotion lives in tiny hearts. On the floor, a passing aide, little as a sparrow, indicates the way. At the desk, a nurse, a white rabbit, peers at a note that has been left. Snow at the window, furious, boils. "Mr. Partham regrets he cannot be here. . . . You wish to see the boy? It's number ten." Swollen feelings lift me down the corridor. I crack the door. "Mother, is that you?" "Yes." "I knew you'd come." "Of course, I came." His hand, at last, is mine. It is the world.

Night after night I come, through blizzard, through ice and sleet, once in a silenced snow-bound city walking more than half the way into a wind with a −40° wind chill against my face, ant-sized under the glitter of infinite distances, at home with the derision of stars. So I push my stubborn nightly way. "You are sleepy," says Mr. Massimo at work. "Why are you so sleepy lately?" I tell him nothing. I can't for yawning.

Bundled in my dark coat, in the shadowy corridor, I sometimes, when Parthams are present, doze. They walk around me, speak to one another, are aware of my presence but do not address it. Denis, once, appearing, stands directly before me; when I lift my head our eyes meet, and they speak and we know it, yes we do. But there is a wall clear as glass between us and if we should fling ourselves through it, it would smash and let us through. Still, we would hurtle past each other. For the glass has a trick in it, a layer at the center seems to place us face to face but really angles us apart. He knows it, I know it. We have been shown the diagram. He nods and turns away.

Several times I see his wife. I recognize her by the newspaper photographs. She is quietly, expensively dressed, with soft shining hair, the one he should have married in the first place. I do not need the coat. Sitting there in the warm room, why do I wear it? The minute the Parthams leave, I shed it. Its dropping from me is real but a symbol also. I am in the room in the same moment.

We hardly talk at all, my son and I. We know everything there is to know already. I sense the hour, almost the minute, when his health begins to flow back again.

We are sitting together on a Saturday morning. Dawn has come to a clear spotless frozen sky. Smoke from the glittering city beneath us, laid out below the windows, turns white. It plumes upward in windless purity. I have been here through the night. We are talking. It is the last time; I know that, too. The needles have been withdrawn from his arms. Soon the morning routine of the hospital will begin to crackle along the hallway and some of it will enter here. I look around me and see what things the Parthams have filled the room with—elegant little transistor radios, sports books and magazines, a lovely tropical aquarium where brilliant fish laze fin and tail among the shells and water plants. Nothing has been spared. He is smiling. His nightmare with the long name—peritonitis—is over. His gaze is weak no longer, but has entered sunlight, is penetrating and can judge.

So much drops away from a sick person; ideas, personality, ambition, interests—all the important Partham baggage. When the pressures of the body turn eccentric and everything is wrong, then they find their secret selves. But once the Partham body returns, it's a sign of laziness not to look around, discriminate, find life "interesting," activities "meaningful"; it would be silly not to be a Partham since a Partham is what one so fortunately is. "Can I come to find you when I get out of here?" my son begs. "Can I, Mother?" "Of course, of course, you can." "I promise to." I am on my way, before the nurse comes with her thermometers or the elephantine gray wagon of trays lumbers in. I am into my coat again, retreating from the Partham gaze. But my insect heart in the unlikely shape of me, almost permanently bent, like a wind-blasted tree, by the awful humors of that phenomenal winter, is incandescent with inextinguishable joy. He will live, he will live. Nothing, nobody, can take that away. I stumble, slip, list, slide down frozen pavements, squeaking over surfaces of impacted snow. In the crystal truth of the day world, the night is done. He will live.

(His name? My son's name? I won't tell you.)

I wing, creep, crawl, hop—what you will—back into my world.

Denis, eventually, seeks me. He comes to find me. A third Partham. I see him at a street end.

He is gray; the winter has made everybody's skin too pale, except, I suppose, the habitual skiers who go up on peaks where the sun strikes. Denis used to ski, but not this year. There he is, gray at the street's end. All has been blown bare and lean by the awful winter. He is himself lean, clean, with gray overcoat and Persian lamb hat, darker gray trousers, brown, fur-lined gloves. "Maureen? Can we go somewhere? Just have a coffee . . . talk a little?" We go to the "bar-b-q" place. It's impersonal there, being on a busy corner; at the pizza restaurant they would want to know who Denis was, and why he'd come and do I have a new boy friend. Also Michel might pass by.

"He thinks you saved him," Denis tells me. "For all I know, it's true. But he thinks more than that. He's obsessed with you . . . can't talk of anything else at times. I don't know what to do, Maureen. He thinks you're a saint, something more than human. Your visits were only half-real to him. They were like—appearances, apparitions." He stops, hesitant. It is the appealing, unsure Denis, absent, I imagine, for most of the time, that I see again as I saw him when we first met, seeking out my eyes, begging for something.

"It must be easy to disillusion him," I say. "You, of all people, could best do that."

"Oh, he's heard all the facts. Not so much from me, mind you . . ."

From his grandmother, I think, and his grandfather and his aunts. Heard all those things he "ought to know."

"I didn't know you went there so often, sat for whole nights at a time, it seems." He is speaking out of a deepening despair, floundering.

"But you saw me there."

"I know, but I—"

"Didn't you know I loved him, too?"

"You loved—" At the mention of love, his face seems about to shatter into a number of different planes, a face in an abstract painting, torn against itself. "To me your love was always defective. You—Maureen, when we were first married, I would think over and over, Now is forever; forever is now. Why did you destroy it all? It frightens me to think of you sitting, in the dark hours, with that boy. You could have pinched his life out like a match."

"I wouldn't do that, Denis. I couldn't hurt what's hurt already." I could have told him what light is like, as I had seen its illusion that day before his accident, how the jagged force tore into my smoothly surfaced vision. I had tried to tell him once: he thought I was raving. Later I smashed a set of his mother's china, and tore up a beautifully tiled wall with my nails, until they split and the blood ran down.

"I thought I had some force that would help him. That's not why I went but it's why I stayed."

"It might not have worked," Denis reflected. "He might have died anyway."

"Then you could have blamed me," I pointed out. "Then I could have been a witch, an evil spirit."

"I don't know why you ever had to turn into a spirit at all! Just a woman, a wife, a mother, a human being–! That's all I ever wanted!"

"Believe me, Denis," I said, *"I don't know either."*

We'd had it out that way, about a million times. Making no real progress, returning to our old familiar dead end, our hovel, which, in a way, was the only home we had.

I was then inspired to say: "It just may be, Denis, that if I'd never left, I could never have returned, and if I never had returned, it just may be that he would never have lived, he would have died, Denis, think of that, he would be dead."

For a moment, I guess he did consider it. His face turned to mine, mouth parted. He slipped little by little into the idea, let himself submerge within it. I will say for Denis: at least, he did that. "The doctors," he said at last, "they were terribly good, you know. The major credit," he said, finishing his coffee, "goes to them."

"Undoubtedly," I said. He had come to the surface, and turned back into a Partham again.

It had been a clear, still, frozen afternoon when we met, but holding just that soft touch of violet which said that winter would at last give over. Its grip was terrible, but a death grip no longer.

I tried to recall my old routine, to show my Partham side myself. "I imagine he will find new interests, once he gets more active. He won't think so much about me. But, Denis, if he does want to hold on to something about me, can't you let him?"

"I wouldn't dream of stopping him. It's a matter of proportion, that's all." He was pulling on his beautiful gloves. "He's practically made a religion of you."

As we were going out, I saw it all more clearly and began to laugh. "Then that's your answer, Denis."

"What is?"

"If I'm to be a 'religion,' then there are ways of handling me. Confine me to one hour a week, on Sunday morning. . . . I need never get out of bounds. Don't worry about him, Denis. He's a Partham, after all."

"Maureen? You're bitter, aren't you? People *have* to live, even Parthams. Life *has* to go on."

We were standing outside by then, at the intersection with my street. He wouldn't enter there, I thought; it was not in accord with his instincts to do so.

"I'm not bitter," I said. "I'm helpless."

"It didn't have to be that way."

It was like a final exchange; it had a certain ring. He leaned to touch my face, then drew back, moving quickly away, not looking behind.

And now I am waiting for the fourth visitor, my son. I think I will see him, at some street corner, seeking me, find him waiting for me in the pizza shop, hear a voice say, "Mother? I promised you. . . ." And before I know it, I will have said his name. . . .

I am waiting still.

Mr. Massimo, one day, leans at me over his portrait camera. "I hear you were married to a wealthy man in Westmount," he says.

"I am a princess in a silver tower," I reply. "Golden birds sing to me. I drift around in a long silk gown. What about you?"

"My father was Al Capone's brother. We rode around when young in a secondhand Rolls-Royce with a crest of the House of Savoia painted on the door. Then we got run out of Italy. The family took another name." He is smiling at me. It is not the story that reaches me, true or false, but the outpouring sun of Italy.

"You'll get me fired," I tell Michel.

"Come work for me," he says. "You can tell fortunes in the back. I'll make you rich."

He's using me again, working in collage–photography plus painting –he needs Mr. Massimo's darkroom. I telephone him when Mr. Massimo is gone and he comes to run a print through, or make an enlargement. When this phase passes, he will go again.

But he creates a picture before that, half-photo, half-drawing. He photographs my hands over a blood-red glass globe, lighted from within. I think the fortune-telling idea has given him the image. He makes the light strong; the veins of my hands stand out in great detail; the bones are almost X-ray visible. "Let me wash my hands," I say, because dirt shows under the nail tips. "No, I like it that way, leave it." So it stays. Watching Michel, I forget to feel anything else, and he is busy timing, setting, focusing. So the hands stay in place as my feelings rock with the sense of the light, and when he shuts it off, finished, we lock the shop up and go home together. Only the next day do I notice that my palm is burned so badly I have to bandage it and go for days in pain. Is the pain for Michel? Damn Michel! The pain is mine, active and virulent. It is mine alone.

The picture, with its background drawing of a woman in evening dress turned from a doorway, and its foreground of hands across a glowing glass, catches on. Michel has others in his package, but none is so popular as this one. He makes enlargements, sells them, makes others, sells those. They go out by the hundreds.

"What is it you carry? *Qu'est-ce que tu as,* Maureen?" Now he is after me, time and again, intense, volpine, impossible, begging from doorways, brushing my shoulder as he passes in the dark. *"Qu'est-ce tu as?"*

"I don't know. *Que t'importe, toi?"*

Among his pictures, a U.S. distributor chooses this one, one of three. If I go to certain shops in New York where cheap exotic dress is sold, incense, and apartment decorations of the lowlier sort, bought for their grass-scented pads by homosexual pairs, or by students or young lovers, or by adventurous young people with little taste for permanence, I will see that picture somewhere among them, speaking its silent language. I will look at my hands, see the splash of red that lingers. The world over, copies of it will eventually stick up out of garbage cans, or will be left in vacated apartments. Held to the wall by one thumb tack, it will hang above junk not thought to be worth moving. It celebrates life as fleeting as a dance.

Yet it was created, it happened, and that, in its smallness must pass for everything—must, in this instance, stand for all.

PRELUDE TO A PARKING LOT

Who are we? Look and see.

Look out from your upstairs window at night, across the cinder alley that leads off the shady street that slants down from Twenty-first Avenue that crosses the west end of Nashville. See us in the lighted bay window below.

We are sitting at the dining room table—round, old-fashioned, with a white cloth—eating strawberries with cream and sugar. Or blackberries maybe. The milk turns purple. Have some more. Not but one or two left. Have you heard and did you know? There's Brother, big and growing, and Uncle, way too fat. There's Mother and my first cousin Janey and me. Uncle and his daughter Janey own the house. Mother and Brother and I moved in after Daddy died. It was too big for two and we had nowhere to go. We hated to stay on in the country. Mother said she could do a lot of things but not farm. She didn't have the slightest notion of how to do it. It's funny because she heard Daddy talk about it for fifteen years, but when Brother accused her of never having heard a word, she finally admitted that was true. "I just never thought I'd need to know," was what she said.

For a long time after I graduated from high school and got a job I was happy to think I was making a living and pulling my own weight. This gave me real satisfaction. My small room, no bigger than a good-sized bathroom, became my domain; my importance filled it neatly, to the crevices. A new kind of lipstick bore itself upright on my dresser with a glistening air of something picked out and knowing it; it could companion me for quite some time. New shoes gave my legs what they wanted to feel about themselves, and I had different feelings for every dress and blouse. I ironed a lot and washed a lot, did my own hair, and for help with my imaginings drew on a stack of books from the library which I was always changing for new ones.

Looking down on us, at the round table, though you can't hear what we say, you may see us laugh. Very few people find each other funny in a good way. We do. We are funny to one another.

All except Janey. But that's another story.

Uncle Jess is the one we all get exasperated with, in an affectionate way. He seems not to take himself seriously enough to get ahead. He has retired into high blood pressure. But really he lacks confidence; he moves timidly, out in the world.

What Uncle Jess likes best is to do something we all will laugh at him about. This way he gets to be himself; it pleases him to be remarked on. But he knows you can't fake it, or you'll just be boring. If you put the radio on and lie out on the little back porch in hot weather on the cot and go to sleep and not hear a word, then you have got to really go to sleep, not just pretend. Then when we call him to supper and he comes in, "What was on the news?" we say. "How are they getting on in Korea?"

"Hard to tell when you don't know none of them names," he says.

"Hard to tell when you're asleep," Brother says.

"Naw, that ain't it. What I need is a map. Look like the war's go' be over 'fore I get it."

"Good Christmas present," Mother says. "A map of Korea."

Janey doesn't say anything. She knows we're having fun but she won't join in. She's got on black lipstick. She has long thin nails, like splinters. The trouble with her not saying anything she makes everybody nervous. And she knows it. She does it for meanness.

Look fast if you want to see us. We seem to be eternal, even though common as weeds—eating and laughing and talking, five in all; but one by one we won't be there. I'm the youngest, and change for me has set in already. It started that very day.

At the firm that afternoon they had sent me upstairs to an executive meeting to take down everything everybody said. It was a day of new shoes (pumps) and good legs, one of my days, hair burnished and lipstick neat. I turned out a cracking good job. It was more than a job; it was also a performance. If they had cast Lana Turner for the role back when she was nineteen or so, she couldn't have been more convincing. I had always been quick in shorthand, like some women can sit in the movies and knit without missing either a stitch or a scene. There had been a shake-up in the law firm because one partner's nitwit brother, who had been holding an office, had at last seen the light and got the message and decided he had better devote himself to raising Tennessee walking horses. Reorganization was now indicated. The law firm was always calibrating itself more and more closely into the needs of certain large businesses it represented. And there were tie-ins with real estate ventures and with powers in the legislature–a top-level meeting removed others from the scene in the wake of the dumb brother. Now they were rechanneling their streams and rerouting their traffic. I sat and did pothooks with my back straight and my legs crossed, feeling pretty.

"Did you get that, Miss Stacey?"

"Yes, sir, shall I read it back?"

"Just that last part, if you don't mind."

And I did.

Somebody eventually sent out for sandwiches and coffee. It was while we were eating that one or two of the men began to ask me questions–where was I from, how long with the firm, where did I live now, what about my family?

"They'll be stealing you next," said Mr. Eric Porter, my boss and not on the stationery yet.

"Not a bad idea," said Mr. Reginald Burns, silver-haired, looking at my knee.

There was general laughter. The feeling was good.

It was late when we broke up and Mr. Eric Porter offered me a lift home. I felt he'd seen me for the first time when Mr. Reginald Burns had said what he did while looking at my knee. Mr. Eric Porter had got nervous with all that shuffling around of big Nashville names, both within the firm and the fabric of society. The business world made him nervous. When he just dealt person-to-person he was calm and able. But mention the world-in-general and something made him swallow, tightened the corners of his mouth, glazed his eyes, reminded him that his office was at the far end of the corridor and had no carpet as yet (though one was ordered). That particular night when what rattled him had been constantly under discussion all day long, he felt the need to be steadied by some outer source of strength. He stopped in front of a house across and up the street from ours for a minute and put his hand on my knee, right where Mr. Reginald Burns's eye had rested.

I felt myself wake up all over, as much or more than if he'd kissed me, and knew that I personally was never going to feel the same about Mr. Eric Porter.

After a time, he removed his hand, plastered a casual kiss on my forehead, and drove on to my front door. "Good night, Miss Stacey," he said as I got out.

After sitting all of a spring afternoon and into the night with my heels deep in rich carpeting, and the smell of oiled mahogany and the discreet cluck of brass-fitted doors and drawers opening and closing, the way our house looked seemed out of the question for a fine attractive bright modern girl like myself to put up with. Mr. Eric Porter had a wife, though the office gossip was that he wasn't happy with her, and she wanted him to do better, and it certainly sounded like all of this and more when they spoke on the telephone. But still, he had her, so I decided I wouldn't even think about him.

But then he asked me for a beer and a hamburger one night when I worked overtime, and then we detoured once on the way home out to Percy Warner Park, which turned out to be a twenty-five mile ride with him telling me his troubles and some kissing thrown in, and I knew I'd better quit that job the next morning. But I didn't.

Percy Warner is a big, beautiful, accessible park and was where I fell in love with Mr. Eric Porter, who wished he was married to me instead of Mrs. Porter but whose career could not, at this point, stand up under a divorce, Mrs. Porter being from a prominent family.

The first year I did nothing but worry, decide and undecide, but the second year I settled down to seeing him without worrying much. The word, I later learned, is accommodation.

The third year Janey got mad at me over a bridge party I had promised to help her with but had only remembered during a movie when it was half over. She then said she had known all along about Mr. Eric Porter. She told Mother out and out, though Mother in some sort of way, not admitting it, had known it too, and she said further that she had a way of getting the word to Mrs. Eric Porter, who was dumb enough to believe her husband was late with important clients once a week, and had joined a volunteer civic group but had to quit, being pregnant.

"Yes, pregnant!" Janey repeated, brows rushing together, sticking her face close out to mine over a bowl of chicken salad.

I hadn't known and couldn't believe it. I couldn't stand to think about it.

Next day at work I got sick and asked to go home early.

"What's the matter?" he said. We'd gotten long ago into an act in the office, blank and professional as strangers.

"Nothing," I said.

A pause.

"Well, it's none of my business," he said.

Another pause.

Then, as we were alone with the door closed, he said: "Tell me anyway."

"Is your wife expecting?"

"Well—I meant to tell you, but I— It doesn't make any difference—"

"Difference! It makes me sick."

He had the nerve to grin. "It made her sick at first, but now it doesn't."

"I'm quitting this job."

"We can't talk now. We'll talk later."

"You've as good as put me in a bucket and run me down a well. You haul me up once a week and look at me, then you put me down the well again."

"I do more than look at you," he pointed out, no quarrel with the rest. "Oh, come on, now," he said, and caught my arm.

The door was opening. Somebody had knocked but we hadn't heard, over in the corner together by the files, quarreling in whispers that went up like steam on a hot stove.

I went out in a streak and left him to make up whatever tale he wanted to tell.

The next day I took the day off. They could fire me or not. I took the bus out of town, out toward the Hermitage. The Hermitage is a big antebellum home built by President Andrew Jackson, "Old Hickory."

I had to get away because, at the house, Mother was wandering around debating what to say to me. I didn't go to the mansion but stopped in a town nearby, had a Coke in the drugstore, and got to talking to an old woman who was sitting on a front porch. She had asked me to close her gate when I went by, and instead of closing myself out I went in. I sat down on the edge of her porch. She did not find this remarkable but said she saw I was worried. I said I had meant to get married and that now I wouldn't be able to, as this man was not only married already but was also expecting a family. I shouldn't have told her all this. She would know somebody and tell. She said I was young and pretty yet, and would get over it. "Go find yourself somebody else," was her advice.

I wondered then what old women sat and thought about and how they could stand it, being old. No new pumps would ever make their legs look good again, no man would ever sigh or catch his breath when he looked at them. This one sat with her knees apart, cotton skirts to her ankles, hands laced together, lying in her lap. She looked happy, she was rocking and smiling now. She had some memories, I guessed, but I wondered if memories, even happy ones, are good enough to live on.

"Don't tell anybody," I said.

"Don't see nobody to tell," she said, which is not a good answer. It meant that if she did see somebody to tell, she would.

I got the bus and went home.

It was fall and getting chilly. There was a smell in the air, a dusty smell, that comes, in our part of the world, from the leaves when they turn color and crumble in the dry air.

The next day, Mr. Reginald Burns called me in and said he had heard about another office which wanted a good secretary rather badly. He said there would be more chance of advancement in this new firm. I nodded and said okay. I agreed with everything he said to keep from crying. All the time I was gathering up my things my eyes kept blurring and running with tears. Mr. Eric Porter wasn't there that day. I thought I'd never see him again. For one minute I considered leaving him a note on a leaf of shorthand paper, but decided that was not the way to say anything.

I did not like the new office I went to as it was a long way by bus in a rather run-down part, over toward Centennial Park where they have a replica of the Parthenon and a lake, too. But now that I had a Past and thought I was making a New Start, I Made the Best of It and I was on the way to Better Things. After a week, Mr. Eric Porter called up and wanted to see me one more time to talk things over, so we started going out to Percy Warner Park again. There didn't seem to be any way to stop because the shade of too many hackberry trees, black by moonlight, the sound of too many little streams, the inside of the big family car, and each familiar touch and word—all belonged to us alone, in the sense we knew them. He said he just couldn't understand it, the way we were, but he thought we were always going to be that way, let's face it. He said his wife had heard some gossip at long last but knew I was out of the way and gone God knew where.

"I told her you'd moved to Atlanta," he said.

"That sounds like the penitentiary," I said.

He said she had always believed he had really had night work and that he had seen me only a few times. He said she didn't know my name and didn't want to know it. He also said she had almost lost her baby. (He said her, not their.)

The next week we were debating with a good deal of cold-blooded happiness just how long after a baby arrived its father could conveniently ask for a divorce. He didn't care if it hurt his career or not, for without me life was not life at all.

Along about then he got a promotion and his wife came into some money. They got a much bigger house, further out in Belle Meade. He had to play at the good life, he said, even if it was only a game. He would always be responsible to me. I was the heart of his heart, and the good life was only a play, but it was the game—did I understand that?—the game that everybody played. You couldn't jump off the world. Anywhere he went he would only be a small-time lawyer, competent, not brilliant. Here in Nashville, all the right names and things collected around him, only here could he play the game. What else could he do?

But I knew the baby had come, and all he was saying was words.

I moved out for a time. I got a room in a section which had a lot of Jews in it, up above Centennial Park. I never knew that part existed. I never knew so many Jews existed, not in Nashville. I thought they were alive and interesting. They were mysterious. The men, though often ugly (sometimes not), looked individually sexy, each in his chosen way. In my world men wear careful masks. Yet I couldn't tell just why these people were doing anything. For instance, when I saw them walking in the streets I wouldn't know for sure where they were going, or why.

For a month in that strange part, among those people, I thought I, too, along with Mrs. Eric Porter, was going to have a baby. I felt sick a good bit and I thought this was why.

I went to see a doctor about an abortion—it was a woman doctor who didn't practice openly. She was in her late forties, I guess, and looked like she must have cried quite a bit herself, from time to time. She was going to do the rabbit test, so I left.

On the way back on the bus, I decided I wouldn't go through with any abortion, I would have that baby instead. This was my Great Decision. I felt very good about it—good forever, a pure sort of goodness. More than that, I felt alive and felt the life in everything we passed. Every driveway and lawn mower and grass blade and doormat had its secret life; and each was shouting silently, giving and giving it. More than the first touch on my knee and all that followed, it wakened me, but in a new way. I would go to another city and have the baby and work for it and that would be my life. I would say its father got killed in the war. I would tell it this.

I stopped back by the old house to see Mother. She was there but not Janey, thank God. Uncle Jess had a job, for a change. Mother had kept up with me on the telephone and I had all the news, but now she told me again as though she hadn't. In a blur of joy, I sat and rocked in time with the world, which was harmonizing like a Grand Ole Opry tune.

That night in my lonely upstairs room in the Jewish section, I found that the child would not be born after all, if it ever had existed. I never knew. I called the woman doctor the next morning to tell her. She said, "That often happens," and click went the phone; so out of my life went the baby, a leaf blown off the steps.

It was the idea that stuck with me: my exaltation, the world's secret life, and the thought of holding on.

My only question: Would I have had the guts to go through with it? My answer: Yes.

For: The high water mark in my own little history had been struck and my soul created. I wanted to leave Eric now. That white, shivering bus ride when I came from out Ward-Belmont way into Twenty-first Avenue and decided not to throw it out with the garbage, this had changed me. Changing me, it had changed the way I felt about Eric.

We argued.

"You wouldn't have had the nerve," he said, and I said: "Just because you haven't got any nerve is no sign I haven't."

You can't get over speeches like that. You think you can, but they are always there, waiting for you to come back to them, purring like two cats, keeping the chairs warm for you.

In those days I used to go on Saturdays which were sunny and warm and sit in Centennial Park, sometimes on the grass. A picture of myself seems to form in my mind, a girl with long dark hair hanging down (I put it up on working days) and legs folded to one side, one arm straight, the wrist pressed into the grass, the other hand lying in my lap. I'm not sure of so much accuracy here, and maybe it only happened once or twice. Maybe other times I sat on a bench, for the ground in autumn and spring is usually cold. Still, the picture endures.

One day I returned home and took my old room back. Nobody had moved into it, though Brother was thinking of fixing it up for a TV viewing room, but Uncle Jess was saying it was too close in there for everybody to get in at once so leave the set in the living room where it belonged. I ended the argument when I came back.

I was happy that first night and cried no more.

In my narrow room, comb, brush, mirror, powder, and lipsticks lined up on the dresser, I was at peace. I felt timeless. This could go on forever, I thought. Why not? I thought.

There is a woman working at the bank on the corner near Peabody College, and she has been there since I can remember. She will stay there till she retires, I guess. Then she will live alone, see the friends she's always had, go to church, read books; one day she will fall ill, go in a nursing home or to a hospital; one day she will die. What's wrong with this? What's to stop life from happening in this peaceful way? Is it so bad? If it is not so bad, why does it make me want to scream with anguish and fear? If I want to scream with anguish and fear, why don't I do it? Instead I come home from work, watch TV, help get supper, help wash up, shampoo my hair, do my nails, read, fall asleep. The one thing I try not to do is quarrel with Janey. Some days I hate her, some days I merely despise her.

Janey is getting married. Her fiancé is younger than she and is from some little hole in the road, he says Yes, ma'am, and No, ma'am, to Mother, but he is an intern at the hospital, from somewhere he got the money to finish med school and being a doctor will put him up in the world. Janey knows this. She also knows why he likes her. So do I. He has plump hands and close-together eyes. Janey doesn't love him, she has never shown love for anybody that I know of, but she is ready to get married. Mother says,

"Janey wants you for her only attendant. We're going to have it at home. She'll wear white. We've all decided to chip in for her. Will you?"

I can't afford it. But it was something to deprive myself to contribute to, just to get her out of the house. I knew I had to anyway. Mother with her little farm income and the house to run always made me feel sorry. She was pretty and ought to have had better. She would put out all she could out of gratitude to Uncle Jess. Brother had got married secretly. (He walked out one day and came back married. He introduced his wife all around, then they left. He came for his stuff later.) We had rented his room for a time to a nice quiet girl.

Twice she went out with some friends and stayed later than we locked up. She had forgotten her key both times, and the second time she swore not to do it again, never, never.

"It's not that important," Mother said. "Don't worry about it."

I thought she was afraid of us, but maybe she was afraid of the world.

"I ought to talk to her," Mother said, "but I don't know what to say."

Then she forgot her key the third time.

It was a freezing cold night. She sat out in the car (she had a little car) alone for three hours, nearly freezing to death, shivering and quaking. I guess she would have stayed there all night but Mother waked up and looked out the window. She put on her flannel robe and went down to let her in.

"Don't worry about it," she said. "It's not important."

The next day when the girl came home from work she went to her room without saying anything. We were all around the dining room table (except Brother, who had got married). There was a long silence, then we heard her door close and presently she appeared in the dining room door. She was thin already, but now she looked drawn, and all I thought was that she was coming down with a cold from sitting out in freezing weather so long and wanted an aspirin. But she just stood there stiff as a cold poker till we all looked up, then she said in a quavering voice:

"I don't understand you. You don't understand me. I don't like any of you. I think you're horrible. You're awful people. It's why I keep forgetting my key. I really don't want to remember it, that's why. It smells funny here. I have to leave."

We got shocked by this, as nobody could think of any way to dispute her. Maybe we were horrible, maybe we didn't understand her, maybe we did (though not aware of it) smell funny, maybe she did keep forgetting her key because she didn't really want to remember it.

Then, for the first time I really missed Brother. I understood him then, his worth. If he had been there he would have had something to say back. I could just hear him.

For instance: "You come on in here and have some of this chocolate cake." (Making her feel better.)

Or, "What a coincidence! We think you smell funny, too." (Making us feel better.)

Or, "Come on, now. Which one of your boy friends stole that key?" (Making her and us both feel better for more complicated reasons; among them: she didn't have any boy friends but would have been flattered to have him pretend to think so.)

Brother could have made all the difference. As it was, it seemed to me later that everything that was changing picked up a vastly accelerated rate after that girl stood there accusing us and we let her get away with it. She was what Mr. Eric Porter, who had majored in literature before he went to law school, called a Greek character, a messenger the gods know about, but you don't. Not till they give you the message. Then you know.

After Janey married and left, Uncle Jess and I used to sit out on the back porch after I came home from work and talk about things. This was the first time we ever did get to talk. Before, he was just somebody there. Like I was born with fingers and toes, so I was born with Uncle Jess. But one day he started talking to me. Maybe he had got tired of reading the paper and listening to the news. He couldn't work (it was understood) because of high blood pressure. In reality, he could never keep a job, but we didn't mention it.

He said, first of all, that he knew I had never liked Janey. Then he said that Janey was not really his own daughter. Her mother, Aunt Edna, now dead, had been playing around with somebody else the summer before Janey was born. Janey knew about herself. This is what had kept Janey from ever having much feeling, she had this about herself and what her mother had done in her mind all the time.

One night Uncle Jess had got drunk, "when you were just a little old thing," he said.

"How little an ole thing?" I asked.

"In yo' *crib!*" cried Uncle Jess.

Well, we'd never had a crib there, but there was an old white-painted child's bed in the attic with a rose appliquéd onto the foot-board, so I let it pass.

"I kept saying to Janey, 'Come here to me, I'll make you mine.' I said it over and over. Being drunk, I couldn't quit once I started. You know what your mama thought? Thought I was trying things on that child."

He was awe-struck at the thought and we both got embarrassed. I fell to remembering the day he had found Brother and Janey out in the garage and had chased Brother around the yard with a bed slat. We did seem like an odd family. But for pointing it out, that girl had dealt us the coup de grâce.

Uncle Jess was a big rounded-out man. He was so perfectly rounded-out that you couldn't tell how big he was at first, then it would dawn on you gradually and rather splendidly, like a sunrise. He was like a girl friend of mine at the office who had taken a European tour said about some cupids in the Vatican at Rome, they just looked like little bitty things, then you would get close and find they were three times as big as you with wrists you couldn't get both hands around. Uncle Jess had a face as big as a close-up on a movie screen; great flat pads for feet—he wore black leather laced-up shoes—and big soft puffy hands. His eyes looked pressed into his face like they'd chosen him a pair too small and then it was too late to swap them. You would never know what color they were, they were too deep in there to see. I can see how Mother might have been horrified with a little child asleep in her white bed, a three- or four-year-old girl in the house, and that big hulk of a brother-in-law, wild drunk, going on about "Come here, I'll make you mine." But just the same I wanted to giggle. I saw it the way Mr. Eric Porter might have. He had a good sense of humor.

But I didn't laugh.

"I built a boat," said Uncle Jess, on another afternoon entirely. "You remember that boat, Sister. Out in the back yard."

I did remember the boat, though my thoughts in those days were all for Mr. Eric Porter.

Also, I forgot to say, Mother had bought the house from Uncle Jess. She had come into a little money when Granddaddy died, out in the country, and she and Uncle Jess had gone through arrangements so complicated it's a wonder to me they ever did get done with them. They filled up three dime-store ruled tablets just with their figuring and calculations. The upshot was that Mother got the house, Uncle Jess invested the money she paid for it, and what with his unemployment check could afford to give Mother money for his room and board. He was also going to do the yard and handy work, painting and all that, just like always. There was a big scramble over who was to pay for upkeep, tools, paint, grass seed, what to do if the garage fell down or the tree died or lightning struck us, no end of considerations. He couldn't have got by with any borrowing of so much as a splinter from our premises to start building on a boat, so he must have scavenged wood from here and there and bought nails, bolts, and hardware out of his pocket money once he quit drinking. Whatever he did, Mother felt she couldn't challenge him about it as he had to have something now he'd given up liquor and she didn't want to start him up again.

At first we didn't even know what it was. It was like one of those puzzles in the paper that you take a pencil to work out. You go from 1 to 2 to 3 and you zig and zag and by the time you get to 59 or 103 you've got a picture of a boat. We suspected that it was a house and that he was going to move out into it only it was too little for him as yet to get more than one foot and leg into it. Then the spar went up and we recognized the curvature of the hull.

"I aim to live on it," said Uncle Jess.

"Out in the back yard?" Mother inquired.

"Don't be a goose," said Uncle Jess. "On the Cumberland River."

We were all at the table (before anybody married) in real hot weather drinking iced tea and eating icebox lemon pie.

"There's people all over the world lives on houseboats. There's just a world of people does it. I don't mean to forget all y'awl. Y'awl can come spend the weekends. Maybe not everybody at once."

"I wouldn't be caught dead in that thing," said Janey.

But Mother thanked him politely. Part of it was, she would have been relieved to have him elsewhere. Brother was a great big boy and felt confined with all of us in one house.

Mother told me years afterward that she thought Brother and Jancy had "something to do" with one another. "She was no blood kin," Mother said, "or so she thought. Brother guessed it, some way or other."

"She believed it," I said. "Uncle Jess told me she did."

"I don't think it was true," Mother said. "I think she was Jess and Edna's child. Edna was scared to death of Jess, just like I was, when he was drinking, only more than me."

There comes a time when you know you're not going to meet anybody in a certain town. It was just that everybody in Nashville had known about Mr. Eric Porter and me, or so I thought for a long time. Then one day I knew and not only knew but told myself right out that nobody in Nashville was going to marry me whether there had been any gossip about Mr. Eric Porter and me or not. I got some proposals but not from anybody I liked. So I joined an agency and, in time, got an offer in Atlanta. A month later I got engaged. It happened sooner than I thought.

I asked Mother, "What makes you think that Janey and Brother had something to do with each other?"

"Well," said Mother, not surprised that five years had elapsed since she mentioned it, "I went up in the attic one warm spring day because I missed them. I'd sent one of them to the grocery and the other to the cleaners and I thought it was time at least one of them was back, if not both. Then it just came to me that's where they were and I'd better get up there quick. I climbed the back stair and opened the attic door and —well, there they were."

"You're kidding!"

"It hadn't gone all that far. He had her black hair wadded up in his fist and her head pulled back, bending over her. She jumped up like turning loose of a spring. She just plain glared at me, and Brother didn't feel like saying much of anything. I just said, 'I thought you all were up here.' And left. I didn't mention it to Jess. How many other times? I kept thinking, lying awake at night. Maybe that was all, though. How do you do."

She said the latter because my fiancé had just walked into the restaurant in Atlanta where he was taking us to lunch. They were meeting for the first time. They said later they were just crazy about each other.

Mother wouldn't move to Atlanta, though we asked her to. It

turned out that all along she'd known how to type, so she freshened up on it and put her card up at Scarritt, Peabody, and Vanderbilt. No end of things came pouring in. Theses, term papers, dissertations, even poetry. She had to put a limit on what she could accept. I sent money home and so did Brother.

It was only Janey wouldn't send any money home. She never came there except about twice a year as a sort of duty. She wore very good-looking clothes, more "outfits" than what you would call ordinary clothes, and she had lovely rings, a gold chain like I always wanted (I had a fake one), three wristwatches—sport, regular, and evening—and alligator bags. Mother never asked her for money. I guess Uncle Jess never asked her either. I guess too it was just as well she didn't come too often. She had a lot of people to talk about up in Jackson, Tennessee—people who belonged to the horse show crowd and the country club, were golfers, too, and went to the West Indies in the winter. Everytime she left, Uncle Jess would be rather afflicted in some way. Mother couldn't say just how, though she understood it. He would mope around, she said. We agreed he was trying to shake her off.

Mother was down in Atlanta to visit us, when she said this. She comes once or twice a year. That night we got a telephone call from the Nashville City Hospital. Uncle Jess was in it. We left right away.

What had happened was strange, but then he was always a strange man. Left all alone, he had gone down to the Cumberland River and tried to drown himself. It was down where he'd hoped to be, I guess, at least had dreamed of, had spoken of, living in his houseboat. And maybe he hadn't tried to drown himself but had just wanted to investigate the depth of the water, the lay of the banks, what it would be like. If so, however, 11:30 P.M. was an odd time to do it.

Some Negroes pulled him out. They'd heard something out in the night splashing and floundering around like a hippopotamus, they said. We had compared Uncle Jess to a lot of things—an elephant, a balloon man that you go to the gas station to have blown up where it says Free Air and then you can't push him over, a baby cupid forty times normal size in the Vatican in Rome, etc.—but had never thought of a hippopotamus. But then we'd never seen him sloshing around in the Cumberland River.

"We had us a time gittin' him outta there," the Negroes told us, when we went down and found them. We wanted to give them something, but they wouldn't accept. "He a big man," was all they kept saying, "He sho' a big man," they said.

At the hospital Uncle Jess looked pale. His hair had got grayer and sparser through the years without our noticing the change. It stuck up against the white pillows. He was talking pretty wild.

"Looks like I can't step out the door something don't happen," Mother said. "Jess," she said, "I ain't ever going to leave you again." (Mother doesn't say ain't but Uncle Jess does; she said it for him.)

He kept on talking wild, but finally we got what he was trying to tell. He'd just been up to the corner for a hamburger at the Krystal Grill—by that he meant at least three of them; it took a lot to fill him up—when he came back to the house and knew it wasn't empty. He thought it was Mother back but he walked into the dining room and there at the table sat Aunt Edna. She was waiting. He'd said she was dead so often he had almost believed it was true. But she had never died. She'd left him, that's all. And left her daughter, too, who was not even his daughter.

He said: "Edna, what on earth you doing here?" And she said: "I've come back to you, Jess. To you and Janey." He said: "But Janey's got married, she's not even here." She said: "All right, then I've come back just to you." And he said: "But why'd you want to do that?" And she said: "Because I love you, Jess."

He felt dizzy and went to the kitchen to get some ice water. He reached to draw the jug out of the refrigerator, and that was the last he remembered.

He didn't remember about the Cumberland River or the Negroes and didn't know anything about how the bottles got into the remains of the old boat hull we still had stored out in the garage. We had put it in there right after Brother left; he was the only one of us that ever had a car.

It is the thought of Uncle Jess wandering around alone and drunk from right after lunch till 11:30 P.M. that I can't get out of my head. It's a home movie that I can't shut off; I can't find the stop button.

The places he went . . . the streets he wandered in and out of . . . the people he passed. . . . The ones who didn't know him . . . the ones who did . . . the dogs he stopped to pet . . . the things he fell over. . . .

It fell my lot to call up Janey in Jackson, Tennessee. She was "out," her maid told me; but finally she was "in."

"Edna's dead as anything," Mother said. "She's buried up in Winchester Cemetery. I read it in the paper. It's true she did go off with somebody else, but in the beginning she did love Jess. She had this disappointment because he could never make do in a job. He thought it was his funny looks, his size and all. It was just a sort of permanent misunderstanding. But she's dead as anybody can be."

But Uncle Jess couldn't get her out of his head. She was part of his reality, or rather his lifelong parade of realities, one after another, the street-length of them, each turning our corner, approaching in full detail, regalia, and flourish, then passing on in time, gone in one way but in another never gone, as each had become its own history. Like Janey and all of us moving in on him and the boat and the war news and the house sale to Mother and the jobs and Janey's marriage (he rented a swallow-tail coat to give her away), Aunt Edna's return was with him forever; it sat in his head, the dining room table and her sitting at it just as he'd seen it when he came in from the Krystal Grill. He has it with him now in the nursing home. That's the only place it is, or can be.

For: The house, the one we used to live in, the one I've talked about all this time, the one that had the table you could look down on and see us all together at, talking and laughing and eating blackberries which make your tongue turn purple—it's sold and torn down. You couldn't even look down on it any more because the house next door where you were has met the same fate. It and ours and two more. They're all a parking lot now. All cemented over, smooth and gray. After surgery comes the neat scar.

When in Nashville, I go to see Mother. She's moved into an apartment in that same neighborhood. She couldn't give up her neighborhood, she says. Then I go to visit Uncle Jess in the nursing home. His mind never came back right, after that day.

I say: "I believe you, Uncle Jess. She was there. And she did love you. That was true."

I can say that so it convinces and soothes him because of that baby I was going to keep. Not those I finally had, but the one that never was, and how I felt about it, that one day.

INDIAN SUMMER

One of my mother's three brothers, Rex Wirth, lived about ten miles from us: he had taken over his wife's family home because her parents had needed somebody on the land to look after it.

Uncle Rex had been wild in youth, had dashed around gambling, among other things, and had not settled down until years after he married. "What Martha's gone through!" was one of Mama's oft-heard remarks. I had a wild boy friend myself back then and I used to reflect that at least Uncle Rex had married Aunt Martha. Furthermore, he did, at last, settle down.

Once stabilized, it became him to be and look like a responsible country gentleman. He was clipped and spare in appearance, scarcely as tall as his horse, and just missed being frail-looking, but he had an almost military air of authority; to me, when I thought of him, I always pictured him as approaching alone. He might be in blue work pants, he might be in a suit; his smart forward step was the same, and his crinkling smile had nothing to beg about. "How you *do?*" was his greeting to everybody, family or stranger. But the place—with its rolling, piny acreage, its big two-story house, its circular drive to the gate—was not his own. He never said this, but his brother, Uncle Hernan, who lived next door to us, said that he never had to mention it because he never forgot it for a minute. "It galls him," was Uncle Hernan's judgment. He was usually right.

The family feeling toward Uncle Rex, which was complicated but filled with reality, had to do, I believe, with his having, when a boy, fallen from a tree into a tractor disk. There was still a scar on his leg and one across his back, but the momentary threat to his manhood, the pity in that, was what gave the family its special tremor about him. If he stood safe it was still a near miss, and gave to his eyes the honest, wide openness of those of our forebears in family daguerreotypes, all the more vulnerable for having died or been killed in the Civil War and yet, at the time of the picture, anyway, not knowing it, that it would happen that way, or happen at all.

To me, even stranger than the tractor disk accident and relating to no photograph of any family member whomsoever, was the time Uncle Rex almost burned alive. He had been sleepy from fox hunting, and out on the place in the afternoon had gone into an abandoned Negro house down in a little hollow with pine and camellia trees around it and built a fire in the empty chimney out of a busted chair and fallen sound asleep on an old pile of cotton—third picking, never ginned. He woke with the place blazing around him and what it came to was that he apparently, from those who saw it, walked out through a solid wall of flame. The house crashed in behind him. He was singed a little but unharmed. Well, he was precious, Mama said, and the Lord had spared him.

Over there where he lived, however, he was a captive of the McClellands; had the Lord spared him for that? A certain way of looking at it made it a predicament. It was better to speak in ordinary terms, that he'd managed the property and taken care of his wife's parents till they died, then had stayed on.

"That farm wouldn't have been anything without you, Rex," I once heard Mama pointing out. "It would have gone to rack and ruin."

"I reckon so," he would say, and brush his hand hard across the sparse hair atop his head, the color having left hold of red for sandy gray, the permanently sun-splotched scalp showing through here and there in slats and angles. "Someday I'll pick up Martha and move in with Hernan." He had as much right, certainly, to live in the old Wirth family home as Uncle Hernan had, for it belonged to all; still, he was joking when he said a thing like that, no matter how many McClellands were always visiting him, making silently clear the place was theirs.

It wouldn't have worked anyway. He was plainer by nature than Uncle Hernan, who loved his bonded whiskey and gold-trimmed porcelain, silver, table linen, and redolent cigars. Uncle Rex's wild days, even, had had nothing plush about them; his gambling had been done not in the carpeted *maisons* of New Orleans, but around and about with hunting companions; he would hunt in the coldest weather in nothing except an old briar-scratched, dog-clawed, leather jacket, standing bareheaded on deer stands through the long drizzles of winter days. Sometimes he got sick, sometimes not. "Come on, Martha," he would snort from his bed, voice muffled in cold symptoms, up to his neck in blankets, while the poor woman went off in every direction for thermometers and hot water bottles and aspirin and boiled egg and tea and the one book he wanted, which had got mislaid. "Come on! Be good for something!"

It was in the course of nature—that and pleasing the McClellands, who were strict—that Uncle Rex had given all his meanness up; he was a regular churchgoer now, first a deacon, then an elder. So all his hollering at Aunt Martha was understood as no more than prankish. Besides, Aunt Martha had been provably good for something; she'd had a son, a fine boy, so everybody said, including me; he'd gone to military academy and now he taught at one.

Once in the winter Mama and Daddy and I drove over to see Uncle Rex and found him alone. It was Sunday. Aunt Martha had gone into town to see some of her folks, who must have had some ailment, else they would have been out there.

"Come on, now," Uncle Rex said, as it was fine weather. "You want to see my filly?" He got up to get his jacket and change into some twill britches for riding in.

"How's she doing?" Daddy asked.

"She's coming on real good, a great big gal. Hope the preacher don't come. Hope Martha's not back early. Just showing a horse, Marilee," he turned to ask me, "ain't that all right on Sunday?" He fancied himself when well mounted and sat as dapper as a cavalryman. In World War I, he'd trained for that, but had never got to France.

"What's her name?" I asked him.

"Sally," he said. "How's that?" He'd put his arm across my shoulder, walking; he didn't have the mass, the complex drawing power of his brother, Uncle Hernan, but his nature was finely coiled, authentic, within him, you could tell that.

We came out to the barn all together, enwrapped (as all around us was) in the thin winter sunshine which fell without color on the smooth-worn unpainted cattle gate letting into the lot. "Mind your step," said Uncle Rex. The cows were out and grazing; two looked peacefully up; the mare was nowhere in sight. The barn stood Sunday quiet. "She must be back yonder," he said.

At the barn he reached up high to unbolt the lock on the tack room door and fling it back. The steps had rotted but a stump of wood had been upended usefully below the door jamb; if you meant business–and Uncle Rex did–about getting in, it would bear a light climbing step without toppling. Uncle Rex emerged with a bridle over his arm. The woods beyond the fenced lot were winter bare, except for some touches of oak. There were elm, pecan, and walnut, a thick stand along the bluff. Below the bluff was more pasture land, good for playing in, I remembered from childhood, handy for hunting arrowheads. It rolled pleasantly, clumped with plum bushes and one or two shade trees, down to the branch with its sandy banks.

Uncle Rex was leading the mare out now. He had found her back of the barn. He re-entered the harness room for the saddle while she stood quietly, reins flung over an iron hook set in the barn wall. Uncle Rex brushed her thick-set neck, which arched out of her shoulders in one glossy, muscular rise; he tossed on her saddle. He brought the girth under, but she spun back. "I'll hold her," Daddy said, and took the reins. "Whoa, there," he said, while Uncle Rex cinched the girth. He gathered her in then, though she wasn't sure yet that she liked it, tapped her fetlock to bring her lower for the mounting, and up he went. We stood around while he showed her off; she had a smart little singlefoot that he liked, and a long swinging walk. I still remember the straightness of his back as he rode away from us, and the jaunty swing of his elbows.

Afterward we returned to the house and there was Aunt Martha's car, back from her folks in town. She acted glad to see us: it was Uncle Rex she was cool to. The McClelland house was a country place, but it had high, white, important sides with not enough windows, like a house on a city street. The McClellands were nice people, a connection spread over two counties, yet the house was different from what we would have had. It was printed all over Aunt Martha what she was thinking; that Uncle Rex had had that horse out on Sunday. And the beast was female, too; that, I now realized, made a difference to both of them, and had all along.

Aunt Martha was pretty, with an unlined plump face, gray hair she wore curled nicely in place. She was reserved about her feelings, and if Uncle Rex had not come into her life, lighting it up for us to see it, I doubt we'd ever have thought anything about Martha McClelland. That day of the mare, she was wearing brown, but summer would see her turned out in fresh bright cotton dresses she'd made herself, trimmed in eyelet with little pleats and buttons cleverly selected. She also picked out the cars they drove; they were always green or blue. It occurred to me years after that what Aunt Martha liked was owning things. Her ownership, which was not an intrusion–she wanted nothing of anybody else's–extended to all things and persons she had any claim on. When she got to Uncle Rex, then I guess she got a little bit confused; did he belong to her or not? If so, in what way? That question, I thought, would be something like Uncle Rex's own confusion over the McClelland property: he had it, but didn't actually own it. He'd certainly improved it quite a bit. But Aunt Martha also could point to improvements; Uncle Rex was so much better than he used to be. For in former days, freshly married, with promises not to still warmly throbbing in the air, he would come in at dawn, stinking of swamp mud and corn likker, having played poker all night while listening to the fox hounds running way off in the woods–some prefer Grand Opera while playing bezique, Uncle Hernan once remarked. I wondered what bezique was. Whatever it was, it wasn't for Uncle Rex.

As we drove away, Daddy said: "She's probably raising Cain about that mare."

"I don't think so," Mama said. "I don't think Martha raises Cain. Andrew is coming home at Thanksgiving. That's keeping her happy. She's proud of that boy."

"Rex is proud of him, too," said Daddy.

"Of course he is," Mama said.

Andrew was a dark-haired square-set boy, and when we used to play, as children, looking for arrowheads in the pasture, climbing through the fence to the next property where, it was said, the high bump in the ground near the old road was really an Indian mound, I would imagine him an Indian brave or somebody with Indian blood. My effort, I suppose, was to make him mysterious and hence more interesting, but the truth is there was never anything mysterious about Andrew. He was a good boy through and through, the way Aunt Martha wanted him. She would have liked him to go in the ministry but he took up history and played basketball so well he was a wonder. He wasn't so tall but he was fast and well set and had a wondrous way of guarding the ball; he knew how to dribble it and keep it safe. After graduating he got a job teaching and coaching at a military academy run by the church. This was not being a preacher but was in no way acting like his father used to act, and Aunt Martha breathed easy once he decided on it.

He was likely to be home in the summers when not working in some boys' camp.

That was all in the late 1940s, post-war. Andrew was younger than me and unlike the boys my age, he had missed the conflict. He was old enough to play basketball but not to be drafted. Somebody—a man of the town—on seeing him win a whole tournament for Port Claiborne, came up afterward to say: "Boy, it's folks like you that keeps us inter-rested here at home. Don't think you ain't doing your part." Aunt Martha was proud of that; she quoted it often and so did Uncle Rex.

With such a fine boy who'd turned out so well, a place running smoothly and yielding up its harvest year by year, a calmed-down husband with a docile wife, it seemed that Uncle Rex and Aunt Martha could sit on their porch in the summer, in their living room by the gas fire in the winter, smiling and smug and more than content with themselves because of the content they felt about Andrew. Next he would get married, no doubt, and have children, and all would be goodness and love and joy forever. But something happened before that and Aunt Martha lost, I suppose, her holy vision.

It happened like this.

One of the summers when Andrew was home sort of puttering around farming and romancing one or two girls in town and reading up for his schoolwork, he and Aunt Martha suddenly got thicker than thieves. They were always out in the family car together, either uptown or driving to Jackson, or out on the place. People leaned in the car window to tell them how much Andrew resembled her side of the family, which was true. The pity (at least to a Wirth) was how pleased they both looked about it. To start really conversing with a parent for the first time must be as strange an experience as falling in love. Daddy and Mama and I love each other but we never say very much about it. Maybe they talk to each other in an unknown tongue when I'm not around. But as for Andrew and Aunt Martha it seemed that somebody had blown up the levee of family reticence, and water and land were mingling to their mutual content.

Late that same summer, Uncle Rex and Uncle Hernan had got together and taken a train trip up to visit their third and older brother, Uncle Andrew, who had lived and worked in Chicago for years, in the law firm of Sanders, Wirth, and Pottle, but who had now retired to a farm he had bought north of Cairo. The trip had renewed the Wirth ties of blood. There is something wonderful about older-type gentlemen on trains. It brings out the good living side of them and makes them relish the table service in the diner, a highball later, and lots of well-seasoned talk. They may even have gambled a little in the club car. The visit with Uncle Andrew must have attained such a joyous and measured richness they would always preserve its privacy.

"It's the property we've looked into these last few days," young Andrew said to his father, on his return. "The possibilities are just great, what with that new highway coming through."

"I think so, too," Aunt Martha said, and served them all the new recipes she was learning. "You've just got to listen to Andrew, Rex."

"I'm still riding the train," said Uncle Rex. "You got to wait awhile before I can listen."

Whether they let him wait awhile or not is doubtful. They were bursting with their plans and designs on the McClelland property. The new highway was coming through. Forty acres given over to real estate was something the farm would never miss. The houses, maybe a shopping center, and even a motel would all be too distant to be seen from the house, yet they glimmered full formed and visible as a mirage in Andrew's talk; and in his thoughts the large pile of money bound to result was already mounding up in the bank.

Andrew had assembled facts and figures, and had borrowed some blueprints of suburban housing from a development firm in Vicksburg. They curled up around his ears when he talked about it all, but nobody had stopped to notice that Uncle Rex had sat the greater part of the time as stiff and straight as if his mare was under him, though the rapport he and that animal shared was not present. He listened and listened and he failed to do justice to the food, and when he couldn't stand it a minute longer he exploded like a firecracker:

"I always knew it!" he jumped up to say. "I never should have moved onto this property."

They looked up with their large brown McClelland eyes, innocent as grazing deer.

"If y'all even think," said Uncle Rex, "that you can sit here and work out all kind of plans the minute I walk out the door you can either un-think 'em or do without me. Which is it?"

"You ought to be open-minded, Father," said Andrew, exactly like he was the oldest one there. He leaned back and let the blueprints roll themselves up with a crackle. "Mother and I have gone to a lot of trouble on this."

"Just listen, Rex," Aunt Martha urged, but her new glow about life was going out like a lamp which has been switched off at the door but doesn't quite know it yet. She spoke timidly.

"I've listened enough already," said Uncle Rex.

He marched out of the room, put on his oldest, most disreputable clothes, and went off in the pickup. He eventually wound up at Uncle Hernan's. We saw him drive up, badly needing a shave. He whammed through the front door of his old home and disappeared. We didn't even dare to telephone. Something, we knew, had happened.

Aunt Martha was so stunned when Uncle Rex hit the ceiling and departed that she shook with nerves all over. She called Mama to come over there (I drove her) and sat and told Mama that everything she had belonged to Rex in her way of thinking, that the Lord had made woman subservient to man, it was put forth that way in the Bible. Did Rex think she would go against the Word of God?

"The land's all yours," Mama said, evidently aware of but not mentioning the wide gap between statements and actions. "I don't think Rex is disputing it. It just comes over him now and then. Maybe Andrew pointed it out to him."

"Andrew ought not to have mentioned it at all," said Aunt Martha. "Oh, I knew that at the time."

"I doubt his coming back to live here now, the way things are," Mama said. "They say the Wirths have got a lot of pride. Especially the men. I just don't know what to tell you. Can you move over to Hernan's with him for a while? Maybe y'all could get more chance to talk things over."

Andrew passed through, knowing everything and not stopping to talk. "He's just hardheaded," he said, in a tone of final authority, and that wasn't smart either. I recalled a saying about the McClellands, that they were so nice they didn't have to be smart. It was widely repeated.

"Hernan's got a whole empty wing," Mama said.

Aunt Martha turned red as a beet and almost cried. She kept twisting her handkerchief, knotting and unknotting it. "Do you imagine a McClelland . . ." she whispered, then she stopped. What she'd started to say was that Uncle Hernan lived with a Negro woman and everybody knew it. It was his young wife's nurse who'd come down from Tennessee with her, nursed her when she got sick and died, then stayed on to keep house. She was Melissa, a good cook—we all took her for granted. But no McClelland could be expected to be under the same roof with that! In fact, Aunt Martha may have thought of herself as sent from God to us, though Mama was also steady at the Ladies Auxiliary and of equal standing.

When we drove back home it was to learn that Uncle Rex had not only departed from Aunt Martha, he had left Uncle Hernan as well, nobody knew for where. He had gone out and loaded his mare in the horse trailer and gone off down the back road unobserved from within, while Aunt Martha was sitting there with Mama and me, crying over him. (We passed a carload of McClellands driving in as we left: at least, we, along with Uncle Rex, had escaped that.)

The next day was Sunday and a good chance for all of us over our way to get together in order to worry better.

"I'm glad I never had any children," Uncle Hernan said. Though he'd apparently had any number by Melissa, he didn't have to count them the way Uncle Rex had to count Andrew.

"I don't think for a minute Andrew and Martha calculated the effect something like this was going to have on Rex," Daddy said.

"It's just now worked to a head," Mama said, "about being on her land and all."

"Hadn't been for Rex wouldn't be much of any land to be on," Daddy said. "The McClellands make mighty poor farmers."

"He knew that," said Uncle Hernan. "He knew that everybody knows it. But the facts speak."

"Wonder where he is right now," Mama said, and from her voice I was made to recall the slight lovable man who was her brother, threatened, in her mind, in some perpetual way.

"Down in the swamp somewhere, with that pickup and that mare, living in some hunting camp," was Uncle Hernan's judgment. "I imagine he's near the river; he'll need a road for working the mare out and some free ground not to get bit to death with mosquitoes and gnats."

"This time of year?" said Mama, because fall was coming early; we were into the first cold snap.

"All times of year down in those places."

"I worry about him, I declare I do," Mama said.

"*You* worry about him. Another week of this and Martha's going to be in the hospital," Daddy said.

"That mare," said Uncle Hernan, searching his back pocket. He drew out a gigantic linen handkerchief, blew his nose in a moderate honk, and arranged his bronze mustache. "She must be getting on for ten years old."

"She was nothing but a filly that day we were over there. You remember that, Marilee?" Daddy asked.

"When was that?" Uncle Hernan asked.

"We drove over there one Sunday," said Mama. "Martha was at one of her folks in town. Rex showed off the mare—nothing would do him but for us to see her."

"Martha came back and caught him fresh out of the lot on Sunday," Daddy said.

"Lord have mercy," said Uncle Hernan. Then he said, "How are you, Marilee?"

I was not so much involved in their discussion. I was over in the bay window reading some reports from the real estate office where I had a job now. School teaching, after two years of it, had gone sour on me. I said I was fine. I was keeping quietly in the background for the very good reason that the fault in all this crisis had been partially my own. I had once suggested to Andrew, who sometimes dropped by the office to talk to me, that the McClelland place had a gold mine in real estate if only they'd care to develop it, what with the new highway laid out to run along beside it. He'd asked me a lot of questions and had evidently got the idea well into him, like a fish appreciative of the minnow.

I knew nobody would ever reckon me responsible, simply because I was a girl in business. A girl in business, their assumptions went, was somebody that had no right to be and did not count in thinking or in conversation. I could sit in the window seat reading up on real estate not ten feet away from them, but I might as well have been reading

Jane Austen for all it was going to enter their thinking about Uncle Rex.

A log broke in the fireplace while we all, for a most unusually long moment, sat pondering in silence, and a spray of sparks shot out.

"Somebody's *got* to find him," Mama said, and almost cried.

"I'd look myself," said Uncle Hernan, "but I'm down with rheumatism and hardly able to drive, much less take a jeep into a swamp. I might get snake bit into the bargain."

"What about Daddy?" I said, and added that I didn't want to go into any swamp either.

"Oh, my Lord," Daddy said, which was his own admission that the Wirth family had never given him much of a voice in their affairs, though it stirred Mama's indignation to hear about it. Daddy knew he certainly might be successful in any mission they sent him on: he was Jim Summerall–a tough little farming man and a good squirrel shot; but though you could entrust a message to him, how could anybody be sure he'd be listened to when he got there? A wild goose chase would be what he'd probably have to call it, with Mama riled up besides.

"Marilee could find him," Uncle Hernan pronounced, and everybody, including myself, looked up in amazement, but didn't get to ask him why he said it, as he picked up his walking cane and stood up to leave. Daddy walked out with him to go down and look at where the soil conservation people were at work straightening the creek in back of ours and Uncle Hernan's properties. There was going to be a new little three-acre patch on their side to be justly divided, and a neighbor across the way to be treated with satisfaction to all. It was a nice walk.

But Uncle Hernan would have found, if not that, some other reason to leave our house. He never seemed in place there. His own house, or rather the old Wirth home where he lived, was pre-Civil War and classical in design; ours was a sturdy farming house. It was within the power of architecture to let us all know that Uncle Hernan was not in his element sitting in front of our fire in the living room, in spite of Mama's antiques and her hooked rugs and all her pretty things. Then it occurred to me that, whether totally his property by deed or inheritance or purchase or not, that house in turn had claimed Uncle Hernan; that he belonged to it and they were one, and then I knew why Uncle Rex had found no peace there either and had left after two days, as restless in search as a sparrow hawk.

When Daddy got back I walked out to speak to Uncle Hernan at the fence.

"What'd you mean, I could find him?" I asked.

"Well, you've got that fella now, that surveyor," Uncle Hernan said. " 'Gully' Richard," he added, giving his nickname.

Joe Richard (pronounced in the French way, accent on the last syllable) was a man with a surveying firm over in Vicksburg whom we'd had out for a couple of jobs. He had got to calling me up lately, always at the office. For some reason, I hadn't mentioned him to anybody.

"You know how he got the name of Gully?" Uncle Hernan asked, looking at the sky.

"No, sir," I said.

"Came up to this country from down yonder in Louisiana and the first job he got to do was survey a tract was nothing but gullies. Like to never got out of there—snakes and kudzu. Says he thinks he's in there yet. Gully's not so bad, Marilee."

"No, sir," I said, and stopped. Let your family know you've seen anybody once or twice and they've already picked out the preacher and decorated the church. But Uncle Hernan wasn't like that. I thought more of him because he'd never commented on anybody I might be going with, except he did say once that the wild boy who had been my first romance could certainly put away a lot of likker. I judged if Uncle Hernan had spoken favorably of Joe Richard, it was because he esteemed him as a man, not because he was hastening to marry me off.

"What's Joe Richard got to do with Uncle Rex?" I asked, but I already knew what the connection was. He'd been surveying some bottom land over toward the river, and, furthermore, he knew people—trappers and squatters and the like. He was a tall, sunburnt, surly-looking man who kept opinions to himself. I had never liked him till I saw his humor. It was like the sun coming out. His grin showed an irregular line of teeth, attractive for some reason, and a good liveliness. He came from a distance, had the air of a divorced man, a name like a Catholic—all this, appealing to me, would be hurdles as high as a steeple to the Summeralls, the McClellands, and the Wirths (except for Uncle Hernan). But any thought that he wanted to get married at all, let alone to me, was pure speculation. Maybe what he would serve for was finding Uncle Rex.

It was a day or so before I saw him. "Will you do it?" I asked him. "Will you try?"

"Hell, he's just goofed off for a while," Joe said. "Anybody can do that. Let him come back by himself."

"He's important to us," I said, "because–" and I stopped and couldn't think of the right thing, but to Joe's credit he didn't do a thing but wait for me to finish. It came to me to put it this way, speaking with Mama's voice, I bet: "Important because he doesn't know he is."

Joe understood that, and said he'd try.

One latent truth in all this is that I was mad enough at Andrew McClelland Wirth to kill him. He'd gone about it wrong: snatching authority away from his father was what he'd obviously acted like.

During the second month of Uncle Rex's absence, with Joe Richard still reporting nothing at all, and Aunt Martha meeting with her prayer group all the time (she was sustained also by droves of McClelland relatives who were speculating on divorce), I drove up to the school where Andrew taught and got to see him between class and basketball practice. "You could have had a little more tact," I told him, when more sense was probably nearer to the point, and what I should have said. The night before I had had a dream. I had seen a little cabin in a swamp that was just catching fire, flames licking up the sides, but nobody so far, when I woke, had walked out of it. The dream was still in my head when I drove to find Andrew.

Andrew and I went to a place across the street from his little school, a conglomerate of red-brick serviceable buildings with a football field out back, a gym made out of an army-surplus aluminum airplane hangar off at the side, and a parade ground in the center, with a tall flagpole. It was a sparkling dry afternoon in the fall, chilly in shadow, hot in the sun. "If you haven't noticed anything about the Wirth pride," I continued, "you must be going through life with blinders on."

"You don't understand, Marilee," he said. "It was Mother I was trying to help. She needs something more to interest her than she's got. I thought the real estate idea you had was just about right."

"It would have been if you'd have gone through Uncle Rex."

"You may not know this, Marilee, but after a certain point I can't do a thing with Father, he just won't listen."

"You mean you tried?"

"I tried about other things. He's got an old cultivator out in back that the seat is falling off of, it's so rusty. You'd have to soak it in a swimming pool full of machine oil to get it in shape, but he won't borrow the money to buy a new one."

"He and Daddy and Uncle Hernan are going in together on one for the spring crop," I said. "It was Uncle Rex got them to do it. Didn't you know that?"

"He won't tell me anything anymore; you'd think I wasn't in the world the way he won't talk to me. I've just about quit."

I recalled that Uncle Rex had told Uncle Hernan that Aunt Martha and Andrew had got so thick he was like a stranger at his own table, but there's no use entering into family quarrels. The people themselves all tell a different tale, so how can you judge what's true?

"Promise me one thing," I said.

"What?"

"If he comes back (and you know he's bound to), glad or sad or mean or sweet or dead drunk with one ear clawed off, you go in and talk to him and tell him how it was. Don't even stop to speak to your mama. You go straight to him."

"How do you know he's bound to come back?" Andrew asked.

"I just do," I said. But I didn't; and neither did anybody else.

Andrew said: "You're bound to side with the Wirths, Marilee. You *are* one."

"Well," I said, "are you trying to break up *your* family?"

He thought it over. He was finishing his Coke because he had to go back over to the gym. He wore a coach's cap with a neat bill, a soft knit shirt, gabardine trousers, and gym shoes. He also wore white socks. All told, he looked to have stepped out of the Sears Roebuck catalogue, for he was trim as could be, but he was too regulation to be real.

"You might be right, Marilee," was his final word. "I'll try."

When I got back to Port Claiborne, Joe Richard was waiting for me. His news was that he had finally located Uncle Rex. He was living in a trapper's house down near the Mississippi River. The horse was there, and also a strange woman.

Indolent at times, in midday sun still as a turtle on a log which is stuck in the mud near some willows . . . at other times, hasty and hustling, banging away over dried-up mud roads in the pickup with a dozen or so muskrat traps in the back and the chopped bait blood-staining a sack on the floor of the seat beside him . . . at yet other times, fishing the muddy shallows of the little bayous in an old, flat-bottomed row-boat, rowing with one hand tight on a short paddle, hearing the quiet separated sounds of water dripping from paddle, pole, or line, or from the occasional bream or white perch or little mud cat he caught, lifting the string to add another: that's how it was for Rex Wirth. In spring and summer sounds run together but in the fall each is separate; I don't know why. Only insect voices mingle, choiring for a while, then dwindling into single chips of sound. The riverbanks and the bayous seem to have nothing to do with the river itself, which flows magnificently in the background, a whole horizon to itself from the banks, or glimpsed through willow fronds–the Father of Waters not minding its children.

At twilight and in the early morning hours when the dew began to sparkle, he rode the mare. He kept a smudge for her, to ward the insects off, sprayed her, too, and swabbed her with some stuff out of a bucket. The mare had nothing to worry about.

The woman was young–likely in her twenties. She came and went, sometimes with sacks of groceries. At other times she fished; sometimes a child fished with her. Another time a man came and sat talking on the porch. She had blond sunburnt hair, nothing fancy about her. Wore jeans and gingham shirts.

"A nice fanny," Joe said.

"Was it her you were studying or Uncle Rex?" I asked him.

"It's curious," he said. "I stayed longer than I meant to. I've got some good binoculars. That old guy might have found him such a paradise he ain't ever going to show up again. Ever think of that, Marilee? Some folks just looking for an excuse to leave?" I thought of it and it carried its own echo for me: Joe Richard had left Louisiana, or he wouldn't be there talking to me.

I thought that if Uncle Rex had wanted to leave forever he would have gone further than twenty miles away; he had the world to choose from, depending on which temperature and landscape he favored. There must be a reason for his choice, I thought, so I went to talk to Uncle Hernan.

"You were right," I said. "Joe Richard found him." And I told him what he'd seen.

"That would be that Bertis girl," said Uncle Hernan at once.

"Who?" I said.

"Oh, it was back before Rex was married. We all used to go down there with the Meecham brothers and Carter Bankston. It was good duck shooting in the winter and we got some deer too if you could stand the cold—cold is not too bad, but river damp goes right into your bones. Of course, we'd be pretty well fortified.

"There was a family we had, to tend camp for us, a fellow named Bertis, better than a river rat, used to work in construction in Natchez, but lost his arm in an accident, then got into a lawsuit, didn't get a cent out of it, went on relief, found him a river house, got to trapping. Well, he had a wife and a couple of kids to raise. His wife was a nice woman. Ought to have gone back to her folks. She had a college degree, if I recall correctly.

"One year, down there on the camp, Bertis came to cook and skin for us, like he'd always done, but he was worried that year over his wife, who'd come down sick. It was Rex who decided to take her to Natchez to the hospital and let the hunt go on. Some of the bunch had invited some others—a big preacher and a senator: at this late date, I don't quite know myself who all was there. It would have been hard to carry on without Bertis and Bertis needed money, too, though I reckon we might have made up a check.

"Everybody was a little surprised at what Rex offered to take on himself. He stood straight-backed and bright-eyed when he spoke up, like a man who's volunteering for a mission and ready to salute when it's granted. Somebody ought to have offered—that was true. But there's the sort of woman, Marilee, can be around ten to a thousand men all together, and every last one of them will have the same impression of her, but not a one will mention it. So we never spoke of what crossed everybody's mind.

"The funny thing was, Bertis never stirred himself to see about his wife. He was an odd sort of fellow, not mean, but what you'd call life-sick. Some people can endure life, slowly, gradually, all that comes, but with enjoyment and good spirit; but some get lightning struck and something splits off in them. In Bertis's case it was more than an arm he'd lost; it was spirit.

"Rex stayed away and stayed away. Not till the camp was breaking up did Bertis come up to me, and I offered to drive him in. We got to the hospital but his wife wasn't there, she'd gone on to Vicksburg and it was late. The next day, on a street in Vicksburg, in an old house they'd made into apartments, we found her. She was sitting in a nice room with a coal fire burning, looking quiet and at peace. She looked more than that. She looked beautiful. Her hands had turned fine, white, delicate as a lady's in a painting, don't you know. She had an afghan over her.

"When we came in, we heard footsteps out the back hall and a door slamming. 'Hello, Mr. Bertis,' was all she said. I drove them home. As far as I recall they never asked each other's news, never exchanged a word. I put them down at the front door of that house out in the wilds, not quite in the swamps but too close to the river to be healthy, not quite a cabin but too run down to call a home–it was just a house, that was all. 'You going to be all right, Mrs. Bertis?' I asked.

"'I reckon I can drive in a day or two,' was what she said. Bertis couldn't do much driving on account of his arm. Though she spoke, it seemed she wasn't really there; she was in a private haze. I remember how she went in the house, like a woman in a dream.

"And there was a little yellow-haired girl in the doorway, waiting for her. That's likely the one's down there now.

"Rex was gone completely for more than a month if I'm not mistaken. He took a trip out West and saw some places he'd always wanted to, though it was a strange time of year to do it, as some pointed out to him when he got back. Married Martha McClelland soon after.

"Marilee, does your mama mind your having a little touch of Bourbon now and then?"

"She minds," I said, "but she's given up."

"The next time you have some bright family ideas about real estate," said Joe Richard, "you better count to a hundred-and-two and keep your mouth shut."

"That's the truth," I said.

We were lying face down on a ridge thick in fallen leaves, side by side, taking turns with the binoculars. I had a blanket under me Joe had dug out of his car to keep me from catching a cold, he said, and I was studying my fill down through the trunks of tall trees–beech, oak, and flaming sycamore–way down to the low fronded willows near the old fishing camp with the weed-grown road and the brown flowing river beyond–and it was all there, just the way he'd said.

I had watched Uncle Rex come up from fishing and moor his boat, had watched a tow-headed child in faded blue overalls enter the field of vision to meet him, and then the blond woman, who'd stood talking in blue jeans and a sweater with the sleeves pushed up—exactly what I had on, truth to tell—taking the string of fish from him, while he walked away and the child ran after him. And I followed with the sights on them, the living field of their life brought as close as my own breath, though they didn't know it—do spirits feel as I did? When he came back, he was leading the mare. She looked well accustomed, and flicked her fine ears, which were furring over for winter, and stood while Uncle Rex lifted the child and set her in the saddle as her mother held the reins. The fish shone silvery on the string against the young woman's leg.

There is such a thing as father, daughter, and grandchild—such a thing as family that is not blood family but a chosen family: I was seeing that. Joe took the glasses out of my hand for his turn and while he looked I thought about Indian summer which isn't summer at all, but something else. There is the long hot summer, heavy and teeming, more real than life; and there is the other summer, pure as gold, as real as hope. Now, not needing glasses, or eyes, either, I saw the problem Rex Wirth must be solving and unsolving every day. If this was the place he belonged and the family that was—though not of blood—in a sense, his, why leave them ever? His life, like a tree drawn into the river and slipping by, must have felt the current pull and turn him every day. Wasn't this where he belonged? Come back, Uncle Rex!—should I run out of the woods and tell him that? No, the struggle was his own. We went away silent, never showing we were there.

Uncle Rex did come home.

It was when the weather broke in a big cold front out of the northwest. It must have come ruffling the water, thickening the afternoon sky, then sweeping across the river, a giant black cloak of a cloud, moaning and howling in the night, stripping the little trees and bushes bare of colored leaves and crashing against the willow thickets. It was like a seasonal motion, too, that Uncle Rex should decamp at that time, arrive back at Aunt Martha's with a pickup of frozen fish packed in ice and some muskrat pelts, even a few mink, the mare in her little cart bringing up the rear.

At least I thought he went home, as soon as somebody I knew out on that road called me at the office to say he'd gone by. If he'd gone to

Uncle Hernan's that would have been a waste of all his motions, all to do again. I telephoned to Andrew.

"Get on out there," I said. "Don't even stop to coach basketball."

But Andrew couldn't do that. If he had started untying a knot in his shoelace when the last trump sounded, he would keep right on with it, before he turned his attention to anything new. So he started home after basketball practice.

There were giant upheavals of wind and hail and falling temperatures throughout the South, the breakup of Indian summer, but Andrew forged his way homeward, discovering along the road that the car heater needed fixing and that he hadn't got on a warm enough suit, or brought a coat.

He went straight in to Uncle Rex. It seemed to me later than anybody could program Andrew, but I guess on the other hand he'd worried about his father's absence and his mother's abandoned condition a great deal, and nobody except me had told him anything he could do about it. He had gone home a time or two to comfort her, but it hadn't worked miracles.

"I'm sorry for what I said about the land, Father," he said right out, even before he got through shivering. "You're the one ought to decide whatever we do."

Then he stopped. The big, white house was silent, emptied of McClellands, by what method God alone would ever know.

Uncle Rex and Aunt Martha were sitting alone by the gas heater. Aunt Martha had risen to greet him when he came in, but then she'd sat down again, looking subdued.

Uncle Rex rose up and approached Andrew with tears in his eyes. He placed his hands on each of his shoulders. "Son—" he said. "Son—" His face had got bearded during his long time away, grizzled, sun- and wind-burnt, veined, austere, like somebody who has had to deal with Indians and doesn't care to discuss it. His hands had split up in half a dozen places from hard use; his nails had blood and grime under them that no scrubbing would remove. "Son, this property . . . it's all coming to you someday. For now . . ."

If you looked deeply into Andrew's eyes, they did not have very much to tell. He said, "Yes, Father," which was about all that was required. When he told me about it, I could imagine both his parents' faces, how they stole glances at him, glowed with pride the same as ever, on account of his being so fine to look at and their own into the bargain. But I remembered that we are back in the bosom of the real family now—the blood one—and that blood is for spilling, among other things.

"Your mother wanted me on this place, Son," Uncle Rex went on, "and as long as she wants me here the only word that goes is mine. She can tell you now if that's so or not."

"But, Father, you left her worried sick. You never sent word to her! It's been awful!"

"That's not the point, Son," said Uncle Rex. "She wants me here."

"I want him here," Aunt Martha echoed. She looked at Andrew with all her love, but she was looking across a mighty wide river.

"You know how he's acted! You know what he did!"

"That's not the point," Aunt Martha murmured.

"Then what is the point?" Andrew asked, craving to know with as much passion as he'd ever have, I guess.

"That your father—that I want him here." She was studying her hands then—not even looking. They were speakers in a play.

As for Andrew, he said he felt as if he wasn't there anymore, that some force had moved through him and that life was not the same. Figuratively speaking, his voice had been taken from him. Literally, he was coming down with a cold. Aunt Martha gave him supper and poured hot chocolate down him, and he went to bed with nothing but the sounds of a shrieking wind and the ticking clock, in the old room he'd had from childhood on. He felt (he told me later) like nothing and nobody. Nothing . . . nobody: the clock was saying it too. There was an ache at the house's core and at some point he dreamed he rose and dressed and went out into the upstairs hall. There he saw his father's face, white, drawn, and small—a ghost face, floating above the stairwell.

"Why call me 'Son' when you don't mean it?"

There wasn't an answer, and he woke and heard the wind.

Uncle Rex—what dream did he have?

"We can't know that," said Uncle Hernan, when I talked to him. "Rex did what he had to. He settled it with those McClellands, once and for all. It was hard for Rex—remember that. Oh yes, Marilee! For Rex it was mighty hard."

THE SEARCH

The man and his wife who put up at the Auberge de la Province on rue St. Denis in Montreal's east end seemed, above everything else, concerned with their own relevance to the world they lived in. She was tall and blond, with hair drawn fashionably back; her loose beige camel's hair coat with the turned-up collar was right for May in Quebec. He was dark and at first glance too slight for her; but his eyes leveled sharply into whatever was before him, suggesting a backup in physical strength that was not at first apparent. He wore muted tattersall suits, or gray slacks with a jacket, and turtleneck shirts in maroon, brown, and green.

The way they came and went, walked out to eat together, ordered soda and ice for their room at six (the desk clerk sent the cleaning boy out for the soda), gave one to understand that they had traveled a lot together and were used to better places. It seemed, in fact, more and more obvious, something finally to get worried about, as they emerged daily at dusk, passing down the steps that dropped from the first-floor entrance over the grimy windows of the rez-de-chaussée to the pavement, that they were in the wrong place for a smart, upper-middle-class American couple to be. True, they escaped the attention of anyone they might know and run into by coming to a second-rate tourist hotel far removed from the fashionable area of town, but they excited public interest in themselves here; for though the street was out of the way, it was busy, and many people who frequented it knew one another.

The hotel was run by two young men whose relationship, the nature of which was obvious, was qualified by a certain considerate quietude;

they were kind to the world. Nonetheless, after the couple, whose name was Davis, had been there a week, one of the owners had to mount the stairs and knock at the door.

Davis opened it. One of the young men was French-speaking and blond; the other, whose dark hair and skin suggested Arab origins, was, by his accent, from England. The French one was in the doorway, smiling agreeably but speaking firmly. Complaints had come from the rooms below and from a neighboring apartment; some sacks of trash, even garbage, had been thrown down into the alleyway from this room.

They had chosen a corner exposure, spacious and sunny. A refrigerator and small stove were evidently useful to them, as grocery sacks and a coffee tin were laid out on a shelf. Their luggage—sophisticated tough canvas with black leather reinforcements, straps, and handles—was scattered about the room, some of it unpacked but open. Davis' wife sat bare-legged on the bed in a loose housecoat of blue crepe and gold slippers, reading a fashion magazine. She glanced up, heard the message, but before it was finished, turned her attention back to the magazine.

"Garbage!" Davis repeated. "Out our window? Don't be crazy!"

"No," the young man said. "I am not crazy. The people below there"—he nodded—"they saw it come down. It broke open."

Davis turned to his wife. "Stella? Did you, by accident—?"

"Of course, I didn't. Don't be silly."

"Obviously, a mistake of some sort," said Davis. But as the young French man lingered, smiling but persistent, Davis suddenly produced five dollars. "So sorry. Won't happen again. . . . Okay?"

The boy looked for a moment at the money. To offer it was to gloss over the issue, to take it was to agree to forget it. Was the choice so important? He was being made to answer this, and evidently judged not, for he accepted at last, bowed to the reading wife (she did not look up), nodded to the man, and withdrew. They could hear his sandals whispering down the stairs.

"What's this all about?" Davis asked, after closing the door.

She did not answer.

"Look, if you're going back into that nervous-breakdown kind of business: 'Get rid of this object, it's accusing me, without it I'll be happy with all these nice objects. . . .' "

"Nothing of the sort," she said, and turned a page. "They have a maid, as we both know. She cleaned up yesterday, must have put all the garbage out but ours, took a short cut–"

"Even so, would she do it more than once? I got the impression it was several times."

"Then it's a mystery. Maybe it didn't happen. How should I know? Maybe he invented it."

Davis sat down. "They've wondered about us," he improvised, half-serious, half-amused. "They've seen we can afford better. It's a shake-down."

"Wondered what?" She joined his game, but idly.

"Anything's possible. I learned that from you. It's possible to imagine, invent, almost anything. Remember how you carried groceries in your arms like babies, remember. . . ."

"You weren't to bring that up again. You weren't to discuss things like that. You know what they said." She threw aside the magazine. "What good can it do to bring those things up?"

"I don't think it matters any more."

She stood, about to move toward the ritual of dress, of drink, of dinner. "We're about to the end anyway."

An hour later, turned out in their always appropriate clothes, they were dining at the street's best restaurant, a candlelit secluded atmosphere, which drew its clientele from far and wide. They had eaten there from the beginning; now, after several evenings they had the comfortable feeling of being old and familiar clients. The proprietor, a soft-spoken Frenchman, felt amiably inclined to sit with them over coffee. He offered them brandy.

"We've liked your food," Mrs. Davis said.

"Certainly have!" her husband agreed.

"You sound as if you go."

"We may," the woman softly began. "Our explorations–our attempt–" She broke off, emotionally stopped.

She's been stopped for years, her husband thought. You plan a child, conceive it, bear it, tend it, rear it. Always, through all the ordinary human motions, you are guiding a future dream. If you are Stella, you are. Stella, hell! Millions of mothers must be at it, envisioning, planning, leaning forward toward golden clouds. The name of their dream was Mary. She went to college, fell in love, eloped, and vanished. First to Montreal, they knew that. . . . Then?

"We had a daughter," he said to the restaurant proprietor, speaking firmly, honestly, ignoring his wife's warning glance. He would enter what he was not supposed to; it was better, now, to do it. "She married a draft evader six years ago and left college with him for Canada. I say married . . . we suppose so. He renounced his citizenship. Later we heard a rumor that he had returned to the States by changing his identity. We don't know if it's true. Since then there's been the amnesty, now the pardon: you've read about it." The proprietor nodded. "We think that she, at least, possibly both of them, could reappear now. But where are they? We've explored before, through channels, all we could use; but this last time, we're doing it personally. We just wanted to see for ourselves, to take a look, no matter how painful, at where they came to."

The proprietor was silent, but his quietness in no way damaged their confidence; in fact, it held them up to its measure.

"You have failed. I am sorry."

"We expected to fail," Davis said. "However, there is something one gains."

"The place itself," his wife said. "Where she was, where they were. We even know the address, a long way from here. The Forum area. We've walked there, gone to grocery stores where she must have shopped, a library, a little park, a movie house. We've wandered around the mountain. The city—it's prettier than New York. It's low, for one thing. You can see the trees and the river." She had started out, bravely intelligent, but when she mentioned the last two things, she began to cry without sobbing or trying to stop her tears. They ran off the rise of her cheekbones, into her smart, severe hairline.

"The winter is a mess," the proprietor remarked. "You're seeing it at its best."

"You're not Canadian?" Davis asked. He laid his hand on his wife's arm.

"From Grenoble. In France. How I landed here, not even any war to escape . . . don't ask me. Still, it is nice. The people are quiet, they ask very little." He had gained permission to smoke, and now, moving toward the ashtray, his intelligent hand hesitated, poised to the catch in his thoughts. "Politics . . . in this world, they reach out. Here, too, they are always reaching. Sooner or later, you are touched, caught up. The damage for some is little; for others, great."

Davis's wife stopped crying. She sipped her brandy, and presently began to smile. "I saw some children today," she recounted. "They were playing some sort of street ball in three or four languages at least. I could hear French, English, and something else—Spanish or Italian—then another I'd no idea about. Yet the game went on."

"A United Nations," the proprietor said. "I respect your confidence," he concluded, rising.

Davis got up and shook hands with him. When he and his wife walked back to the small hotel, they were talking with animation. They had always loved to travel. They did not eat at the restaurant again.

The restaurant proprietor heard a good many secrets, but told none. This was partly because of his own nature, which was thoughtful, inward. He sought no chorusing community to bear out opinions he might express, then later doubt himself. He ceased to think about the American couple. Then, one evening, while helping a waitress clear what had been their table, he remembered them. Their daughter, he thought. They were almost finished with her. Almost.

On the drive back to the States at twilight, Stella Davis suddenly put her head in her hands. They were passing a rushing mountain stream in the Adirondacks. "What's the matter, sick?" her husband asked.

"I was thinking of a story I read once, or saw on TV—no, I read it. It was about some people searching for someone—dear to them, or lost, who needed them. And they came closer and closer and finally they saw her in a wood and then they lost sight of her. They came out of the wood onto some sand beside a little river and found her footprints and followed them, one step appearing regularly just before the other. Then the steps stopped. They didn't turn toward the water or anything, they just weren't there any more. There was no sign of a struggle, no sign of a body. There was just nothing."

"Bad story," her husband said, trying to tease. "Stella, stop remembering bad stories."

"I just wonder," said Stella Davis, "if she ever existed at all."

"Do you want her not to have?" he asked. It was a remark that might have caused another man to draw off the road, confront her. But he drove steadily on.

His wife put her hand to her head once more. "I just want to be rid of my anguish . . . my anguish. I want to lose it forever."

Davis kept driving, profile like the blade of a knife cutting steadily through life. "That garbage incident . . . why, that's it."

"What do you mean, that's it?"

"That you did it . . . it *was* you, after all."

She did not answer, but her silent nod reached him. She could not answer because she was crying too completely now, a different, more relieving sort of tears.

PORT OF EMBARKATION

It was nearly noon of the day my father went back to his unit and thence to overseas service in World War II that I saw the horses. They were coming up the hill from the field, and all I could see first was the delicately scalloped, chestnut tips of their four ears all set forward, which showed their effort, one pair lower than the other. Then their forelocks and long, down-plunging, toiling heads rose to view, the chins dipped low and lather from the bits splashing down, to foam across the twinned chests. I saw the black harness, heard the shout of the driver, and had the impression of a heavily laden wagon, though who the driver was—somebody working for us? a stranger?—and what the wagon carried, I did not know.

The team of great strong chestnut horses lingered in my mind's vision even after I woke on the bed in the far corner of the sleeping porch where I had gone to cry myself to sleep, not wanting anyone to see my tears. The hill up from the field was blocked from my view by the whole of the house, which lay between. But caught in the dream, I lay still in the midday July heat, willing for a time for it to extend its power. There was indeed a moment of further increase when I knew that the nearer horse had white-stockinged hind legs, and that the hill, though steep, was nothing to the power of the team which nobly crested it.

And this was all.

In the center of the house I ran into my mother, who also showed signs of having been crying, but who at once asked where my brother was. He had said he was going somewhere, but I had forgotten where. We went into the kitchen together, trying to act as if it were any other day—we were a reserved kind of family—and found that my brother had already gotten into the lunch and had eaten most of it. We would have to scramble eggs, or drive uptown to the grocery, and we preferred not to have to go out and talk to people. An alternative was to locate my brother and get him to bring us something, but this would undoubtedly provoke a quarrel between him and my mother. My brother was stubborn and seemed to be unfeeling with us all, but I had caught the worst of his nature, for, being smaller and younger I was the object of bullying and threats.

In the hallway to which I had returned, to look past the white front porch, across the positive, relentless sun glare of the yard, toward the fall of the hill, to where I had dreamed the horses ascending, I could hear my mother's and brother's voices. Though he had missed my father's departure with us in the car to the airport, he had been somewhere around, it would seem, all the time.

"That food you got into, that was mine and Estelle's lunch. You knew that, didn't you?"

"No, I didn't know it. How would I?"

"You must have heard us say we didn't want to go out, we'd have a cold lunch, I'd make the potato salad and an aspic, then stuff some eggs. You said you wouldn't be here. There's not enough left for one, now, much less both of us."

"Can't you just fix some more?"

"I certainly don't want to, I guess I can. . . ." The down-turning of their encounter was like fire in a log smothering down to smoke; then (I knew it would come by the tension in my middle), my mother's voice flared up like flame.

"Why can't you be more considerate! That's all I ever want to know. You're the man of the house now. Your father told you that, last night at dinner. We'd like to count on you, we need to count on you, but you . . . ! What do you care?"

"The way you tell it, I don't care about nothing."

"Do you? I'd dearly love to know."

"What you want me to do? You want me to go uptown and get something for your nourishment?"

My mother started crying. He was that sarcastic. "Oh, we'll manage. We'll manage somehow."

Mother eventually found a can of crab meat and made another salad and we sat down to a good lunch. Iced tea, crisp and lemony brown, is comforting after you've been crying, especially on a hot day. It soothes out your feelings.

"We're going to be stuck here all summer," I remarked, "with the way he acts. It's all on purpose," I added, which was not a good thought to give her.

She put her hand to her head. "I think he has problems," she said. "I think something worries him deep down."

"Like what?" I asked.

"How do we know each other's problems unless we tell them? How do I know? Maybe there's some girl he likes who doesn't like him, maybe he doesn't know what to do with himself, maybe he hates it about your father and doesn't want to show it."

"Maybe he's just mean and doesn't like us and wants to show that."

"I wish you wouldn't talk like that," Mother said. She looked frail and she was upset, but she could come out with things full force. "It may interest you to know, Missy, that I love you both the same. I've always said that, and it's true. Your brother knows I love him. He'd have to know that."

That afternoon Mother and I went to the picture show in a neighboring town. Our town was too small to have anything but a flea bag for a movie house, so we generally went over to a larger town. The larger towns, having more pavement and less shade, were hotter than our own. We parked between two white slanted lines, each a paintbrush wide, and walked to the movie house. The sidewalk burned through the soles of our shoes.

"If anybody sees us and asks," Mother said, "I'm going to say we went just to get our minds off everything."

"I'll say that too," I said.

Movies in those days were not, I think, air-conditioned, but they were air-cooled, which was not a bad substitute. They had large concealed fans, almost silent, which blew over ice, so that a constant breeze was stirring, moist and pleasant. If something in this apparatus broke, as it sometimes did, you sat there in the dark, sweltering and wondering whether or not the movie was interesting enough to hold you in discomfort.

That day nothing broke and the movie, *Up in Arms,* with Danny Kaye and Dinah Shore, seemed to be making the war a great big joke. We were complete suckers for what they were doing and sat there shaking with laughter.

When we went out together we heard a voice from the lobby where a wave of hot air was coming in through the front door which the matinee crowd was pushing open.

"Hey, wasn't that swell?"

It was my brother, standing in a knot of other boys. He was laughing and talking out to us. Mother stood stock still when she saw him and I almost laughed aloud, not at the movie, but at them, because she was good and ready in her mind to bless him out for going to a movie the day his father went to port of embarkation, but then, there she was herself. The only difference was that she had her excuse ready and he, undoubtedly, did not.

"Got a ride home now," Brother said to the boys he was with. He came over to us. "Lemme tag a ride," he said. Then he flung an arm around each of us. You could think he was showing off for the benefit of the boys. But, as always with him, you couldn't altogether tell why he was doing anything. He was just doing it, that was all. "I'll buy you girls a Coke," he said.

We went next door to a little hamburger shop and sat in a booth. We ordered Cokes and glasses of ice, the way we all liked them. Then we went to the car, where hot air had to be let out before we could even get in; and Brother drove us home.

All during the time we had been sitting and drinking the Cokes together he had kept laughing and talking about the movie. "It's that scat singing," he said. "I can't see how he does it, 'less they speed up the sound track. I tried it but it didn't work."

"You tried to sing!" my mother exclaimed. "I never knew you to sing a note."

"Oh, I got talents. I got lots of talents." He was laughing at both of us. We might have been people he knew slightly. He was almost sixteen and I was just twelve.

After supper that night my father telephoned to cheer us up. "I've been talking to some of the other officers," he said. "They don't see how the war can go on more than another year at the most. I may not even get there."

I was on one phone, Mother on the other, but we couldn't get my brother to hear us as he was moving the furniture in his room, making an awful racket. Wasn't it important that they spoke? No matter what my father said, we all knew the war was reaching its height. He was heading straight to its heart.

"What's going on there?"

"It's Brother," Mother said. "He's started changing his room around. Wait, I'm going to call him again."

"There're a hundred people lined up to use this phone. I've got to get off it in three minutes or my name is mud. Listen, Ginny, you and Estelle both, don't bother that boy."

"We're going to try to do everything right," Mother said. "Don't you worry, not about anything."

"You let him be his own way. Just let him be."

"I promise, Nat. Oh, I do!"

Then we were hollering good-by, this morning all over again, until the phone clicked off. From my brother's room, immediately after the click, something fell and smashed.

My mother and I rubbed ourselves with 6-12 and went to sit out on the porch in the dark. We hadn't done much of anything, but I felt tired to death.

Neighbors' lights glowed through the trees. Down the hill, the fields slept densely under dewfall. Lightning bugs drifted against a black row of bushes at the field's distant edge. In all that lay out there, I knew the road where I had seen the horses in my dream was rising up as it always did, but I couldn't make it out.

"I had this dream this morning after Daddy left," I said. I told her about the horses, the wagon, and driver.

She didn't say anything, and I wondered if I should have mentioned it. I hadn't tried to think what it meant, if anything.

Finally she said, "It's funny what you dream." I wondered whether she would ever think of it again. Maybe she would.

We heard a door slam above us and my brother's heavy steps, coming downstairs. I felt the powerful sway of her promise to my father on the phone, his demand for it all the greater by coming through from afar, as though from an unseeable beyond: *Let him be his own way. Just let him be.*

I heard her talking to herself, whispering that she would try.

THE GIRL WHO LOVED HORSES

She had drawn back from throwing a pan of bird scraps out the door because she heard what was coming, the two-part pounding of a full gallop, not the graceful triple notes of a canter. They were mounting the drive now, turning into the stretch along the side of the house; once before, someone appearing at the screen door had made the horse shy, so that, barely held beneath the rider, barely restrained, he had plunged off into the flower beds. So she stepped back from the door and saw the two of them shoot past, rounding a final corner, heading for the straight run of drive into the cattle gate and the barn lot back of it.

She flung out the scraps, then walked to the other side of the kitchen and peered through the window, raised for spring, toward the barn lot. The horse had slowed, out of habit, knowing what came next. And the white shirt that had passed hugged so low as to seem some strange part of the animal's trappings, or as though he had run under a low line of drying laundry and caught something to an otherwise empty saddle and bare withers, now rose up, angling to an upright posture. A gloved hand extended to pat the lathered neck.

"Lord have mercy," the woman said. The young woman riding the horse was her daughter, but she was speaking also for her son-in-law, who went in for even more reckless behavior in the jumping ring the two of them had set up. What she meant by it was that they were going to kill themselves before they ever had any children, or if they did have children safely they'd bring up the children to be just as foolish about horses and careless of life and limb as they were themselves.

The young woman's booted heel struck the back steps. The screen door banged.

"You ought not to bring him in hot like that," the mother said. "I do know that much."

"Cottrell is out there," she said.

"It's still March, even if it has got warm."

"Cottrell knows what to do."

She ran water at the sink, and cupping her hand, drank primitive fashion out of it, bending to the tap, then wet her hands in the running water and thrust her fingers into the dusty, sweat-damp roots of her sand-colored hair. It had been a good ride.

"I hope he doesn't take up too much time," the mother said. "My beds need working."

She spoke mildly but it was always part of the same quarrel they were in like a stream that was now a trickle, now a still pool, but sometimes after a freshet could turn into a torrent. Such as: "Y'all are just crazy. Y'all are wasting everything on those things. And what are they? I know they're pretty and all that, but they're not a thing in the world but animals. Cows are animals. You can make a lot more money in cattle, than carting those things around over two states and three counties."

She could work herself up too much to eat, leaving the two of them at the table, but would see them just the same in her mind's eye, just as if she'd stayed. There were the sandy-haired young woman, already thirty—married four years and still apparently with no intention of producing a family (she was an only child and the estate, though small, was a fine piece of land)—and across from her the dark spare still young man she had married.

She knew how they would sit there alone and not even look at one another or discuss what she'd said or talk against her; they would just sit there and maybe pass each other some food or one of them would get up for the coffeepot. The fanatics of a strange cult would do the same, she often thought, loosening her long hair upstairs, brushing the gray and brown together to a colorless patina, putting on one of her long cotton gowns with the ruched neck, crawling in between white cotton sheets. She was a widow and if she didn't want to sit up and try to talk to the family after a hard day, she didn't have to. Reading was a joy, lifelong. She found her place in *Middlemarch,* one of her favorites.

But during the day not even reading (if she'd had the time) could shut out the sounds from back of the privet hedge, plainly to be heard from the house. The trudging of the trot, the pause, the low directive, the thud of hoofs, the heave and shout, and sometimes the ring of struck wood as a bar came down. And every jump a risk of life and limb. One dislocated shoulder—Clyde's, thank heaven, not Deedee's—a taping, a sling, a contraption of boards, and pain "like a hot knife," he had said. A hot knife. Wouldn't that hurt anybody enough to make him quit risking life and limb with those two blood horses, quit at least talking about getting still another one while swallowing down pain-killer he said he hated to be sissy enough to take?

"Uh-huh," the mother said. "But it'll be Deborah next. You thought about that?"

"Aw, now, Miss Emma," he'd lean back to say, charming her through his warrior's haze of pain. "Deedee and me—that's what we're hooked on. Think of us without it, Mama. You really want to kill us. We couldn't live."

He was speaking to his mother-in-law but smiling at his wife. And she, Deborah, was smiling back.

Her name was Deborah Dale, but they'd always, of course, being from LaGrange, Tennessee, right over the Mississippi border, that is to say, real South, had had a hundred nicknames for her. Deedee, her father had named her, and "Deeds" her funny cousins said—"Hey, Deeds, how ya' doin'?" Being on this property in a town of pretty properties, though theirs was a little way out, a little bit larger than most, she was always out romping, swimming in forbidden creeks, climbing forbidden fences, going barefoot too soon in the spring, the last one in at recess, the first one to turn in an exam paper. ("Are you quite sure that you have finished, Deborah?" "Yes, ma'am.")

When she graduated from ponies to that sturdy calico her uncle gave her, bringing it in from his farm because he had an eye for a good match, there was almost no finding her. "I always know she's somewhere on the place," her mother said. "We just can't see it all at once," said her father. He was ailing even back then but he undertook walks. Once when the leaves had all but gone from the trees, on a warm November afternoon, from a slight rise, he saw her down in a little-used pasture with a straight open stretch among some oaks. The ground was spongy and clotted with damp and even a child ought not to have tried to run there, on foot. But there went the calico with Deedee clinging low, going like the wind, and knowing furthermore out of what couldn't be anything but long practice, where to turn, where to veer, where to stop.

"One fine afternoon," he said to himself, suspecting even then (they hadn't told him yet) what his illness was, "and Emma's going to be left with nobody." He remarked on this privately, not without anguish and not without humor.

They stopped her riding, at least like that, by sending her off to boarding school, where a watchful ringmaster took "those girls interested in equitation" out on leafy trails, "at the walk, at the trot, and at the canter." They also, with that depth of consideration which must flourish even among those Southerners unlucky enough to wind up in the lower reaches of hell, kept her young spirit out of the worst of the dying. She just got a call from the housemother one night. Her father had "passed away."

After college she forgot it, she gave it up. It was too expensive, it took a lot of time and devotion, she was interested in boys. Some boys were interested in her. She worked in Memphis, drove home to her mother every night. In winter she had to eat breakfast in the dark. On some evenings the phone rang; on some it was silent. Her mother treated both kinds of evenings just the same.

To Emma Tyler it always seemed that Clyde Mecklin materialized out of nowhere. She ran straight into him when opening the front door one evening to get the paper off the porch, he being just about to turn the bell or knock. There he stood, dark and straight in the late light that comes after first dark and is so clear. He was clear as anything in it, clear as the first stamp of a young man ever cast.

"Is Deb'rah here?" At least no Yankee. But not Miss Tyler or Miss Deborah Tyler, or Miss Deborah. No, he was city all right.

She did not answer at first.

"What's the matter, scare you? I was just about to knock."

She still said nothing.

"Maybe this is the wrong place," he said.

"No, it's the right place," Emma Tyler finally said. She stepped back and held the door wider. "Come on in."

"Scared the life out of me," she told Deborah when she finally came down to breakfast the next day, Clyde's car having been heard to depart by Emma Tyler in her upstairs bedroom at an hour she did not care to verify. "Why didn't you tell me you were expecting him? I just opened the door and there he was."

"I liked him so much," said Deborah with grave honesty. "I guess I was scared he wouldn't come. That would have hurt."

"Do you still like him?" her mother ventured, after this confidence.

"He's all for outdoors," said Deborah, as dreamy over coffee as any mother had ever beheld. "Everybody is so indoors. He likes hunting, going fishing, farms."

"Has he got one?"

"He'd like to have. All he's got's this job. He's coming back next weekend. You can talk to him. He's interested in horses."

"But does he know we don't keep horses anymore?"

"That was just my thumbnail sketch," said Deborah. "We don't have to run out and buy any."

"No, I don't imagine so," said her mother, but Deborah hardly remarked the peculiar turn of tone, the dryness. She was letting coast through her head the scene: her mother (whom she now loved better than she ever had in her life) opening the door just before Clyde knocked, so seeing unexpectedly for the first time, that face, that head, that being. . . . When he had kissed her her ears drummed, and it came back to her once more, not thought of in years, the drumming hoofs of the calico, and the ghosting father, behind, invisible, observant, off on the bare distant November rise.

It was after she married that Deborah got beautiful. All LaGrange noticed it. "I declare," they said to her mother or sometimes right out to her face, "I always said she was nice-looking but I never thought anything like that."

Emma first saw the boy in the parking lot. He was new. In former days she'd parked in front of nearly any place she wanted to go—hardware, or drugstore, or courthouse: change for the meter was her biggest problem. But so many streets were one-way now and what with the increased numbers of cars, the growth of the town, those days were gone; she used a parking lot back of a café, near the newspaper office. The entrance to the lot was a bottleneck of a narrow drive between the two brick buildings; once in, it was hard sometimes to park.

That day the boy offered to help. He was an expert driver, she noted, whereas Emma was inclined to perspire, crane, and fret, fearful of scraping a fender or grazing a door. He spun the wheel with one hand; a glance told him all he had to know; he as good as sat the car in place, as skillful (she reluctantly thought) as her children on their horses. When she returned an hour later, the cars were denser still; he helped her again. She wondered whether to tip him. This happened twice more.

"You've been so nice to me," she said, the last time. "They're lucky to have you."

"It's not much of a job," he said. "Just all I can get for the moment. Being new and all."

"I might need some help," she said. "You can call up at the Tyler place if you want to work. It's in the book. Right now I'm in a hurry."

On the warm June day, Deborah sat the horse comfortably in the side yard and watched her mother and the young man (whose name was Willett? Williams?), who, having worked the beds and straightened a fence post, was now replacing warped fence boards with new ones.

"Who is he?" she asked her mother, not quite low enough, and meaning what a Southern woman invariably means by that question, not what is his name but where did he come from, is he anybody we know? What excuse, in other words, does he have for even being born?

"One thing, he's a good worker," her mother said, preening a little. Did they think she couldn't manage if she had to? "Now don't you make him feel bad."

"Feel bad!" But once again, if only to spite her mother, who was in a way criticizing her and Clyde by hiring anybody at all to do work that Clyde or the Negro help would have been able to do if only it weren't for those horses—once again Deborah had spoken too loudly.

If she ever had freely to admit things, even to herself, Deborah would have to say she knew she not only looked good that June day, she looked sexy as hell. Her light hair, tousled from a ride in the fields, had grown longer in the last year; it had slipped its pins on one side and lay in a sensuous lock along her cheek. A breeze stirred it, then passed by. Her soft poplin shirt was loose at the throat, the two top buttons open, the cuffs turned back to her elbows. The new horse, the third, was gentle, too much so (this worried them); she sat it easily, one leg up, crossed lazily over the flat English pommel, while the horse, head stretched down, cropped at the tender grass. In the silence between their voices, the tearing of the grass was the only sound except for a shrill jay's cry.

"Make him feel bad!" she repeated.

The boy looked up. The horse, seeking grass, had moved forward; she was closer than before, eyes looking down on him above the rise of her breasts and throat; she saw the closeness go through him, saw her presence register as strongly as if the earth's accidental shifting had slammed them physically together. For a minute there was nothing but the two of them. The jay was silent; even the horse, sensing something, had raised his head.

Stepping back, the boy stumbled over the pile of lumber, then fell in it. Deborah laughed. Nothing, that day, could have stopped her laughter. She was beautifully, languidly, atop a fine horse on the year's choice day at the peak of her life.

"You know what?" Deborah said at supper, when they were discussing her mother's helper. "I thought who he looks like. He looks like Clyde."

"The poor guy," Clyde said. "Was that the best you could do?"

Emma sat still. Now that she thought of it, he did look like Clyde. She stopped eating, to think it over. What difference did it make if he did? She returned to her plate.

Deborah ate lustily, her table manners unrestrained. She swabbed bread into the empty salad bowl, drenched it with dressing, bit it in hunks.

"The poor woman's Clyde, that's what you hired," she said. She looked up.

The screen door had just softly closed in the kitchen behind them. Emma's hired man had come in for his money.

It was the next day that the boy, whose name was Willett or Williams, broke the riding mower by running it full speed into a rock pile overgrown with weeds but clearly visible, and left without asking for pay but evidently taking with him in his car a number of selected items from barn, garage, and tack room, along with a transistor radio that Clyde kept in the kitchen for getting news with his early coffee.

Emma Tyler, vexed for a number of reasons she did not care to sort out (prime among them was the very peaceful and good time she had been having with the boy the day before in the yard when Deborah had chosen to ride over and join them), telephoned the police and reported the whole matter. But boy, car, and stolen articles vanished into the nowhere. That was all, for what they took to be forever.

Three years later, aged thirty-three, Deborah Mecklin was carrying her fine head higher than ever uptown in LaGrange. She drove herself on errands back and forth in car or station wagon, not looking to left or right, not speaking so much as before. She was trying not to hear from the outside what they were now saying about Clyde, how well he'd done with the horses, that place was as good as a stud farm now that he kept ten or a dozen, advertised and traded, as well as showed. And the money was coming in hard and fast. But, they would add, he moved with a fast set, and there was also the occasional gossip item, too often, in Clyde's case, with someone ready to report first hand; look how quick, now you thought of it, he'd taken up with Deborah, and how she'd snapped him up too soon to hear what his reputation was, even back then. It would be a cold day in August before any one woman would be enough for him. And his father before him? And his father before him. So the voices said.

Deborah, too, was trying not to hear what was still sounding from inside her head after her fall in the last big horse show:

The doctor: You barely escaped concussion, young lady.

Clyde: I just never saw your timing go off like that. I can't get over it.

Emma: You'd better let it go for a while, honey. There're other things, so many other things.

Back home, she later said to Emma: "Oh, Mama, I know you're right sometimes, and sometimes I'm sick of it all, but Clyde depends on me, he always has, and now look—"

"Yes, and 'Now look' is right, he has to be out with it to keep it all running. You got your wish, is all I can say."

Emma was frequently over at her sister-in-law Marian's farm these days. The ladies were aging, Marian especially down in the back, and those twilights in the house alone were more and more all that Deedee had to keep herself company with. Sometimes the phone rang and there'd be Clyde on it, to say he'd be late again. Or there'd be no call at all. And once she (of all people) pressed some curtains and hung them, and once hunted for old photographs, and once, standing in the middle of the little-used parlor among the walnut Victorian furniture upholstered in gold and blue and rose, she had said "Daddy?" right out loud, like he might have been there to answer, really been there. It had surprised her, the word falling out like that as though a thought took reality all by itself and made a word on its own.

And once there came a knock at the door.

All she thought, though she hadn't heard the car, was that it was Clyde and that he'd forgotten his key, or seeing her there, his arms loaded maybe, was asking her to let him in. It was past dark. Though times were a little more chancy now, LaGrange was a safe place. People nearer to town used to brag that if they went off for any length of time less than a weekend and locked the doors, the neighbors would get their feelings hurt; and if the Tylers lived further out and "locked up," the feeling for it was ritual mainly, a precaution.

She glanced through the sidelight, saw what she took for Clyde, and opened the door. There were cedars in the front yard, not too near the house, but dense enough to block out whatever gathering of light there might have been from the long slope of property beyond the front gate. There was no moon.

The man she took for Clyde, instead of stepping through the door or up to the threshold to greet her, withdrew a step and leaned down and to one side, turning outward as though to pick up something. It was she who stepped forward, to greet, help, inquire; for deep within was the idea her mother had seen to it was firmly and forever planted: that one day one of them was going to get too badly hurt by "those things" ever to be patched up.

So it was in outer dark, three paces from the safe threshold and to the left of the area where the light was falling outward, a dim single sidelight near the mantelpiece having been all she had switched on, too faint to penetrate the sheer gathered curtains of the sidelight, that the man at the door rose up, that he tried to take her. The first she knew of it, his face was in hers, not Clyde's but something like it and at Clyde's exact height, so that for the moment she thought that some joke was on, and then the strange hand caught the parting of her blouse, a new mouth fell hard on her own, one knee thrust her legs apart, the free hand diving in to clutch and press against the thin nylon between her thighs. She recoiled at the same time that she felt, touched in the quick, the painful glory of desire brought on too fast—looking back on that instant's two-edged meaning, she would never hear about rape without the lightning quiver of ambivalence within the word. However, at the time no meditation stopped her knee from coming up into the nameless groin and nothing stopped her from tearing back her mouth slathered with spit so suddenly smeared into it as to drag it into the shape of a scream she was unable yet to find a voice for. Her good right arm struck like a hard backhand against a line-smoking tennis serve. Then from the driveway came the stream of twin headlights thrusting through the cedars.

"Bitch!" The word, distorted and low, was like a groan; she had hurt him, freed herself for a moment, but the struggle would have just begun except for the lights, and the screams that were just trying to get out of her. "You fucking bitch." He saw the car lights, wavered, then turned. His leap into the shrubbery was bent, like a hunchback's. She stopped screaming suddenly. Hurt where he lived, she thought. The animal motion, wounded, drew her curiosity for a second. Saved, she saw the car sweep round the drive, but watched the bushes shake, put up her hand to touch but not to close the torn halves of the blouse, which was ripped open to her waist.

Inside, she stood looking down at herself in the dim light. There was a nail scratch near the left nipple, two teeth marks between elbow and wrist where she'd smashed into his mouth. She wiped her own mouth on the back of her hand, gagging at the taste of cigarette smoke, bitterly staled. Animals! She'd always had a special feeling for them, a helpless tenderness. In her memory the bushes, shaking to a crippled flight, shook forever.

She went upstairs, stood trembling in her mother's room (Emma was away), combed her hair with her mother's comb. Then, hearing Clyde's voice calling her below, she stripped off her ravaged blouse and hastened across to their own rooms to hide it in a drawer, change into a fresh one, come downstairs. She had made her decision already. Who was this man? A nothing . . . an unknown. She hated women who shouted Rape! Rape! It was an incident, but once she told it everyone would know, along with the police, and would add to it: they'd say she'd been violated. It was an incident, but Clyde, once he knew, would trace him down. Clyde would kill him.

"Did you know the door was wide open?" He was standing in the living room.

"I know. I must have opened it when I heard the car. I thought you were stopping in the front."

"Well, I hardly ever do."

"Sometimes you do."

"Deedee, have you been drinking?"

"Drinking . . . ? Me?" She squinted at him, joking in her own way; it was a standing quarrel now that alone she sometimes poured one or two.

He would check her breath but not her marked body. Lust with him was mole-dark now, not desire in the soft increase of morning light, or on slowly westering afternoons, or by the night light's glow. He would kill for her because she was his wife. . . .

"Who was that man?"

Uptown one winter afternoon late, she had seen him again. He had been coming out of the hamburger place and looking back, seeing her through the street lights, he had turned quickly into an alley. She had hurried to catch up, to see. But only a form was hastening there, deeper into the unlit slit between brick walls, down toward a street and a section nobody went into without good reason.

"That man," she repeated to the owner (also the proprietor and cook) in the hamburger place. "He was in here just now."

"I don't know him. He hangs around. Wondered myself. You know him?"

"I think he used to work for us once, two or three years ago. I just wondered."

"I thought I seen him somewhere myself."

"He looks a little bit like Clyde."

"Maybe so. Now you mention it." He wiped the counter with a wet rag. "Get you anything, Miss Deb'rah?"

"I've got to get home."

"Y'all got yourselves some prizes, huh?"

"Aw, just some good luck." She was gone.

Prizes, yes. Two trophies at the Shelby County Fair, one in Brownsville where she'd almost lost control again, and Clyde not worrying about her so much as scolding her. His recent theory was that she was out to spite him. He would think it if he was guilty about the women, and she didn't doubt any more that he was. But worse than spite was what had got to her, hating as she did to admit it.

It was fear.

She'd never known it before. When it first started she hadn't even known what the name of it was.

Over two years ago, Clyde had started buying colts not broken yet from a stud farm south of Nashville, bringing them home for him and Deborah to get in shape together. It saved a pile of money to do it that way. She'd been thrown in consequence three times, trampled once, a terrifying moment as the double reins had caught up her outstretched arm so she couldn't fall free. Now when she closed her eyes at night, steel hoofs sometimes hung through the dark above them, and she felt hard ground beneath her head, smelled smeared grass on cheek and elbow. To Clyde she murmured in the dark: "I'm not good at it any more." "Why, Deeds, you were always good. It's temporary, honey. That was a bad day."

A great couple. That's what Clyde thought of them. But more than half their name had been made by her, by the sight of her, Deborah Mecklin, out in full dress, black broadcloth and white satin stock with hair drawn trimly back beneath the smooth rise of the hat, entering the show ring. She looked damned good back of the glossy neck's steep arch, the pointed ears and lacquered hoofs which hardly touched earth before springing upward, as though in the instant before actual flight. There was always the stillness, then the murmur, the rustle of the crowd. At top form she could even get applause. A fame for a time spread round them. The Mecklins. Great riders. "Ridgewood Stable. Blood horses trained. Saddle and Show." He'd had it put up in wrought iron, with a sign as well, Old English style, of a horseman spurring.

("Well, you got to make money," said Miss Emma to her son-in-law. "And don't I know it," she said. "But I just hate to think how many times I kept those historical people from putting up a marker on this place. And now all I do is worry one of y'all's going to break your neck. If it wasn't for Marian needing me and all . . . I just can't sleep a wink over here."

("You like to be over there anyway, Mama," Deborah said. "You know we want you here."

("Sure, we want you here," said Clyde. "As for the property, we talked it all out beforehand. I don't think I've damaged it any way."

("I just never saw it as a horse farm. But it's you all I worry about. It's the danger.")

Deborah drove home.

When the workingman her mother had hired three years before had stolen things and left, he had left too on the garage wall inside, a long pair of crossing diagonal lines, brown, in mud, Deborah thought, until she smelled what it was, and there were the blood-stained menstrual pads she later came across in the driveway, dug up out of the garbage, strewed out into the yard.

She told Clyde about the first but not the second discovery. "Some critters are mean," he'd shrugged it off. "Some critters are just mean."

They'd been dancing, out at the club. And so in love back then, he'd turned and turned her, far apart, then close, talking into her ear, making her laugh and answer, but finally he said: "Are you a mean critter, Deedee? Some critters are mean." And she'd remembered what she didn't tell.

But in those days Clyde was passionate and fun, both marvelously together, and the devil appearing at midnight in the bend of a country road would not have scared her. Nothing would have. It was the day of her life when they bought the first two horses.

"I thought I seen him somewhere myself."

"He looks a little bit like Clyde."

And dusk again, a third and final time.

The parking lot where she'd come after a movie was empty except for a few cars. The small office was unlighted, but a man she took for the attendant was bending to the door on the far side of a long cream-colored sedan near the back fence. "Want my ticket?" she called. The man straightened, head rising above the body frame, and she knew him. Had he been about to steal a car, or was he breaking in for whatever he could find, or was it her coming all along that he was waiting for? However it was, he knew her as instantly as she knew him. Each other was what they had, by whatever design or absence of it, found. Deborah did not cry out or stir.

Who knew how many lines life had cut away from him down through the years till the moment when an arrogant woman on a horse had ridden him down with lust and laughter? He wasn't bad-looking;

his eyes were beautiful; he was the kind to whom nothing good could happen. From that bright day to this chilly dusk, it had probably just been the same old story.

Deborah waited. Someway or other, what was coming, threading through the cars like an animal lost for years catching the scent of a former owner, was her own.

("You're losing nerve, Deedee," Clyde had told her recently. "That's what's really bothering me. You're scared, aren't you?")

The bitter-stale smell of cigarette breath, though not so near as before, not forced against her mouth, was still unmistakably familiar. But the prod of a gun's muzzle just under the rise of her breast was not. It had never happened to her before. She shuddered at the touch with a chill spring-like start of something like life, which was also something like death.

"Get inside," he said.

"Are you the same one?" she asked. "Just tell me that. Three years ago, Mama hired somebody. Was that you?"

"Get in the car."

She opened the door, slid over to the driver's seat, found him beside her. The gun, thrust under his crossed arm, resumed its place against her.

"Drive."

"Was it you the other night at the door?" Her voice trembled as the motor started, the gear caught.

"He left me with the lot; ain't nobody coming."

The car eased into an empty street.

"Go out of town. The Memphis road."

She was driving past familiar, cared-for lawns and houses, trees and intersections. Someone waved from a car at a stoplight, taking them for her and Clyde. She was frightened and accepting fear, which come to think of it was all she'd been doing for months, working with those horses. ("Don't let him bluff you, Deedee. It's you or him. He'll do it if he can.")

"What do you want with me? What is it you want?"

He spoke straight outward, only his mouth moving, watching the road, never turning his head to her. "You're going out on that Memphis road and you're going up a side road with me. There's some woods I know. When I'm through with you you ain't never going to have nothing to ask nobody about me because you're going to know it all and it ain't going to make you laugh none, I guarantee."

Deborah cleared the town and swinging into the highway wondered at herself. Did she want him? She had waited when she might have run. Did she want, trembling, pleading, degraded, finally to let him have every single thing his own way?

(Do you see steel hoofs above you over and over because you want them one day to smash into your brain?

("Daddy, Daddy," she had murmured long ago when the old unshaven tramp had come up into the lawn, bleary-eyed, face bloodburst with years of drink and weather, frightening as the boogeyman, "raw head and bloody bones," like the Negro women scared her with. That day the sky streamed with end-of-the-world fire. But she hadn't called so loudly as she might have, she'd let him come closer, to look at him better, until the threatening voice of her father behind her, just on the door's slamming, had cried: "What do you want in this yard? What you think you want here? Deborah! You come in this house this minute!" But the mystery still lay dark within her, forgotten for years, then stirring to life again: When I said "Daddy, Daddy?" was I calling to the tramp or to the house? Did I think the tramp was him in some sort of joke or dream or trick? If not, why did I say it? Why?

("Why do you ride a horse so fast, Deedee? Why do you like to do that?" *I'm going where the sky breaks open.* "I just like to." "Why do you like to drive so fast?" "I don't know.")

Suppose he kills me, too, thought Deborah, striking the straight stretch on the Memphis road, the beginning of the long rolling run through farms and woods. She stole a glance to her right. He looked like Clyde, all right. What right did he have to look like Clyde?

("It's you or him, Deedee." All her life they'd said that to her from the time her first pony, scared at something, didn't want to cross a bridge. "Don't let him get away with it. It's you or him.")

Righting the big car into the road ahead, she understood what was demanded of her. She pressed the accelerator gradually downward toward the floor.

"And by the time he realized it," she said, sitting straight in her chair at supper between Clyde and Emma, who by chance were there that night together; "—by the time he knew, we were hitting above seventy-five, and he said, 'What you speeding for?' and I said, 'I want to get it over with.' And he said, 'Okay, but that's too fast.' By that time we were touching eighty and he said, 'What the fucking hell'—excuse me, Mama—'you think you're doing? You slow this thing down.' So I said, 'I tell you what I'm doing. This is a rolling road with high banks and trees and lots of curves. If you try to take the wheel away from me, I'm going to wreck us both. If you try to sit there with that gun in my side I'm going to go faster and faster and sooner or later something will happen, like a curve too sharp to take or a car too many to pass with a big truck coming and we're both going to get smashed up at the very least. It won't do any good to shoot me when it's more than likely both of us would die. You want that?'

"He grabbed at the wheel but I put on another spurt of speed and when he pulled at the wheel we side-rolled, skidded back, and another car coming almost didn't get out of the way. I said, 'You see what you're doing, I guess.' And he said, 'Jesus God.' Then I knew I had him, had whipped him down.

"But it was another two or three miles like that before he said, 'Okay, okay, so I quit. Just slow down and let's forget it.' And I said, 'You give me that gun. The mood I'm in, I can drive with one hand or no hands at all, and don't think I won't do it.' But he wanted his gun at least, I could tell. He didn't give in till a truck was ahead and we passed but barely missed a car that was coming (it had to run off the concrete), and he put it down, in my lap."

(Like a dog, she could have said, but didn't. And I felt sorry for him, she could have added, because it was his glory's end.)

"So I said, 'Get over, way over,' and he did, and I coasted from fast to slow. I turned the gun around on him and let him out on an empty stretch of road, by a rise with a wood and a country side road rambling off, real pretty, and I thought, Maybe that's where he was talking about, where he meant to screw hell—excuse me, Mama—out of me. I held the gun till he closed the door and went down in the ditch a little way, then I put the safety catch on and threw it at him. It hit his shoulder, then fell in the weeds. I saw it fall, driving off."

"Oh, my poor baby," said Emma. "Oh, my precious child."

It was Clyde who rose, came round the table to her, drew her to her feet, held her close. "That's nerve," he said. "That's class." He let her go and she sat down again. "Why didn't you shoot him?"

"I don't know."

"He was the one we hired that time," Emma said. "I'd be willing to bet you anything."

"No, it wasn't," said Deborah quickly. "This one was blond and short, red-nosed from too much drinking, I guess. Awful like Mickey Rooney, gone and gotten old. Like the boogeyman, I guess."

"The poor woman's Mickey Rooney. You women find yourselves the damnedest men."

"She's not right about that," said Emma. "What do you want to tell that for? I know it was him. I feel like it was."

"Why'd you throw the gun away?" Clyde asked. "We could trace that."

"It's what I felt like doing," she said. She had seen it strike, how his shoulder, struck, went back a little.

Clyde Mecklin sat watching his wife. She had scarcely touched her food, and now, pale, distracted, she had risen to wander toward the windows, look out at the empty lawn, the shrubs and flowers, the stretch of white-painted fence, ghostly by moonlight.

"It's the last horse I'll ever break," she said, more to herself than not, but Clyde heard and stood up and was coming to her.

"Now, Deedee–"

"When you know you know," she said, and turned, her face set against him: her anger, her victory, held up like a blade against his stubborn willfulness. "I want my children now," she said.

At the mention of children, Emma's presence with them became multiple and vague; it trembled with thanksgiving, it spiraled on wings of joy.

Deborah turned again, back to the window. Whenever she looked away, the eyes by the road were there below her: they were worthless, nothing, but infinite, never finishing–the surface there was no touching bottom for–taking to them, into themselves, the self that was hers no longer.

Wayne Grady, editor

THE PENGUIN BOOK OF CANADIAN SHORT STORIES°

In this collection of Canadian short stories the very best Canadian writing is sampled. This vast range of stories offers something for every taste and colourfully reflects the rich diversity of one country's literary heritage.

'. . . the short story has developed into Canada's healthiest and most versatile literary genre. Several of our novelists—Morley Callaghan and Hugh Garner, for example—are better known abroad for their short stories than for their novels. And many of our best writers write virtually nothing but short stories: Mavis Gallant, Norman Levine, Alice Munro, W. D. Valgardson, and others.'—*from the preface by Wayne Grady.*

These twenty-eight stories have been carefully selected and introduced to provide both entertaining reading and an insight into the dominant themes and directions of Canadian literature from its beginnings in the early nineteenth century right up to the present day.

THE PENGUIN BOOK OF MODERN CANADIAN SHORT STORIES°

This anthology is presented as a companion volume to the highly acclaimed *Penguin Book of Canadian Short Stories,* and focuses on the period from the early 1960s to the present, two vital decades in the development of Canada's most important literary genre.

The twenty-four stories have been carefully selected from both published and unpublished material to reflect the broad diversity of the modern Canadian short story, as well as to provide an overview of its dominant and recurring themes. Stories by such major authors as Alice Munro, Brian Moore, Margaret Atwood, Norman Levine, Elizabeth Spencer, and Margaret Laurence are included. French-Canadian short fiction is represented by Anne Hébert, Gabrielle Roy, Gérard Bessette, and Jacques Ferron (the latter two by stories appearing here in English for the first time). Recent work by these writers is accompanied by stories from the newer generation—Sean Virgo, W. D. Valgardson, Matt Cohen, and W. P. Kinsella.

As in the *Penguin Book of Canadian Short Stories,* editor Wayne Grady has brought together stories that provide a valuable and entertaining collection for both the student of Canadian literature and the casual reader.

° Not available in the United States

Robertson Davies

THE REBEL ANGELS

A cast of unforgettable characters is featured in this rich and vivid novel of passion and murder smouldering beneath the surface of a sophisticated Canadian university. Maria Theotoky, a ravishingly beautiful graduate student is pursuing a hopeless affair with her professor; Simon Darcourt, a professor of Greek is pursuing a hopeless affair of a different sort; Clement Hollier, a renowned scholar and professor nurtures a passion for the darker side of medieval psychology; John Parlabane, an unstable and defrocked monk whose miserable existence ends tragically; Arthur Cornish, a wealthy young businessman who inherits a troublesome bequest of priceless works of art. The reader is drawn spellbound into a mystical plot where he is effortlessly entertained and instructed, puzzled and amused . . . an enchantingly mysterious novel by Canada's pre-eminent man of letters.

'The Rebel Angels stands by itself as a remarkable achievement.'—*Toronto Star*

'Fascinating and witty . . . he is a first-rate storyteller and a real moralist with a crackling sense of humour.' *Newsweek*

'The Rebel Angels is a wonderful book . . . human, hilarious, whimsical and wicked.'—*Calgary Herald*

'One of the most learned, amusing and otherwise accomplished novelists of our time.'—*John Kenneth Galbraith*

THE DEPTFORD TRILOGY

Robertson Davies

FIFTH BUSINESS

Fifth Business might be described simply as the memoirs of a Canadian schoolteacher named Dunstan Ramsay. But such a description would not even suggest the dark currents of love, ambition, vengeance, and death that flow through this powerful novel. As Ramsay writes, he reveals his influence on other people—on Boy Staunton, who, one day in 1908, threw a snowball with a stone in it; on Mary Dempster, whom it hit; on Paul Dempster, her son, born prematurely because of the blow; and on the ravishingly beautiful Leola Cruikshank, whom Staunton grew up to marry and, eventually, to destroy.

THE MANTICORE

The Canadian David Staunton enters Jungian analysis in Switzerland because of his father's strange death. (Was it an accident? Or suicide? Or homicide?) As the analysis proceeds, the manticore—a monster with the head of a man, the body of a lion, and the tail of a scorpion—is among the symbols that emerge, and David learns surprising things not only about himself but also his father, about the schoolmaster Dunstan Ramsay, about the libidinous Liesl, and about the warped and gifted Magnus Eisengrim.

WORLD OF WONDERS

Magnus Eisengrim is a master illusionist, the most celebrated magician of his age. Together with his old friends Dunstan Ramsay and Liesl Naegeli, he is ensconced at Liesl's castle in Switzerland, where he is enacting the title role in a film about the legendary French illusionist Robert-Houdin. Off-camera and after shooting sessions, the film's great Scandinavian director, Jurgen Lind, becomes intrigued with Magnus and—together with the producer, the cameraman, the incomparable Liesl, and Ramsay himself—draws from him an account of his life story, a story as rich in color, drama, comedy, and gripping tension as any in recent fiction.